Praise for C.E. Murphy's

URBAN SHAMAN

"Murphy's *Urban Shaman* is a solid,
enjoyable, quick read."
—*Storyteller Magazine*

"Joanne's scrambling efforts to learn to use [her]
talent and stay alive are highly entertaining, an
excellent start to a new series."
—*LOCUS* magazine

"Tightly plotted and nicely paced,
Murphy's latest has a world in which ancient and
modern magic fuse almost seamlessly....Fans of
urban fantasy are sure to enjoy this first book in
what looks to be an exciting new series."
—*Romantic Times BOOKclub*

C.E. MURPHY

THUNDERBIRD FALLS

LUNA™
www.LUNA-Books.com

LUNA™

First edition May 2006

THUNDERBIRD FALLS

ISBN 0-373-80235-8

www.LUNA-Books.com

Printed in U.S.A.

Once more, thanks are due to both my editor,
Mary-Theresa Hussey, and my agent,
Jennifer Jackson, for making this a better book;
and to cover artist Hugh Syme, whose artwork
I am still delighted to have my book judged by.

They are further due to Silkie,
for research above and beyond the call of duty
(especially since there was no call of duty at all!); to
Trip, for making me think harder than is my natural
inclination; and to Anna, who is responsible for any
geography I got right in Seattle.

As for the rest of it, if I started listing
my support structure in detail, there wouldn't be
room for the book. Still, to my family, especially
Ted and Shaun, who respectively keep me fed
and keep the kitchen clean, thank you.

This one's for Alex Trebek.

(Really.)

CHAPTER ONE

Thursday, June 16, 6:19 a.m.

Two words I never thought would go together: Joanne Walker and 6:00 a.m.

Never mind that that's actually four words, five if you spell out ante meridiem. If you're going to get technical, you're going to lose all your friends. The point is, it was Oh God Early and I was not only up, but at work. Not even at work. I was *volunteering*. Volunteering my own precious sleeping time, five hours before I was supposed to be at work. I was so noble I could kill myself.

While I was busy admiring my nobility, a bunch of protesters linked arms and waded toward the police line I was a part of. There were considerably more of them than there were of us—hence me being there at all—and the power of authority as granted to us by the city of Seattle wasn't pulling a lot of weight with them. They weren't violent, just determined. I spread my arms wide and leaned into the oncoming mass, blowing a whistle that was more noisome than effective. The protesters stopped close enough that I could count the individual silver hairs on the head of the man in front of me, who stood there, Right In My Personal Space.

People have gotten shot for less.

Not, however, by me, and besides, as one of the city's finest, I wasn't in a position to be shooting people just for getting in my personal space. Instead, I took a step forward, trusting my own presence to be enough to cow them. It was; the silver-haired guy in front of me shifted back, making a bow in his line. I pressed my advantage, arms still spread wide, and they all fell back a step.

I let go a sigh of relief that I couldn't let them see, herding them back several more steps before I let up, and backed up again myself. They watched me, silent, sullen, and short.

I was working on a theory that said all environmentalists were short. I knew it was wrong—Al Gore is a tall man—but it gave me something to do while I played push-me-pull-you with the protesters. Of course, most people are short compared to me: I stood a smidge under six feet in socks, and the sturdy black walking shoes I wore put me an inch over.

Behind me lay the summertime glory of the Seattle Center, where a symposium on global warming was being held. Representatives from every oil company, every car manufacturer, every corporation that had ever been fined for too many dirty emissions being pumped out into the air were gathered there to argue their case against the bleeding-heart liberals who thought a little clean air wasn't asking too much.

Sarcasm aside, the greenies were losing major ground and had been since the symposium had opened two days earlier. The federal administration favored big money and big companies, and those companies were taking as much advantage as they could.

My own sympathies lay a whole lot more with the protesters and their concerns about details like global warming. It was already in the high seventies and it wasn't yet seven in the morning, which was just wrong for mid-June.

But it wasn't my job to have an opinion about who was right and who was wrong. It was my job to keep the several thousand men and women who were gathered at the Center from breaking through and rending the Armani suits from the bodies of the corpulent pigs managing the slaughter.

"Officer?" A woman's voice, high-pitched with worry, broke me out of my cheerfully spiraling cynicism. I turned toward her, one hand still lifted in warning against the crowd. I suspected a trick: distract the cop for a minute while everybody surges forward, therefore losing the law a few precious feet of land. There were more physical barriers than just the police officers keeping people off the Center grounds—bright orange, cordoned sawhorses surrounded the entire place—but it was its own sort of psychological warfare.

The woman held a pale-cheeked sleeping girl in her arms. "She fainted," the woman said. Her voice was thready with concern and fear. "Please, I think she needs a doctor."

Right behind the bottom of my breastbone, centered in the diaphragm, a coil of energy flared up, making a cool fluttering space inside me. It demanded attention, making my hands cramp and my stomach churn. I rubbed my sternum, swallowing back the wave of nausea. I'd gotten good at ignoring that sensation in the past several months, pretending I couldn't feel it wrapped around my insides, waiting for me to give in and use it again. Having it crop up so sharply made me feel as pale as the girl. My hand, without any conscious order from my brain, reached out to touch her forehead. Her skin was cold and sticky with sweat.

For the first time since I'd nearly burned out in March, I lost the battle with the energy within me. It shot through me, making silver-tinted rainbows beneath my skin, and strained at my fingertips, trying to pass from me into the chilly-skinned child. Had she been an adult, I might have been able to pull back and refuse yet again to acknowledge its existence.

But she was a kid, and whether I wanted the power and responsibility I'd unintentionally taken on, a six-year-old didn't deserve to suffer for my stubbornness. Silver-sheened magic told me in the most simple, nonmedical terms possible, that the girl was suffering from near heatstroke.

To me—a mechanic by trade, even if I was a cop by day—that meant her engine had overheated.

Fixing an overheated engine's not a hard thing. You pop the hood, pour new water into the radiator and try not to get burned by the steam, then do it again until the radiator's full and the engine's cooled down.

Translating that to a child sick with heat was surprisingly easy. The energy inside me boiled with eagerness to flow out of me and into the girl, but I made it drip instead of pour, afraid of what might happen if her system cooled down too rapidly. I could actually envision the steam hissing off her as heat gradually was replaced by my cool silver strength. It seemed a wonder that no one else could see it.

I was glad she was asleep. At her age she probably had very few perceptions about how health and illness worked, but it was a whole lot easier to heal somebody who couldn't consciously disbelieve that what you were doing was possible.

The bitter truth of the matter was that I had to believe it was possible, too, and I didn't want to. What I wanted and what was, however, were two very different things. Right through the core of me, I knew that cooling down an overheated little kid was only the bare edge of what I was capable of.

I let my hand fall off the girl's forehead. There was a little color in her cheeks now, her breathing somehow more steady and less shallow. She was going to be all right, though an IV drip to help get her fluids back up would probably be a good idea. From the outside, it looked as if

I'd touched the girl's forehead as an assessment, then said, "I'll escort you out." I was the only one who knew better, and I was grateful for that. Headlines blaring *Cop Turns Faith Healer!* would not endear me to my boss.

The girl's mother, bright-eyed with tears, whispered her thanks. I led them through the crowd, radioing for an ambulance as we walked.

Watching them drive away half an hour later, I realized I could breathe more easily than I'd been able to in months. I rubbed the heel of my hand over my breastbone again, irritably, and went back to work.

I left at nine, which was cutting it way too close to expect to get back to the university by nine-thirty. The traffic gods smiled on me, though, and I slid my Mustang into a parking spot outside the gym with a whole two minutes to spare.

I have never been what I would call the athletic sort. Not because I'm uncoordinated, but because I was never very good at working with a team in high school. I hadn't improved at it since then, for that matter. The basketball coach had been endlessly frustrated by me. Alone I could shoot hoops till the cows came home, but put nine other people on a court with me and I got sullen and stupid and couldn't hold on to the ball.

So fencing, which I'd started shortly after wrassling a banshee to ground, was the first sport I'd ever really pursued. I was surprised at how much I enjoyed it, even with sweat leaking into my eyes and my own hot breath washing back at me against the mask.

Metal clashed against metal, a twitchy vibration running up my arm, even through the heavy canvas gloves. Block and retreat, block and retreat, lunge and attack. I blinked sweat away as I extended.

My épée scraped along the other blade and slid home, thumping my opponent solidly in the ribs. For a moment we both froze, equally startled. Then through the mesh of her mask, I saw her grin as she came back to a full stand. She pulled the mask off, tucking short damp hair behind her ears, and saluted me. I straightened and yanked my mask off. My shadow splashed against her white tunic, my hair a hedgehog of sagging points.

"We might just make a fencer of you yet, Joanne."

Panting and grinning, I tucked my mask under my arm, transferring my épée to my left hand, and offered Phoebe my right. She grabbed it in an old-fashioned warrior's handshake, wrapping her fingers around my forearm, the way she always shook hands. She was small and compact, like a Porsche, and had muscles where I didn't even have body parts. Most days she made me feel large and lumbering and slow.

Of course, on a bad day, Godzilla could make me feel large and lumbering and slow.

"That's my plan." I shook Phoebe's hand solidly before falling back a step, rubbing a thumb over my sternum. Phoebe's dark eyebrows knitted. It was very nearly her dark eyebrow knitting, but I was afraid to even think that too loudly, for fear she'd hear me and beat the tar out of me.

"Why do you do that?"

My hand dropped as if weighed down by a concrete brick, and I twisted it behind my back guiltily. "Do what?"

"You're the worst liar I've ever met. Every time somebody makes a point against you and every time a match ends, you rub your breastbone. How come?"

"I had…surgery a while ago." I took a too-deep breath, trying to will away the sensation of not getting enough air. "I guess it still bothers me."

"Heart surgery?"

"More like lung."

Phoebe's eyebrows went up. "You don't smoke, do you?"

"No." I hadn't snitched since January, when a steely eyed cab driver refused to give me a smoke because his wife of forty-eight years had died of emphysema. I could learn from other people's lessons. That was what I told myself.

Quitting smoking had nothing to do with the crushing sensation of being unable to breathe from having a sword stuffed through my lung. I told myself that, too. It turned out myself was a skeptical bitch and didn't believe me. Even so, I tried hard not to think about the truth: that the sword had been wielded by a Celtic god, and in a shadowland between life and death, a Native American trickster called Coyote offered me a choice between the two.

I had no idea what I was getting myself into when I chose a life and became a shaman. I felt that coil of energy bubble up again inside of me, and squelched it. There was no one around who needed healing right now. Nobody but myself, anyway, and I didn't deny I had a lot of self-healing to do.

Actually, I denied it all the time. Which was part of why I was learning to fence, instead of sitting somewhere quietly, as Coyote would like me to, focusing on my inner turmoil and getting it all sorted out. Inner turmoil could wait, as far as I was concerned. External turmoil seemed inclined to stick me with pointy things or otherwise try to do me in. Under those circumstances, I figured learning how to parry was a much better use of my time than fussing over things I'd rather let lie.

I rolled my shoulders, pushing the thoughts away. "It wasn't cancer. Sort of more hereditary. It's fine now. Just kind of bugs me sometimes. I think it's mostly mental." I knew it was mostly mental. I didn't even have a scar.

"Is that why you started coming here?" she wondered. "A lot of people find martial arts to be a great way to center themselves after they've had a life-changing experience."

I ducked my chin and let out a breathy laugh. "Something like that, yeah. Plus I could use the exercise."

"I thought cops were supposed to be in good shape."

I looked back up through my eyebrows. "Don't know many cops, do you? Speaking of which, I better hit the shower and get to work. Thanks for the lesson, Phoebe." I headed for the locker room, Phoebe taking the lead and holding the door for me.

"My pleasure. I like beating up on the big girls. Makes me feel all studly."

"You are all studly. And you're not that small."

"Compared to you I am."

"Compared to me Arnold Schwartznegger is small."

Phoebe laughed out loud. "*You're* not *that* big."

I grinned as I struggled out of my tunic. I was pretty sure it had a secret mission in life to strangle me as I undressed. "Nah. I lack the shoulders." Phoebe turned the showers on, drowning out anything else I might say. Once I got loose of the tunic, I followed her, standing to the side while the pins-and-needles water pelted from cold to too hot.

The beauty of university showers is that they never run out of hot water. I stood there, leaning my forehead against the wall, until my skin turned boiled lobster-red. Phoebe turned her shower off with a squeak of faucets, and in the fashion of community showers everywhere, the water in mine got significantly hotter. Turning it down didn't help. That was the flip side of never running out of hot water: the only way I'd ever found to keep a public shower from being too hot was to run more than one at a time. "Ow. Turn that back on, would you?"

"Sorry." The faucets squeaked again and after a few seconds my shower faded back to a bearable heat. Water lapped over the top of my feet, and I pushed away from the wall with another groan, listening to Phoebe slosh to the drying area.

"Thanks." I reached for my shampoo, scrubbing a palmful through my hair. If I weren't so fond of standing mindlessly in the hot water, it would only take me about thirty seconds to shower. A minute and a half if I used conditioner, which my hair was too short to bother with except occasionally. But I wasn't quite late for work, so I luxuriated in the heat. Water crept up around my ankles. "I think the drain's plugged."

"Check," Phoebe said. "I'll call maintenance if it is."

"Okay." I rinsed my hair, turned the water off, and wrapped a towel around myself as I slogged through the shower room in search of the drain.

Two stalls down from me, a naked black girl, her skin ashy blue with death, lay with her hip fitted neatly in the hollow of the drain.

CHAPTER TWO

"Phoebe," I said, amazed at how calm my voice was, "call the cops."

"You are the cops," she said. I could hear the grin in her voice in the suddenly echoing shower room.

"Phoebe!"

"Yow, okay, what's wrong?" Phoebe didn't call the cops. She splashed back through the showers, rewetting her feet. "What's wrong, Joanne?"

"There's a dead girl in the shower," I said, still very calmly. "Please go call the police, Phoebe."

"There's *what?!*" Phoebe looked around the edge of the shower stall and went pale under her olive skin. "Oh my God. Oh my God, we have to do something!" She surged forward. I grabbed her shoulder and pulled her back.

"We have to call the cops," I repeated. "She's dead, Phoebe. Look at her color. There's nothing we can do. We shouldn't touch her."

"You *are* the cops!"

"I'm also the one who found the body. Again," I added in a mutter.

"Again?" Phoebe's voice rose and broke.

"I found a murder victim in January," I said. My boss was going find a way to blame me for this. He was convinced I lived out each day with the deliberate intention to piss him off. Some days he was right, but it hadn't been in my game plan today. I didn't get up at five in the morning to volunteer at protests with irritating my boss in mind. Rather the opposite, in fact, not that I'd admit that out loud.

I took Phoebe's other shoulder and steered her away from the body. "Shouldn't we at least check to make sure she's dead?" she demanded, voice rising. I exhaled, nice and slow.

"She's dead, Phoebe. Look, okay." I let her go and waded to the dead girl. She looked like she'd been posed for a photograph, her back against the tile wall, her bottom leg and arm stretched out long and her top leg folded gracefully forward into the water, bent at the knee. Her head was thrown back, slender neck exposed, as if she were laughing without inhibition. The edge of the drain was just barely visible beneath her hip, all of the drain holes covered. I wondered who would take that kind of picture, then remembered that if nobody else would, the police photographer would have to do the job.

"Christ." I crouched and pressed two fingers against her neck, below her jaw. She was on the cool side of luke-warm, the skin pliant, and had no pulse. I tried a second time, then a third, shifting my fingers slightly. "She's dead, Phoebe." I stood up again, wiping my fingers against my towel. I'd never touched a dead body before. It hadn't felt like I expected it to. "Go call the cops."

"What're you going to do?" Phoebe's voice trembled as she backed away, water splashing around her ankles.

"I'm going to go get dressed." I turned to follow Phoebe, who continued to back up, still staring at the dead girl. "Watch where you're go—"

I lunged, too late. Phoebe's heel caught the curb of the shower area and her feet slid out from under her, kicking water into my eyes. My fingers closed on empty air as she shrieked and crashed to the tile floor with a painful crack. My own feet slid on the wet tiles and for a moment I thought I'd dive after her. My arms swung wildly and I caught my balance, heaving myself upright with a gasp. Phoebe, her mouth a tight line, stared up at me, then let out an uncharacteristic soprano giggle. I stepped over the curb and offered her a hand up.

"I take it you're okay, then."

Phoebe wrapped her fingers around mine in a strong grip and I hauled her to her feet. "No, I'm not okay." Her voice squeaked as high as her giggle had. "We just found a dead girl in the showers and I think my butt's going to be bruised for a month." She giggled again, then set her mouth and pressed her eyes shut, inhaling deeply through her nostrils. "I'm okay," she said after several seconds. I nodded.

"I'll call the cops. You get dressed."

"Okay." She gave me a pathetically grateful look that I didn't like from my fencing instructor, and left me alone with the dead girl. I stole a glance at her over my shoulder, feeling power flutter behind my breastbone, urging me to use it.

I could think of one good reason to disregard it. Well, one reason. Good was debatable, especially since even in my own head I heard it as a whine: *but I don't want to be a shaman!*

Except, possibly, when it meant I could save little girls from heatstroke. I sighed and went back to the dead woman, kneeling in the cooling water. The bottom edge of my towel drooped into it, sucking up as much as it could, and I debated running to put some clothes on before doing anything else. Only then I'd be soaking up water with my uniform, which, unlike a towel, wasn't designed for it. It wasn't like the police would arrive in the thirty seconds I intended to be out.

"Arright," I muttered. "One healthy little girl for one esoteric death investigation. I guess that's fair." Five more minutes before calling the cops wasn't going to make a difference to the body. "I'm here," I said out loud, "if you want to talk."

There was a place between life and death that spirits could linger in, a place that, with all due apology to Mr. King, I'd started calling the Dead Zone. If I could catch this young woman's spirit there, I might just be able to learn something useful, like how she'd ended up filling a drain at the University of Washington's gym locker rooms.

Reaching that world was easier with a drum, but somewhere in the shower room a shower leaked, a steady dripdrop of water hitting water. It was a pattern, and that was good enough. I closed my eyes. The sound amplified, deliberate *poiks* bouncing off the bones behind my ears. I lost count of the drops, and rose out of my body.

I slid through the ceiling, skimming through pipes and wires and insulation that felt laced with asbestos. The sky above the university was so bright it made my eyes ache, and for a few seconds I turned my attention away from the journey for the sake of the view.

The world glittered. White and blue lights zoomed along in tangled blurs, each of them a point of life. Trees glowed in the full bloom of summer and I could see the thin silver rivers of sap running through them to put out leaves that glimmered with hope and brightness. Concrete and asphalt lay like heavy thick blots of paint smeared over the brilliance, but at midmorning, with people out and doing things, those smears of paint had endless sparks of life along them, defying what seemed, at this level, to be a deliberate attempt to wipe out the natural order of the world.

Don't get me wrong. Not only do I like my indoor plumbing and my Mustang that runs roughshod over those dark blots of freeway, but I also think that a dam built by man is just as natural as a dam built by a beaver. We're a part of this world, and there's nothing unnatural about how we choose to modify it. If it weren't in our nature, we wouldn't be doing it.

Still, looking down from the astral plane, the way we

lay out streets and modify the world to suit ourselves looks pretty awkward compared to the blur of life all around it. Humans like right angles and straight lines. There weren't many of those outside of man-made objects.

But even overlooking humanity's additions to the lay of the land, there was something subtly wrong with the patterns of light and life. I'd noticed it months earlier—the last time I'd gone tripping into the astral plane—and it seemed worse now. There was a sick hue to the neon brilliance, like the heat had drawn color out, mixed it with a little death, and injected it back into the world without much regard to where it'd come from. It made my nerves jangle, discomfort pulling at the hairs on my arms until I felt like a porcupine, hunched up and defensive.

The longer I hung there, studying the world through second sight, the worse the colors got. Impatient scarlet bled into the silver lines of life, black tar gooing the edges of what had been pure and blue once upon a time. I had no sense of where the source of the problem was. It felt like it was all around me, and the more I concentrated on it the harder it got to breathe. I finally jerked in a deep breath, clearing a cough from my lungs, and shook off the need to figure out what was wrong. I suspected it had more to do with procrastination than anything else. I'd been warned more than once that my own perceptions could get me in trouble, in the astral plane.

It wasn't that I was scared. Just wary. Apprehensive. Cautious. Uneasy. And that exhausted my mental thesaurus, which meant I had to stop farting around and go do what I meant to do.

Coyote had told me that traveling in the astral plane wasn't a matter of distance, but a matter of will. It seemed like distance to me, always different, always changing. Seattle receded below me, darkening and broadening until the Pacific seaboard seemed to be just one burnt-out city, the sparks of life that colored it faded and scattered with distance. Skyscrapers that seemed to defy physics with their height leaped up around me and crumbled again, and the stars were closer.

A tunnel, blocked off by a wall of stone, appeared to my left, and I felt him waiting there. Him, it—whatever. Something was there, and it tugged at me. It laughed every time I forged past it, and every time I did I felt one more spiderweb-thin line binding me to it. The first time I traveled the astral plane I almost went to him, compelled by curiosity and a sense of malicious rightness. The second time, the stone wall was in place, my dead mother's way of protecting me from whatever lay down that tunnel. This time I knew he was there, and it was easier to ignore him.

Someday I'm not going to be able to.

The tunnel whipped away into a wash of light, the sky bleeding gold and green around me. New skyscrapers blossomed into tall trees, filled with the light of life, but here that light was orange and red, not the blues and white I was used to. I grinned wildly and lifted my hands, encouraging the speed that the world swum around me with.

Under the gold sky, palaces built like where the Taj Mahal's wealthy older sister grew up. A tiger paced by, sabre-toothed and feral, watching me like I might be a tasty snack. A man's laughter broke over me, and the world spun into midnight, the sky rich and blue and star-studded. I relaxed, letting myself enjoy the changing vistas, and in the instant I did, the shifting worlds slammed to a stop.

A red man stood in front of me. Genuinely red: the color of bricks, or dark smoked salmon. His eyes were golden and his mouth was angry. "Haven't you learned anything?"

I gaped at him, breathless. "What are you doing here?"

"You're making enough noise to wake the dead."

"That was kind of the idea."

"Siobhán Walkin—"

"Don't call me that."

"It's your name."

"Don't," I repeated, "call me that. Not here."

I'd become uncomfortably protective of that name: Siobhán Walkingstick. It was my birth name, the one I'd been saddled with by parents whose cultures clashed just long enough to produce me. My American father'd taken one look at *Siobhán* and Anglicized it to Joanne. Until I was in my twenties, no one had called me Siobhán except once, in a dream.

The last name, Walkingstick, I'd abandoned on my own when I went to college. I'd wanted to leave my Cherokee heritage behind, defining myself by my own rules. I was Joanne Walker. Siobhán Walkingstick was someone who barely existed.

But whether I liked it or not, that name belonged to the most internal, broken parts of me, and flinging it around astral planescapes made me vulnerable. I had learned to build protective shields around it, the one thing I'd managed to do to Coyote's satisfaction over the past six months. I saw those shields as being titanium, thin and flexible and virtually unbreakable, an iridescent fortress in my mind. They were meant to protect my innermost self from the bad guys.

So I didn't like having the two names rolled together in the best of circumstances, and I resented the shit out of having them flung around the astral plane as a form of reprimand by the very same brick-red spirit guide who'd insisted I develop the shields in the first place.

The spirit guide in question flared his nostrils, inclining his head slightly, and inside that motion, shifted. A loll-tongued, golden-eyed coyote sat in front of me, looking as disgruntled about the eyes as the man had.

"Dammit," I said, "I hate when you do that."

"This is not about what you hate," the coyote said, in exactly the same tenor the man owned. His mouth didn't move, and I was, as ever, uncertain if he was speaking out loud or in my mind. "You haven't got the skill for this, Joanne."

I wet my lips. "Looks to me like you're wrong."

"Do you really understand what you're doing?" The coyote's voice sharpened, making my chin lift and my shoulders go back defensively.

"I'm just trying to see if she can tell me anything about what happened, Coyote."

"There are more mundane ways to find out. You are a policeman, are you not?"

"I'm a beat cop," I said through my teeth. "Beat cops

don't get to investigate dead bodies in the women's shower."

Coyote cocked his head at me, a steady golden-eyed look that spoke volumes. Then, in case I'd missed the speaking of volumes, he said it out loud, too: "Then maybe you shouldn't."

Which comedian was it who said wisdom came from children, especially the mouth part of the face? I felt like he must have when he first thought it: like it would be nice to wrap duct tape around the talking part until nothing more could be said.

Coyote snapped his teeth at me, a coyote laugh. "Wouldn't work anyway."

"Oh, shut up." Yet another incredibly annoying thing: he heard every thought I had, and I heard none of his. "This is supposed to be my dreamscape. Why can't I hear your thoughts?"

He cocked his head the other way, wrinkles appearing in the brown-yellow fur of his forehead. "First," he said, "it's not your dreamscape. Haven't you learned even that much? The astral plane is a lot bigger than just you or me."

"I thought it was all basically the same," I muttered. "How'm I supposed to know?"

"By studying," Coyote suggested, voice dry with sarcasm. "Or is that asking too much?"

For one brief moment I wondered if it was possible that Coyote might also be my boss, Morrison.

"I'll have to meet him someday," Coyote said idly. I winced.

"Sure, he'll like that a lot. Talking coyotes from the astral plane. That'll go over well." Morrison made Scully look like a paragon of belief. Once upon a time, our skepticism for the occult was the only thing we had in common. Then I'd done some unpleasantly weird things, like come back from the dead more or less in front of him, and now the only thing we had in common was neither of us was happy about me being a cop, though our reasons were different. "What was the second thing?" I asked, unwilling to pursue any more thoughts of Morrison.

For a moment Coyote looked blank as a happy puppy. Then he shook himself and stood up to pace, the tip of his tail twitching. "Second, you can't hear my thoughts because I have shields, and I can hear yours because even after six months of study your shields are rudimentary and poorly crafted."

"Thank you," I said, "would you like me to lie down to make it easier to kick me?"

Coyote stopped turning in a circle and flashed, seamlessly, into the man-form. He had perfectly straight black hair that fell down to his hips, gleaming with blue highlights even in the star-studded blackness near the Dead Zone.

I closed up my thoughts like all the windows rolling up in a car at once, and privately admitted to myself that Coyote was a hell of a lot easier to deal with as a coyote. As a man he was almost too pretty to live, and I mostly wanted to look at him, not listen to him.

"Joanne, you took on a great power when you chose life."

"If you say, 'With great power comes great responsibility,' so help me God, I'm going to kick you into last week."

He gave me the same unblinking gaze that the coyote could. "Try it."

A beat passed in which we neither moved nor spoke, until Coyote dropped his chin, watching me through long dark eyelashes. "You accepted this life months ago, Joanne. Why do you insist on fighting it?"

"I'm here, aren't I?" I snapped. "Isn't that something?"

"Something," he agreed, but shook his head. "But not enough. Speaking with the dead is a dangerous art, and you're not even doing that. You're just opening yourself up and offering yourself as a conduit for anybody who has a piece to speak."

"Yeah, so?" I admired my mature rebuttal. High school debate teams would weep to have me. "It's all I know how to do." Ah, a defensive attack. *Good, Joanne,* I said to myself, and hoped the windows of my mind were still sealed tight enough that Coyote didn't hear me. *That'll show him you're really the It girl.* Any moment now legions of cheerleaders would leap out and rah-rah-rah their support of my rapier wit and keen discussion skills.

"That," Coyote said with more patience and less sharpness than I deserved, "is my point. Has it occurred to you, Joanne, that I'd prefer it if you didn't get yourself killed out here?"

I blinked, and swallowed.

"Why are you so afraid?" he asked, much more softly.

There are questions a girl doesn't want to answer, and then there are the ones she doesn't even want to think about. I reached out, around Coyote and beyond him, for the Dead Zone.

The stars shut down and the world went blank.

CHAPTER THREE

In time, stars began winking in and out again, solitary dots of light that made me feel like a single extremely small point on an endless curve of blackness. I was cold beneath my skin, but when I touched my arm, my body temperature seemed normal. I didn't remember the chill in the Dead Zone before. It was as if it was tainted, too, with the same subtle wrongness that had marred Seattle.

I held my breath and turned, one slow circle, reaching out with my hands and my mind alike. The former felt nothing.

The latter encountered pain.

It rolled through me, a bone-cold ache that settled in my spine at the base of my neck, creating a headache. Ice throbbed into my veins with every heartbeat. My skin was flayed from my flesh and my flesh from my bones, knives thrusting into my kidneys and cutting out my heart. My bones broke, crushed by a weight of regret that lay heavier than the sea. It dragged me down to my knees, too weak from a hundred billion lifetimes of mistakes to bear up any longer.

And rapture shattered through me, turning the ice in my blood to golden heat. I staggered to my feet again, fire in my lungs so pure it seemed I could breathe it. Burning tears scalded my face, tracks following a thin scar to the corner of my mouth. I swallowed them down, not caring that they seared my throat.

Disbelief caught me in the belly, a bowel-twisting moment of realization that culminated in the words, "Oh, shit," when I knew I couldn't stop the *carcrashbombexplosionrunawayhorsetrainwreckshipsinking* followed by relief and dismay, to put down the burden of a body after *secondsminuteshoursdaysyearsdecadescenturieseons* of life.

Dimly, I was aware that I was connected, hideously and intimately, to everything that had ever died.

More immediately, I understood that now *I* was going to die. Again. For good.

Then somebody hit me in the face. New, fresh pain blossomed, shattering all the old. I clapped both hands to my nose, doubling over and shrieking.

Note to self: grabbing a broken nose does not, in any fashion, help. Lightning shot through my head in blinding stabs of agony. I made a retching noise and fell to the ground, knocking my forehead against the featureless planescape. Brightness flashed in my eyes. I closed them, grateful for the ache in my skull that took a little away from the shards of pain in my nose. "Mother of Christ."

I rolled onto my side, panting, and gingerly put my hand over my nose, envisioning a Mustang with a dented hood as I did so. Undenting it was easy: stick a suction cup over it and ratchet up the pressure until it popped back into place. In my mind's eye, the dent banged into shape. I opened my eyes, relieved.

Pain slammed through my nose and stabbed me in the pupils. I shot to my feet, clutching my nose more cautiously, and stared accusingly at Coyote.

"This is the realm of the dead, Joanne," he said with a shrug. He was back in coyote form, his narrow shoulders twitching lankily. "It's not a place for healing."

None of the things that came to mind were very ladylike. I managed to hold my tongue, but Coyote tilted his head at me and gave a very human snort of derision. "Nice girls don't think things like that."

"Thank you for getting me out of that," I said without the slightest degree of genuine gratitude. I hadn't felt even a hint of the healing power that normally boiled behind my breastbone when I envisioned fixing my nose. I should've known it hadn't worked.

"You're welcome," Coyote said, not meaning it any more than I had. "Can we go now?"

"No, we're here. I might as well see if I can find her."

Coyote sighed, a tremendous puff of air. "All right. What's her name?"

"I don't know."

I didn't know dogs could look scathing. I thought they

were supposed to be all about supportive looks and hopeful puppy eyes. Coyote turned a scathing look on me anyway.

"I'm not," he said through his teeth, which seemed larger and whiter and much pointier suddenly, "a dog. How do you expect to find someone in the realms of the dead if you don't even have a name to start with?"

"The others just met me here," I said uncomfortably. Coyote said something in an Indian language I didn't know, but I didn't really need a translation. The tone was enough.

"When you get out of here," he went on, "if you don't find a teacher I'm going to…" He snapped his teeth.

"Bite me?" I supplied, as helpfully as I could. He snapped his teeth again.

"The others met you here," he said, instead of completing the threat, "because you invited them to contact you. They drew you here through their skill. This time you're on your own."

"Am not. I have you."

This time he said, "Ministers and angels of grace defend us," in English, and shifted back into his human form, stepping forward to put his hands on my shoulders. I blinked. Aside from hitting me in the face a few minutes ago, I couldn't remember him having touched me before. "Have you no sense of self-preservation at all, Joanne? Are you—" Sudden clarity lit his gold eyes to amber, and his chin came up with evident surprise. "Ah," he said more quietly, and let me go.

"What? What? Am I what?"

"I think we'd better try to do what you came to do, and get out of here." He stepped away from me. A strangled sound of frustration erupted from my throat. "This is a dangerous place for you, in more ways than one. Tell me what you know about this girl, and we'll see if we can find her."

I told him what I knew: young, black, dead in the shower of the women's locker room. It was pathetically little, and I began to feel embarrassed. "Focus on her," Coyote said. "Focus on what she looked like. If we're lucky she won't have lost her body sense yet, and we'll be able to find her that way."

"And if we're not?"

"Then we're going home and you're going to have to do your research the old-fashioned way. I don't want you to be here."

I muttered under my breath as I closed my eyes, constructing an image of the dead girl behind my eyelids. She'd been pretty, with round cheekbones and a pointed chin. Her hair was short with kinky curls, a few of them bleached and dyed fire engine-red. She was dark-skinned, even in death, and I tried to imagine away the ashy blue that had tinged full lips and discolored her fingernails.

A chill slid down my back, slow and thick, like cold blood wending its way around my spine. Fine hairs stood up all over me, sweeping in waves until I shivered and shook my hands. "I'm sorry," I said, eyes still closed. "I can't do any better."

Coyote's voice came from a long way away, echoing as if through a cavernous chamber. "I think you've done more than well enough."

I opened my eyes.

Snakes.

Snakes were everywhere, winding through the empty blackness of the floor like sanguine rivers, curdling in spots and making pools of heart's-blood red. They wrapped around my ankles and crawled up my thighs, invasive and intimate. One twisted itself around my waist and ribs and lifted its face to mine, a hissing, flickering tongue tasting my breath. Smelling me and seeing me. Fangs curved dangerously past its wide-open lower jaw, drops of venom forming and splashing away. It didn't blink; I couldn't. "Coyote?" I could barely hear myself.

"I can't help you." He sounded even farther away. I dared to turn my head, the smallest motion I could manage, very aware that doing so exposed my jugular to the snake. It hissed softly, dropping its jaw wider.

Coyote was no longer off to my right. No, he was, just at an impossible distance, a speck of man-shape among the sea of snakes. They roiled and bubbled over one another, making the floor a living thing, and as I watched they began to drip from the emptiness above me.

I was caught in a Salvador Dali painting gone horribly wrong.

I laughed. It reverberated, short and broken, off the nonexistent walls of the Dead Zone. The snake around my middle tightened and hissed, bringing its head closer to my throat. My laughter cut off with a shudder.

Garter snakes, crimson and russet, crept up my body, tangling around my fingers and extending like writhing talons. They nestled through my hair until I could see them wriggling in my line of vision, making me a modern-day Gorgon. "Coyote, what's happening?" My voice was scared and thin, just the way I hadn't liked hearing Phoebe sound.

There was no answer from the trickster.

The snake at my waist still watched me. I felt my pulse jumping in my throat like a frightened mouse and ducked my head, trying to hide it from the snake. "What do you want?"

It drew its head back, flaring a hood, and hissed at me. My knees locked up, keeping me from bolting, but I didn't know if that was good or bad. "What do you want?" I managed a second time. The snake spat, venom flying past my face so close I thought I could feel it burn. Then it twisted its head away from me without releasing its grip around my middle, focused on something I couldn't see.

The Dead Zone heaved with a bloody mass of bodies, seething and knotted reptiles washing around one another in sea-sickening motion. A wave broke through them, like a submarine cruising just beneath the surface, displacing water without being visible. Then the surface ruptured, spraying frightened, twisting snakes through the air. They wriggled frantically, clutching at unsupportive sky, and collapsed soundlessly back down into the melting mess of serpents.

The thing that looked down at me was not at all like a submarine. *Monster* leaped to mind, and then a narrower classification: *sea serpent*. Why I was worried about the very specific kind of monster I was facing was beyond me, but the label hung in my thoughts as the thing reared up above me.

It was massive. It had a weight to it unlike anything I'd seen in the Dead Zone, a heaviness that seemed to bear down like the guilt and pain I'd experienced moments ago. There was no sense of being dead about the serpent. I wasn't sure I'd ever seen anything so alive or so filled with purpose. It lived, and it lived to kill.

Its scales were black, fastened together like intricate armor, and gleamed so hard against the darkness of the Dead Zone they hurt to look at. It flared out a ruff, exposing gills that glittered and sparkled with hard edges. Tentacles, like Medusa gone mad, waved around its head. It had no legs, but the word *snake* fell pitifully short. Ridges crested its back, sharp and deadly. Even in the half-light, it looked as if the spires glistened with poison. It coiled higher, enough strength visible in its body to crush a ship. If this was the kind of thing that had inspired ancient mariners to their warnings of *Here Be Dragons,* I couldn't blame them for wanting to avoid the unknown areas of the sea. It opened its mouth to hiss at me.

Its fangs were nearly as long as I was.

I wondered if I would stop feeling right away, or if I'd be alive a while inside the serpent's maw, feeling the muscle of its throat crush me as it swallowed me down.

The smaller snakes began to drop off me, slithering down my arms and legs again and falling to the floor. I couldn't blame them: I didn't want to be facing their lord and master, either. One wriggled under my shirt and down my spine, then panicked, thrashing around, when it met the taut muscle of the snake around my ribs, blocking its passage. The snake around my ribs whipped its head around, pinning my arm against my body as it sank its teeth into the littler one under my shirt. The smaller reptile spasmed, flailing under my shirt in its death throes. Its cold terror seeped in through my skin, leaving me in an icy sweat. I stared up at the monster, feeling the snake die, little and boneless against the small of my back.

The rib-hugging viper began to unwind from me. Above me, the giant serpent swayed and moved closer, snakes below it squirming away from the weight of its huge body.

"Coyote," I said once more, but this time I knew he wasn't going to answer. The viper fell away from me. For the second time that morning, my hand reached out without consulting my mind. I caught the creature at the base of the neck, below its jaw, like I'd seen snake handlers do on the Discovery Channel. It hissed and spat and writhed, effectively neutered.

The thing above me went still.

"Oh good." My voice cracked like a teenage boy's. "You're not a cannibal."

It hissed. I wanted to look down to see if it had tiny impotent arms like a T Rex, waggling angrily at me, but I didn't dare. Around me, the sea of snakes backed away, making a circle of blackness with the sea serpent at its head. Like their master, the ones closest to me reared up, and unlike the monster creature, swayed menacingly, as if to remind me I wasn't the one in charge here.

I really didn't need the reminder.

"So maybe now we make a bargain," I said. It blinked

at me, an action that in another creature might have read as surprise. In the giant serpent, it only served to make me aware that I could see my entire body reflected in the empty blackness. "You let us go," I said hopefully, "and I'll let it go."

"Usssss." The serpent's voice was a river of sound, pounding behind my ears.

"Us," I said again. "Me and Coyote." Distance and space in the Dead Zone were malleable. I'd learned that the first time I'd visited, though I hadn't been able to deliberately affect it. Now I swallowed against the tightness in my throat, clung to the idea of Coyote, and told the universe to change.

My feet went out from under me like I'd hit a patch of ice. My gut lurched with panic and I tightened my stranglehold on the snake in my fist. Space contracted into a needle point, then expanded again, snakes slithering down into that point like a sucking drain, and reappearing all around me. The dragon-thing slid with me, and so did the snake I held knotted in my fingers, but all the other snakes were new.

How I recognized one wriggling field of snakes from another, I didn't know, but there it was.

The sea serpent flicked its tongue, long enough to wrap around me, and at my elbow, Coyote growled, "What," and in an audible pause I heard him not saying "the hell" before he finished, "do you think you're doing?"

"Rescuing us," I said with all the confidence I could muster. My voice didn't break again, so I counted that as good enough, and brandished my captive snake. "It for us," I said to the waiting sea serpent. It flickered its tongue again, weaving back and forth to examine me from one side, then the other.

"There isss one of it," it answered. "There are two of you."

Crap. I'd been afraid it would notice that. "I don't suppose you'll give me time off for good behavior?"

It stared at me, unblinking.

Crap.

"Joanne," Coyote said, a warning in his voice.

"Then let this one go," I said, jerking my head at the red man beside me.

"Jo," Coyote said again. "Don't."

The monster flattened its snout, tongue darting out, as if it were flaring its nostrils. "The sssacrifisse is ssweetesst when the victim isss willing."

"I'm willing." I waved the smaller snake at it. "This little guy for Coyote, and I'm all yours."

"Done," it said.

I released the little snake and shoved Coyote away from me with all my will, like the recoil from a car crash.

For an instant, Coyote resisted. He knew me; he knew that I work through the medium I know best, cars. In fact, he'd taught me to do that. So for a moment, the recoil of that car wreck was met by his own image, the steadfastness of a mountain, absorbing the energy I tried pushing him away with.

Then power surged through me, blood-red and deep and cool, a link from the serpent as it bent its will to the same ends I pursued. There was no metaphor to its desire, only the intent to remove that which it had promised to.

Coyote flickered like the serpent's tongue, and disappeared.

The viper I'd dropped whipped around and hissed at me, striking forward so quickly I didn't stand a chance.

The serpent spat, venom splashing over the smaller snake before it completed its attack. It shrieked, a high thin sound, and flipped onto its back, writhing and whining in pain.

"Yeah!" I spat at it, too, to much less effect. "I'm only a meal for the big guy!"

The serpent lifted its head and spread its hood, staring at me. It struck me that gloating was not a snakely trait. I cleared my throat. "Never mind. It's just, you know, if you've got to go out, might as well get taken out by the…never mind."

It reared up and doubled forward, jaws gaping. As I stared into its descending maw, my last thought was, *isn't there a Shel Silverstein poem appropriate to this situation?*

CHAPTER FOUR

A meaty hand, warm and callused, clamped onto my shoulder. My eyes popped open and I looked blankly at the cream-colored tiles above the dead girl. This was not what I imagined the inside of a snake to look like.

"Walker?"

I twisted my head up. The warm hand on my shoulder was attached to the wrist, arm, shoulder, and ultimately, beefy body of my immediate supervisor, Captain Michael Morrison of the Seattle Police Department, North Precinct.

Morrison always made me think of a superhero starting to go to seed: late thirties, graying hair, sharp blue eyes, a bit too much weight on the bones. I'd never been so glad to see a seedy superhero in my life, and said the first grateful words that came to mind: "This isn't your jurisdiction."

"And that sure as hell isn't your uniform." Morrison smirked and took his hand off my shoulder.

Goose bumps shot up all over my body and I clutched my arms around my towel. This was not the outfit I'd have chosen to summon the police in. And if I'd been out long enough for the cops to get here, time had gone funny in a way I wasn't used to. I took refuge in defensiveness, staring up at Morrison. "What the hell are you doing here?"

"I was on my way into work when the call came across the scanner. I just couldn't resist the words 'Officer Joanne Walker' and '10-55' in the same sentence."

"Yeah. You might've gotten lucky and the dead body might've been mine." If he'd put his hand on my shoulder half a second later, it would've been. I didn't like to think about the implications of that. "What happened?"

"You were in a trance, or something," Phoebe blurted from somewhere behind Morrison. "I thought you were following me, but you didn't, so I came back to look and you wouldn't wake up when I shook you, so I called the cops. You woke up as soon as he touched you."

I didn't like to think about the implications of that, either. I climbed to my feet instead. Cold water trailed down my shins in rivulets. Something even colder slid down the back of my towel and hit the water with a plop.

"Jesus Christ! What the hell is that?" Morrison all but levitated away, moving back across the other side of the curb with a smooth bound that did the aging superhero look proud. My neck stiffened, preventing me from looking at what had fallen.

"It's a snake," I said in a small voice, then checked to be sure I was right.

Sometimes I hate it when I'm right.

The first time I visited the astral plane, I came home with a leaf that shimmered blue and white in the darkness. I thought that was a much nicer souvenir than a dead albino garter snake.

I crouched and picked it up. "Put that down!" Morrison barked. "It's part of the crime scene."

"It is not. It's contaminating the crime scene." I scowled at him from my crouch. "Unless you think I did it."

"Did you?" he snapped.

I groaned. "No."

"Fine. Then tell me why the hell you're carrying a snake in your tow—"

Look, in his shoes, I wouldn't have been able to make it through that sentence, either. Morrison broke off, choked, then guffawed, while I put my elbow on my knee and my forehead against my hand and waited for him to laugh it out. Phoebe, the traitor, giggled, too, although she tried to hide it by clapping both hands over her mouth.

It took a long time for them to stop laughing.

"Get dressed," Morrison said eventually, still grinning. "That's no way for the department to be represented when members of other forces are on their way."

There was nothing I could say that wouldn't sound like fishing for a compliment, so I bit my tongue, took my snake, and got dressed.

Answering questions about the body I'd found turned out to be a lot less unpleasant when I was wearing a police officer's uniform than it had been when I'd been wearing jeans and a sweater. For one thing, the university police didn't seem to think I'd done it, which was a huge improvement. There was a bit of *quel coincidence* that a cop had found her, but hey, those things happened. Phoebe and I took turns answering questions, neither of us any more helpful than I'd been with Coyote in the Dead Zone.

The detective in charge, a knockout Southerner named Renfroe, kept saying, "Uh-huh," and, "Huh," and scribbling things down, including my phone number. I thought I saw her checking me out as I walked away when we were finally dismissed. I resisted the urge to call back, "It's a snake in my pocket," but since not even Morrison had brought up the snake, I wasn't about to.

Morning sunshine and heat were already swimming up off the pavement as I walked outside, escorted by Morrison. My eyes started watering and I lifted a hand to shade them, squinting down the parking lot for my car, now hidden among dozens of others in the lot. Morrison held the yellow crime scene tape up for me. I ducked under it, half-expecting him to let it fall and entangle me, like we were in grade school. I snorted at myself. As if he read my mind, Morrison snorted louder. "You're welcome."

"Thanks. I wasn't trying to be rude." There. Politeness to a superior officer. Go me.

"No, it just comes naturally to you."

A higher-ranking officer, anyway.

No, that just wasn't true. Morrison was a better cop than I was. It went beyond petty and right into sheer stupidity to suggest otherwise. "Is there anything I can say that would convince you I wasn't trying to be an asshole?" There was another word that should be used somewhere in that sentence. Oh yes: "Captain?"

"'I quit' would be right up there at the top of the list," Morrison said. "You need a ride to the station?"

For a moment I stared at him. Not up at him: we were exactly the same height, and in police-issued street stompers, neither of us had the shoe advantage.

I'd passed the Academy with not-entirely-shameful marks and got a job for the department doing what I was good at: fixing cars. Almost a year ago I'd taken some personal leave that went on too long. I couldn't blame Morrison for hiring somebody to replace me—well, I could and did, but that wasn't the point—but as a woman of Native American descent, I looked too good on the roster to fire. So he'd made me a real cop, put me on the street and hoped I'd bolt.

I'd rather have poked my eyes out with a shrimp fork than give him the satisfaction.

My feet toughened up after a few weeks, and I admit a certain vicious pleasure in ticketing SUVs in compact car parking spaces, but I still missed being elbow deep in grease and oil. This was not how my life was supposed to go.

The coroners wheeled the body—Cassandra Tucker, age twenty, a college junior, recently broken up with her boyfriend, mother of a little girl whose name wasn't written on the back of her photo, and possessor of an illegal

photo ID, all of which would have been helpful in the
Dead Zone—past us.

Maybe my life wasn't so bad after all. With that in mind,
I pasted on a bright smile for my captain. "No, I've got Petite. Want a ride?"

The corners of Morrison's mouth tightened. My smile
got brighter. "I didn't think so."

"I want to talk to you in my office when you get to work."

That put a hitch in my jaunty swagger away. I looked
over my shoulder. Morrison's mouth was still tight. "Yeah,
all right, boss," I said, more subdued, and went to find
Petite.

She was the root cause of the trouble between Morrison and me. There are few cars as sweet as a 1969 Mustang, but how any red-blooded American male could
mistake one for a 1963 Corvette was beyond my ken. I'd
been merciless in teasing him about it.

It turned out mocking a newly promoted captain wasn't
a great idea, especially since it turned out that he was also
newly assigned to the precinct I worked in, and therefore
my new boss. It wasn't the best way to start a working relationship, and it had only degenerated from there.

The worst of it was I'd eventually learned that Morrison's real problem with me was that he thought I was
wasting my potential as a mechanic. He might've put me
on street duty to get me to quit, but it'd backfired. I was
bound and determined to prove myself to him now, a
stance as contrary as any Irishman could take.

The idea that he'd suspected I'd react that way and had
reverse-psychologied me into doing what he wanted

didn't bear thinking about. I pulled out of the parking lot behind him and drove to the station at a sedate pace.

"Where did the snake come from?" The question sounded over the click of the door; I'd already noted with trepidation that the Venetian blinds were lowered over the glass wall that faced the rest of the office. I put my palm against the door frame as if to make sure it was closed, but mostly it was to steady myself before I turned to face Morrison.

"You wouldn't believe me if I told you." I left the door and sat down, rubbing my fingers over the scar on my cheek. Morrison's eyebrows quirked.

"Try me." Arizona deserts had nothing on the dry spell in his voice.

"My new boyfriend's got kind of a kink about snakes," I said, as straight-faced as I could. I liked that idea better than the truth anyway.

A Colorado thunderstorm swept Arizona dryness from Morrison's face. "Walker."

I flinched. Dammit.

"Even," Morrison said through his teeth, "if I thought the odds of you sharing intimate sexual details with me for any reason was within the realm of possibility, I've been here long enough to know that the odds of you having a boyfriend are even *less* likely—"

I felt heat burning up my jaw and into my cheekbones. "Okay," I said tightly. "My new girlfr—"

"Walker!"

Apparently I was incapable of getting any from either

side of the street. How incredibly depressing. I closed my eyes and slumped in my chair. "I took a quick trip into the astral realm to see if I could find out anything from Cassandra Tucker about who'd killed her. I ran into a bunch of snakes instead. That one came back with me."

Deadly silence filled the room. I counted to ten, then forced my eyes open. Morrison looked at me, expressionless. I counted to ten a second time, then a third, and he said, "I liked the boyfriend story better. Get back to work."

I stood up by degrees and nodded, my jaw clenched. "Yes, sir." I felt like I had an iron pipe rammed up my spine as I turned away. I got the door open half an inch before he said, "Walker."

I waited.

It was harder for Morrison than me. Silence stretched like hot glass, then shattered: "Did you learn anything?"

That he even asked—well, I said he was a better cop than I was. "No, sir. Sorry."

A deaf man could've heard the relief and vindication in his voice: "Then leave the detecting to the detectives, dammit, and get back to work."

"Yes, sir."

It wasn't a direct disobeyal of orders to drop by Detective Billy Holliday's desk and hitch myself up onto a corner of it. I was in uniform. The door was mere yards away. Not my fault I got caught up in a bit of conversation.

Morrison wouldn't have bought it, either, but he was still in his office. Billy frowned up at me, displaying a big hand with his fingers wide-spread. "The truth, now. Do you think the pearlescent polish is a bit much?"

Billy Holliday had been saddled by loving if cruel parents with one of the more unfortunate names a boy could be given. To the best of my ability to tell, part of his retaliation was growing up to be a cross-dresser. He had better dress sense than I did, and over the years the department had gotten used to him showing up at the Policeman's Ball in drag. Even normally conservative cops could learn to take a lot in stride, although it probably didn't hurt that his wife made Salma Hayek look like the redheaded stepchild.

He was also, metaphysically speaking, on the far end of the spectrum from Morrison. Where I was a reluctant believer, Billy was a True Believer, and once upon a time I'd ragged him endlessly about that. It wasn't until my own world turned upside-down that I thought to ask why he was a believer, and I'd seen enough by then to not wholly discount his claim of being able to see ghosts. Especially when he'd reported that the ghost of a dead little girl had claimed I had no past lives to haunt me, and my own spirit guide had independently confirmed it. The entire idea still made me squirm with discomfort, but Billy'd been very generous in not giving me a ration of well-deserved shit over the past few months. There wasn't much doubt that he was a far better person than I was.

"It's nice." I peered at his nails. "Subtle."

Billy looked smug. "Thought so. Just enough to throw 'em off."

Curiosity reigned. "Is that why you do it? To throw suspects off?" I'd never nerved myself up to ask before.

"Nah," Billy said. "But it doesn't hurt. You're trying to look winsome, Joanie. What do you need?"

"To work on my winsome look, apparently." I wrinkled my nose and Billy laughed. "Know anything about the significance of snakes on the astral plane?"

"I love how you do that," he said, fighting down a grin that threatened to turn into veritable beaming. "All casual-like. Nonchalant. How much does that cost you?"

"I grind my teeth flat and featureless every night while I sleep," I assured him. Unfortunately, it wasn't far from true. I'd had to get a mouth guard two months ago. No wonder I couldn't get a boyfriend. The image of me with a translucent green plastic guard was enough to set *me* off my feed.

"I weep to hear it," Billy said, much too cheerfully. "Snakes, huh? Not a whole lot. The old gut," which, I observed, was distinctly larger than it had been a month ago, "says betrayal, uncertainty, choices lying ahead."

"Billy," I said, staring at his belly, "is Melinda pregnant again?"

I never saw anybody blush as hard as Billy did right then, not even myself under Morrison's gimlet eye. Not that I'd actually seen that.

"Shit," Billy said with embarrassed enthusiasm, "I'm not supposed to tell anybody for another month. How'd you know?"

I cackled, then straightened up and cleared my throat, trying not to sound self-satisfied. "Sekrit Shamanic Knowledge," I said, imbuing the words with as many capital letters as I could. Billy squinted at me. I cackled again, clapping a hand over my mouth. "You've put on weight," I said behind my fingers. "Last time she was pregnant you gained forty pounds."

"I lost it again!"

"How much weight did *she* gain?"

Billy's lower lip protruded in a sulk. "About seventeen pounds. I think it's a Jedi mind trick."

I grinned and clapped him on the shoulder. "I won't tell. And congratulations. I won't tell. But you might want to stop hitting The Missing O."

"Snakes," Billy said grouchily. "Why do you want to know about snakes?"

"I had a weird encounter this morning."

Billy lit up. "Yeah? We could go over to the O and you could tell me abou—"

Morrison strode out of his office and down the hall. I scrambled to my feet. "No O for you," I told Billy, "and streetwalking for me." He made the obligatory snicker and I rolled my eyes. "I'll tell you about it later, okay?"

"I'll try to find out about snakes," Billy called after me, and I ducked out of the station with Morrison hot on my tail.

CHAPTER FIVE

Morrison didn't catch up with me. He didn't have to. I spent the rest of the morning reciting what he would've said in my head, anyway. It was a bad sign when I'd bawl myself out and save my boss the trouble. I found myself writing more parking tickets than were strictly necessary. There was a kind of quota about them. Too many meant I was being overzealous, but not enough meant I was slacking. Being the sympathetic sort—at least when it came to cars—I usually erred on the side of slacking, but I was taking a mean vengeance against the universe by overdoing it today. I slapped a ticket on a double-parked cab and stalked by, muttering at the Morrison in my head.

"Lady, I cannot believe you just did that."

My shoulders rose toward my ears of their own accord

and my face wrinkled up until it felt like a raisin around my nose.

"I mean, after all I done for you, you go and write me a ticket? A…Christ, lady! A sixty dollar ticket?"

The raisin of my face started to split with a grin. I peeked over my shoulder. Leaning on the cab I'd just ticketed was the most solid old man I'd ever seen. His massive gray eyebrows were lifted toward an all-white hairline, and even squinting into the sun, his gray eyes were bright as he grinned.

"Gary," I said, trying not to let my own smile slide into "idiotic." "I thought you were calling me 'copper' these days."

"I just can't get the hang of it," the cabbie admitted. He shoved away from the cab, holding the ticket as if it were something two weeks dead, and arched his bushy eyebrows more sharply. "You ticketed me, Jo. Doncha love me anymore?"

I snatched the ticket and stuffed it in my mouth, chewing. Two gnaws in, the flat gray taste of the paper and the sharp blue of the ink stung my tongue, and my mouth went all Mr. Magoo while I tried to figure out what to do with it now. "I didn't know you were back," I croaked, and spat the gooey ticket into my palm. "Don't try that," I advised, then grinned stupidly again. "You look good."

"'Course I do," Gary said with pleasant arrogance. He still had the build of the linebacker he'd once been, and deep-set Hemingway wrinkles assured the world he knew the score. "How's my crazy dame?"

"Fine," I said automatically, considered, then nodded.

"Yeah, I'm okay. You look like California was good for you. You're tanned."

Gary's expression closed down, some of the brightness dying from gray eyes. "First time I'd been since Annie died."

A cord of loss knotted around my heart, for all that I'd never met his wife. Gary'd walked into my life—or I'd climbed into his cab, more accurately—six months ago, the day everything went to hell. Somehow he'd become the most real thing in my life since then. "Was it tough?"

"Yeah. Sometimes. But she woulda hated the thought of me sittin' around until I was rotted enough to die, so I figured I better get off my duff and go see some of the world again."

I exhaled a snort. "Gary, *I'm* going to rot before you do."

He squinted up at the sky. "In this heat, you're prob'ly right. If I'd known it was gonna be ninety by noon, I mighta stayed in San Diego. At least the girls there wear bikinis."

I put on my best indignant look. "Are you cheating on me, Gary? Running around with bikini-clad bimbos?"

"Yeah," he said, good humor restored. "Blond ones."

"You're breaking my heart." I smiled so I'd fool myself into thinking I wasn't just a little bit jealous of a seventy-three-year-old's romantic notions.

"Guess I better invite you over for dinner, then," Gary said with aplomb.

"It's a date," I said instantly. "Wait. You're not cooking, are you?"

He let out a shout of laughter. "Like you can complain about my cooking. I know what you live on."

"Hey, you've got me eating frozen Italian dinners instead of mac and cheese. All your nagging did some good."

"I don't nag."

"You do too. Italian dinners have vegetables in them. I haven't eaten vegetables without nagging in my whole twenty-seven years."

"Arright, if you say so, Jo." He gave me a good-natured grin, like he knew he was humoring me.

Actually, it was true. I'd started eating better—frozen entrees *did* qualify as better than an endless diet of macaroni and cheese—in part because *I* wanted to look as good as he did at seventy-three. Hell, I'd be glad to look as good as he did at twenty-eight. "I get off work at seven, barring disaster."

Gary's bushy eyebrows drew together. "Been any lately?"

I hesitated, then brushed the answer away with a wave of my hand. "I'll tell you at dinner."

"Arright." Gary beamed at me. "Look, I gotta take off, there's this crazy lady cop who wants to ticket my cab. Call when you're on the way over. Dinner at seven-thirty."

"It's a date," I repeated. "See you tonight."

Gary gave me a broad wink and climbed into his cab. I stood on the sidewalk, smiling stupidly as I watched him drive away.

Gary being back in town lifted my spirits despite the oppressive heat. With a dinner date to look forward to, I stopped writing so many tickets and grabbed a doughnut for lunch. I wanted to drop into the astral realm to apologize to Coyote, and a real meal would take too long. Besides, I was on street beat, which I told myself gave me license to eat anything I wanted because I'd walk it off. So far I believed me.

Doughnut in hand, I scurried down to the garage, my favorite place in the station. The smell of gasoline and motor oil soothed the savage beast, or at least the savage Joanne.

Not everyone down there would meet my eye. I still hadn't gotten used to that, especially from Nick, who'd been my supervisor and a pretty good friend not all that long ago. His greeting was made up of shoving his hands in his pockets and lifting his shoulders as he dropped his chin, turning him into a no-neck wonder. He kept his gaze fixed firmly on the wall as I gave him a tentative smile. Tentative didn't used to be in my vocabulary around the boys in the garage. We'd worked together for three years, and I'd thought I was just one of the guys. But in January I'd invited the Wild Hunt into the garage's office, and two months later I'd collapsed on the stairs, bleeding from the ears. Since then things had been a little touchy when I came down to visit. I hoped if I just kept it cool everybody would relax again, but so far it hadn't worked.

Still, hope sprang eternal. I strengthened my smile for Nick and said, "Hi," as normally as I could. My voice squeaked and broke, which at least made him look at me. I cleared my throat and smiled again, wishing it didn't feel plastic. "I was wondering if I could hang out in the office for a little bit."

Nick's gaze snapped back to the wall and he shrugged his shoulders higher. "Sure. Whatever."

Not the most ringing endorsement I'd ever heard. Nick stalked off to harass one of the other mechanics, who gave me a wry look and rolled his eyes. It made me feel better, and I said, "Thanks," to Nick's retreating back before turning to discover my arch nemesis, Thor the Thunder God, standing about eight inches behind me. Thor—whose real name was something dull like Ed or Eddie or Freddie—had been hired to replace me in the motor pool. He was blond, about six foot five, and had shoulders that Thor himself would envy. I figured him taking my job gave me license to call him whatever I wanted. For some reason he didn't like it.

We both stepped the same direction, trying to get out of each other's way. We both hesitated, then lurched the other way. By the third twitch, I was grinning. "Shall we dance?"

He took a deliberately large step backward and gestured me by with a sarcastic flourish. My smile fell away. "Thank you, O Mighty God of Thunder." I saw his mouth twist as I headed for the office. It was the one place in the station I thought I could slide into the astral realm without the help of a drum. I was comfortable there, and back in January I'd done enough—

This shaman thing was getting to me. I'd almost thought *done enough magic there* without the idea even making me hitch. I sat down with a shiver and tried to push the thought away. Despite everything, I didn't like being comfortable enough with the idea that magic was real to just think it casually. Having oatmeal for breakfast was casual. Doing magic was not.

Then, excruciatingly aware of the irony, I relaxed and thought of my garden.

The bottom fell out of the world and I slid into a tunnel, twisting and bumping over earthen ridges, fast enough to make my nose tickle from the vibrations. It reminded me of the defensive driving course at the academy, rattling over speed bumps placed too closely together.

The tunnel shot to the left, leveling out and narrowing. I was aware that, like the tunnel, I became smaller and smaller as I scurried along it. In what little studying I'd done, I'd read that shapeshifting inside one's own psyche was the first step toward a complete and physical shapechange. The book had talked earnestly about transforming into an eagle, a bear, a wolf—the usual World Wildlife Fund Charismatic Megafauna sorts of creatures. Nothing I'd read ever mentioned people turning into badgers or earthworms.

I realized with a dismayed jolt that the tunnel had disappeared entirely and I was grinding my way through the earth blindly, gnawing on dirt to move forward.

Earthworm. I really needed to learn to be careful about what I was thinking in trance states.

Badger, I thought encouragingly, and a few seconds later burst upward through the earth in a flurry of dirt and strong claws. I scrambled out of my tunnel and shook myself all over, bits of grass and soil plopping to the grass around me.

Everyone has an inner landscape, shaped by the events and thoughts that make a life. The first time I'd been in mine, it had been stiff and parched. Now it looked distorted, seen from only several inches above the ground and in faded grayscale. To the right was a thick, shimmering pool of mercury, ripples wobbling over the surface to break against the shore. Behind it was a tall granite-streaked bluff, too high to easily see the top of from a badger's vantage point. To the left, a lawn manicured so short it was nearly dead spread out, a handful of dark-leafed hedges sprouting up in asture blocks of green. Stone pathways and stone benches made straight lines through the garden.

Possibly, just possibly, I still had some inner-garden nurturing to do.

Immediately behind me, my badger hole folded in on itself and smoothed out again, leaving lawn behind. "Well, that's something," I said out loud, as the world around me stained with color. The pool faded from mercury to clear, its earthy bottom refracting brown through reflected gray skies. I rolled onto my back, briefly missing the extraordinary strength of the badger's legs, and closed my eyes. "Coyote?" I tried to picture him, long-legged and golden-eyed, then laughed silently as the image slid between Coyote-the-man and Coyote-the-coyote. Straight black hair drooped over perked furry ears. He looked like a character from Disney's *Robin Hood* gone terribly wrong.

A rustle hissed over the grass like wax paper sliding against itself. I sat up, grinning. "You're always reading my mind," I said. "So get a load of how I think of…you?"

A rattlesnake swayed in front of me, black eyes reflecting the sudden paleness of my skin.

A snake in my garden.

For one hysterical moment I looked for an apple tree. Then panic took over and I crab-walked backward, elbows and knees going everywhere. It took another few seconds to make myself stop by asserting enough control to dig my fingers into the earth. "My garden," I croaked. "You can't be here."

The rattler slithered forward a few inches, dry scrape against the short grass. "You can't *be* here," I repeated. It lifted its head and hissed at me, long tongue darting in and out. I shot to my feet, barely keeping myself from leaping to one of the stone benches and screaming like a '50s housewife. It was my garden. My rules were supposed to apply. I bit the inside of my cheek and closed my eyes, reverting to the car metaphor I was most comfortable with. Rolling up the mental windows and making a shield of glass around myself reminded me of movies where the venomous animal was kept away from the actors by a sheet of glass.

The snake bonked its nose against the glass, striking out and coiling back as I opened my eyes. Its tongue thrust out again, and it reared back, expressionless flat eyes somehow looking offended. I grinned in a breathless combination of triumph and fear, and waggled my fingers at it. "G'bye, then."

For once I let myself forget the vehicle metaphor, and instead spun glass. Heat poured off my body as I willed it to soften the shield between myself and the snake. I blew air through pursed lips and the glass expanded, spilling clear and delicate over the lawn as I protected my garden. The snake squiggled backward, forced to the edges of the garden.

I nearly had the thing vanquished when it shifted.

It didn't change like Coyote did, inside a blink. Instead it reared up, making a long slender line of itself, balancing on a single coil of muscle. A hood flared, cobralike, then widened farther, broadening until it became shoulders. The body thickened, arms sprouting and waist narrowing. Hips splayed, legs splitting from the expanding breadth of muscle that had been its body. The coil upon which she had balanced became feet, small and bare. I jerked my eyes up to her face.

The rattlesnake's dead eyes gazed back at me; like Ra, she was human-shaped with a snake's head, large enough to fit the body. She flicked her tongue at me once more and completed the transformation into a brisk-looking Native American woman whose age I couldn't judge. Her eyes were still very black, though bright with reflected sunlight. She had salt-and-pepper hair and wrinkles around her eyes. Her cheeks were round over a thin mouth that looked like it was used to smiling, but which was at the moment pushed out in a thoughtful moue. "Well, you certainly are a handful."

"What?"

"You're a handful," she repeated. "Sliding around the astral realm, leaving psychic debris all over the place, and with such terrible shields I could walk right in here. I can see what needs to be done. At least you have potential," she added, shaking her head. "You nearly pushed me out just now."

I set my teeth and reared my head back, reestablishing the crystalline wall. It glimmered, becoming a solid curve of glass between the snake woman and myself. Her eyebrows—straight and slightly angled, like Spock's—rose a fraction of an inch, and she took a step back. "You see?" She sounded pleased.

"Who are you? And what are you doing here?"

"My name is Judy Morningstar," she said. "I'm going to be your teacher."

CHAPTER SIX

"The hell you are." Guilt mixed with incredulity in my voice. Coyote'd just finished telling me I needed a teacher, and I hated to admit he might be right. "Get out of my head. I'm doing just fine on my own." Ah, yes. The petulant, spoiled child tone. That always went over well.

Judy sat down with irritating grace, as if she'd had it drilled into her by a dance instructor when she was too small to protest. "You've regressed from what your abilities six months ago were," she disagreed. "Even three months ago. You haven't accepted your power or the responsibility that comes with it."

"What the hell are you talking about? I stopped Cernunnos, didn't I? I fought the banshee. That all took power."

"Oh yes." She nodded. "In the moment of crisis, you did

what had to be done, with the tools at hand. You used enormous power, but without regard for the consequences."

A thin trickle of apprehension dribbled down my spine. "I was careful. The hospitals and the airport, all the power stayed on so people would be okay." Chills swept over my arms regardless of the heat, oppressive even here in my own garden. I tried rubbing the goose bumps away without success.

"Consequences aren't always so easily seen as that, Joanne. You know there's something wrong, yet you ignore it."

The discolored streets and life-lights I'd seen with my second sight flashed through my memory, streaky vision of wrongness. "I saw it," I said reluctantly. "I don't know what it is, though."

"It's you," Judy said. "The power you used six months ago disrupted weather systems all over the world, and worst of all in Seattle. How long did it take the snow to melt, Joanne?"

Seattle, not notorious for snow, had seen a storm that began the week after I gained shamanic powers and hadn't stopped worth mentioning until April. When spring hit, it did so overnight, temperatures soaring into the seventies. There'd been flooding for weeks, and since then it'd been drier than bones. I wrapped my arms around myself, shaking my head. Denial: it wasn't just a river in Egypt. The worst part was the uncomfortable, shoulder-hunching suspicion that she was telling God's own truth. I knew something was wrong, and I hadn't been able to find its center. I also hadn't looked at myself. Dammit.

"You've left a mess to clean up, Joanne. You used tremendous power once or twice, and what have you done since then?"

My shoulders hunched again, without my permission. I hated body language. Most of it didn't pass through my brain for a spot-check on what I wanted to give away.

It wasn't that I'd done *nothing* with the gifts that had been catalyzed in me. I'd done detail work, fixing up chips in peoples' paint, so to speak. My coworker Bruce got a hairline fracture on his ankle and the doctors had been astounded at how quickly he healed. Not quite overnight, but within a few days he was running again, without discomfort. I took a perverse pleasure in smoothing over hangnails and papercuts when I shook hands. One of the books I'd read said those who needed healing had to believe the healing could be done. I'd discovered that for small physical injuries, being unaware that healing was taking place was just about as good.

But none of it was earth-shattering, world-saving stuff, and the truth was, most of it made no long-term difference to the people I'd helped.

My shoulders inched farther toward my ears. "Look, I promise I'll do better, okay? Go away."

"I can't do that, Joanne. I'm committing myself to teaching you, and unlike you, I take that responsibility seriously."

Anger flared in my belly, sending blood up to stain my cheeks and make my ears hot. "It's not that I don't take it seriously. I just never asked for this in the first place—"

"But you accepted it." There was a note of smugness in

her voice, almost as unlikable as my whining. "Do you accept me as your teacher, Joanne Walker?"

I scowled at the pond. Coyote wanted me to have a teacher. "Did Coyote send you?"

"I beg your pardon?" Genuine surprise filled her voice. "You called out for help twice today. Traditionally it takes three cries, but I thought you might not want to wait. You expected someone as powerful as Coyote to send you a teacher?"

My shoulders couldn't hunch any farther, so I tightened my arms around my ribs. "It seemed likely. Anyway, I didn't know I was yelling for help."

Judy pursed her mouth. "I'm sorry," she said after a moment. "If you're on casual terms with Coyote, maybe I misinterpreted your need for help." She got to her feet as smoothly as she'd sat, bowing her head toward me. "I hope I'll see you again, Joanne." She began to fade, again not like Coyote, but as if she were a ghost.

I gritted my teeth and dug my fingers into my ribs. "Wait."

The fade stopped and she lifted her head again, one eyebrow raised in question. I clenched my jaw a couple of times before asking, "Who are you? I mean, how do I know you're qualified to teach me? Do you even exist outside here?" I swept the fingers of one hand in a circle, more meaning to encompass the astral realm than my garden.

Judy gave me a very brief, wry smile. "You mean, would I answer if you dropped me an e-mail message? Not usually. I'm terrible about checking it. As for qualified…" She spread her hands and lifted her shoulders in a shrug.

"I've practiced magic for most of my existence. We could try a handful of lessons and you could decide if I'm the teacher for you."

"Most of your existence?" I thought that was a weird word to choose, and it showed in my voice. Judy's smile went less wry and more open.

"You, of all people, should know that *life* is too limited a term for those who walk in other realms."

I remembered, quite vividly, a sour-faced shaman who was irritated at her untimely death because she was young in the practice of shamanism, and others who had been tolerant of her because they had far more experience, even though some of them looked much younger in years. I rubbed my hand over my eyes. "Yeah. I guess so. All right." I pressed my lips together and looked at her again. "All right, fine. We'll see how it goes for, like, three lessons, okay? And then I get to reevaluate." The crystal wall I'd built had dimmed during our conversation, a physical sign that I was relenting mentally.

Judy smiled and ducked her head in another semi-bow. "Wonderful. We'll meet here tomorrow at six to begin."

"Six? In the *morning?*"

"The mind is clearer and less burdened after dreaming."

I groaned. "Okay. Six. God."

Judy grinned, took one step backward, and disappeared.

"Out of sight, out of mind," I muttered. I wished I thought I'd accomplished ridding myself of her, but it was painfully clear that she'd opted to leave on her own. I curled a lip grouchily and cast out my consciousness, calling for Coyote.

There was no answer.

I opened my eyes again, watching the clock mark away seconds in clicks that hadn't seemed loud when I went under. I had fifteen seconds of lunch break left, and a sour lump of doughnut in my belly.

The second hand swept to the top. I got to my feet and walked out of the office, saying, "Hey," unbidden when Thor accidentally met my eyes. He jerked his head in a nod, a startled, "Hey," following me up the stairs.

Another "Hey," caught my attention as I headed for the front doors, Billy swinging around a corner to grin beefily down at me. "Joanie. There you are. Snakes are good juju. Thought you'd like to know."

I stared at him for a couple of seconds, then shook myself. "Could've fooled me. What do you mean?"

"Looked 'em up on the Net, but I really should've known it before. I mean, think about it. The Hippocratic symbol—"

"—a staff with the snakes twined around it. Duh."

Billy grinned. "Yep. Duh. So, yeah, basically, good vibes. They're symbols of healing and renewal and change."

I thought of Judy, shifting from snake to woman in my garden, and tried to smile. "Great. Good. I could use some."

Billy's eyebrows drew down. "You okay, Joanie? You look like you lost your best friend."

Memory hit me in the sternum, so real and immediate that my breath stopped. I lifted my hand, pressing the heel against my breastbone, trying to clear the tightness. My heart pounded in fast, thick pulses that brought the doughnut back up to the gagging point, making me swallow heavily. Color burned my cheeks, and I resented my fair skin all over again.

"Joanie? Are you okay?" Billy caught my shoulders, concern wrinkling his forehead. My vision was cloudy, a haze settling down between us. For a few seconds all I could do was remember.

I was fifteen and my father and I had been living in North Carolina for over a year, by far the longest time I'd ever lived in one place in my life. I'd never been anywhere long enough to make good friends; that pretty, petite Sara Buchanan had chosen me as a best friend was a source of regular amazement and pleasure to me. But in memory, her eyebrows were drawn down over angry hazel eyes, and the golden-brown skin that I envied so much was suffused with furious red.

She'd said she didn't like him. I was already terrified by what I'd done in trying to fit in, trying to make a boy like me. I hadn't meant for things to go as far as they did, and I only wanted someone to tell me it'd be okay. She'd said she didn't like him, and when I'd whispered that, confused and frightened, she'd barked derisive laughter at me. *I lied! God, what was I supposed to say, yeah, I like him? How obvious is that? God, Joanne, don't you know anything?*

"No." I whispered it now, just like I'd done then. No, I didn't know anything. I'd grown up solitary enough, with my father rather than girls for company, that I'd honestly had no idea that her hair-tossing denial had been a front.

Tiny black spots of panic swam at the corners of my vision, etching around the memory of Sara until she stood out, full of vibrant color, against an inky background. There was fear in my stomach, more potent than what I'd felt with the boy. The First Boy; even in memory I didn't let myself think his name. Panic edged through me, so I could feel the flow of blood fluttering through my heart, little missed murmurs that I couldn't catch my breath to banish. Like the tide coming in, sound thrummed against my eardrums, blocking out Sara's words, although I could see them in the shape of her mouth.

I'm never speaking to you again.

And she didn't.

She watched me with cool disdain that turned into hate when I began to show a few months later. The First Boy went back to his mother's people in Canada, and none of us, not me, not Sara, certainly not the Boy, ever told anyone he was the father. When the twins were born and the little girl died, I tried to ask Sara to speak for her. She looked through me as if I wasn't there. I'd lost my best friend.

And even now, almost thirteen years later, tears stung my eyes as I shook off Billy's hands. "I'm all right."

I didn't sound all right, my voice thick and stuffy and coming through my nose. I was afraid to blink, for fear those tears would roll down my cheeks. Billy's whole face turned down like an unhappy Muppet and he put his arm around my shoulders.

"Come on. A cold washcloth will help." He walked me down the hall, blocking me from the other officers' view with his body, and ushered me into the men's bathroom. I let out a stressy little giggle.

"I don't think I've ever been in a boy's bathroom before. I thought they were supposed to be all dirty and gross." The words spilled out in a too-high, too-fast voice, but it was better than bursting into tears. Billy smiled, pulling paper towels out of the dispenser and running water over them.

"Here you go. You really think Morrison'd let us keep the bathroom all dirty and gross?"

I buried my face in the cold towels, pressing the wet paper against my eyes. "No," I admitted hoarsely. My shoulders dropped as the coolness pulled some of the burning from my eyes and cheeks. I snuffled, lowering the papers to find Billy leaning against a sink, arms folded over his chest as he frowned at me.

"You okay, Joanie? You want to tell me what that was all about?"

I wiped my nose on my wrist and snuffled again, looking away. "I'm just being stupid." I was suddenly tired, the price of sudden and high emotion. And maybe the price of using a power that I'd been doing my best to ignore for several months. I'd been uncharacteristically emotional the day I became a shaman, too, now that I thought about it. "It's been one of those days. I've been up and down and all over the place."

"That girl this morning a friend of yours?"

"What?" I looked at him, then dropped my shoulders, relieved for an excuse to hang my behavior on. "No. No. I guess I'm just a little more freaked out about it than I thought." It was as good an excuse as any.

"Happens to the best of us," Billy said. "You need a drink."

My eyes bugged. "I'm on duty."

"Hot chocolate with mint," he said, still firmly. "Wash your face again and I'll buy you one."

A little bubble of happiness burst through my misery. I shuffled forward to turn the cold water on again, splashing it over my face, and reached blindly for a dry paper towel, which Billy put into my hand. "You're a good friend," I said into the towel.

"I just know your comfort food hot buttons," he said, pleased with himself. "Come on, Joanie. It'll be okay."

Billy was right. Just going outside did me some good, even if it was ninety-three degrees and about equal humidity. I felt sorry for the protesters down at the Seattle Center, and wondered how the little girl was doing.

I ended up with an Italian soda, because it was way too warm out for hot chocolate, but the very normal act of getting a drink and getting back on my beat did a lot to restore my equilibrium. I had a tentative teacher, which would make Coyote happy, and snakes were good juju. The Internet said so, and if you couldn't believe the Internet, who could you believe?

The rest of the day was blessedly normal, except I was so grungy and sticky with sweat by the time work was over I called Gary and told him not to have dinner until eight. He said, "Aw, damn, and me with the microwave heatin' up already," which kept a grin on my face until I arrived on his doorstep, newly showered and wearing as little as humanly possible. For me, that meant a strappy tank top with one of those built-in bra thingies and a pair of shorts that I considered to be cut daringly short, although I had nothing on Daisy Duke. Gary arched an eyebrow and gave me a grin that was better than words, even if he was seventy-three years old. I momentarily wished I had long hair so I could fluff it. Then reality kicked in: if I'd had long hair, I'd have cut it off by now in an attempt to cool down, so it didn't really matter.

The house didn't smell like he'd been cooking. I kicked my sandals off and padded through the living room into the kitchen, where cold cuts and crackers and fruit and a pasta salad were arranged rather elegantly on a platter. I stole a piece of ham, wrapped it around some cheese, and nibbled. "You do this yourself or you buy it?"

I could all but hear the old man's offended look as he came in behind me. "Did it myself. Donno about you, but I think it's too hot to cook or eat hot food. I got salmon in the freezer, but you're gonna have to wait till the heat breaks."

I grinned over my shoulder at him and picked up the platter to bring it out to the living room. There were picture windows that went all the way up to a vaulted ceiling overlooking an expansive front yard full of lilacs and other flowering things I couldn't identify. There was enough actual lawn that the kids next door tended to spill out onto it, having water balloon fights as they hid behind the hedges. Gary and Annie had owned the place since about 1965, though he'd been living in an apartment, having the place modernized and refurbished when I met him. Between that and the endlessly climbing real estate value in Seattle, I couldn't imagine what the market value of the place was now. Gary could probably retire rich, if he wanted to move out. Or retire.

"Lemonade or water?" Gary asked from the kitchen. My mouth puckered up at the very idea of lemonade, so I requested it happily as I put the food platter on the coffee table. The furniture was leather, but there were hand-sewn quilts thrown over everything, so a person could sit down in the armchair without sticking to it. I did, and Gary came out of the kitchen with a jug, two glasses, and a finger pointed at me accusingly. "Get outta my chair, kid."

I laughed like a guilty five-year-old and squirmed out of Gary's chair to kick back on the couch. "I had to try."

He snorted and sat down, pouring juice into glasses that clinked with just a couple of ice cubes. "You always try. Arright, Jo, so what's going on now? I go away for a few weeks and miss all the good stuff?"

"Only you would think it's the good stuff." I squished farther into the couch and, between bites of crackers and meat, told him about my day. Six months ago Gary'd thought I was a hundred percent insane when I climbed in his cab in search of a woman I'd seen from an airplane. By the end of that same morning I'd come back from the dead and he was determined to stick with me on the logic that I was the most interesting thing that'd happened to him in years. Things I could barely handle, like the very idea of the power that'd awakened inside me, he took in stride, shrugging off improbability with easy axioms about old dogs needing to learn new tricks, or they'd just up and die. By that standard, I suspected I'd been dead for half my life already.

"You think she's right?" Gary asked, bushy eyebrows elevated as I finished. "About the heat wave being somethin' you did?"

"Gary, if I thought I could affect global weather patterns, I would go home and hide under the bed for the rest of my life." I stared gloomily at the pasta salad, my appetite suddenly gone. Gary noticed and harrumphed.

"So you think she's right."

I sighed and sank a few inches farther into the couch. The quilt slid down over my shoulder, blocking most of my view of Gary. I felt like a Kilroy, peeking over it at him. "So what do I do?"

Gary gave me an incredulous look that made me want to pull the quilt all the way up so it covered me entirely. "You fix it, Jo. You go listen to this dame and you learn what you gotta do to fix it."

I pushed the quilt back up over the arm of the couch and reached for my salad again, picking at it without enthusiasm. "I hate it when you're right."

Gary beamed. "You got a lotta hate going on, then, darlin'. No point in bein' an old dog if you can't be right."

A wheeze of a laugh erupted up through my throat, quick jolts that were more like a cough than laughter, but a grin spread across my face. "Yeah, yeah yeah. All right, fine. Be that way. I'll show you."

"You will?"

"Yeah." I got up from the couch, heading for the kitchen again. "I'm going to eat all your ice cream. So there."

"What makes you think I've got any?"

"You've always got ice cream." I pulled open the freezer and took out a carton. "Gary! It's rocky road. You know I don't like rocky road!"

I heard him kick the footrest up on his chair, and when I looked over my shoulder he had his arms folded behind his head, expression smug as a cat's. "Now who showed who? Get me a bowl, wouldya? And if you dump it on my head like you're thinkin' about," he added a minute later as I came out with his bowl of ice cream, "I won't tell you where that raspberry-chocolate stuff you like is hidden."

I stopped with the bowl tilted at a precarious angle and stared down at him. He grinned up at me genially. "Youth and good looks are no match for old age and treachery, doll. Who wins?"

"You do, you old goat."

Gary's grin expanded exponentially. "Garage freezer."

I went out, trying not to laugh as I grumbled dire imprecations loudly enough for him to hear me. Gary's chortles followed me all the way into the garage.

CHAPTER SEVEN

Friday, June 17, 5:58 a.m.

6:00 a.m. two mornings in a row was more than any civil-
ized person should have to bear. Or me, for that matter. I
sat at the edge of my garden's pond, not looking behind me.
I could feel Judy, ten steps away, standing in the middle of
the very short lawn. The grass looked, if anything, worse
than it had the day before. Clouds hung thick and low over
the cliffs that made up the northern boundary of the garden, full of the promise of rain. I felt like that myself, on
the edge of overflowing with tears. It bothered me that I
still felt that fragile after spending the evening at Gary's and
eating an entire pint of chocolate-raspberry swirl ice cream.

Judy sat down beside me on the pond shore, close

enough that I could feel the warmth of her skin next to mine. I leaned away semiconsciously, the clouds above darkening with displeasure. I might need a teacher, but that didn't mean she had to come barging into my personal space.

"Where does the power come from?" she asked in a light, lilting tone. It reminded me of my neighbor's cat, which habitually sat beside the sink and stared at the faucet while she washed dishes. When she turned the water off, he would thrust his head beneath the faucet, as if trying to figure out where the water came from.

"Everywhere," I said, able to answer Judy, if not the cat. "Every living thing carries power within itself. A shaman is a conduit, a focus, for that power. We can use what's given to us to affect changes. To heal. That's what we're supposed to do, is heal."

"At least you've learned something." She didn't sound particularly pleased.

"Go me." I waved an imaginary flag. Judy's gaze slid sideways toward me, then away again.

"Asking you what your spirit animals are would be rude," Judy said. The implication that I should tell her anyway was clear, but instead I scowled at the water and shrugged.

"Haven't got any." I glanced at Judy, whose stare all but bore a hole into my head. "What?"

"You have no spirit animals? You've never done a quest for one?" Her expression was indecipherable.

"I've done a couple. Nothing came to me, or whatever's supposed to happen." It irritated me that my half-hearted attempts to summon a spirit animal felt like failures. The truth was I wanted my cake and to eat it, too. I didn't want to admit any of this shamanic nonsense was real, but I also wanted to be able to snap my fingers and make it so. I was pretty sure I'd thwarted my own questing experiments with the mental equivalent of concrete bunkers of disbelief.

"Is this really so hard for you to resolve?" Judy asked. "You've been a part of these other realities. Why do you reject them so fiercely?"

"No sense in being Irish if you can't be thick," I muttered. It was a cop-out answer, but it made Judy's mouth quirk.

"Maybe we can wear some of that thickness away. I can guide your search for spirit animals, if you think it might help."

I mumbled so incoherently even I didn't know what I was trying to say. Judy's smile broadened. "I'll take that as a yes." She opened her hands, a skin drum appearing in them. "I'll drum us under," she said. "Are you ready?"

It was different.

The drumbeat rang in my blood, tasting like copper. I ran up a mountainside, nimble as a goat, leaping from one stone to another without hesitation or fear. The sky above was pale, washed-out blue, so thin a sparkle of stars shone through it.

To the west I saw a glint in the sky, gold sheering through the paleness like godslight.

The air was rarefied, burning my lungs as I swallowed down deep breaths. I crossed some unseeable barrier as I climbed, and snow began gleaming in cold soft spots around me. I kicked it up in puffs and slid through it as I scrambled higher.

The shadow of a bird passed over me, blue against the snow. I squinted up into the sky, but the bird was gone again.

I couldn't see or feel Judy anywhere, and wondered if she'd managed to come on this journey with me at all. My hands were hot, excitement pounding through them. I touched the frozen ground as I clambered upward, leaving steaming prints deep in the snow.

A sharp, almost sheer cliff face rose up in front of me. I dug my hands into the snow, pulling myself up, my breath whisked away in little clouds of heat. Ice stung my palms and drops of sweat rolled out of my hair and into my eyes. I lost track of time, inching up the cliff. My arms burned, fingers splaying wide in search of handholds, and then I folded my hand over a distinct edge. Panting with triumph, I swung my leg up and hauled myself onto the top of the mountain. I stayed on my hands and knees, head hanging down while I wheezed, then pushed myself to my feet, bracing myself on my thighs.

There was nothing on the other side of the mountain.

The world fell away, straight and featureless into pale blue sky. Clouds drifted miles below me, and rushing wind made my hair stand up straight from my face. I leaned into it, trusting the strength of the wind to keep me from plummeting off the edge of the world.

About a million miles below me, an eagle, gold as sunrise, rose and fell on the updrafts. I tilted farther into the wind, trying to catch my breath as it was ripped away from me. The eagle shadowed in and out of distant clouds, lighting them from within with its own golden strength. It twisted, playing in the updrafts, then folded its wings and dove out of sight, a predator dropping beyond the edge of the world.

The wind stopped.

I pitched forward with one fruitless flail of my arms. The mountain face zipped past me, streaks of granite dark behind me, miles of sky in front of me. I spread my arms and legs, swallowing against panic and sickness, trying to slow my fall. I couldn't see land below me, only blue that faded into stars.

Wind slammed into me again, so hard it drove me upward a few feet before I began to fall again. Another updraft tossed me higher, then cut out from under me so fast I screamed, leaving my stomach yards above me. It happened again, then again, buffeting me through the sky like a feather.

I was flying.

A giddy laugh erupted from my throat as I banked into the wind and soared, always losing sky. I rolled onto my back, looking for the top of the mountain, already so far away it seemed to go on forever. I arched my back, spilling upside-down through the sky, eyes closed against the rush of air.

Talons pinched closed around my outstretched arms.

I opened my eyes to the brilliance of the golden eagle's belly above me. Its belly alone was wider than I was tall, and tilting my head to squint at its length made me feel like a doll in the hands of a child. The wings, stretched to their fullest, were so broad that the tips faded into invisibility from my vantage point, and the feathers looked as if they'd been deliberately crafted of the purest gold. Even its down was etched in distinct soft threads.

Eagle. The thought came to me with embarrassing clarity. Not even I, deliberately unaware of Native American mythology, could fail to recognize the incredible animal that had caught me. Creator, destroyer, all-around magnificent totem creature, so far beyond the ordinary I cringed at myself again. I'd thought a *thunderbird* was a lousy *eagle*?

The thunderbird screamed, a high sweet sound that could have been rage or pleasure. Its claws snapped up to its belly, flinging me out of its talons with bone-jarring strength. I flew upwards for a few disconcerting seconds, flipping end over end through the cold sky.

Then its beak crushed my ribs and we fell through the air, the thunderbird tearing me apart and eating me.

The drumbeat was steady and calm. My eyes popped open to a gibbous moon, hanging low and fat in the carmine sky. There were jungles, thick and lush, heavy green vines hanging against black tree trunks, and the air smelled of rich earth and old rot. There was no sign of the mountain or the pale blue sky that went on forever, and certainly no thunderbird. I shook myself, turning and staring around in confusion. I remembered some pain, and more fear, and the blackness that was the inside of the thunderbird's belly, but—

"How'd I get here?"

Judy stepped up to my side, smiling. "It can be confusing for someone else to lead the spirit journey. You'll get used to it, and then you'll learn to do it on your own. As we traveled down I asked for those who were willing to guide you to join us. These are those who have answered my call on your behalf."

She lifted her right hand. A copperhead snake, eyes bright and black, wound up around her arm and opened his mouth wide to me. "The strengths that snakes have I share with you," he said. Its s's were sibilant and hissed, stretched out long enough to make chills rise on my arms.

"Thank you." I didn't want a snake guide. My whole feeling about snakes was very mixed, after the encounter in the Dead Zone. I couldn't think of a polite way to say that, though.

The snake flicked his tongue at me and twisted his way up to Judy's shoulder, piling himself into tall coils there. As I watched, he changed, head growing rounder, shoulders appearing. Wings sprouted, a chest and spindly legs shaping out of the coils. His darting tongue stretched and became glossy and hard, until a raven perched on Judy's shoulder, only its bright eyes the same as the snake's. The raven stretched his throat and cawed, a sound of raucous music, before he cocked his head and stared at me one-eyed. "The strengths that ravens have, I share with you," he said.

I found myself smiling. "Thank you. You're beautiful," I added impulsively. He puffed out his feathers, preening with satisfaction, then leaped off Judy's shoulder, wings fanning out to encompass the shadows dropped by the enormous moon.

Darkness swept up into him, broadening his chest and lengthening his body. His wings buckled forward, becoming legs, his tail feathers extending into long black hairs. His neck elongated again, face shattering from a bird's delicacy to the fine weight of a horse's head. He snapped his tail over his sides as if brushing off a coating of dust, and pranced a time or two with his front feet, before inclining his head. His forelock fell over bright black eyes. Looking for all the world like an impatient kid, he tossed his head before saying, "The strengths that horses have, I share with you."

"Thank you," I said a third time, then, searching for some appropriate response, asked, "How can I honor you?"

The horse snorted and stomped his feet again, two solid thumps into the dark ground. From one hoof print, the snake coiled up again, winding itself around the horse's leg. From the other, the raven exploded forth in a flurry of feathers and cawing, then winged around to settle on the horse's head, between his ears. "How may I honor you all," I amended hastily, "for sharing your gifts with me."

"By heeding the words of your teacher," the snake suggested.

"By seeking truth." The raven gave the snake a one-eyed look, then turned it on me. I felt inexplicably guilty. No, not inexplicably: I could explic it perfectly well. I just didn't like to.

"By accepting." The horse's voice had a raw tenor to it that shivered down my spine, making me cold despite the jungle heat. Hairs stood up on my arms, making me shiver a second time. I met the horse's eyes for a few seconds, feeling exposed and vulnerable under its black gaze.

Months earlier, there'd been a moment of clarity, a moment when I'd understood that as a shaman, I could make a real difference in the world. The confidence had slipped away almost immediately when the conflict with Cernunnos had ended, and I'd let it. The world was simpler without the responsibility I'd taken on, and not believing was easy when there weren't otherworldly monsters to fight every day. I took a deep breath, closing my eyes and struggling to remember the certainty that had filled my bones and my breath for a few hours.

I couldn't. It was a struggle, like trying to bring a face to mind clearly. Instead of holding it, I could only grasp at the edges, knowing I'd had it and lost it again. Every time I tried, it slipped farther away, until my hands were shaking from a wholly different exertion.

"Can you tell me?" I asked, my voice small as I opened my eyes again. "Can you tell me how many times I'll have to remind myself, or relearn what I can do, before I believe it without question?"

The raven made a derisive sound, a sort of trill that seemed to come from behind his eyes. "To be without question is to be dead."

"Thanks," I said, equilibrium temporarily restored by wryness. "Very reassuring."

"Every day," the horse said. "Until the hour comes when your first breath tells you the aches of the world and your first exhalation heals them, every morning you'll have to fight to believe." He inclined his head, making the raven grip his forelock and spread his wings to keep from sliding off. "Your nature is not that of an easy believer, but that's not a flaw. It only means that when you accept the truth—" He snorted, tossing his head with very horselike amusement.

"That wild horses won't be able to drag me from it?" I asked, smiling a little.

"Even so," the horse agreed. The raven cawed, clearly irritated at having been outclevered. I looked down at the snake, wound around the horse's leg, and sighed as I kneeled.

"What about you?" I asked him. "Do you have an answer for me?"

He stuck his tongue out at me. "Ssstudy. Your mind is closed to the possibility that this is real, even when you live it. Ssstudy will help open those doorsss. Then you will not look back, only forward, and you will go with strength. Heed your teacher. Heed your elders. Heed your ssspirits. When faith wavers, look to the things that have crossed over with you."

An electronic beeping broke through the last of the snake's words, an ugly counterpoint to the drum that still thumped in the background. "It's time to go back," Judy said. "We'll meet again tomorrow morning."

"Thank you," I said, more to the spirit animals than to the woman who'd brought them to me. "I'll try to remember what you said and honor your words and advice."

"Honor your alarm clock," the raven suggested, and I opened my eyes to find out I was already late for work.

CHAPTER EIGHT

I'd bite my own tongue off before admitting it to Morrison, but I actually sort of liked being a beat cop. Motor oil was good for the soul and all, but the truth is that as a mechanic I didn't get out much. The only time I saw a new face was when there was a new hire, and let's not even talk about the exercise regime I didn't follow. I'd lost twelve pounds since I'd been stuck on patrol duty, and I felt like She Who Was Not To Be Messed With as a result.

The North Precinct covered a huge area, thirty-two square miles above and around the University of Washington. It ran the gamut of neighborhoods, from very nice to very bad, and I'd walked more of them than I'd ever dreamed possible. I had two favorite beats: the first was through some bad sections of Aurora, which was nobody's sensible idea of a favorite beat. Still, it passed under the no-longer-guttering streetlight that had started me down the path I was on now. Given my usual bad temper about the whole shamanism business, I wasn't sure why I was drawn back to the place that kicked it off. Moth to flame, I guessed. Either that or the less flattering "humans are stupid," but I thought maybe I'd stick with the metaphor.

The other one I liked was University Avenue. I lived on its far north end, and working that beat always seemed like something of a reward, like I was keeping my very own personal neighborhood safe from hooligans.

I imagine every big city has at least one drag strip like the Ave. To my mind, University Bookstore was its linchpin. Spreading out from it on either side were restaurants and storefronts ranging from burger joints to tofu houses and from The Gap to bohemian, incense-filled shops filled with Indian imports. Young people—I observed them that way, like I was hitching along with a walker—spilled out of coffee shops to sit under sun-faded umbrella tables, chatting up every topic from Kant to Britney.

Police patrol was heavy along the Ave, increasing every fall when new students arrived to wreak havoc on unsuspecting Seattle. It used to be that any undercover cop could score the drug of her choice on the Ave. It was a matter of departmental pride that these days it was widely acknowledged that there was too much heat to risk turning a little illegal profit. The Ave was a battle against chaos, and for once, order was winning.

I usually got a friendly nod or two from store owners, particularly the restaurants I frequented. When I'd first begun patrol duty, I'd had to argue extensively with Mrs. Li, owner of my favorite Chinese place, who was convinced that all that walking would wear me away to a stick. She kept trying to give me "a little snack"—usually enough to feed two for a day—on the house, to keep my strength up. I finally convinced her that as a police officer I couldn't take what she offered without compromising myself, and she retaliated by feeding me twice as much when I came in to the shop off-duty.

I waved at her through the restaurant window and grinned my way up the street. A long-nosed bicycle messenger zipped past me, illegally riding on the sidewalk. I barked, "Hey!" He shot a nasty glance over his shoulder at me and didn't stop. At the corner, he bounced his bike off the curb and down into the street, careening across the avenue to ride on the correct, if not right, side. Rather than chase him down on foot, I punched 411 on my generally despised department-issued cell phone and got the number for the company he worked for. It took the length of waiting for one stoplight to register a request for disciplinary action. I crossed the street with the rest of the herd cheerfully. If I was lucky, I'd see his bike ahead of me and get to ticket it for vehicular misuse.

It was a sad, sad state when I was glad about carrying a cell phone and considered the opportunity to ticket a bicycle to be good luck.

Bells on a shop door behind me chimed urgently as someone pushed and held it open. "Excuse me. Officer Walker?"

I blinked over my shoulder. A girl of about twenty

leaned in the door, vibrating it enough to keep the bells ringing. "Er, yeah? I mean, yes?"

Relief brightened her face. "Oh good. I had a premonition, you see, a dream about you, but I wasn't sure if Walker was your last name or if it was just that you were a walker." She gestured at me. "Foot patrol, see?"

I backed up a step and glanced at the name above the shop. It did not, as I half expected it to, say Lunatics "R" Us. Actually, it bore the innocuous name of East Asian Imports, although the girl whose leaning continued to jangle the bells was about as East Asian as Queen Elizabeth. She was blond and on the slightly chunky side of curvy, with brown eyes and a hopeful expression. For an unkind moment I thought of golden retrievers. "What can I do for you, miss?"

"My name's Faye." The door bells quivered with excitement. "I need your help."

Fishwire tightened around my chest, making it difficult to breathe. "My help specifically, or the police in general?" Adrenaline made the tips of my fingers cold and tingly and slid the world into sharper focus. Given Faye's opening statement about dreams, I wasn't surprised when she said—

"Yours specifically. See, a friend of mine died yesterday, and I dreamed about you—"

Adrenaline abandoned my fingertips to turn into a festering pit of nausea in my belly. "Who was your friend?"

Tears welled in Faye's eyes. "Her name was Cassie. Nobody even knows what happened yet." She narrowly escaped wailing, mouth turned down in misery. "She couldn't just *die* like that, could she? She was only twenty, and she couldn't just *die!*" The bells shivered and banged and rang. I set my teeth together and stepped forward, not quite touching Faye's elbow.

"How about if we go inside for a minute?" Because if we didn't, I was going to shoot the bells right off the door. Faye sniffled miserably and backed into the store. It was poorly lit after the brilliant morning sunshine. I tripped over a solemn wooden monkey carved out of dark wood that sat precariously near the door. It wobbled ponderously. I slapped my hand on its flat head—maybe it was a plant stand—and left it complacently back in its place as I edged farther into the store.

"It's okay." Faye snuffled and wiped her hand under her nose, which would have been considerably more endearing if she'd been three. "Everybody does that."

"Why don't you move it, then?"

"He likes to be able to see out the door."

I consider it a matter of great pride that I didn't abandon the store right there. I paused, gathered up the several things I wanted to say, admired them briefly, then moved on as manfully as I could. "Ms.—" She hadn't given me her last name. "Faye," I said somewhat reluctantly, not wanting at all to get personal with the girl. "If you know something about Cassandra Tucker's death, you should be talking with UW police, not with me."

Faye's gaze snapped to me, her big brown eyes seeming much less golden-retriever-like suddenly. "I didn't mention Cassie's last name."

Crap. "No, you didn't, but police departments do talk

to one another." I really didn't want to confess to being the one who found her friend's body. It seemed likely that it would get messy after that, and she was already snorfling all over the place. I made a slow circuit of the store, wedging myself between narrowly placed shelves and trying not to knock any more bric-a-brac over. I wondered if the place was up to fire code.

Faye, evidently mollified, kept pace with me on the other side of the skinny shelving unit. It, like the monkey, was carved of some kind of dark wood, and a price tag was wrapped around one of the supports. I wondered what would happen to all the stuff it held if someone saw fit to buy it. "I dreamed that you could help us," she said.

"Us?" I picked the lid off a small pot and peered inside. Black enamel paint gleamed at me. Faye looked uncomfortable.

"Me and some friends. Friends of Cassie's."

I set the lid back on the pot with a distinctive click, remembered Morrison's magnificent scowl, and said without a trace of guilt, "Cassandra's death isn't my jurisdiction, Faye. I'm very sorry, but my captain would hang me by my toes to dry if I got involved. The best I can do is offer to bring you down to the Udub police so you can talk to them, and I can't really even do that until my lunch break." I twisted my arm, peering at my watch, a big black clunker of a thing that no longer told me what time it was in Moscow. "Which is in about three hours. Want me to come back then?" Maybe a little twinge of guilt.

"I dreamed you had darkness wrapped around your

heart and that light shone through it so powerfully it cracked and shattered letting goodness into the world and the goodness said to me that your name was Walker and that without you all hope was lost and that I had to wait and watch today so that I could stop you and ask you to help and I didn't know if I would even know you because all I really saw in the dream was a woman with a walking stick but as soon as I saw you I knew you were the one from the dream because you're confident and strong and you move like the woman in the dream and anybody with eyes to *see* can tell that you've got power so *please* won't you help us?" Faye clutched the corner of the shelves, staring up at me as she dragged in a deep breath. I gaped at her.

Rationally, not one of the things she said should have swayed me. Hell, not *all* of the things she said should have swayed me, not even with the breathless, desperate delivery. I snapped, "All right," and shoved my hand through my hair. "Dammit."

Faye's eyes widened. Maybe good police officers didn't say "dammit." I'd have to check the handbook. Meantime, I said, "Dammit," again for good measure, and raked my hand through my hair again. "All right, look, Faye. What's your last name?"

"Kirkland. Why?"

So I can look up your police records. "I like to know people's names when I agree to get in over my head. Look. I will come talk to you and your friends, all right?" My speech was getting more precise, indicating to me, if not to Faye, who, after all, didn't know me very well, that I really meant what I was saying. "However, I want you to promise me that if, after speaking with you, I believe that what you have to say might be of use to the university police department, you and your friends will come with me to talk to them. Do we have a deal?" The last words were so clipped that Faye's eyes widened again.

"Okay. Honest, I don't think it'll be any help, but if we are, yes, okay, I promise." Swear to God, if she'd had a tail she would've wagged it. I dropped my chin to my chest.

"All right. All right, fine. Dammit," I added again for good measure. "Where should I meet you?"

"We'll be at the reading room for the graduate library on campus at seven tonight. Can you come then?"

I stood up. "I don't get off work until seven. Is it okay if I'm late?"

Faye nodded, backing up so she could abandon the narrow shelving area for the slightly roomier front counter. "It'll be fine. Maybe you shouldn't come in uniform." She gave me a critical sideways glance that took the wind right out of the She Who Was Not To Be Messed With mindset.

"Maybe I *should*," I said. "It might make people more willing to talk to the university police, if I'm not scary."

Faye eyed me dubiously. "If you think so," she said with such exaggerated politeness that I knew I'd be succumbing to peer pressure. I closed my eyes momentarily and scolded myself for being a weenie, then put on a fake smile.

"Or not. Okay. I'll see you tonight, then."

Faye beamed, tongue lolling out just like a retriever's.

Well, no, but boy, she looked happy. "Thank you, Officer Walker. We'll see you tonight."

"It's Joanne," I said, resigned, and let myself out to the jangling of bells. Morrison was going to kill me.

CHAPTER NINE

Friday, June 17, 5:15 p.m.

I rapped twice on Morrison's door frame, cautious taps, and said, "Captain?" before screwing my face up in a wince. Knocking was about the sum total of politeness Morrison could typically expect from me. Bringing his title into the conversation before it even began gave him warning to be wary.

And the look he gave me as he glanced up from paperwork was, indeed, wary. "What do you want?"

I sighed and hunched my way into his office even though there'd been no invitation issued. "I am not investigating Cassandra Tucker's death," I offered as my initial foray. Morrison's eyebrows beetled down. "But I was wondering if we knew anything else about it yet." I set my teeth together in a grimace and added, "A friend of hers approached me today."

"Approached you." Morrison got up from his desk and walked around me, closing the door with a final-sounding click. I watched him over my shoulder as he stood there with his mouth held in a thick purse, then jerked my gaze forward again as he turned back around. "Sit," he said from behind me, and I did as he went back to his desk. "Approached you," he repeated.

I sank down into the chair and pressed my fingertips against my eyelids, speaking into the cover my palms made. "While I was on patrol. She said…" I trailed off long enough to sigh, then lifted my eyebrows over the protective steepling of my fingers, eyes still closed. "She said she'd had a dream about me and she was waiting for me. She wanted me to meet some of Cassandra's friends tonight."

"A dream." Morrison's voice sounded exactly like mine would have in his position: exasperated, frustrated, and annoyed. I felt sorry for him. I'd have felt sorry for myself, too, except world-weary resignation seemed to have overcome the self-pity. Morrison dragged in a deep breath and said, "You're telling me this because…?"

I dropped my fingers to look at him. "Because you told me specifically to stay away from this case, and whether you believe it or not, I'm actually trying to follow orders. Except the case may not want to stay away from me."

"A case," Morrison said through his teeth, "is not something that makes choices about who it's assigned to, Walker."

"No, sir, not normally." I'd spent the better part of the day since encountering Faye trying to find a way around having this conversation with Morrison. The only alternatives I could come up with were considerably worse than having it. Somehow the inevitability made me less antagonistic than I usually would have been. "But under the circumstances, I don't really think it's coincidence that this girl came to me."

"Under what circumstances?"

I turned my hands palm-up, a shrug, and said, "Me."

Tension spilled through Morrison's expression, aging him years in a few seconds. I looked away, uncomfortable with seeing him look so defeated. "What the hell is that supposed to mean?" he said, but we both knew the growl in his voice was only for show. I pressed my lips together, daring to glance back at him, but only for a moment. He still looked aged and unhappy.

"It means something's wrong with Cassandra Tucker's death, sir." I really didn't want to say *I think magic may have been involved, sir,* and I was pretty sure Morrison didn't want me to say it, either.

He didn't let the possibility of clarification linger on the air, snapping, "Of course something's wrong. She was twenty years old and ended up dead in a locker room. There's nothing right about it."

"That's not what I mean, Captain." I didn't want to push it any more than that, but I felt like I had to at least say that much. "I'd like your permission to go talk to her friends."

He gave me a baleful glare. "Are you going to do it anyway?"

"Yeah," I admitted, "but at least I'm trying to be above-board here, Morrison. Doesn't that count for anything?"

He sighed explosively. "They're doing an autopsy. It's being investigated as a homicide. Right now that's all I know." He clenched his jaw, muscle working. "Get back to me if you learn anything."

I said, "Yes, sir," and got the hell out of his office before we were forced to acknowledge the elephant in the room.

Friday, June 17, 7:25 p.m.

The graduate library's reading room was dim and dark, which wasn't unusual. What was unusual was that the dimness came not from clouds overhead, but from smoky torches that couldn't possibly meet fire code. I hung in the doorway, squinting into smoke and trying to get the lay of the land before anyone noticed me, but Faye clapped her hands, letting out a squeal of delight. "You came! I knew you'd come! This is Joanne Walker, everyone. She's the one I dreamed about." Her voice lowered portentously with the last several words, but I was the only one who seemed to notice.

The rest of the group took Faye's lead, climbing to their feet and encircling me. There were eleven or twelve of them, all of them smiling politely and offering me their hands to shake. With the exception of a man and a woman both in their fifties, and another man in his thirties, the median age of the gathered group appeared somewhere below the legal drinking age.

I said, "Um, thank you," with every handshake and introduction and welcome, a little taken aback. I wished I'd brought along a tape recorder so I could be sure of everyone's names. Faye hadn't turned up a police record—not even so much as a driver's license—but I wasn't above doing a quick investigation on all her friends, too. When everyone was done greeting me and I'd forgotten most of the names already, I asked, "Faye told you why I was coming here tonight, right?"

They all exchanged glances, amusement suddenly coloring the air. "Of course," one of the young men said. He was Garth; I remembered that because he didn't look at all like Garth Brooks. Maybe it wasn't the greatest mnemonic device ever, but it worked for me. Garth-not-Brooks went on, "She dreamed that you would come to lend us your power. With Cassie's death—" A ripple of pain, tangible, went through the little gathered crowd. I drew in a sharp breath, pushing their loss away long enough to get through the conversation, at least. It was possible I could do something later to ease the sharpness of grief, but I thought it was a bad idea. Only a day after Cassandra Tucker's death, none of them would have had the time to work through it naturally. Mucking about with it at this stage struck me as premature.

Maybe I was learning something after all.

While I was thinking all that, Garth continued, "—we don't have a Mother anymore. You must be her—Faye dreamed you."

"A mother? I don't know what you're tal—"

There are phrases that I never think describe a real feeling until I experience them myself. "The words turned to dust in my mouth," was a new one on me, but it happened. My saliva shriveled up, leaving my tongue feeling thick and dry. My throat constricted, and the taste of ashes, flat and sticky, filled my mouth. I choked and coughed, and one of the young men leaped up and got me a cup of water. Faye hovered at my side, patting my back in concern as I drank. It still took a few long moments before I was able to croak, "Mother. Maiden. Crone." The older woman's mouth twisted wryly as I said the third word.

"You're a coven."

If I expected this to come across as an earth-shattering revelation, I was badly disappointed. Everyone exchanged glances again, and Faye laughed, a bright musical sound in the gloomy hall. "Well, yes. What did you think?"

My voice rose and cracked. "I thought you were going to give me any information you might have about your friend Cassie's death. That's what we discussed this morning."

Faye went from laughter to kicked puppy dog, her brown eyes mournful. "And I told you I didn't think we'd be able to help you very much, but you promised to come anyway. I told you," she said, eager again, "we need you. You must be the Mother. I dreamed you and you were there, and you have power, and we don't have anybody else for the part. There are already eleven of us, and you're the twelfth. You *must* be the Mother."

"I thought a full coven had thirteen." I let the words come as a barrier to thought, but it didn't work.

Two children. *From my womb untimely rip'd.* I closed my

eyes. They'd come early, but twins often do. Neither was strong as they lay together, fragile and tiny. The girl's last breath seemed to strengthen her brother.

Somewhere in the distance, I heard Faye explaining that *he,* whoever *he* was, was the thirteenth. He led and completed the coven, and there were twelve of us, so I must be the Mother.

Adoption papers signed and the boy—Aidan, though I expected his adoptive parents would change his name— taken away. I knew who his new parents were; the Eastern Cherokee Nation simply wasn't that big. But I was only fifteen, and I never saw him again. I stared into my water glass, shivering and unwilling to meet anyone's eyes.

"She's the Mother," the Crone said. I felt the older woman's hand brush my hair. "Leave her alone. She'll be all right. Come." She urged me to my feet. "Come and rest a while."

"Faye doesn't mean to be insensitive," she said a moment later, when I was safely tucked into a nook in the wall, invisible from the rest of the coven. "She's just very young. I'm Marcia. I know there were a lot of names to remember."

"There were. Thanks." I glanced up at her, trying to get a feel for her.

She was reasonably tall and attractive, threads of gray through brown hair and wrinkles settling in around her eyes. She could stand to lose fifteen or twenty pounds, but carried the weight comfortably, letting it round her cheeks where age had begun to take the flesh away. There was a sense of strength, of connectedness, about her. "Are you a witch?"

She smiled, thin and only a little amused. "Are you?"

"I don't think so." I had no idea, really. I just assumed Coyote would've called me a witch if that's what he'd woken up in me. "If I'm not a witch, I can't do you any good, can I?"

Marcia's smile grew, spreading through her voice. "You might be able to. Witchcraft is spellcrafting. We use one kind of spell to call up power that Gaia, the goddess Earth, lends us, and another kind to focus that power and create with it. Spells and witchcraft can be learned."

"What kind of spells? I don't think I do spells." I knew I could borrow power from people and objects if my own wasn't enough, and drumming was a sort of ritual to get myself into the mindset, but Marcia sounded like she was talking about something else entirely.

"The basic tenement of witchcraft is *do what thou wilt, an' it harm none*," Marcia said. "We try to use spells to create, to heal, and to nurture."

I could get with the healing. I knew something about that. "Create and heal and nurture what?"

Marcia smiled, almost impishly. "The world."

A startled laugh burst from my throat. "That's a tall order, Marcia." My laughter faded as I remembered that six months ago I'd thought it was a tall order I might be up to accomplishing. If not the world, Seattle, at least. "You think you can do that?" I asked, more subdued.

"We do. Beginning with this heat wave. It's not natural, no more than the long winter was. Maybe you've sensed that, too."

A chill that had nothing to with the air-conditioning settled over me and sank into my stomach, making the power centered there flutter and dip. "Yeah," I said in a low voice. "I've gotten that idea. You think your spellcrafting can help fix it?" I was beginning to think I lived in a world in which there were no coincidences. The universe appeared to be lining up the support I needed to deal with the heat wave. Unless I wanted to turn my back on it all, the spirit horse was probably right and I'd better accept what was being offered.

Nobody said anything about *liking* it, though. The bitchy little thought hung around the edges of my mind and I gritted my teeth against it. At some point I was going to have to come to terms with all this, and whining incessantly wasn't going to win me any friends. More to the point, it was starting to annoy *me,* and I had to live with me all the time. I preferred it when I got along with myself.

"It can," Marcia said with utmost confidence, but then she faltered. "It could have," she corrected, "but we do desperately need a Mother figure, Joanne. Cassandra took that role, but now…"

I remembered the picture of the little girl in Cassie's wallet, and nodded, then looked up, a sick feeling gurgling in my gut. "When did Faye dream about me?"

Marcia's eyebrows drew down. "She only told us about the dream this evening, before you arrived. Why?"

My shoulders relaxed. "Nothing. Just an ugly thought."

It must have shown in my face, because Marcia's eyes widened with surprise I thought genuine. Her pupils dilated, color gone from her cheeks, and she shook her head, the action verging on violence. "We would have succeeded with Cassie in place, Joanne. No one would do something like this in order to replace her with you. It couldn't be hidden from the coven. Our power would be forever tainted, and anything we tried would go terribly wrong, or fail entirely."

I got to my feet, shaking my head. "I hope you're right."

"Join us in tonight's ceremony," Marcia suggested, voice caught somewhere between rigidity and hope. "It'll prove our innocence to you."

I sighed and nodded. "Yeah. All right. I'm still going to have to talk to everyone about whether Cassandra had any enemies, even if you're all pure as the driven snow." Telling Morrison I'd eliminated people as possible murderers via psychic investigation was not going to go over well.

"The police have already done that," Marcia said.

"Oh." I wanted to say *I am the police*, but I was only here on Morrison's forbearance, and the elephant we'd been ignoring was the fact that psychically was exactly how I was most useful in this investigation. That made me feel a little bit better, so I lifted my chin, put on a stiff upper lip, and went to participate in my very first witchcraft session.

I was marked with red wine, a circle written on my shoulder by Faye's determined finger. The wine symbolized a woman's first blood and the blood of childbirth, they told me, and the circle represented the full moon, the sign of the Mother. Marcia wrote a crescent moon, waxing, onto Faye's shoulder, and reluctantly, I completed the ritual by writing a crescent moon waning onto Marcia's.

We stepped together in the center of a circle of coven members, standing back to back and shoulder to shoulder. My right shoulder, inscribed with the full moon, pressed against Marcia's left, Faye's right shoulder with her crescent moon against my left shoulder. Marcia took one more small step backward, pressing her right shoulder against Faye's left, and power, like an electric current, slammed through me.

We made a tiny triangle with our backs to one another, a small empty space between us. In that space, light shot up, crashing into the ceiling like it would burst through and illuminate the world. I heard Marcia and Faye's indrawn breath, sharp as my own, and from the coven came whispers of awe.

I tingled. From my toes to the top of my head, I tingled, light coursing through me until I thought it would pour out my fingers and eyes. My hair felt as if it was standing on end, waving in the air of its own accord. I cranked my head up by degrees, looking up into the light.

It spilled across the ceiling, pooling outward like water meeting resistance. It rippled toward the walls, pure and white, then slithered down them, coating the room in brilliance. It made the air cleaner, so fresh and cold that it hurt to breathe in. *Like knives in my lungs,* I thought, then laughed without humor. I knew what a knife in the lung felt like, and it was nothing like this.

The laugh reverberated through the light, bouncing and waving. A few of the coven glanced at me and the white light flexed outward, testing its limits. That brought the coven's attention back to it, and the containment field that lined the room strengthened again. At least, that's what I thought was happening. I couldn't see the coven's power the way I could usually see my own, but the light washed farther down the walls and crept across the magically reinforced floor, moving in toward us. I watched it, mesmerized, as it swept over the outer ring of witches, glazing them in shimmering waves.

It reached my feet, and began to climb up my body. Clarity ripped through me, pulling me apart on the cellular level, exposing everything I'd ever hidden away. It snuggled into my core, warm and reassuring, and dug through me like a rat scrabbling for food, tearing away layers of old pain and joy indiscriminately. My body felt lighter than air, like a deep breath would launch me into the sky, and my head fell back, exposing my throat to the white light.

A sense of exultation and glee swept through me, settling in my bones. It crowed, smug and powerful, then hissed, *"Yesss!"* in such deep-voiced satisfaction that it rumbled through my stomach, making me sick.

I jerked convulsively, breaking contact with Faye and Marcia. The light disappeared with a silence that was louder than sound, and I fell to my knees, barely locking my arms in time to keep from meeting the floor with my face.

CHAPTER TEN

"Did you see him?" The question was delivered zealously, before I even pushed back to my heels.

"Did you see him?" Garth asked again, avidly. I heard a "Shh!" and the distinct sound of someone elbowing his ribs. I hadn't known, until that moment, that rib-elbowing had a specific sound.

"Leave her alone," followed the shushing. Faye. "Are you okay?"

"I'm fine." I shook my head, trying to clear it, then sat back on my heels, looking up.

Eleven worried faces peered down at me. I couldn't help it: I giggled. Half the faces exchanged worried for offended, and the other half for relieved. "I'm fine," I repeated.

"What happened?" someone chirruped, full of hope and curiosity. I thought his name was Sam. He looked like an underwear model, with full pouty lips and long eyelashes.

"You guys didn't hear him?"

They all looked back and forth at one another, above me. I'd never seen so many chins in my life. "No." Marcia spoke for all of them, and they all looked back down at me.

"He guides us," Faye gushed, "but we rarely hear his voice. You are blessed among us, Joanne!"

Hoo boy.

"All he said was yes," I said. "I don't think it's that big a deal. Who is he?"

"Our master. Our guide," Garth said reverently. I groaned and sat up, putting my hand over my nose.

"His name is Virissong," Marcia offered. "He's our thirteenth."

"Doesn't that mean he should be here?"

Marcia sat down beside me. The others took their cue from her and settled down all around me. I felt like the main attraction at P. T. Barnum. "He's caught between worlds," she explained. "We're working on a spell to free him."

"Uh-huh. Why?"

"As a beginning to restoring balance to this world," Marcia said with utmost confidence. "His power will help guide us."

I sort of thought that kind of power might just bowl them over. "Does that happen every time you get all shoulder to shoulder?"

Faye and Marcia locked gazes for a moment before Marcia looked back at me. "I've never joined with a Maiden and Mother with that intensity. I believe Virissong chose very well when he guided Faye to you."

That was all well and good for their Virissong, but it wasn't any use at all to the police department. I was afraid the whole visit with the coven, while literally enlightening, had been a complete waste of time. Either they were all very good liars both verbally and magically, or there wasn't anything here. I hadn't felt anything wrong in the power that had contained the white light, and I thought I could recognize a taint if it was there. More to the point, I was pretty sure Marcia could, and I didn't think she'd protect somebody who'd murdered Cassie.

I sighed, and let myself get drawn into my own curiosity about the surge of light and power we'd felt. Marcia'd been very specific, so I asked, "What happens when the male aspect calls the magic?" Male aspect. I was so proud of myself. I could sound New Agey with the best of them.

"Our power's different," the Elder said. "You women have the power of creation."

"Lemme guess. You guys have the power of destruction and your light is black and what we really want to do is blend it so it's all gray."

"More like a yin-yang," Garth corrected. "In balance, black and white, instead of losing them both to grayness."

"But it's nothing like the kind of power displayed here tonight," the Elder went on.

"So I what, kicked it up a notch?" I asked, then compulsively added, "Bam!" Garth laughed out loud. Everybody else stared at me. "Never mind," I said, grinning at Garth.

"I'd like to try again," Marcia said, and I said, "Like hell but hell no," which got the stares again. "A single huge burst of unexplained flashy power is all the fun I can handle in one evening."

"Oh." Marcia looked like I'd taken her favorite toy away. "All right. Perhaps tomorrow night."

"Do you meet every single night?"

A chorus of *no*s met me. "But the solstice is coming," Faye concluded, as if it explained everything. I gave her my best look of incomprehension, and she patted my shoulder. I felt like barking. "Virissong believes he can break through to this world on the solstice. Every day until then we'll meet to guide him with our power. It's a beacon of light," she said without the slightest hint of irony. "It shows him his path."

"Whoa, whoa, wait a minute. Break through to this world? You didn't say anything about people coming through from other worlds. You said you wanted to stop the heat wave." I stared at Marcia, full of accusation.

"We aren't strong enough by ourselves. We need Virissong's strength to do it," she said patiently.

"I don't like things breaking through to this world." I had a small amount of familiarity with this kind of thing. In my experience, it meant I wanted to be armed with a sharp pointy object. I blessed the impulse that led me to taking classes from Phoebe, and leaned toward Marcia. "Are we talking about a god here, Marcia?"

"Oh, no. Virissong is powerful, but not a god."

"Mythologically important? Like a Coyote or Grandfather Sky figure?" I asked. I did not want to be messing with power on that magnitude if I could avoid it.

"No, no. They're archetypes, like Gaia herself. Virissong was human once, a hero among his people, but he lost an epic battle and was banished to the Shadowlands."

I let out a slow breath. "And he's your leader."

Everyone beamed at me. I felt like a kid who'd been successfully potty-trained under the watchful gaze of an entire community. "Exactly," the Elder said.

"So he's a witch," I said. Silence met my statement, but I didn't mark it. I was busy thinking. I didn't know beans about witches in Native American culture, but I did know one thing: if Virissong was in Marcia's "Shadowlands," I could probably reach him. Maybe he could lead me toward some kind of information about Cassie's death. It wasn't exactly what I wanted to bring back to Morrison, but it might do. I puffed out my cheeks and glanced around. "Can I suggest something?"

They all looked at me expectantly. I was beginning to feel like I was inside a goldfish bowl. "Go gently. We called up an awful lot of power there. I'm not really sure I understand what's going on." I knew perfectly well I didn't know what was going on. I just hoped putting it on myself might make them more open to the idea that *they* didn't know what was going on.

"You'll learn," Faye promised. "You'll come to understand. We all have."

Guess that approach wasn't going to work. "Be careful anyway," I muttered, climbing to my feet. "Look, you've told me an awful lot and I need to take some time to absorb it, okay?" I also needed to talk to Judy, to see if she could tell me anything about Virissong. I had a teacher now, and I was by God going to take advantage of that. I'd had enough of fumbling in the dark.

"You'll come back, won't you?" Faye asked. "We need you. Virissong guided me to you with my dream. I know you're the one we need to complete the coven."

My nostrils flared. "I'll think about it," I said. "That's all I can promise right now."

The coven parted, reluctant as Romeo and Juliet, and let me go.

Wisdom dictated that I go home and go to bed, since I had to be up at what I considered an obscenely early hour. Instead, Petite drove herself over to Gary's house without bothering to notify me about the change of plans. I sat there in his driveway, trying to explain to my car that it was eleven at night and Gary's job as a cabbie got him up at four in the morning. There was no way he'd be awake. Then the living room light flipped on and he peered at me through the picture windows before coming out to the porch to stand there in shorts and a T-shirt, arms akimbo.

I'd always been a leg girl. When the Olympics were on TV, I'd be the one watching the speedskaters and saying, lustfully, "Look at those *thighs*." Gary, standing there in boxers, could've given those skaters a run for their money, even if he was seventy-three years old. Him standing up there was like having Paul Bunyan waiting on me expectantly.

I didn't realize I was leaning on the steering wheel, gazing dreamily at his thighs, until he stomped down off the porch and came to lift his bushy eyebrows at me through the driver side window. "Jo? You arright?"

I said, "You have great legs," which in no way answered the question, but made him chortle with delight and open Petite's door for me.

"You come by in the middle of the night to tell me that?"

I laughed as I climbed out of the car. "Not really. I didn't mean to come over at all. Petite wanted to visit."

Gary gave the car a sly smile and a pat on the roof. "I'm flattered, darlin'. It ain't every day a pretty girl half my age wants to drop by late at night to see me."

Now there was a man who knew how to treat a girl. I beamed at Gary. "Love me, love my car." Or maybe it was the other way around, but he treated her like a lady, and that was what mattered. "She is half your age, too, isn't she?"

"Yep." Gary ushered me toward the house. "Guess this old dog hasn't quite lost it yet."

"Gary, you're still going to have it when I'm a withered old wisp."

"Flattery," he pronounced, "will get you everywhere. What's goin' on, Jo? These ain't your usual visiting hours."

I screwed up my face and kicked my shoes off as I went into the living room. "I know. Sorry if I woke you. It's just that I just got back from a—" My throat seized up. There were things I just hated to say, and it disconcerted me when they started pouring out from my mouth like it was natural. I sighed, took a deep breath, and tried again: "A coven meeting."

Gary's eyebrows shot up with surprise, moving his white hairline back half an inch. I didn't think he looked anything like Sean Connery, but for a moment he reminded me of the sexy old Scotsman. "'Scuze me? Coven? With witches?"

"With witches." I dropped into the couch and pulled a quilt over myself.

"What'd they want? How come you didn't invite me?"

"They wanted to open up a passage between worlds and invite an ancient American Indian spirit into this one to help end the heat wave as a precursor to saving the world." I thought that summed it up pretty nicely. "Oh, and I didn't invite you because I'm an ingrate."

"I love ya anyway." Gary leaned forward, sitting on the front edge of his comfy chair, big hands laced together. He wasn't exactly Rodin's *The Thinker*, but he looked solid and practical and made me feel better. "What's the catch?"

I dragged the quilt over my head. "They need my help."

Gary chuckled. "Hiding ain't gonna make it go away, doll. Wasn't it just yesterday you were sayin' this heat wave might be your fault? Sounds like you got your work cut out for you."

I pulled the quilt down again and looked at him unhappily. "I don't like this, Gary."

"C'mere, darlin'."

I got up, trailing the quilt after me like Linus, and sat down on the arm of his chair. Gary put an arm around my hips and gave them a hard hug. "Someday all them walls you got built up are gonna have to come tumblin' down, Jo, and when they're ready there's gonna be nothing you can do about it. Might be easier on you if you start pryin' some of the bricks out now."

"Might be," I said very cautiously. This was bordering on the territory of Things Joanne Didn't Talk About. "But I wouldn't count on it." I didn't want to be nasty. I just didn't want to open up that conversational path right now. Gary gave my hips another hug.

"I reckon you're gonna do what you have to do, sweetheart. In the meantime, whaddaya think you're doin', showin' up at this hour and interruptin' an old man's beauty sleep? Get goin'. I'll see you tomorrow."

I didn't point out he'd been awake when I arrived, and got going, feeling like I'd dodged a bullet. Gary'd never made mention of being actively aware there were things I didn't want to talk about, and I didn't know what I would've done if he'd pressed it. Everyone else who'd pushed me about them had been on a psychic plane, and I couldn't just disappear from Gary's living room the way I could from my garden or the Dead Zone. I wasn't ready to deal with my personal demons yet. It was kind of nice to know, though, that Gary would be there when I was.

Petite deigned to drive me home, and I went to bed trying hard not to think about the things I didn't want to think about.

Saturday, June 18, 5:50 a.m.

For the second morning in a row, I was early. I was very impressed with myself, especially since this made three whole days I'd been up early, and I didn't yet seem to be suffering from the mind-numbing tiredness that had accompanied my previous shamanic experiences. Maybe I was getting better at this.

"I think that's the idea," Judy said good-naturedly. I nearly flinched out of my skin, which was an unfortunately realistic possibility on this level of existence. I got my psyche under control and settled back into my skin before getting to my feet.

"Judy. I'm glad you're here. I need some answers."

"Again," she said, "I think that's the idea." Her eyes were bright with amusement, despite their blackness.

"Yeah, but don't be difficult, okay? I'm good with all of the openness and the accepting and the learning." Okay, I wasn't really, but that wasn't the point. The skies over my garden darkened perceptibly and I scowled at them. "I'm trying to be, okay? Look." That was back to Judy, who sat down on a bench and folded her feet up under herself cozily. She looked more at peace in my garden than I did. It was annoying. Thunder rumbled, and I set my teeth together, trying to find the reasonable voice that I knew had to be buried somewhere inside me. "I need to know about someone named Virissong."

Judy's entire body language changed, her head tipping to the side, birdlike, anticipation and curiosity in the set of her shoulders and the way she leaned forward. "Where did you come across *his* name?"

I let out an explosive breath. "So you've heard of him?"

"Certainly. Anyone who travels the astral realms enough eventually meets or hears of him. I didn't think you had the experience, though."

"I'm full of surprises. What can you tell me about him?"

Judy smiled. "I think I can introduce you to him. It'll mean another journey to the Lower World. Are you ready?"

I glanced skyward inadvertently, wondering if I'd get another glance of the thunderbird if I tried another Lower World journey. "Yeah, I think so."

"He isn't always easy to contact," Judy warned. "This may take all of your lesson time today, and it's not really what you need to be learning right now."

"Tomorrow," I promised. "Tomorrow we can do whatever comes after power animals."

"More power animals," she said with another smile. "But this time we'll do it as a healing journey. You'll be searching for an animal to help someone else."

"Who?"

Judy shook her head. "That remains to be seen. Are you ready to begin this journey?"

I straightened my shoulders and nodded. "Let's do it."

There was no side trip to the Upper World, no thunderbird visitation. The drumbeat caught me, and I fell, chasing after Judy, into the Lower World. When I hit the earth—rich and loamy, full of nightcrawlers and clicking bugs—a jolt went through me, one part connection to the Lower World and one part disappointment that I hadn't been moved to sneak away again.

"There's more ritual," Judy was telling me, "to asking someone like Virissong to come to you than there is in calling power animals. Begin with a power circle. Start in the north."

I bit my tongue on asking which way was north, and tried to figure it out on my own. The Lower World felt flatter than the real world, as if I might be standing on the face of a compass. I closed my eyes, trying to feel the world around me through the darkness. After a moment I felt light and heat to my right, and turned that way.

The sun broke over the horizon, very fast and very large, coloring the sky in a flare of white that faded to red. I bowed toward it, like it had risen just to help me find my directions.

I'd never drawn a power circle before, and had no idea what was involved. No, not no idea. I had enough sense to thank the spirits of the north and invoke their protection. I did it again for the other three directions, making a circle around Judy, who looked pleased, and myself, who felt absurd.

There was a little burst of power as I thanked the last spirits, to the west, like a forcefield coming online around me. I pressed my palm against the air, then yanked it away again as I encountered resistance. Behind me, Judy laughed. "You have so little faith." She sounded impressed. "Don't worry. I'll help you come to believe."

Just what I always wanted. My own personal savior. "Now what?"

"Now the offering." Judy looked expectant. I looked around.

"Of what?" I asked after a while, when nothing seemed to be happening.

"Didn't you bring a gift?"

"Gosh, no. Fresh out of gifts. Nobody left me a memo."

"No cornmeal? No water or tobacco?"

I shifted uncomfortably. Judy twisted her mouth in disapproval. "I thought you wanted to meet Virissong."

"I do," I protested.

"But you came without gifts?"

"I didn't know I was supposed to bring any!"

Judy sighed. "I'm surprised you've lived this long. All right. We'll have to make do. Give me your hand."

Chagrined, I gave her my hand. "The point of the gift is to make an offering connected with the earth, so Virissong knows we respect him and will listen to our call," she said. "Do you understand that?"

"Yeah." Grumpy Jo. I sounded like a sullen teenager. "Yes, I do," I said more politely.

"There's one thing you carry within you at all times that's connected to the earth and holds great power."

"There is?" I asked, but instead of answering, Judy took a knife from the small of her back and laid my palm open to the bone.

CHAPTER ELEVEN

"Jesus motherfucking Christ!" I yanked my hand back, but Judy held it with a painfully solid grip, twisting my wrist so the blood pooling between my fingers dripped to the earth.

"Careful!" she snapped. "If it splashes onto the power circle, the shields will come down. Blood is power, Joanne Walker. Blood is the most precious gift that can be given. Now think of Virissong, and ask for him to visit us!"

"Jesus *Christ*," I said again. Judy let my hand go and I turned it up, curling my fingers around the wound. It hurt, but not as badly as I thought it should. It was a dull, thick pain, like my joints were tired instead of the clear sharpness I associated with a blade cut. I wrapped my other hand around it, trying to cut off the blood flow, but even as I watched, it began to heal, the blood congealing between my fingers. "Jesus Christ." I thrust my jaw out and turned away from Judy, anger hunching my shoulders as I tried to clear my mind and think of England. Or Virissong.

An unexpected feeling of well-being swept over me. The ache faded from my hand and the air around me cleared, brightening in a way that had nothing to do with the rising sun. "Virissong," Judy said in a warm voice. "We welcome and greet you."

My anger couldn't stand up under the onslaught of warm fuzzies. I turned, still clutching my injured hand, to face—

Well, it wasn't a god. That much I knew. It was powerful, much more powerful than any person I'd met, but it didn't carry with it the raw, primal forces of chaos that Cernunnos had.

Had I not met Cernunnos, though, I'd think I was facing a god. He was small and slender and the very air he exhaled was charged with energy. Power crawled over his skin, glittering white in the close morning sunlight. He was human, but only just. The hairs on my arms stood up, and I held my ground through conscious effort. "Thank you for answering our call," I said. He turned to smile at me.

Was there a rule that otherworldly beings had to be gorgeous? He was dark-skinned and black-eyed, his broad features full of passion. "Joanne Walker." His voice washed over me, a warm tenor that ought to have been filling concert halls. It raised the hairs on my arms just like Caruso's voice might've, making me feel as if I might take wing and be transported somewhere else entirely by their lift.

"It is a very great pleasure to know you." His voice dropped on the "know," and I felt myself blush as I got all Biblical about it. I clearly needed a real-world relationship.

"It's nice to meet you, too. I, um…"

"Had questions for me," Virissong put in. I smiled crookedly, relieved I didn't actually have to say that myself. It seemed presumptuous. "Will you walk with me?" he asked. I glanced at Judy, who spread her hands slightly.

"I think I should stay inside the power circle," I said apologetically. His eyebrows lifted fractionally and he put his hand against the invisible wall between us. It bowed slightly under the pressure, but it held.

"Are you always so cautious?" he asked, not bothering to hide a smile. Great. I was being teased by three-thousand-year-old Indian witches. I wrinkled my nose.

"No, but it's never too late to learn." I'd been hanging out with Gary too much. Any minute now I was going to start calling myself an old dog.

He chuckled, liquid musical sound. My arm hairs gave up trying to escape and lay down flat, like a cat's ears, and I rubbed my hands over them. My right hand didn't hurt anymore. I turned it up to find the bone-deep slice across my palm had healed over entirely. "Very well," Virissong said. "I'll stay. Ask your questions, Joanne Walker."

"I need to know your purpose." Even as I said it, the sheer arrogance of it came back and hit me in the teeth.

Virissong's eyebrows shot up and he looked beyond me at Judy. She said nothing, though I saw her shrug from the corner of my eye. Virissong looked back at me.

"I don't think anyone's ever been quite that bald-faced about it," he said. "My purpose, you say."

I twisted my shoulders uncomfortably and let them fall again. "I've met some people who believe they can bring you back into our world, and that to do so will help restore a balance of life. They think they need my help to do it, and I need to know what I'm getting into before I commit to it."

"Wise of you." I got the impression he was teasing me again, but that there was also some small degree of respect in it.

"I've had a little experience with this sort of thing."

"Yessss." He drew the word out, and suddenly I recognized his voice as the same one that had come out of the light the night before. I relaxed and tensed all at once. it was good to know I was dealing with the right demi-deity, but the exultation of power that had hit me the night before made me cautious. "Yes," he repeated. "We have some knowledge of that."

"We?" I looked around. "Royal we?"

"Universal consciousness we," he said, straight-faced. "A step above royal."

He was like Coyote, only more so. I thought one was enough. "I'm also trying to find out about a girl who died suddenly. One of the group that's trying to bring you across."

Virissong's black eyes darkened further. "Cassandra

Tucker. Her poor daughter, left without a mother so young."

It took active effort to keep my jaw from dropping open. "You know about her?"

He lifted his eyebrows. "The coven has been working toward bringing me back into the Middle World for months, Joanne. I've tried to participate in it as much as possible." He made a moue, then shrugged. "My ability to do so is limited, but I certainly know who's involved. I had always sensed Cassandra had a weak heart. I was concerned being the Mother might worsen the damage, but she laughed off my warnings. I lacked the power to strengthen her while still trapped in the Lower World. It's a loss I'll regret for a long time."

"She had a heart attack?" I lost the battle and my jaw fell somewhere around my ribs. "And the coven never noticed anything was wrong?" To be fair, I wasn't sure how I would tell if someone's heart was defective, so maybe I couldn't blame the coven. "Why didn't you tell them? Magic can do that to somebody?"

"Magic," Virissong said, rather sternly, "has its price, just as everything else does. It can become as much a burden as physical labor, with the same results."

Having been pleased only minutes earlier about my lack of sleep deprivation, I felt a little chastised. I should've known that, or at least put it together on my own. Virissong gave me a brief understanding smile, then added, "I did try to warn Faye. I gathered they were close. But as much as I want to, my ability to communicate with those in the Middle World is limited. She may never have heard my warning."

I thought of Faye's quivering sorrow and anger over Cassie's death, and nodded. "Guess not."

"As to the other, though. As to my purpose." Virissong folded himself down suddenly, with much the same grace Judy had displayed when she arrived in my garden, and gestured for me to do the same. My shoulder brushed the shield as I sat, glimmers wavering around the circle. Judy sat behind me, half-visible from the corner of my eye. The sun crept higher in the sky, and no one said anything. Just before my patience gave out, Virissong lifted his head and began to speak, more to the too-close horizon than to me.

"I was born, as men reckon it, some three thousand years ago, south of what you now call Seattle."

I refrained from comment on his grasp of colloquial English in favor of listening, and he gave me a look like he'd heard what I was thinking.

"Things were different then. Not perfect, as some people of your age want to believe, but different." He saw the wryness of my smile and gave me a quick grin in return. "My people were generally at peace, both with each other and with the world. But there came a time of great darkness and great coldness. We starved and grew cold and died, and nothing we did seemed to appease our gods and ancestors. We became desperate. We made offerings of everything—what little we had, and still our people died and froze and starved. I was very young then, a youth of less than twenty summers."

He hesitated, then put out his hand toward me. "Are

you sure you will not cross the power circle, Joanne Walker? If I could take your hand I could show you these things, rather than only tell them."

I looked at Judy. Her forehead wrinkled with uncertainty and she shook her head. "The decision isn't one I can make for you, Joanne. I can't forbid you to take risks."

"Do you think it would help?" I asked. "To be able to see it?"

"It might," she said reluctantly. "It's always easier to believe, when you've seen."

I thought of the black-eyed Horse spirit, ordering me to try, and curled my fingernails against my palm. The healed skin opened again, easily. I put my hand against the barrier, bringing the shield down with a shudder. Virissong's eyes glittered. "Thank you," he said. "Your trust will not go unforgotten."

"I hope it goes unregretted, too," I said, and put my bloody hand in his.

Hunger bit through my belly like a knife, embarrassingly sharp. Part of me knew I had to have eaten recently: otherwise the need for food would have been reduced to a dull ache, ignorable. It was only after a feast that the famine struck so hard. Another part of me knew my twenty-first century self had never known the real meaning of the word "starving," and that was where the embarrassment came from. I knew, back home and safe in my own time and body, that I'd still claim to be starving from time to time.

The cold cut in then, daggers slicing through the tough,

warm leathers I wore, ignoring the flesh and setting up shop in my bones. I looked to my left, chill stiffening my neck. Virissong sat beside me, young and handsome and with his jaw thrust out like a petulant child's.

"They are wrong, Nakaytah," he said. The body I was in reached its hand out and put it on his arm. Apparently I was Nakaytah. Good to know.

"They're the elders, beloved," I replied. "You must trust them."

"No! It isn't right that we starve and freeze and do nothing. I've found a way," he said, suddenly eager, and turned to me. He wasn't, I realized, all that handsome after all. His features were lighted by a fierce zealotry, and that gave the wide bones of his face and the darkness of his eyes a compulsion that was easily mistaken for good looks. "I can make the spirits come to me."

Horror drained down my throat in an icy sluice, colder than the wind, and pooled in my belly. "But you're not a shaman. Not called, not trained—"

"But I *am* called," he protested. "How else could I make the spirits come? I *am* called, Nakaytah. It is only that my family is not a favorite, not born to the shaman line—"

Reluctant agreement thawed the horror inside me. Virissong's father and grandfather had both pleaded to study with the shamans, convinced that they, too, carried within them the power to visit the spirit world. Their pleas had been denied; no true shaman, the elders said, would have to struggle so hard to prove his position. A spirit journey would show their true paths, and the journeys hadn't led Virissong's family to the powerful shaman spirits. Now they were shunned and a little ridiculed, for their delusions of grandeur. My hand crept out and wrapped itself around Virissong's. "What do the spirits tell you?"

Virissong sat back, relief sagging his shoulders. He tightened his fingers around mine, then withdrew them. I tucked mine back inside my leathers; it was too cold to hold hands in the frozen wind. "They say there is a great and terrible battle raging in the spirit world. They say that the monsters the spirits fight are so strong the battle spills into the Middle World, and this is why it's so cold, and why game is so scarce. Only we are stubborn—" Virissong broke off with a crooked little grin, adding, "—or foolish enough to stay."

Disbelief bubbled up in my stomach. "You can't mean the spirits want us to leave here!"

Comic dismay popped Virissong's eyes wide. He shook his head, reaching to catch my hand again. "No, no. The spirits admire our stubbornness a little, I think. No. They say that to end the cold and bring the game back, we must end the battle that's being fought in the spirit world."

My chin dropped to my chest, cold leather tucking against the warmth of my neck as I stared at Virissong. "We have to bring the monsters to this world," he said enthusiastically. "Here, men can hunt and slay their bodies, weakening them so that in the spirit world they can be defeated."

Slow admiration began to course through my veins, warming me despite the freezing air. "Like in the stories of the First People," I said wonderingly. Virissong did his best to look modest, but excitement burned in his eyes. "You'll be remembered forever as a great hero!"

Virissong ducked his head, smiling. "That isn't why I do this," he said. Not even my host entirely believed him, so when he lifted his head, expression bright and hopeful, to say, "Perhaps a little of why," it made us both laugh. "I want to prove myself," he went on in a low voice, when the laughter had faded. "I want to show them that even if the family is not a long line of shamans, our power should not be denied. But I also want to help our people, Nakaytah. We freeze and starve and die, and I do not want this to be the end of us."

"Then we will." I put my hand in his again, still warmed from laughter and admiration. "Even the elders will see that they were wrong, and warmth and food will come back to us. I'll help you, if I can."

In the Lower World, Virissong took his hand from mine. I startled awake, blood sticky in my palm, to find him looking away, tightness around his mouth. "If you must see the rest I will show you," he said in a low voice. He'd lost the familiar colloquial speech patterns and was more cautious now, formality masking distress. "It is…painful. Nakaytah died, helping me."

"Oh my God. What happened?"

"Something I didn't anticipate. The monsters were more cunning than I thought. We built a power circle," he said, idly drawing one in the earth in front of him. "We called the spirits to protect us, and we drummed to catch the monsters' attention. We wanted to draw them into the circle, where we could slay them and free our people."

I nodded, clutching my hand closed over the wound in it. "What went wrong?"

"The monsters tried to become us," Virissong said. "They tried to take the places of our own souls. My spirit protectors were strong, and rejected the monster that tried to take me. But Nakaytah…"

"She wasn't strong enough." I felt dizzy, as if I'd lost far more blood from the cut than I thought I had. "What happened?"

"She leaped at me with tooth and nail," Virissong said. "She took my knife from my belt as we struggled, cutting me here, and here." He pushed up a sleeve, showing a strong white scar across his forearm, and then another across his belly as he pulled his shirt out of the way. "I carry these scars forever, to remember her by."

My fingers found their way to my cheek, brushing over a thin scar that ran from my eye socket to the corner of my mouth. "I understand," I said. Virissong nodded, letting his clothes fall back into place.

"I took the knife from her," he went on after a few seconds. "I was stronger and larger and trained in hunting, if not war. She…ran forward. Onto the knife. I pulled it away, but it was already inside her. Blood went everywhere. It brought down the power circle, as you did a little while ago." He nodded at me, an acknowledgment of repeating patterns. "I saw the monster that had infected her fly free, beyond the power circle and into the world. I vowed that day I would never rest until I had brought it to its death."

"And three thousand years later you're still trying." My voice was tight and choked. Virissong inclined his head.

"I chose to spend many lifetimes in the Lower World, waiting for a time when I had a chance against the monster again. I think the tide of the Middle World is changing, now. I think there are many who look to embrace a better way of life. I think now is the time I must make my final challenge. But I've grown weak, being away from the Middle World for so long. It's why I need your help, and the coven's help. With the power you lend me, I can become whole again, joining spirit and body together as they are meant to be."

"And the monster?"

"Together we'll track it down and destroy it," Virissong said, voice flat with ancient emotion. "And from that, I hope a new world will be born. A better one."

I nodded slowly. "What happened to your people, Virissong? Did the cold end?"

"It did. The spirits were right. With the battle no longer shaking the Lower and Upper Worlds, the Middle World became safe and normal again."

"That's good. But—" Something nagged at me, a prickle at the base of my neck. I frowned vaguely at Virissong, then at Judy, who sat quietly beside me.

Virissong's eyebrows rose. "But?"

"But what—" Another tickle ran down my spine, like an elementary school fire alarm buzzing in the distance. I frowned less vaguely and rubbed the back of my neck. "What happ—"

The tickle turned into a shrill that broke through my

trance, finally recognizable as the phone ringing. I stumbled to my feet and picked up the receiver, my voice groggy with disuse. "Hello?"

"Joanne Walker?" The voice was unfamiliar, even if I wasn't half-asleep.

"Yeah?"

"Do you know a Gary Muldoon?"

I woke all the way up inside of an instant, cold making an ugly burp of nervousness in my stomach. "Yeah. What's wrong?"

"This is Dr. Wood at Northwest Hospital. We'd like you to come down right away. Mr. Muldoon has had a heart attack."

CHAPTER TWELVE

Saturday, June 18, 6:33 a.m.

I didn't know how I got to the hospital. I didn't know if I even hung up the phone. All I could hear was my heartbeat and the memory of the day I'd met Gary, when a human banshee called Marie told us both that Gary wasn't going to die any time soon. Soon. What was soon? Was six months soon? It seemed soon to me. How far in advance had her ability to see death coming worked? She hadn't said, and it was much too late to ask her. I remembered her body, lying across her living room floor, the heart torn out, and I wondered if six months was soon.

The doctor I'd spoken to on the phone met me in the

waiting room. She was short, with dark sympathetic eyes and a quick reassuring smile that I didn't buy for a minute.

I felt like I was watching myself from a safe distance of several feet. From out there, the pain and fear couldn't really get to me. All I could really feel from out there was the itch in my nose that made me want to sneeze, something that happened every time I went into a hospital.

In there, inside my body, everything was tunnel-visioned and I kept asking, "A heart attack? Not a stroke? A heart attack?" as if it were important, but I couldn't figure out why it would be. In there, there wasn't enough room to breathe, like someone'd sat on my lungs. I wanted to stay out here, distant, where it was easier to breathe. The doctor—I had to look at her name tag to remember it was Wood—sat me down and put her hands on my shoulders.

"A heart attack. He's very weak right now," she told me. "He's weak, but he's awake," she said. "He wanted to see you, Ms. Walker. Can you do that?"

I snapped back into my body so hard it made me cry out loud, a sharp high whimper. Blood flow tingled through my fingertips, painfully, but the pain gave me something to focus on. "Yeah." My voice was all rough again. "Yeah, of course. Is he gonna be okay, doctor?"

She nodded and gave me another reassuring smile. "He realized very quickly what the attack was and got to the hospital before significant damage had been done. That was a few hours ago. I called as soon as he was stabilized."

"I'm sorry." I had no idea why I was apologizing.

"It's okay." The doctor smiled at me. "You all right?"

"No." My voice cracked, and I put on my best brave smile in return. "But I can pretend."

She patted my shoulder. "Come on, then."

"There's my girl." Gary's voice was too thin, his gray eyes dulled, but he smiled as I put my hand into his. Power fluttered very gently inside me as we touched, and I nearly burst into tears at the realization that there might actually be something I could do. I held off for a minute, though, hanging on to Gary's hand.

"Your girl, huh?" I sat down on a stool beside his bed, trying not to sniffle. "When'd I graduate from being a crazy dame to being your girl?"

"Right about the time my arm started tingling and aching," Gary said. He looked like he'd lost thirty pounds in the eight hours since I'd seen him. His skin was ashy, the Hemingway wrinkles that I found so reassuring now deep and haggard around his mouth and eyes. "You look like hell, Jo."

I gave a shaky laugh. "*I* look like hell? Anybody shown you a mirror, Gary?"

"They don't need to. I'm feelin' like the old gray ghost."

"Yeah, well." I tightened my fingers around his. "No giving up that ghost, okay? Not for a while yet."

Gary snorted. "You kidding? You've only just gotten started. I'm not plannin' on checking out for a while yet. I want grandkids," he said with a wink and a sudden grin. My heart lurched.

"That's why you're hanging around, huh? Nice to finally find out there's a reason." My attempt at levity fell flat, but Gary smiled anyway, then let his eyes close, which told me as much as anything how tired he was. I'd never met a more open-eyed kind of guy than Gary. We stayed like that for a few minutes, me trying to memorize him while he breathed, then I closed my own eyes, hoping I wouldn't cry.

"Lissen, Jo."

My eyes popped open again. Gary was wearing his serious face. His really serious face, so serious I'd never seen it before. Nerves twisted in my stomach. "Yeah?"

"The grandkids, y'know I'm joking. But—"

"God, Gary, don't. Okay? Don't get all maudlin on me." I managed a feeble smile. "At least wait until you're sitting up again, okay?" I made the smile brighter, even though tears stung my eyes, and I bent over his hand. "Anyway, I know, okay?" My voice squeaked. "I know. Me, too, huh? Okay? Me, too." I blinked back tears, keeping my head lowered over his hand. Gary reached over himself with his left hand, clonking my head with the oxygen sensor on his middle finger as he ruffled my hair. "Ow."

He chuckled. "Sorry. Okay. Arright, Jo. Now you gotta keep me up to date on what's goin' on out there, all right? I hate missin' things."

I sat up laughing and brushed my hand over my eyes. "I know. I will, I promise. Like, here, you'll like this. I was talking to Virissong, the spirit guy the coven wants to bring across, when the hospital called."

Gary's eyebrows retained their bushiness even when the rest of him looked smaller. "What's he like?"

"He seems okay. I guess I'm going to do this."

"Man," Gary said, "I gotta get out of here. I'm gonna miss all the good stuff."

"Only you think it's the good stuff." I gave him a watery smile. "When're they letting you out?"

"I donno. A cute blond nurse says I gotta go to physical therapy. Me, physical therapy. I'm seventy-three years old. What kinda crap is that?"

"The kind that's going to make sure you live to see seventy-four," I said sternly. Gary's eyes brightened, as if chastisement was better for him than sympathy. It probably was.

"You're gonna keep me in line, aren't you," he grumbled, without disguising the note of pleasure in his voice.

"Damn straight." I took a deep breath. "And I'm going to do a little laying on of hands, and then I'm going to ask a power animal to keep an eye on you."

If somebody'd said that to me, it would've made me even crabbier. Gary lit up again. "Yeah? What animal?"

"I'll know when it comes. Tomorrow morning." The part of me that knew I wouldn't really turn my back on shamanism stung me with cold guilt. If I'd studied maybe I could've seen this coming and done something to prevent it. Preemptive healing.

"Stop it," Gary said. I twitched and blinked at him. "You're lookin' all guilty," he said. "Knock it off. I'm an old man, Jo. I ain't gonna last forever, and there's nothing you or anybody else can do about that. But I'm not checkin' out just yet, so just stop it, you hear? You want to find this old dog a little spiritual support to shore him up, I'll appreciate it, but don't go thinkin' you can stop nature in its tracks. You hear me?"

"I hear you." I smiled a little. "I'm just not sure I'm ready to listen."

He squeezed my hand. "Fair 'nuff. Women always take their own sweet time makin' up their minds to see sense."

I nodded, then straightened my spine. "Hey!"

Gary cackled, breathier than usual, but still his own laugh. "There's my girl," he said again, and let himself slip back into resting. I waited until he slept, then dug down inside me for the power that lay behind my breastbone.

It flickered and murmured, responding sluggishly. I wasn't too sure how to go about repairing a broken heart. Cosmetic changes, like visualizing a new paint job, seemed inadequate, and the patch replacement that I'd used to fix the hole in my own lung struck me as somehow dangerous. I'd been dying at the time. Screwing up would have only finished the job. If I messed up now, Gary, who wasn't dying, might. My car analogy was turning out to have limitations I didn't like.

In the end the best I could do was to share my own essence, the way Billy had done with me back in March. I thought it would help, just by giving him more than his own depleted energy to draw from as he healed. It took a while to formulate, but I slipped a small, delicate ball of silver rainbows inside Gary's chest, and wished it Godspeed and good luck.

Then I stayed until a nurse came to usher me out, and went back to my apartment to sob in the shower.

Routine brought gratifying numbness. I wrote tickets and walked my beat, nodding at locals and stopping to give directions to tourists. I didn't have to think, which was a godsend. Thinking put me back into that place where it was too hard to breathe. Gary might've believed there wasn't anything I could've done, but I wasn't so sure.

At lunch I went back to the station instead of stopping on my beat to get a bite to eat. I wasn't hungry, and I needed comfort smells, grease and oil and gasoline. I went down to the garage, even though I didn't think I was up to watching Nick carefully not look at me.

It was almost a relief that Thor was the only one around, lying on his back beneath a vehicle. I stood there by his feet until he slid out to get a wrench from the toolbox by the car. His eyebrows, grease-smeared, rose a little as he saw me. I looked around, unable to meet his eyes as I mumbled, "Wondered if there was anything I could help out with for a while."

He frowned at me. I looked somewhere else again. "Please."

"Yeah." His answer was so gruff and so long in coming that I flinched, startled out of trying to think of where I was going to go when he said no. "Rodriguez got his wheels out of whack again. Get some coveralls and take a look." He gave me the faintest smile possible and slid under his work-in-progress again. I was left staring at his legs, stunned. I'd warned him about Rodriguez's axle alignment problems six months earlier. Maybe good ol' Thor wasn't so bad after all.

Rodriguez didn't really spend hours beating his vehicle's axle out of alignment, even if I'd accused him of doing so in the past. I'd never yet checked his vehicle and found the alignment outside of factory tolerances, which didn't mean he was wrong. Some drivers are more sensitive to the variations in alignment, and Rodriguez was like the princess with the pea. The camber and casting readings on his vehicle were a full degree side to side off, enough to cause a pull.

And that was something I could deal with. Methodical, straight-forward work could fix an alignment problem. It took my mind off everything, and I finished the job with reluctance, not wanting to leave the garage and face the world again.

Thor, still on his back, rolled out from under the car he was working on and pushed up on an elbow, watching me. I wiped my hands down on the cleanest towel I could find and stripped the coveralls off. I'd done it a thousand times—just about literally—with the guys in the shop there. I'd never felt self-conscious before, too aware of Thor watching me. Big and thick and clumsy: that was the Joanne from high school, too tall and too poorly socialized. I fumbled the coveralls as I tried to put them back on their hook and caught a new handful of grease. I closed my eyes, sighed, and shoved my hand back through my hair before my brain caught up with my actions.

Thor's laughter, deep and out loud, made hairs stand up on the back of my neck. I looked over my shoulder, mouth twisted. Propped up on an elbow, still on the creeper, he looked like a beefcake calendar picture, except in a pinup he'd be in jeans, stripped to the waist, and glistening with baby oil instead of wearing tar-smeared coveralls. "You know where the shampoo is."

My mouth betrayed me and the corners turned up in a tiny smile. "That bad?" I headed for the washroom, not expecting an answer. Thor's voice followed me anyway.

"Well, they said you're Native American, but I think war paint's supposed to be different colors."

I stopped. "War paint can be black. They?"

He shrugged the shoulder his weight wasn't on. "People talk."

"About me?" I wasn't sure if I was pleased or alarmed.

He gave a sharp snort. "Don't sound so surprised. Replacing you's like trying to replace David Lee Roth."

"Hagar was better." For a moment we stared at one another, caught in an unexpected camaraderie. "I gotta wash up," I said abruptly. Thor slid back under his car. He didn't come back out when I jogged through the garage a few minutes later, my hair still damp. The summer day was already heavier than the air-conditioning could defeat, and I figured I'd be back outside and dried off before anyone could comment.

Morrison caught me two halls away from the front door and gave me a scathing look. "You smell like a grease pit, Walker. I thought you were on beat."

The fragile sense of well-being garnered in the garage evaporated and I clenched my fists, fixing my gaze on the floor. Heat prickled at the back of my eyes, and the flutter in my stomach didn't have anything to do with magic, for once. It was just plain old-fashioned nausea, all knotted up in a ball of misery. "Lunch. On my way back out now." I knew I sounded sullen, but that was better than bursting into tears.

Morrison stepped aside, surprising me. For a second I didn't know what to do, stings prickling the inside of my nose, another precursor to embarrassing tears. I hunched my shoulders and flared my nostrils, trying to press the tingle away without being so obvious as to use my hands, and bulled past him.

"You all right, Walker?" There was a note of what sounded like genuine concern in Morrison's voice, and it pushed me even farther off-balance.

"No." I hadn't given my mouth permission to tell the truth, and bit my lower lip hard in admonishment. "I'm fine."

"Which is it?" He came back around me, frowning, and for a few seconds Captain Michael Morrison clearly didn't know what to do with his hands. Even with my gaze locked on the floor I could see him reach for my chin, like he'd tilt it up so I had to meet his eyes. Then the sheer inappropriateness of that gesture hit him, even as it made me look up, the knot in my stomach giving a sick thump.

His fingers brushed my jaw because I moved, the contact making his hand drop like a dead weight. The breath in my lungs went with it, my chest beginning to ache because I didn't seem to be able to remember how to inhale again.

"Walker." Morrison was not a man I thought of as uncertain or unprepared, but his voice was tight and he held himself in such a way that I thought maybe he'd forgotten how to breathe, too. That began to concern me. Surely we couldn't just stand there, not breathing at one another, all afternoon. My heart was pounding much too loudly in

my ears, like it was determined to drown out whatever
Morrison might say next. But he didn't say anything, only
kept watching me as if he wasn't entirely sure what to do
with me. My palms began to ache with the need to do
something, but the obvious thing to do with a man in my
personal space.

"Joanie!"

I drew in a sharp breath, air startlingly cool in my
lungs as guilty color burned my cheeks. Morrison
stepped back as if he'd been released from confinement,
and Billy came lumbering around the corner with a sticky
note in hand, his voice raised. "The reason the department gives you a cell phone is so you can be called on it.
The hospital's been trying to get through to you. They've
got some paperwork you need to sign. Excuse me, Captain," he added, perfunctorily.

Morrison grunted. "Hospital?"

"That's what I was just trying to tell you," I snapped,
not at all fairly. Refuge in anger. Good, Jo. I watched the
indecipherable thing go out of Morrison's expression, to
be replaced by far more familiar irritation. Unexpected regret lanced through the general nausea in my stomach,
turning my voice even more acid. "My friend Gary had a
heart attack last night. What do they want to talk to *me*
for?" I addressed the last to Billy, who thrust the sticky
note at me.

"You're down as next of kin, I guess. Insurance wants
you to sign off on his physical therapy stuff."

I reached for the note with a hand gone so numb I
couldn't feel the paper. It stuck to Billy's fingers as he

tried to let go, and the edge sliced a thin gash in my index finger. I stared at the blood welling up, waiting for the sting of pain. "Next of kin?"

"That's what the lady said. You and the old man didn't get hitched, did you?"

I didn't trust myself to look at either of them, especially Morrison. "No." Out of the corner of my eye, I saw Billy wince as his joke fell flat. "Thanks for taking the message." My voice was too hoarse. "I'll call the hospital and see if I can get over there tonight."

"Take half an hour if they need it right now," Morrison said, more gracefully than I deserved after snarling at him. "Otherwise, get back to work." That, too, sounded more like sympathy than an order, though he turned a scowl on Billy. "You, too, Holliday. I'm not running a messenger service here."

Billy said, "Yessir," as we both watched Morrison stomp down the hallway. Then Billy turned to me, squinting. "Did I interrupt something there?"

Sometimes it was nice to have friends who demonstrated more sensitivity than the average male was reputed to. Other times, not so much. I said, "No," because there was no other answer I could reasonably give, and Billy didn't look like he believed it for a minute. "Thanks for the message."

I went out into the June sunshine to get my phone and call the hospital.

CHAPTER THIRTEEN

Saturday, June 18, 10:18 p.m.

"Officer Walker?" A young man's surprised voice sounded in my ear, welcome distraction from the eye-crossing insurance paperwork I was trying to fill out. I looked up, catching a glimpse of myself in a window reflection. My hair had wilted from the cute spikes it'd dried in after my shower. A boy who looked vaguely familiar was also dimly reflected in the window, standing behind my chair. I twisted around to frown up at him.

"Garth," he said. "Garth Johannsen. From the coven?"

"Oh!" I blinked at him, my frown getting deeper. "Hi, Garth. What're you doing here?" I hadn't even changed out of uniform before coming to the hospital. The nurse I'd talked to said I didn't need to come during work, but if I could come immediately after that would be great. I'd picked up the paperwork and visited with Gary until he started dozing off, then retreated to the lobby to go through it. It was after ten now and I was sticky and uncomfortable.

"You weren't at the meeting tonight." He came around to sit one chair over from me, leaving an empty space between us. I was grateful on a variety of levels, the most basic of which being that I was too damned hot to want to deal with someone's body next to mine. "We were worried," he added.

"And so you what," I said, "hunted me down at the hospital? How'd you do that, magic?" I set my teeth together and flopped my head against the padded plastic chair back. The kid was earnest and polite and didn't deserve to be the victim of my sarcasm. "Sorry," I muttered, then straightened up, convincing myself that I would be more gracious from here on out. "I forgot about the meeting."

"You forgot?" All the injury and dismay in the whole world were conveyed in those two words. "But this is *very important*."

"Garth," I said in what I felt was a reasonable tone, "a very close friend of mine had a heart attack last night while I was chasing down your goddamn Virissong. Forgive me if your priorities are not my priorities." So much for courtesy.

"Oh." Garth's voice went all hollow. "Oh, I'm sorry. I didn't mean to be a jerk."

I *had* meant to be a jerk, and now I felt like even more of one. Venting at Garth struck me as being on about the same level as kicking puppies. I was going to have to consider the possibility that it'd be better if I never spoke to anyone again as long as I lived. "It's not your fault. Sorry I snarled."

"You didn't," he assured me hastily, which was nice, if blatantly untrue. "Is your friend going to be okay?"

I sighed and looked down at the paperwork. "Yeah, if I can get all this stuff filled out so they'll put him in PT." I shuffled the stack, then shook my head. "Did you really magic up my location?"

Garth looked guilty. "No."

I frowned up at him. "Then what're you doing here?"

Garth brightened a little. "Visiting somebody. Come on."

I eyed my paperwork, then groaned and stood up. "Anything for a break."

The sordid truth was I expected Garth to lead me through the hospital to meet some handsome, starry-eyed young intern who he would euphemistically introduce as "my friend." Instead he took my hand and tugged me up to the cancer ward, where we stopped at the reception area and Garth leaned on the desk without letting go of my hand. "We're here to see Colin."

The man behind the desk waved us on without looking up, then followed us with, "He'll be glad to see you, Garth."

"You come here a lot?" I asked. Garth nodded, knocked on a room door, then pushed it open. Despite the hour, the young man in the bed sat up and smiled wearily as we stepped inside.

"Garth, man, who's this? You didn't tell me you were dating an Amazon." His voice was thin, rising and falling on shallow breaths. He was good-looking, even through the bloat of weight that cancer treatments had put on him. His eyes were hazel and cheerful, and the handshake he offered was full of concentrated strength. "I'm Colin," he said. "Garth's my big brother."

It wasn't quite full light when I left the cancer ward with Garth. The sky was hazy and light gray, a promise of another beautiful day to come. The air was cool for the first time in forever, although I privately admitted I wasn't usually up at five-thirty, the past few days notwithstanding. Possibly it was always perfect at this hour on a summer morning. Garth walked out onto the medical center steps with me, hands jammed in his pockets and head lowered. Neither of us had spoken since we left Colin's room.

"So what's the deal?" I finally asked. We'd stayed in Colin's room most of the night, both of them offering up absurd answers to questions on the insurance forms, Garth watching his brother when he slept. Between naps and paperwork, I tried to convince Colin that I was neither an Amazon nor Garth's girlfriend. He cheerfully refused to believe either.

Garth sat on the steps, not looking at me as he answered. "He's had leukemia his whole life, pretty much. Since he was eight. We thought he had it beat, but then a few months ago it came back, and he's been pretty sick since."

"How old is he?"

"Seventeen."

I blinked. "How old are you?"

"Twenty-two."

I didn't say he seemed younger. "I just want him to be okay," Garth said, without noticing my lack of input. "I tried praying for a long time, and when Colin was getting better I thought it was working, but then he got sick again and God doesn't seem to care."

"So you looked for something else?" I ventured. Garth nodded, dangling his hands between his knees.

"Mom couldn't handle Colin being sick again. She split a while ago, so even trying to hang together with family didn't work. Dad and me live about five minutes from here. So yeah, it's how come I got involved in the Craft." He studied his hands, while I bit my tongue from asking, *you got involved in the Craft because you live five minutes from here?* "I thought maybe…well, the Goddess is supposed to do magic, right?" Garth went on. "Witches and everything. I thought maybe…"

"Maybe magic could help." I put my fingertips over my eyes and rubbed. "It's not really that simple, Garth."

"I found that out. I was gonna give up, but then I heard Virissong, see? In the coven, I heard him talking to me. He said that when he came back and was strong again, he could heal the earth, and heal my brother, too."

"Virissong isn't a god, Garth."

"I think he's an aspect of the god."

"The God?" I pointed upward.

"That God and the god and the goddess are all one and the same. It's just kind of hard to see it with modern religious trappings." He sounded like he'd learned it by rote and believed it to the core of his being. "But Colin's getting worse. I know the solstice is soon and Virissong will come then, but—" He broke off, took a deep breath, and spoke very quickly: "But you have real power. We all felt it. I hoped maybe you could help Colin hang on just a little longer." The breath whooshed out of him and his shoulders deflated as he curved in on himself.

"Jesus, Garth." I leaned over, putting my head on my knees.

If I let myself—and I had been careful, on some level, not to—I could feel the hospital behind me. Not just the hospital, but each individual, patients and doctors alike, interns and nurses, newborns and the dying. Sometimes they were one and the same. I could feel places in them that needed healing, sometimes physical, very often psychological. There was too much for me to heal at once, even if those who were in need would allow me to try, and not all of them would. Young doctors, determined to prove that they could hack the harsh realities of the medical world, wouldn't let someone like me near them, for a multitude of reasons. Skepticism was only the easiest; a fear of showing weakness was the worst.

I wondered for the first time if I'd always avoided hospitals because I caught some sense of the meteoric emotional highs and lows, even before I was rudely awakened to a world that wasn't quite like the physical one I was comfortable with. Tuning into that sensation didn't even require any particular supernatural skill or belief. Hospitals carried a lot of psychic whammy.

"I'll try to help him, Garth," I said to my knees. There wasn't really any question about it from the moment I stepped into Colin's room. I could shrug off responsibility to the faceless masses for months at a time, as I'd less-than-admirably proven already. Individuals, though, in need of help, aching for it with every breath, even if they couldn't ask for it out loud—I wasn't a monster, and I was a long way from being that hard. "I can't promise anything," I said, lifting my head. "Okay? I can't promise anything. But I can try."

"Thank you." Garth's voice cracked and he crashed his shoulder against mine as he leaned over to hug me. "Thank you. I know you can help him. I think that's part of why Virissong called you to the coven. He knew you could help Colin hang on just a little while longer. Until he comes to help everyone."

I felt very old as I hugged Garth back. I knew Virissong wasn't a god any more than I was, but he didn't seem to want to hear it. Maybe some things just had to be taken on faith.

"Go on," I said, giving Garth a little shove. "I'll see you at the meeting tonight. I've got to think about how I'm going to do this." My inability to know how to heal Gary only seemed enormously compounded when facing something as invasive as a cancer. There had to be a way to do it. If I'd spent the past several months studying, I'd probably know what it was.

"Okay." Garth climbed to his feet, nodding, and wobbled down the steps, leaving me alone to my planning.

I didn't really need to plan. I had Gary's spirit quest to

do in a matter of minutes; making it home in time would be a crunch. A bit of memory floated through my mind, something about traditional shamans using sleep deprivation as a tool to enter their trances. That was good: in my current state, one or two deep breaths ought to put me under. I watched Garth walk away, then pushed to my feet. For once I had a clear path to follow and no qualms about following it. I went to find Petite.

CHAPTER FOURTEEN

Sunday, June 19, 6:00 a.m.

I wasn't early. I wasn't late, either, but I wasn't early. My garden was as hazy as I was, fog rolling through it. The trees were all budded with brand-new leaves, visible if I looked straight at them and a green, unfocused blur if I looked away even a fraction of an inch. On the one hand, the whole new life symbolism of the budding branches seemed like a good one. On the other, it seemed likely that the blooming trees were more going for the fuzzy green-ness than making a statement about my psychic prepar-edness for a new day. I yawned so hard my eyes teared up and I toppled over on my side. Judy sniffed in disapproval this time. "The weariness of the body should be left behind, Joanne."

"You'll have to teach me how to do that." I pushed myself upright again, still yawning until my vision sparkled and blurred. "And what is this with Joanne, Joanne, Joanne all the time. Everybody's all formal." I'd gotten used to Gary calling me Jo, a name I never thought I'd like. For a few seconds an image of my father glittered in my tears: watchful almond eyes with neither patience nor humor in them. He called me Jo, like he wanted a boy if he wanted a child at all.

I blinked away tears and visions alike. Judy's eyebrows were lifted. "Is there something else you'd rather be called?"

I studied her for a few seconds, gauging my response to that and to her. "No. Joanne's fine." Even Joanie, which most people called me, seemed a little more personal than I wanted to get with Judy just yet. "Let's get started. There's a lot to do this morning."

Judy smiled. "So there is. Is there someone specific you'd like to do a spirit quest for?"

"A couple people. Do I have to tell you who?" My recalcitrance surprised me, but it surprised Judy more. Her eyebrows darted up again.

"Not if you don't want to. It'll make it harder for me to help guide you."

I held my breath, staring at her for a while. "All right. One of them's a kid named Colin. He's a cancer patient, a friend of mine's brother." Friend. I'd known Garth two days and doubted I'd ever see him again after the solstice.

If that constituted a friend, I needed a lot of work on my interpersonal relationships.

Not that that was really much of a surprise.

"And the other?"

I found myself holding my breath again. "Let's start with Colin. He's pretty sick." Gary *was* my friend, and I felt a gut-deep reluctance to invite Judy along to guide me to finding a spirit animal for him. I'd screwed up all on my own with Gary, as far as I was concerned. I was going to find a way to help him on my own, too. It wasn't the right shamanistic spirit, but despite that, it felt right. My heart hurt, tiny sharp beats that made breathing hard. I shook my head, an attempt at literally shaking the feeling off. "Colin first."

I was getting good at plunging into the Lower World. This time I went through my little garden pond, too impatient to take a slow burrow through the earth. Cold gray water surrounded me, my lungs burning although I knew if I needed to I could draw a breath and not drown. Doing so seemed like cheating somehow. I thought the price of gasping to the surface was only the first step I should take toward finding a healing place.

I burst up through the earth, rich loam splattering every which way, as if it were water. I planted my hands in the dirt, treating it like a lakeshore, and pulled myself out of the ground, neither wet nor mud-encrusted. Maybe, just maybe, I was getting a little better at this. Judy appeared at my side, having taken a different path to the Lower World, and nodded with what I thought might be faint approval.

This time I didn't need to be told to draw a power circle. The sun was already high, burning very close to us in the red sky. I greeted it without even feeling ridiculous, and bowed in each direction, asking for guidance and protection in my quest. Judy settled down beside me in the circle, looking pleased.

"It's not unlike doing a search for yourself," she said as I sat down. "But rather than asking for the spirits to come and guide you, think of your friend Colin. Ask for the help of any who will come. Focus on him." She lifted a drum I hadn't seen her carrying and began to beat a rhythmic tang. I took a deep breath and let my eyes close, wondering if there was a difference between sleeping and trances in the Lower World.

The too-close sun bore a bright spot through my closed eyes, making my eyelids burn a brighter crimson than the sky. I built an image of Colin around that brilliance, turning the whiteness into his fair hair and remembering the hollowness of his eyes beneath it. The darkness around the image felt cloying and sticky, as if his sickness affected the picture I had in my mind. It was uncomfortable, like picking my feet up and slogging through tar, but I'd made a promise. More, I wanted to help him. Maybe needed to.

Please. Making a word of the need startled me. *He's just a kid, and his strength is almost gone. If there's anyone who's willing to lend him your strength, I'll guide you to him. He's a good kid.* I felt the heat of tears press through my eyelashes and swallowed against them. *Please,* I said again, then drew a sharp breath, trying to settle my thoughts into silence.

Not thinking was harder than it sounded. Judy's drum helped, the beat mixing with my heartbeat and filling my blood with hope. The sunspot in my eyelids drifted up, then away, telling me that time passed. Comforting blackness wrapped around me, the drum as its pulse. The thickness of the dark stayed with me, until I couldn't feel myself breathing anymore. I took a deeper breath, trying to make my lungs and ribs expand so much that I couldn't help but feel them, and instead I lost Colin's image from my mind. Retrieving it was slow work, pulling it from the sticky darkness piece by piece.

I didn't know why I opened my eyes: nothing that I could sense on any physical level had changed. But I did, and found a massive serpent coiled inside the power circle, its blunt nose mere inches from my hooked one. It had the same bright black eyes as its predecessor, watching me with deadly calm. My heart lurched, making a pit of sickness in my stomach.

"You ssseek," it murmured. "I anssswer."

Did it have to be a snake? I tried to keep the thought stuffed deep in my brain where no one, particularly the snake, could hear it. Its flat expression didn't change and I let out a relieved breath. "Thank you." *Snakes are a symbol of healing,* I reminded myself. *This is a good sign.* I kept that thought stuffed deep in my brain, too. "Judy?" My voice had only the slightest quaver to it. I was proud of myself. "How come it's *inside* the circle?"

"To bring its power back to your friend, it has to become a part of you," Judy said with a trace of impatience.

"You're a conduit, Joanne. How on earth did you manage to make it this far with so little education?"

Heat crept up my cheeks. I *knew* shamans were conduits. I'd invited the snake in to the power circle with my thoughts. How else did I expect to guide it to Colin? "Sorry," I muttered, still scarlet. "I knew that."

To the snake, I said, "I'm not with the one who needs your help. Will you let me carry you to him?" I put out an arm, trying not to notice the goose bumps that shivered up my skin as I made the offer. The snake ducked its head, flicking its tongue over the fine hairs on my arm. Then it shot forward, putting its head over my shoulder. I gathered it up as carefully as I could, settling its weight over both my shoulders. It slithered down my right arm, coiling around it, and as I lifted its tail, that coiled around me, too. The thing was at least as tall as I was, powerful muscles bunching and releasing against my skin. I fought down terror for a few seconds, trying desperately to remind myself that it was there to help. Its weight was enough that I considered stopping for the day right there, and simply heading back to the real world so I could deliver the snake's strength to Colin.

"Oh." My voice sounded loud and startled to my own ears. The strength I'd just been afraid of was exactly what the creature was offering to Colin. My fear broke apart, making the next breath I took easier, and suddenly the snake's weight seemed much less significant. "Thank you," I said again to the snake. "But I have a question. Will carrying you with me make it harder for me to do a spirit quest for another friend? I have a lot to do this morning."

The snake twined its way back up my arm and stuck its tongue in my ear. I tried not to squirm or shriek as it hissed, "Perhaps. I have come to help. Shall I help more than one?"

My heart slowed down as I considered the offer, my thoughts long and careful between one beat and the next. "No," I said after a few echoes had pounded through my body. "I think Colin will need all the strength you can spare him. I think I need to do another quest for my other friend."

"Very well." The snake slid down off my shoulders and wrapped itself in a loose circle around my folded legs, not touching me. "When you have completed your quesssst, we shall all return together."

"Thank you," I said, surprised at how much I meant it. "Judy, would you drum again, please?"

She pursed her mouth, lifted the drum, and began a new beat. I took a deep breath, smiling briefly at her, but her concentration was for the drum. I shrugged, tilting my head back as I closed my eyes, and fell into darkness again.

It felt different this time. The darkness behind my eyelids was cool and slick, like black water. I could hear my heartbeat more clearly than Judy's drum, and my breathing was easier. My ribs creaked as I inhaled, and I enjoyed the sensation. I knew Gary a lot better. Maybe that was why it was so much easier.

Focusing on Gary took less distinct concentration. I was able to remember the funny gray eyes and bushy eyebrows, the deep-set wrinkles and the shock of white hair and the strong white teeth without carefully rebuilding the image in my mind every few seconds. The width of his shoulders, which, if they'd lessened with age, made me wonder how big a man he'd been in his youth, and the carpe diem strength that made me feel like a piker in my own life.

Mostly, though, what I held on to as I put a second call out into the void wasn't physical. It was his heart, the periodic gruffness that overlaid tremendous caring and the steady thrum of his soul, the V-8 engine that charged him. *Please,* I found myself whispering again, into a darkness that hadn't decided to answer yet. *He's a terrific old man. I wouldn't have made it this far without him. Is there anyone who will help him?*

Tiny floating spots of brightness began appearing behind my eyelids, little explosive fireworks. They danced around, staying at a safe distance, which made me wonder how I could tell distance in the space between my eyes and their lids. They—the lights were a *they,* not the usual floaties I got when I closed my eyes under a bright light source—were waiting for something. For once I wasn't at a loss as to what it was.

I need him, too. I felt a painful smile curve my mouth just a little, and my bright lights swam as tears burned against my eyelids. *I know spirit quests for someone else aren't supposed to be for selfish reasons, but…I need him, too. Please,* I asked one more time. *Lend your strength to an old man whose time shouldn't be now. Not yet.*

Half a dozen of the lights erupted, leaping toward me from out of the darkness. I twitched, keeping my eyes closed. Behind my eyelids, animals warred playfully with each other, glowing from within as they jumped and pounced and batted at one another. A wolf stretched into downward-facing-dog, baring his teeth and wagging his tail frantically at a bear that lifted a heavy paw in mock warning. They charged one another, hitting in a spray of fireworks that shot blue and gold through the backs of my eyes, so bright it hurt. I let out a startled yell, flinging my arm over my eyes, which didn't help at all.

A thick-shouldered ram lowered his head and charged a lion who sat lashing his tail and watching the goings-on with interest. The ram crashed into its shoulder, sending both animals head over heels. The lion roared, a sound like laughter, and together the two creatures rolled into the still-sparring bear and wolf. Another volley of sparks ensued, as crackly and noisy and bright as a static-filled blanket on a dark winter night. An eagle joined the fray, winging down out of the blackness behind my eyelids to slam into the rolling, chortling mess of animals, its claws curled harmlessly into fists as it battered the others with its wings. Below all of them, a badger erupted up from the darkness, making me laugh out loud. It scrambled up the bear's hide, clearly wanting a chance at the eagle.

Distantly, I heard Judy's drum falter when I laughed, but my own heartbeat was strong, and the spirit animals rumbling to see who got to help Gary made me feel tremendously better. I took a breath, about to speak to them, when I felt a bump against my foot. It wasn't the same physical ponderousness that had made me open my eyes when the snake appeared. It felt more like the arrival of these spirit animals, a shower of sparks that lit different parts of my body. I looked down to discover a tortoise waiting patiently at my toes. I crouched, smiling as the other animals continued their playful war. The tortoise blinked slowly at me, and it was everything I could do to keep from picking it up and hugging it. I had the idea tortoises weren't big on hugs. "Thank you," I whispered to it. It bobbed its head and put one of its front feet on mine, which I took as an invitation to pick it up, carefully.

My hand touched the shining patterns on its shell, and light slammed into me so hard I lost consciousness.

CHAPTER FIFTEEN

The first thing I noticed was my head hurt so badly it felt like the top was coming off. Blood pounded in my temples hard enough to make me put stacked odds on being upside-down, but I was afraid to open my eyes and find out. Light seared into me from all sides. I was pretty sure if I opened my eyes, I'd discover that my bones would be dark shapes in my lit-up flesh. The air I breathed was hot, much hotter than the Lower World air, and tasted of dryness. Sand, I thought, and my eyes opened without consulting me on the matter.

At first there was nothing to see, just whiteness so intense it made my eyes try to turn around and crawl into my head. Tears streamed down my forehead and into my hair. I was almost certain I heard sizzling as they beaded and hit the ground somewhere below me. Crushing my eyes closed didn't help any: the light smashed right through my eyelids as if they weren't even there, prying out all the imagined places of shadow where my vision was trying to hide. I peeled my lashes open in the tiniest squint I could manage.

The light didn't recede, but after a dozen head-pounding heartbeats my vision adjusted very slightly. It took a long time to get my eyes all the way open. By the time I had, I could feel sunburn setting into my skin, so deep it felt like my bones were burning.

The sky was white with heat, cloudless and stretching to approximately forever, where it ran into a horizon as blindingly white as the ground below me. The sun was too close and much too hot. If it hadn't been for the fact my hands were tied behind my back, I'd have thought I could touch it.

I was trussed up like a chicken for Sunday dinner. My ankles were bound together and I hung upside-down from what appeared to be the only tree in Creation. It was about twelve feet tall and so extremely dead that I was astounded its bleached branches could hold my weight. The ground, crystals of sand too tired from the weight of the sun to even glisten, lay about six inches above my head. There were tiny indentations directly below me where my tears had hit and evaporated.

"Help?" My throat was already dry and parched. I swallowed nervously, squinting to eye the sun and the horizon. If it was anything like at home, the distance between the two suggested I'd be dead long before night came. I wriggled around in my ropes, earning myself burns on my ankles and wrists, and a slight swing to change the monotony of just hanging there.

Seattle Cop Found Dead In Apartment—Suffered From Sun, Rope Burns. I could see the headline. I wondered what Morrison would think. I wondered where the hell I was. I wondered if I could possibly get myself out of it. I wasn't panicked; the heat had smashed panic right out of me and pushed me well into numb. But there had to be something I could do before the sun cooked my brain for good. It'd be embarrassing to die here in the white desert without even trying to get out of it.

Start with what I knew. I closed my eyes, not that it did any good against the light, to help myself focus.

I knew I was hanging upside-down on the verge of horrible death by dehydration, according to the backs of my eyelids. "Goddamn it," I croaked, and opened my eyes again to stare at the expanses of white. One baked crystal gleamed at me. I wondered briefly if it was salt, not sand. Because that made it all better somehow. *Shut up and concentrate, Joanne.*

My vision started doing interesting things, swimming in and out as it tried to make depth out of featureless grains of sand. I listened for my heartbeat; last time I'd been in a desert of the mind, I'd been dying and my heartbeat was a painfully slow drum. But no: it was bumping along steadily, pounding in my ears and now making me notice the headache all over again. That was probably a good sign.

Choice. The word whispered itself to me. I had a worried moment of wondering whether I was hearing voices or if my own tiny mind had come up with that direction all by itself. After another moment I decided it didn't matter, as long as I got out of here. If I continued to hear voices, I'd thank them nicely for pointing me in the right direction, and then get medication.

One of the fundamental concepts of shamanism was choice: choosing to believe, choosing to heal, choosing to accept. Once, choosing to accept something that someone else had forced on me had allowed me the power to change it and escape. I let my eyes close again and began the task of acceptance.

It turned out hanging upside-down from a bleached tree in the desert wasn't the best place to start on the whole acceptance thing. Time wore on and the sun kept burning me. I swallowed on a dry throat more times than I could count, trying to work up a little moisture. Whether I managed to accept my position or if the part of me that held on to disbelief simply dried up and blew away, eventually I started to feel as if I belonged there, the Hanged Joanne in the desert. There was a Tarot card like that. The Hanged Man, not the Hanged Joanne. I remembered Billy enthusiastically telling me about Tarot in general a couple years earlier, while I rolled my eyes and generally behaved like a jerk. I reminded myself to apologize to him—again—if I got out of this. Then I spent a while wondering what it was that the Hanged Man signified, anyway.

Once in a while I tried to will the tree to fall over, or the rope to stretch and put me on the ground. I was starting to feel very at home there, like a nineteenth-century out-law waiting for the coyotes to come nibble his eyeballs out.

Coyotes!

My eyes popped open. "Coyote! Hello? Help? Look, I know I never call, I never write, but I've been kind of busy the last few days." I wasn't in daily contact with my spirit guide anyway, but since last time I'd ended up in a desert—one completely unlike this one—he'd been the one to get me out, I figured it was probably my best shot. "I got a teacher!" I yelled. "That's a good sign, right?" The desert swallowed the shouts up without effort. "Hello? Coyote?"

There was no answer whatsoever, and I started to wonder if doing a spirit quest would wake my spirit guide up to my predicament. While I wasn't exactly in a sweat lodge, the out-of-body surreality surrounded me in spades, which seemed like a good place to start. For a few seconds I got distracted by how many levels removed from my body I actually was, then decided down that path lay madness. Assuming I wasn't already totally nuts. Either way, I certainly wasn't going to get back to myself by hanging around in a desert wondering when the hero was going to show up and rescue me.

After another ten seconds, I realized I was holding my breath and waiting for Morrison to interrupt my trance, as if my thoughts could conjure him.

Another ten seconds after that I couldn't decide if I was relieved or horribly disappointed that they hadn't. I sighed and closed my eyes, trying out a crooked half smile at my-self. I could afford that here, somewhere so deep and private that nobody but me was ever going to see it. My shoulders relaxed and I sighed, drifting past caring whether or not my skin was burned to the bone or my wrists were numb from the ropes around them. My mouth was too dry to make any saliva at all. When I swallowed it felt like double-sided tape closing together and trying to pull apart again. My shoulders relaxed again, falling another centimeter toward my ears. If I could just take a little nap, it'd turn out all right, whether Morrison rode in to save the day or not.

If my inner self had any sense of dignity at all, it would allow my brain to cook to a crisp rather than let me wake up, go to work, and face Morrison with the knowledge that he'd featured heavily as the White Hat in my damsel-in-distress fantasies.

Someone sucked all the air out of the desert. I inhaled and began coughing, the air suddenly so much hotter that it was like sticking my head in a furnace. Tears rolled down my forehead again as I pried my eyes open. The whiteness of the sun and earth was no longer what I had to struggle against. Now the heat itself stuck my eyelids together and pressed my eyeballs farther back into my head. I whimpered, a genuinely pathetic sound, and the heat added thunder.

It was a physical presence, pushing into my body with a rumble I couldn't even hear, only feel. I couldn't breathe. Spots swam through my vision, black and red boxes with sharp edges like pain. The air itself had malicious intent, squeezing down on me. Lightning split the empty white sky, a bolt of brightness against the already impossibly bright world. My eyes ached, but the heat had seared away the last of my tears. I tried to think of last words, sure that the thunder and air and lightning would crush me into lasting oblivion.

"Well, fuck this," I croaked. A final show of defiance would have to do. Go, Joanne.

A coyote trotted out of the desert.

It wasn't my coyote.

This one took up more space than my coyote, although he wasn't, at an upside-down glance, any bigger. When he breathed, the air seemed to expand around him, shimmering like a heat mirage. Every piece of fur on his body gleamed and bristled, like they'd each been individually dipped in gold and bronze and copper. The play of muscle under the gold-dipped fur was incredibly precise, as if every bunch and release was calculated and thought-out ahead of time. Coyotes, with their long legs and skinny bodies, weren't animals I thought of as beautiful.

This one was.

The air he brought with him was cooler, just within the upper ranges of tolerable. He sat down six inches from my head and I gasped in a grateful breath, never once thinking he was there to rescue me. It was probably a little late to judge somebody who's already been hanged, but the coyote was jury, judge and executioner. His eyes were gold-flecked, stars in blackness. He felt a little like Cernunnos, and more like the thunderbird. I could only see the surface, but if I relied on the knots in my belly instead of my eyes, I could feel that he tapped into something much larger, part of the raw primal force that made up the universe.

"Oh, for sweet pity's sake," I said in a normal enough voice that the shock of it sent racking coughs through my body. When I finally undoubled—and doubling up to cough while suspended by your feet is not something to be recommended—the coyote was watching me with his head cocked very slightly to the side. Exactly like my coyote, only much, much bigger, metaphysically speaking. "I honor you," I grated. My throat tasted like I'd swallowed a cup full of iron filaments. It was a flavor I associated with running, and it made bile splash in my stomach.

Coyote tilted his head the other way, looking amused. I wrinkled my eyes shut, trying to think of what I'd said, and if it had been wrong. "You honor me?" I tried. "How can I honor you?" I opened one eye. Coyote still looked amused. "Oh, for Christ's sake, what do you want? Nobody ever gave me lessons in talking to archetypes, but honestly, I respect the shit out of you and I'd really like to go home now, please."

Coyote barked and snapped his teeth, which looked very large and very white and very much like Little Red Riding Jo should stay far away from them. I swore I could hear the dried earth crackling and breaking apart when he snapped his teeth together. "I've already been eaten once recently. You don't have to do it again. Really." I cranked my head up, wondering if the thunderbird might fall out of the sky and rescue me.

It didn't. I let my head drop back down and sighed. At least with Coyote for company I'd regained some equilibrium. "What do you want from me?" I asked again, more subdued.

Coyote—I was going to have to find something else to call *my* coyote; after this, calling him Coyote would be like calling a mountain lion "kitty"—Coyote leaned forward until my eyes crossed, and put the slope of his forehead against mine.

Fragments of memory shot through my brain, sharp as shrapnel.

Sara Buchanan's angry eyes, blaming me for a decision that already terrified me.

A desolate garden coming to life.

A dark-haired woman with a silver choker and a ready laugh.

Dusty highway roads stretching in front and in back of us as far as I could see. My father, slender-shouldered, quiet and thoughtful, tapping out a tune against the steering wheel. I didn't know where we were going, didn't recognize where we might've been. The story of my childhood, never belonging, in a more literal sense than most lonely kids feel. A bitterness old enough to feel tired filled my throat. I turned my head away from Coyote, dry spitting the taste of resentment from my mouth.

The images blasted on, undeterred by breaking contact with Coyote.

A baby boy, his sister too small to live.

Getting off a plane in Dublin, searching for features that might be at all like mine. Not finding them, even when the mother I didn't know touched my arm and asked, "Siobhán?"

SIOBHÁN

I flinched so hard my whole body cramped up. My name thundered through the recesses of my mind again, echoing and slamming against the inside of my head. I doubled again, trying to twist my arms around somehow to protect myself from the huge sound. My own *name* tore at me, pulling images from beneath my skin, faster, like tenterhooks with no regard for pain.

—a tunnel of darkness leading into somewhere I was afraid of, astral lights bluing the path—

—a beautiful man, high-cheekboned and grim-mouthed standing with a gun to my head—

—a horned god standing over me, sword lifted for a killing blow—

—Morrison, white with pain, shouting at me—

—Gary grinning over his shoulder at me, pulling away from the airport in his cab, apparently driving by use of the Force—

—a thin scar on my right cheek, running from my eye to just below the corner of my mouth—

—tearing across flat earth in Petite, the speedometer clocking over a hundred and forty—

—a banshee's head held in my hand, dangling from its hair—

—bone-wearying exhaustion, like sleep had come to weigh on me with all its strength—

—*a baby boy, his sister too small to live*—

—a diploma, the name I'd abandoned written on it: Joanne Walkingstick—

WALKINGSTICK.

I began to scream.

—a race against the Wild Hunt—*a snake's bright black eyes, staring at me*—a kiss I'd waited years to taste—*a graveyard with a new marker, and me on my knees beside it*—another grave—*another*—a bewildered child wailed and flung herself at coffin-bearing men—*me, squalling and waving angry red fists in the air, a man's brogue saying, "And there she is, our wee Siobhán, welcome, alanna, welcome," as he lifted me into the air*—and another voice, one I knew somewhere in my bones, saying, "Already?" before my own voice, cracked with age or pain, replied, "It had to happen sometime," and coldness settled over me—*a dark-haired teenage boy, expression neutral and calm*—a cauldron bubbling with the stench of death—*a raven with a woman's eyes*—a mantis, preying—

a baby boy, his sister too small to live!

"STOP IT!" My eyes flew open and I thrust Coyote away with everything I had, all my heart put into the rejection. He exploded in a burst of white that seared my eyeballs, pain so intense I thought I could feel the nerves sizzling and spitting into decay. I flew backward from the force of the blast, driven farther by the strength of my own pain and fury, and slammed back into the Lower World so hard I jolted over backward. The snake that encircled me lifted its head and spat with annoyance, then slithered out from under me to coil itself tall beside Judy. My eyes burned as I sat up again, holding my head and squinting at them. The light still dazzled my eyes, and the two of them were inversed, their black eyes glowing white. Judy's skin was black and almost featureless, like shadows had come to live on it, and the snake's scaled hide spun between purples and dark greens. I swallowed down nausea and turned my head away, looking for something that was a normal color.

The sky provided; it was deep cerulean, almost too dark for nature, but less disturbing than Judy's shadowy skin. Only when my gaze went to the sun did I realize that it was black, too, and that in the Lower World the sky should be crimson, not blue. I pressed the heels of my hands over my eyes and shuddered. "I have to go back." My voice still sounded parched to my own ears, and I didn't want to look at Judy to see if her expression said I sounded odd to her, too. "…snake, will you come with me?" I didn't know how to address it, and I didn't want to look at its swimming patterns, either. It hissed with ill-concealed annoyance, but slithered forward and climbed up my body to wrap around my shoulders. "Thank you," I whispered, grateful to not have to look at it. My hands pressed against my eyes were making sparks that reminded me: "Where's—"

I didn't finish the question before I felt the presence I was looking for. The tortoise appeared behind my eyelids again, its colors bright and proper, unlike everything around me. "There you are," I whispered. "Thank you."

It bobbed its head agreeably and I swallowed against sickness again. The snake wanted me to carry it on my shoulders, but the tortoise seemed satisfied to come along for the ride behind my eyelids. "Tomorrow," I grated at Judy. "I'll come back tomorrow."

I couldn't close my eyes any harder, but I tried, and fell upward through my bellybutton back home.

CHAPTER SIXTEEN

The snake wasn't actually coiled around my shoulders when I opened my eyes in my dark living room. I could feel its weight, but my fingers brushed my arms as I folded them around myself, not meeting any scaly resistance. My head hurt. My *skin* hurt; I tested it with my fingertips, trying to feel heat. There wasn't any, but the papery dryness of sunburn was there. I got up and walked through darkness to turn the shower on, not bothering with the lights. The single window in the bathroom was curtained, but enough morning light leaked through the shade to keep me from killing myself as I stepped into the tub.

The hot water was too hot. I turned it down again, then again, until it was lukewarm and cooled my skin. I felt vaguely sick to my stomach, more exhaustion than genuine illness, and wondered what time it was. Maybe I could nap before work.

No, I couldn't. I groaned and put my face against the shower wall. The tile was cold, shocking my cheekbone. I groaned again, in appreciation, and turned around to lean against the tile, letting cool water run down my front. I *felt* sunburned, all over, my skin too thin and too hot. I wondered if I had any aloe vera, and then I slept for a while, standing there with my feet lodged against the far edge of the tub so I wouldn't fall down.

I woke up when the lukewarm water turned cold, with no sense of how much time had passed. Last time I'd done that—and the fraction of my brain still capable of thought decided it was a bad sign that there was a last time for falling asleep in the shower—Coyote had visited me. My coyote. Not this time. A sudden surge of energy hit me and I jolted out of the tub, grabbing a towel in the semidark and scrubbing it over my face.

Then I sat on the toilet and whimpered for a while until my sunburned skin stopped protesting the rough abuse from the towel. Getting dressed was going to hurt. But I had to. Even if I called in sick to work, which Morrison wouldn't believe because it was going to be another beautiful day, I still had to deliver the spirit guides to Colin and Gary. And if I was going to get dressed at all, I might as well go to work instead of calling in with the Blue Sky Flu.

The red numbers on my clock flared an inversed blue when I wobbled into my bedroom: 9:37. I flipped the light on and it went black in my eyes before reasserting itself in the more normal yellow-white bulb light. I rubbed my eyes gingerly and went to find my uniform. Coyote's little explosion trick was leaving a mark.

Halfway through getting dressed I noticed my skin wasn't visibly sunburned. It still *felt* burned: I kept involuntarily flinching away from cloth brushing my skin, and the idea of putting on a vest made my head pound even harder. I glanced at the clock again; a quarter to ten. I had forty-five minutes to get to work. I might be able to tear by and visit Colin, who was the sicker of the two. Maybe I could see Gary at lunch. Either way, I wasn't going to be left with enough time to plop down on my bed and see if I could get rid of the ache of sunburn with the idea of a new paint job, or the funky vision with a little windshield wiper fluid. It could wait till tonight. I could suffer until then. I went back into the bathroom, drank three glasses of water, put my contacts in, and determined that my reflection was haggard, horrible, and not in the least sunburned. It didn't seem fair somehow.

The phone rang on my way out the door. My stomach seized up and I ran back, snatching it out of the cradle. A woman demanded, "Are you alive?"

"What?" God, my voice sounded as dreadful as it had in the desert. I cleared it and tried again. "I mean, yes."

"This is Phoebe. You were supposed to be here fifty minutes ago. Fencing lesson?"

"Oh. Oh, God. I'm sorry. Last night got kind of weird." I felt the snake's weight slither around my shoulders, settling more comfortably. That was just so totally not cool I couldn't even begin to express it. The tortoise was much more circumspect. I knew he was there somewhere, waiting for me to need him. I liked that a lot more than the slithery snake. "I just got home. I'm on my way to work. I completely spaced it."

"Everything okay?" I could hear the frown in her voice.

"Yeah. More or less. Look, I've really got to go, so I'll call you back and reschedule later, okay?"

"Yeah, okay. I just wanted to be sure you were okay."

I wondered what she'd say if I said, "Sure, fine, except the sunburn that isn't there, the lack of sleep, the thirty-pound snake on my shoulders, and the way the lights keep imploding their color." Fortunately for both of us, I didn't really want to say it, and instead said, "Thanks for checking up on me. I'll call. Bye." I hung up and made a break for the great outdoors and Petite.

The sky went yellow and the sun went black when I stepped outside. I flung my equipment bag into Petite's passenger seat, dropped into the driver seat, and fumbled for my sunglasses, wondering if the traffic lights were going freak out the way the rest of the lights were. That would be a real pain in the ass. I tried to remember if the order was red-yellow-green or red-green-yellow as I drove down the street.

It was red-yellow-green, but watching the yellow burst into incandescent blue was so interesting I ran the light and nearly T-boned a Camero. I didn't blame the guy for leaning on his horn. After that I bit my tongue and paid significant attention to what I was doing.

By the time I reached the hospital I'd figured it out. The color inversion wasn't a constant: it just happened when light changed, and then faded back to normal. I'd be okay for the day as long as I was cautious, though I'd have to hope I wouldn't need to identify any runaway vehicles, because my first glance at anything seemed to come up with entirely the wrong colors.

Colin's pale hair looked black and silky as death, for example. It faded back into blond as I sat down by his bed, grinning crookedly at him. He opened one eye and lifted an eyebrow. "Couldn't get enough of me, huh?"

"Guess not." My voice fell into that irritatingly quiet hospital voice that people use. "How you doing?"

"Better, with an Amazon visiting me. They killed off their sick and weak, you know. For the good of the tribe."

My eyebrows went up too. "I didn't know. I don't think they mentioned that in the comic books."

"Different kind of Amazon. You could be one of that kind," he said, looking me over critically. "Except, no offense, you've got nothing on Lynda Carter."

I laughed out loud, shaking the hospital voice off. "You're not old enough to know who Lynda Carter is."

"Dude," he said, sincerely, "I'm not *dead*."

I laughed again. "And 'not dead' is all it takes?"

"Damn straight," Colin said with a nod, then sank back into the covers, looking weary.

"Hey," I said, quiet again. "I can only stay for a minute, okay? But I wanted to come by and say hi. Say a couple words of Amazon healing over you, that sort of thing, huh?"

Colin smiled without opening his eyes again. "Every little bit helps. Thanks, Joanne."

I put my hand on his shoulder. The snake didn't need

telling; it just coiled its way down from my shoulders to wrap itself around Colin's.

My vision smashed into inversion, the walls and bed, Colin's white skin and blond hair, all going black with hard shimmering blue edges. The lights overhead seemed to pop out, emitting blackness, and for a moment I could see the spirit-snake, his pale tans and browns all gone to blue and greens like they had in the Lower World. I jerked my hand off Colin's shoulder and put it to my head. He opened his eyes, frowning. "Joanne?"

"It's…I've got something weird going on with my vision this morning. It's okay. It just went all freaky." The effect was fading now, although the edges of things seemed a little dimmer, still hanging on to their reversed colors.

"You've probably got a brain tumor," Colin said cheerfully. I gaped at him, then laughed silently, shoulders shaking.

"Thank you. Thanks, Colin, that makes me feel a lot better." *Please,* I asked the snake. *Give him the strength and protection he needs. Thank you. I'll do my best to honor you.* I smiled, partly for the snake and partly for Colin. *I'll heed my teacher.*

My vision popped black again, and I fumbled my way out of the hospital, hoping I'd make it to work on time.

I clocked in no more than two minutes late. The precinct building lights snapped to inverse colors every time I opened a door, and I tripped over backwardly shadowed stairs and my own feet three times trying to get to the front door. Getting outside into the heat and morning sunlight was almost a relief. At least it was consistent, even if every breath I dragged in tasted of overheated street tar and dust.

At lunch I radioed Bruce at the front desk and asked him to punch me out so I'd have more time to go visit Gary. He told me that was illegal and did it anyway.

I felt a little silly pulling into the hospital parking lot in the patrol car, as if there ought to be a dire emergency that justified the black and white. A couple of visitors gave me curious looks as I strode through the parking lot, suddenly in a hurry to see the old man.

He was in PT when I got there. A critical nurse examined me from head to toe before asking, "Are you his daughter?"

Out of the various questions I'd expected upon showing up in uniform, that wasn't one of them. I tried counting on my fingers how old Gary'd have been when he fathered me if I were his daughter and came up with a reasonable number as an answer. "Yes. I'm also on lunch break, so do you think I could maybe see him, please?"

"Well." The nurse tapped lacquered nails against the desk, examining me again. "I suppose. But if the therapist says no, you'll have to go immediately, miss."

For the first time in my life I had to swallow the urge to correct her with "Officer." It took a couple of seconds, and then I put on a cheery smile and said, "Sure, of course."

Her expression said I wasn't fooling anyone. "Second floor."

"Thank you." I got out of there at a brisk pace, uncertain how long my bout of transparent politeness was going to last.

The PT room had half a dozen patients in it. None of them looked particularly patient, least of all Gary, who bore the expression of a constipated rhino as he trod a treadmill. A cute blond woman sat in a chair beside the treadmill, saying, "Two minutes," in a voice that wasn't so much encouraging as it was uncompromising. She gave me a gimlet stare and I pointed to a chair near hers, eyes wide in a question. She pursed her lips, eyed her watch, and nodded once, sharply. I scurried past Gary to the chair, giving him a broad wink that I was pretty sure the PT couldn't see. He cracked a slow grin that brightened him up all over, and picked up his pace a bit.

He looked better. Much better, like the vitality I was used to seeing in him had been replenished wholesale and the only reason he was there was because they wouldn't let him go home yet. A little bubble of joy lit up inside me. I hadn't been able to properly fix his heart, but maybe the energy I'd lent him had done some good. Even with my vision flipping inside-out, he looked better. I sat there grinning stupidly until the therapist said, "Cool down," and slowed the treadmill. After another minute, she glanced from her watch to me to Gary. "Five minutes. Drink water." Then she got up and left, leaving me grinning after her.

"Does she ever use sentences of more than two words?" I got up to get Gary a cup of water while he plunked down in the chair next to the one I abandoned.

"Pretty much no," he said. I came back with the water

and he enveloped me in a bear hug. I hung on and tried not to spill water, either from the cup or from my eyes. I was getting to be a real soft touch in my old age.

"You look better," I mumbled against his shoulder. He shoved me back into my chair, sort of like I was a big dog, and ruffled my hair, undoing the complete lack of styling I'd spent so much time at this morning.

"Feelin' better," he announced. "'Cept the food's terrible, and nobody'll sneak me in a Big Mac." He eyed me hopefully. I grinned through embarrassingly bright eyes.

"Like hell. Here, have some water instead."

Gary snorted but took the cup and drank greedily. "So what'm I missin', Jo? Didja bring me back a bear? This place is worse than a crypt for gettin' news in."

We both looked around, and after a couple of seconds, he said, "Mebbe not that bad. So, a bear?" He looked as enthusiastic as a kid at Christmas, gray eyes bright and eyebrows bushing eagerly. I thought of the tortoise, tucked somewhere safe behind my eyes, and laughed.

"No, but it wasn't for lack of trying on the bear's part." I realized, once more to my embarrassment, that I had no idea how to transfer the more subtle tortoise to Gary. Colin's snake had just crawled off me, but this was entirely different. "Think your PT would object to a couple minutes' meditation?"

"No," she said from behind me. I jolted and twisted around, trying to arrange my face into a "sure, I knew you were there" expression. "I'd approve," she said. "Meditation's healing. Releases stress. Go ahead." It was like listening to a very determined and very precise woodpecker.

I was so busy counting the number of words it took me several seconds to realize she'd given permission. Then I straightened up, beaming at her.

"Thanks! Except I don't have a drum," I said.

"You could sing for me," Gary suggested, grinning. "Think you said you don't scare the neighbors." I laughed.

"Just close your eyes and stop being a pain." Actually, I wanted him to continue being a pain for another fifteen or twenty years. He closed his eyes, still grinning. I folded one leg under me and took his hands, letting my own eyes close.

"Concentrate on your breathing," the PT said, her voice soft and soothing and completely unexpected. My eyes flew open, vision flattening, going negative, and reversing itself back to normal. God, I was getting to hate that. Gary'd opened his eyes, too, and we both blinked at the PT, whose eyebrows rose slightly. "No drum," she said with a shrug. "Listen to me instead."

"Right." I smiled at her, trying not to look as startled as I felt, and Gary cleared his throat in the best gruff manner available. We closed our eyes again, and concentrated on our breathing. "I'm going to guide you," I said, barely audible beneath the PT's calm voice. "I want to bring you to a place of healing, where the transfer will do the most good." I was working on instinct, my body feeling heavier and heavier with every breath. "Imagine sinking through—"

I plunged through my tailbone and went on a greased slide through about a zillion layers of earth. The ground came up and caught me with a muffled crash, and I found myself staring upward, looking for the hole in the sky I felt like I'd fallen through.

There was no sky, only thick, healthy tangled trees arching over my head. I closed my fingers on the earth, prickles tickling my palms, and looked around to discover I was sitting in a cushioning heap of moss. I was stuck a good eight inches into it, my knees pointed awkwardly at the trees above. I pushed up for a fruitless moment, trying to get unstuck. Somewhere in the wriggling, I took a deep breath, and forgot all about trying to get free.

This place smelled alive and rich. Clean air and a little bit of wind, carrying the scent of green all the way into my bones. It had rained nearby, close enough for coolness to still be in the air, although my moss hump was dry. The slight chill settled into my skin, making me remember the ache of bone-deep sunburn. That ache was gone for the moment, and hairs on my arms stood up in appreciation of the mild temperature.

With my eyes closed I could hear the busy hum of bugs and birds going about their business, and water burbling somewhere relatively nearby. A branch cracked a few steps away from me, a burst of wings sounded, and I opened my eyes again to find an amused, broad-shouldered man standing above me. He wore an olive green army uniform, a black tag with bright yellow letters on it above his left breast pocket. He looked at ease and confident, hands in his pockets as he slouched over me.

He was on the good side of ageless, laugh lines starting to crinkle around gray eyes. His hair was dark, cut military short to go with the uniform, but his eyebrows were already starting to get away from him. His nose had been broken at least once, taking away any chance at beauty but leaving behind a sort of cheerful ruggedness that made me forget how to breathe. He stuck a big hand out, encompassing mine entirely as I put it in his. My hands weren't small, but his made me feel delicate as he pulled me to my feet with an easy surge.

"Don't look so surprised, Jo. How many times do I gotta tell you, old dogs learn a trick or two along the way?" His voice was a delicious rumble, not quite what I was used to hearing, but then, I'd never heard someone's voice from inside his own head before.

"*Gary?*"

He glanced down at himself, then spread his hands in a wide-shouldered shrug. "Guess how we see ourselves never really changes. What, it's that bad?" His grin was familiar, self-deprecating and crooked.

"*Bad?* No, jeez, bad? You're *gorgeous.*" He wasn't exactly gorgeous, not in a movie-star sense, but he was a whole lot better than "not bad." The Hemingway look hadn't settled in yet; that was more an effect of age than his own bone structure. I gazed up at him, completely besotted.

"And you're tall," I added faintly. He was taller than me back in the real world, too, but the internal Gary was still young, and age hadn't taken any height from him yet. And maybe, just maybe, he was a little bit better than the reality had ever been. I grinned at him dippily. He grinned back, pleased as the cat who stole the cream. I was suddenly terribly, terribly envious of his wife, Annie, who would've known him when he was the handsome cock of

the walk I saw now. It was easy to see them dancing together, him in uniform and her in one of the full-skirted
party dresses worn during the war. For a moment I tried
putting myself in her place, then let it go in another little
wash of envy.

"You sayin' I wasn't always?" he teased.

I actually blushed. "Which, gorgeous, or tall?" That
didn't help any. Gary laughed out loud, and I blushed
harder. "This is your garden?" I blurted, gesturing around
before stepping away to take a look. I hoped investigating would keep me from fluttering at the old man.

It wasn't a measly garden. It was an entire inner landscape, forests that went on farther than I'd ever be able to
explore. It was lush and startlingly healthy, given that the
man had just had a heart attack. It was like the attack had
come out of nowhere: there was nothing hinting at it in
his garden. No dead trees thinned the forest, and everywhere I looked the earth was soft and rich and mossy. I
could hear water running, and I felt envy all over again.

"I thought I was going to bring you to my garden." I
folded my arms around myself, looking through the trees
until the distance became a green blur. "This is…a better
place."

"Jo." Gary put his hands on my shoulders, standing just
a few inches behind me. His hands were warm and big
enough to make me feel small. "Different don't mean better. I'm an old man, and this place has taken a lotta years
of living to build. You gotta let the sunshine in, sweetheart.
Nothing can grow in the fog."

"I thought I was supposed to be here to help you." My

voice was tight, though I tried to put a smile in it. It must've worked: Gary chuckled and stepped a little closer, putting his arms around my waist. I held my breath until he poked me in the ribs and I let out a laugh that verged on tears.

"Maybe it's all one and the same, darlin'. We got some time."

I turned around in his arms to hug him, and maybe to hide the tendency for tears against his chest. "Plenty of time," I promised in a hoarse voice. My tortoise passenger had already left me, making its own slow way through the mossy forest toward the river. "Lots of time," I repeated, and Gary tightened his arms around my shoulders like a promise in return.

CHAPTER SEVENTEEN

I left the hospital feeling a bit lighter of heart, Gary's semi-outraged protest at being protected by a tortoise still ringing in my ears. I'd pointed out tortoises lived a hundred and fifty years, which had silenced him into a slow grin that reminded me of the garden Gary. It was almost as if I was a competent human being.

Of course, a competent human being would have already told Morrison that Cassandra Tucker had apparently died of a heart defect aggravated by the use of magic, but I hadn't found it in myself to try. I didn't know which was worse: him believing me, or not. Either way, I could put it off a little longer, because I still had an afternoon beat to walk.

The heat was making people either crabby or listless.

I busted up more than one burgeoning fight on the Ave, glad I wasn't working someplace more dangerous. My vision behaved itself all afternoon, and between that and Gary, I genuinely felt up to attending the coven event that evening. I went back to the precinct building to clock out and to shower, too disgusting with sweat to wait until I went home. My equipment bag had shorts and a tank top, far more suited to the weather than wool pants and a cotton shirt. I jogged out of the building with my duffel slung over my shoulder, thinking about running home to start laundry before I met up with the coven.

"Walker!"

I turned warily. Morrison shouting for me wasn't usually a good sign. Especially since he should've gone home by now. *Especially* since I'd been avoiding him all day, and the sound of his voice was a sharp reminder I'd been expecting him to show up and rescue me from the desert.

He looked tired, not much like a desert-searching hero, and not much like he wanted to talk to me. Neither of those was unusual, but I was oddly disappointed. After all, if he was going to feature heavily in my subconscious fantasies, the least he could do was be pleased about seeing me. Not that I had the slightest intention of telling him he was apparently my own personal champion. And not that he'd arrived on the scene to rescue me, which sort of annoyed me when I thought about it.

I slung my duffel over my back, holding on to the strap with two fingers, as if the oversized action would force my internal nattering out of mind. Morrison really did look tired, or maybe angry, his mouth a thin line and blue eyes squinted against the sun. I should've been used to him looking irritated, but the underlying weariness sent a pang of compassion through me. "Everything okay, Captain?"

He cut off whatever he was about to say and eyed me suspiciously for a few seconds. I tried to keep my expression neutral: *no, boss, I really mean it. Is everything okay?* He'd never believe it.

"Yeah," he said after enough time that I wondered if he was going to answer at all. "Tomorrow—"

I got ready to blow up. Tomorrow was my day off. "—is Cassandra Tucker's funeral," he said. I choked on my own indignation and stared at him as he concluded, "I thought you might want to go."

I wet my lips and looked around, anywhere but at my captain, so that I could work off being embarrassed over my near blowup. "Thank you," I finally said, awkwardly. "I really appreciate that. Look, does that mean they know what happened to her? Because—"

"Congenital heart defect," he said shortly. "No murder investigation. I assume you didn't get anything from your...sources."

For some reason, it didn't make me at all happy to have Virissong's explanation verified by a coroner. I stared at Morrison for a long time without really seeing him, then wet my lips. "Nothing substantially different."

"Substantially?"

I should have known better than to put an adverb into my response. I wet my lips again and shook my head.

"Someone thought it was brought on by an overload of…" I felt like Michael Keaton trying to tell Kim Basinger his secret. If Morrison would only turn around so I couldn't see his face, I was sure I could finish saying, "Doing magic." What I said instead was, "It doesn't really matter, does it? The cops and the freaks are in agreement on this one."

Morrison's expression had gone sour as I approached the end of my first explanation, as if he knew perfectly well what I wasn't saying. Then it changed from sour to genuinely disapproving, and I had to stop myself from backing up a step. "Don't do that," he said.

I hadn't moved. "Don't do what?"

"Belittle yourself. Or anyone else, for that matter."

I gaped at him. "I'm sorry, Cap, but when did you get on the it's-okay-for-Joanne-to-be-a-super-shamanic-weirdo bandwagon?"

"I didn't," he said very evenly. "I don't like what you can do at all. But I like you setting yourself up for the sucker punch even less. It's degrading, and you're better than that. I won't tolerate it."

I felt like my world had taken a sharp swerve and dip to the left. "Morrison, you rag on me all the time." He did. He said I was a pain in the ass, which was true, and to not darken his doorstep again, which I always did, and a variety of other blustery *you bother me* sorts of comments.

But I couldn't think of one single time where he'd outright insulted me, or anyone else, for that matter. I stared at him some more, trying to fit that piece of information into the Morrison-shaped prejudices I carried around, and then looked at a wall and reached for safer ground. "Do you know when and where Cassandra's funeral is?"

"I do," he said, still very evenly, as if the last bit of conversation hadn't happened. "I'm going. Should I pick you up?"

My gaze snapped back to him. "*You're* going?"

"We were the first two officers on the scene, Walker. I visited her mother." Morrison's voice was strained. I found myself staring at him again.

"Jesus, Cap. Shouldn't the UW police have done that? I mean, not your juris—"

"I was the ranking officer," he said. "It was my duty."

My vision didn't go all inverted again, but rather, for an instant, I saw with extreme clarity. The worst job anybody could have is telling a parent that her child is dead.

Morrison'd done it to spare somebody else having to.

Color burned along my jaw and up into my cheekbones and ears, a bewildering rush of pride to be working for this particular police captain. I swallowed and straightened my shoulders. "What time should I be ready?"

Maybe it was my imagination, but I thought Morrison relaxed almost imperceptibly. "Nine-thirty. Funeral's at ten."

"I'll be ready. Morrison?"

Morrison, already turning away, went still, and looked at me like he expected the other shoe to drop.

"Thanks."

For a few seconds he looked as if he was waiting for the follow-up smart-ass remark. Then he nodded, a short, sharp motion, and walked away.

Sunday, June 19, 7:14 p.m.

There was no time to get laundry started. I dashed to campus, stopping at the pizzeria to buy two slices of pepperoni and olive pizza. They offered me a soda large enough to swim in for a mere sixty cents more. Being a red-blooded American, I bought it and had vague guilty thoughts about exercise.

I was still licking pizza grease off my fingers when I ducked into the room the coven had been held in two nights earlier. Contrary to the smoky gloom of that night, it was bright and well lit and distinctly empty of both torches and witches. I said, "Um," out loud to the empty room, and stood there with my soda feeling a little foolish. That was me, Joanne Walker, the world's sneakiest undercover cop. Not that I was undercover, because Morrison had given me permission to case these people, although I suspected I might be going further than he meant me to. It didn't matter. This was all on my own time.

Just like Cassandra Tucker's funeral would be.

"I thought you'd be here," Faye said from behind me. I flinched two inches to the left and whipped around, wishing I had something dangerous and sexy in my hand instead of a sixty-four ounce soda cup. My vision blurred again for the first time since I'd seen Gary, fluorescent lights above me twisting into purple streaks, and I pressed the heel of one hand against my left eye. I could feel the under-the-skin sunburn again, as if coming out of the daylight had made it more intense.

"Sorry," Faye said. "I didn't mean to scare you."

"Are you sure?" I asked petulantly. She smiled as I peeled one eye open to look at her. The light stabilized and I cautiously removed my hand from my other eye.

"Of course. I didn't have your number to call, and you weren't with us last night so you couldn't know that we don't usually meet in the same place twice in a row. I thought I'd drop by and get you."

"I'm in the phone book." I still sounded tetchy. Faye looked surprised.

"I didn't think of it."

I muttered, "Of course not," and came back to the door, slurping my soda. "Where're we going?"

"Ravenna Park."

I blinked. "Not on campus?" Ah, yes. A brilliant deduction. "Won't the park be busy?"

Faye herded me out of the room. "D'you have a car? I don't. It'll be busy, but no one will notice us."

"Yeah, in the south lot. They won't?"

Faye shrugged. "People look around magic a lot. I don't know why. It's like a big blind spot in humanity." She beamed suddenly. "But we're going to change that, Joanne. We're going to make a real difference in the world. Starting tonight."

There are certain phrases people like to hear. Mechanics, for example, are fond of, "The transmission's okay, so the insurance company says fix it instead of totaling it out." At least, they are if they don't work for a cop shop that pays the same amount no matter how much work you do or don't do, which wasn't the point. "Elise will make tamales if you come over and look at the Eagle," was another nice one, although possibly that only got mileage from mechanics who knew my friend Bruce. And every mechanic I knew liked, "She's a beauty. Did you do the work yourself?"

That was not what Faye said when she saw Petite. Faye squealed, "Oooh, purple!" and leaned over the hood to see if she could see her reflection in the gilt-flecked finish. She could, in fact: I'd spent a lot of hours working depth into the rich paint, but the usual rush of smug pride wasn't available with this go-around of appreciation.

I was too busy thinking about phrases that cops didn't like.

"Starting tonight" was way up there, particularly when the cop in question thought she had another three days before the big bang. I drove down to Ravenna Park without listening to Faye's chipper conversation, cranky at the inverted light and how much attention I had to pay to driving. It was probably a bad sign I didn't normally pay that much attention to driving, but I was in no mood to think about that.

Tonight was a lot sooner than I wanted to participate in anything. I was working myself up to doing it, but I'd thought I had a few more days. Part of me wanted to just not show up. From what Faye and the others had said, without me they might not have enough power to pull their stunt off.

But every time I thought about doing that, an image of Colin, whose cancer I didn't know how to heal, flashed behind my eyes. Virissong might be able to pull off what I couldn't, and I wasn't sure I had the right to stand in the way of that happening. Not just for Colin, but for the whole overheated Seattle metropolitan area, and maybe the world.

I pulled into the lot at the north end of the park, still uncomfortable, and reached over to lock Faye's door before getting out of the car. "Lead on, Macduff."

Faye gave me a look of complete incomprehension. I rolled my eyes. "Never mind. Let's just go."

A stream large enough to be considered a river in some parts of the country ran through Ravenna Park. People were strewn along the banks, kids shrieking happily as they played in the water. I had no idea how a coven meeting was going to proceed undisturbed. I envisioned small children dashing through the sacred circle, then wondered if they'd be able to, or if there'd be some sort of mystical force field that they'd bounce off. The thought cheered me and I stuffed my hands in my pockets, whistling jauntily as I strode along behind Faye.

"Please don't," she said.

"Mmm?"

"Whistle. Please don't whistle. Whistling brings down the walls between this world and the next."

I stopped midwhistle, my mouth pursed. "You're kidding."

She glanced over her shoulder at me. "No. The tonal qualities and pitch are a bridge between worlds."

"Fascinating. Isn't that what we're trying to do?"

Faye sighed, developing the very patient tone that isn't. "Yes, of course. But we want it to be controlled, Joanne. Bridging worlds isn't something that should be done lightly, and you've felt the kind of power we're dealing with."

That much, at least, was true. I stopped arguing and whistling both, and slunk along like a properly chastised new coven member.

Well, I would've if I could've kept my mouth shut for more than three steps. "What d'you mean, we're starting to change the world tonight?"

Faye looked over her shoulder again, dimpled, and fell into stride with me. "The world has to be prepared for Virissong's arrival," she explained. "Tonight we'll begin to thin the walls, and over the next few days humanity will become accustomed to the otherworld mixing with this one again."

"It will?" My eyebrows climbed. "Humanity takes longer than a few days to get used to most things, Faye."

"There's a core of belief in all of us," she said airily. "All we're going to do is let the world start looking like that core expects it to."

Several things, the nicest of which was, "Isn't that a little naive?" went through my mind. I didn't know I'd said it out loud until Faye gave me a dirty look.

"Maybe, but haven't you always wanted to live in a world where magic was real?"

I was so startled I laughed out loud, a sharp derisive bark. Faye's expression skidded into insulted anger and she tossed her hair, flouncing ahead of me. "Crap. Faye, wait up." I jogged a few steps to catch up with her, then had to lengthen my stride to stay in step. Given the height advantage I had, that was a little embarrassing, but I did it anyway.

"Look, I'm sorry, I didn't mean to be rude. The truth is, no, I've never wanted to live in a world with magic. I like my world to make sense. I hate this mucking with magic thing."

Faye whirled on me, eyes bright with emotion. "But you're really powerful, Joanne! How can you say that? We all felt it, the power you command. You could change the world."

"I know." I looked down at her, searching for words. "Look, you ever notice how in movies or TV the one guy who gets the phenomenal cosmic power is the one guy who doesn't want it? Maybe the universe sets itself up that way as a fail-safe. Maybe that's why I ended up with all this power, instead of somebody who'd been pursuing it her whole life."

Faye's mouth tightened into a thin line. Great, I'd done it again. "Faye, I wasn't trying to be insulting—"

"It doesn't matter," she said flatly. "You're a part of the coven now. We'll help guide you into your powers, and when Virissong has returned to this world you'll see that it's better the way that we're trying to make it. Come on. We're going to be late." She turned and stalked off again, leaving me with nothing to do but walk away or follow.

I followed, feeling oddly abandoned. Tromping around parks preparing for coven meetings wasn't my usual evening routine, and after the past few days I felt distanced from what I considered my real life. I wanted to hang out with Gary and maybe go see a movie, or go drink beer with some of the guys from the shop. Normal things, which I didn't seem to have time for. Failing that, it would be nice to fit in with the coven in some fashion, but here I was, studying the angry swing of Faye's hair as she marched ahead of me. I couldn't imagine asking for a shaman's gifts, or wanting the responsibility of trying to save the world, whereas the coven seemed very into that idea. Cars. I was happy being responsible for the state of someone's vehicle. Their spirits or souls—that was a calling I wasn't at all happy with.

Then again, my power animals hadn't charged me with being comfortable with what I was and what I could do, only to accept, honor, and study. Curiously, that made me feel better.

"Joanne, Faye. There you are." Marcia's voice interrupted my train of thought and I blinked. We stood in a copse of trees, blocks of sunlight sliding through the trunks in golden, dust-littered chunks. The coven, looking mobbish and happy, surrounded me, and I hadn't even noticed approaching them. Garth and Sam were building an entirely illegal fire.

"Nice trick," I said. "How do you do that, the hiding in plain sight thing?"

"It's a matter of expectation. I'm surprised you didn't see us." Marcia sounded ever so slightly accusing. I shrugged.

"I was thinking about something else. Aren't we going to get in trouble for that fire?"

"No one will notice," she promised me.

Another matter of expectation, I presumed. My own personal expectation was that somebody out of her sphere of influence would see smoke rising from the park grounds and call the cops, but I didn't say that out loud. I sat down a few feet away, watching the fire build. "So I thought this was all going down on Tuesday."

"Tuesday's the grand finale." Garth straightened out of his crouch, dusting his palms against his jean shorts.

"Okay. Tonight's spirit, Tuesday's the grand finale. What's tomorrow?" At least I could be better prepared once.

"Tomorrow we give the spirits body."

I must've looked as bewildered as I felt, because another coven member—a girl whose name I thought was Roxie—said, "So they can walk the earth as they did when the world was young."

"We can do that without a full coven?" I asked cautiously. Around me, guarded looks were exchanged.

"We think so," Marcia finally said. "It would be better with the thirteenth, but with you—"

What was I, the Energizer Bunny? "I'll try," I said. I felt like I had to. I wanted to do what I could to end the heat wave. Smiles met my words, and I ducked my head to hide a grimace. I hadn't meant to sign on for changing the face of the earth, spiritually or otherwise. "Did it," I started, then cut myself off as curious faces turned to me. "Never mind."

"Did it what?" Roxie, if that was her name, had a headful of tight curls and a cant to her stance that invited openness.

"Did it ever occur to any of you that there might be a reason the spirits don't walk the earth anymore?" I sighed. "Maybe a good reason?"

Blank expressions met my words. I nodded. "That's

what I thought. Just thought I'd bring it up. Never mind. Carry on."

"We turned our back on the spirits a long time ago," Marcia said. "They moved away, to wait for us to recognize our need for them. Now that we have, we'll share that knowledge with the rest of the world, and balance will be restored." She sounded utterly confident.

"And you don't think eleven people making a decision for six billion others might be a little...arrogant?" Man. My mouth just wouldn't shut up.

"Of course it is." Marcia smiled, and Faye's eyebrows drew down into a scowl. "If we're truly arrogant and this is truly not the correct path, I believe that the Goddess will not allow us to succeed."

"And if she does, it's okay?"

Marcia nodded. The Elder stepped up beside her, as confident in his bearing as Marcia was in her words. "I admire your caution, Joanne. It shows wisdom."

I grinned a bit. "A trait not normally seen in the young?"

He flashed me a smile in return, without nodding. For an unexpected moment, my vision deepened, setting aside the mundane world for the spirit world the coven was so eager to call up. The Elder blazed with power, a V-8 engine stuffed into a body designed for a V-6 at best. He was connected to the earth in an almost literal fashion, glowing lines of strength flowing from his spine, from his hands and feet, and burying themselves in the ground. When he stepped away from Marcia, it was with a profound sense of centeredness, as if nothing could knock him from his feet unless he permitted it to. The earth itself held him in its grasp, sure as the earth was in the sun's thrall. Seen this way, he was gorgeous, serene colors of confidence connecting him to the world.

At least, I hoped they were serene colors of confidence. My vision clung to the inverted, and his power lines were weirdly spiked, black centers with glowing outsides that filtered from one shade to another. He *felt* honest and true, but my eyes couldn't prove it.

Faye had real power as well, glowing a horrible lime-green against the black circle of the setting sun. I thought it might be sunlight yellow against the genuine gold of the sunset, if my vision'd been behaving. Garth, to my surprise, spiked with power, too, his a murky brown that I thought might really be green. My head was beginning to pound, but I didn't dare blink as I looked from one coven member to another.

The others were duller, even the Father, their magic buoyed by their faith in the Goddess more than their own ability to command power. They were, I thought, what the strength of the coven needed: support. I blinked away from them toward Marcia, wanting a read on the final living member of the six named positions in the coven. She stepped into a shaft of sunlight as I looked her way, and inverted color inverted again, flaring from black into gold. Tears sprang to my eyes from the brilliance. By the time I'd blinked them away again, I'd lost the sight, and Marcia was smiling down at me. "Do you think you're ready, Joanne?"

I wasn't ready at all, but I climbed to my feet. "Yeah. Yeah, all right, let's do this thing."

CHAPTER EIGHTEEN

I had no idea why the cops weren't coming down on us like a load of bricks. The flames, pushed to a bonfire, sent heat pouring over us. Everyone but me sang in a language I didn't know. I wasn't sure it was a real language, but after a few minutes of listening to the high, sweet tones, it didn't matter. It was like Gregorian chants wrapped around wind chimes. Their voices got under my skin, lifting goose bumps. Faye's soprano skirled up, pure enough to tangle with thin blue wood smoke, and dropped away again, leaving the air sharper and harder to breathe, like someone had brought a winter chill into the smoky summer air. Garth's tenor matched her for a few notes, then was overrun by the Elder's deep baritone.

Whistling, I thought, had nothing on this performance.

I could feel what they were doing, all the way into my bones. Their singing had the same power as the drum, breaking down thought into the pure joy of sound. And, like the drum, it was meant to dilute the walls between the worlds, allowing the merely mortal to pass into the Upper and Lower Worlds. It made me gasp for air and grin at the fire while I struggled not to dance for the sheer delight of being alive. I leaned into the music, catching vowel sounds and carrying them up into the smoke, driven to participate without wanting to disrupt.

The six of us began by holding hands. We women had the symbols of the moon painted on our palms with sticky red that flared black in my wretched vision. The men stood between us, their own symbols—sword, scythe, skull—painted on their palms. When we joined hands, power spasmed through us, an electrical connection that lingered even after we stepped back from the fire. The other coven members joined us one at a time, taking up the empty spaces between our shoulders. Each new addition changed the power flow, a brisk shock that went through my body and pooled in unexpected places. I'd never thought about magic making a girl horny. Suddenly the reputed Wiccan practice of performing witchcraft "skyclad" sounded pretty entertaining.

Too bad, the irreverent and sane part of my mind said, *that the garden Gary isn't around.*

It was too bad Gary wasn't here, period. He would've loved the pageantry. I grinned, bumping my shoulders against the people next to me. I'd have to enjoy it for him, and tell him about it in the morning.

We made a tight circle around the fire. *Ring around the rosy*, I sang to myself, not wanting to interrupt the music the others still made. My feet had begun a bright, excited dance entirely of their own volition, and the coven as a whole circled the fire, crushing half steps closer to the flame.

Power built in its heart, a core of white expanding. I wanted to kneel down and touch it, but the under-the-skin ache of sunburn stopped me. My own powers, meant for healing or not, wouldn't stop me from developing some lovely third-degree burns if I stuck my hand into a bonfire.

I was almost dancing in the fire now as it was, singing the few bright sounds I could anticipate. I closed my eyes, tilting my head back, and lifted my hands up toward the sky. The music made me feel like my feet were only bound to the ground by habit. I wondered if that was how Virissong felt: bound by time and habit to a world he fled to in hopes of saving his own. It was too late now; his world had been gone for eons.

For a moment, that thought seemed very important.

The coven's song reached a crescendo, and ended.

Silence thundered in my ears, so loud my eyes flew open.

And my goddamned vision inverted again, the flames turning white with flickering gray cores. Blackened branches glowed crimson and white, the fire's center bubbling a malicious, murky purple. I shook my head, trying to clear away the reversal of colors as I realized the song had been more than just music. It was a spell.

Power exploded upward.

It erupted from the heart of the fire, slamming into the atmosphere so hard it cracked the sky. Darkness boiled down from the stars, shredding the evening sky. Somebody screamed.

Things poured out of the darkness. They were pale, wraithlike, blues and grays and whites against a blackness so encompassing I couldn't breathe. The fire was a single point of illumination, but even its colors were wrong, struggling through my reversed vision. Sheets of flat color ripped through the sky, like I imagined the aurora to look, only in grayscale or shades of purples and blues that seemed too deep. Spirits leaped from the colored sheets, in shapes and forms I had no frame of reference for. They were horrible, distorted and cruel, their faces pulled long to accommodate teeth meant for tearing and rending. They were neither human nor animal, and sometimes not even something in between. They taloned their hands, clutching at me, at the coven, then whisked away through the black power. They were made up of legends: names for some of them settled behind my ear bones, painfully intense knowledge that forced its way into the front of my mind. Stone giants called *a-senee-ki-wakw;* flint-winged monsters from the stars; *mistai* who haunted the dark and sad places.

They hated. Trapped for more time than I could comprehend, they only wanted to be free and to wreak destruction on a world that had rejected them. Panic surged up in my stomach, making me cold as I scrabbled for a foothold against them, anything that could help me build a wall and stop Hell from being unleashed on Earth. I had no support from the coven: they held fast, pulling the edges of darkness farther open. I spared one glance around the fire, hoping to find the desperation I felt in at least one face.

Instead, I found ecstasy.

Faye's blond hair was strung out wildly, her mouth open and head flung back. Her skin glowed blue, as if she stood under black lights, her eyes dark pits and her open mouth swallowing down, or injecting, power. She looked like she was screaming, but her expression held fierce joy, not fear.

At the third point of the triangle, Marcia stood with her teeth bared, a terrible grimace distorting her face. But I could see and feel the power emanating from her; there was no rejection in her. From one face to another, I saw the same things. Even Garth, whose earnestness I had trusted, cried out in silent, joyful abandon, tears spilling down his cheeks.

I set my teeth together and prepared to dig down to the core of my being, and call up the power to stop this. There was a gut-level certainty in me: even if the earth itself were willing to share power with me, the effort would kill me. I wished, desperately, that I'd said goodbye to Gary.

And then, like Pandora's Box, hope came.

Nothing outward changed: the silence still shrieked in my ears, the sky still boiled black. But the *intent* of the specters pouring out of the black hole we'd created seemed to change. The body-confused chill of sunburn swept up from my bones, making me shiver, making a bubble of sickness in my tummy. I swayed, and the boy next to me, more aware than I expected, put his hand under my elbow, supporting me. I glanced at him; his eyes shone with hope and excitement, even through my distorted vision.

Spirits like the ones who'd tumbled and mock-fought over Gary filled the sky. One caught my eye, a lion with tufts missing from his mane, and I wondered if the badger was nearby, carrying a tawny victory prize. More fantastical creatures, *honochenokeh* who were benevolent spirits; *oni* which had no visible form, but were life-force personified; other beings, some nearly human and some from pure legend, rolled out of the gap, chasing down their nightmare counterparts and disappearing into the sky. I looked for the thunderbird, and for Coyote, but saw neither of them in the mad rush. Even so, a sense of safety overwhelmed me.

The fire burned out in one impossible burst, swallowing the sparks it had thrown at the stars just one breath earlier. The column of power cut off, and all around me the coven members collapsed to their knees, as if they'd been supported by nothing more than the sky-rending light. The rip of blackness sealed shut, leaving twilight skies again, and suddenly I could hear distant voices.

They weren't laughing anymore. They were raised in alarm and confusion: the overhead activity hadn't gone unnoticed, even if our bonfire had. I stared up at the sky, trying to grasp the implications of what we'd done, when Garth grabbed my arm.

"It's time to go," he said in a low, urgent voice. I startled and shook him off, staring first at him and then at the other coven members, who were scrambling to their feet and hurrying away.

"What? Why?"

"Because that was way too much magic to hide. Can't you hear people coming? We'll get in trouble if we're found around the smoking ruins of a bonfire in the middle of the park." Garth was smiling brightly at me, his colors fading from inversed. "Did you see it, Joanne? Did you see what we did?"

I looked back up at the healed sky. "We let monsters into the world."

"Light and dark," he said earnestly. "We can't have the good without the bad. You felt all the goodness, too, didn't you?"

I nodded slowly. The strength of the spirit animals and benevolent ghosts still lingered beneath my skin. I remembered Colin's snake, and Gary's tortoise, and smiled suddenly. They'd have a lot of company now.

My vision went completely black, and I fell over.

Monday, June 20, 5:04 a.m.

I woke up around dawn, more feeling the time in my sunburned bones than actually knowing it. The ceiling above me was unfamiliar, gold sparkles mixed in with the ridges of plaster. The corners of the room seemed dim, which, after a few moments' consideration, I realized was due to the lights being off. I thought about my whole body, from toes to the top of my head, and decided that while I needed about eighteen weeks of sleep, I didn't hurt, so probably all was well. I pushed up on an elbow.

Like a sledgehammer crashing into the side of my skull, a headache announced its disapproval of my moving. I groaned and put a hand over my eye, trying without much focus to will the headache away. What qualified as a headache for a car? Being too cold to start in the morning? The body rusting out? I settled on the too-cold analogy and tried to think my car warm again. Absolutely nothing happened.

Faye appeared in a flurry of worry, sitting down on the edge of the couch I lay on and feeling my forehead. I groaned again, even though her hands were cold and felt good. "Where am I?"

"My apartment. You passed out last night. We were worried. I thought you might not want to go to Garth's, and nobody knew where you lived."

"What time is it?" I didn't trust the internal chronometer.

"I don't know, like five in the morning. The sun's rising."

Guess I should've trusted it. "Have you been up all night?"

"Mostly. I napped a little, but I was worried about you. We all were. Are you all right, Joanne?" Her eyebrows drew down over her puppy dog brown eyes. I tried to work up a smile, got as far as a grimace, and gave it up as a bad job.

"I—" I started, then yawned so big it felt like my head was going to split open. I groaned again. "Do you have any aspirin?"

"Sure." She leaped to her feet and scurried to get some. I sat up gingerly, surprised to discover that my head didn't hurt as much when I was in a sitting position. Maybe the barometric pressure was different two feet farther off the ground. Faye hurried back with aspirin and a huge glass of water. I took both gratefully.

"I didn't sleep last night," I said when I'd drained the

glass. "Or the night before, whatever. And it was kind of a long day. I guess last night's little powwow was too much."

"You put an awful lot of power out," she said sympathetically. "It exhausted all of us. But think of what we're doing, Joanne! Think how different things will be. Maybe there'll be no more war, once we understand better how connected we all are."

I grinned tiredly at her. "Faye's a good name for you. You've got a lot of faith." She smiled, and I resisted the urge to pat her on top of the head. "I hope you're right."

"I am," she said with confidence. "You felt what followed the nightmares last night. All the hope and goodness."

"Yeah." I nodded a bit, then did it some more, noticing that my head didn't hurt nearly as much. Either it was wonder-aspirin, or I'd been very badly dehydrated. "Look, where are we meeting tonight? I've got a million things to do today, so I should get home." Well, I had at least four things to do today. That was sort of like a million. I admired how much better my head felt after just a glass of water. "You didn't put anything in that water, did you?" I asked. Faye's eyes widened.

"No!"

I held up a hand, grinning. "I didn't think so. It just helped a lot. Thanks. Look, how far are we from the park? I'd like to go pick Petite up."

"Petite? Your car?"

I nodded.

"Oh," Faye said blithely, "I drove it home last night."

My vision went all tunnelly and red in a way that had

nothing to do with the annoying inversions that had been bothering me for the last day. "You drove. My car. Here?"

"Sure," Faye chirped. "I thought you'd like it to be here."

"You don't even have a driver's license! You drove *my car*," my beautiful, wonderful, delicate Petite, "without my *permission,* and *without a driver's license?!*"

It began to dawn on Faye that she had perhaps made a tactical error. "Well, I—it wasn't so hard—"

"You drove my *1969 Mustang* WITHOUT PERMISSION AND WITHOUT A DRIVER'S LICENSE?"

Faye shrank in on herself and squeaked, "I'm sorry." Then her eyebrows wrinkled down and she straightened up a little. "How'd you know I didn't have a driver's license?"

"BECAUSE I'M A COP!" I thundered. "Now GIVE ME MY KEYS!"

She handed them over and I stomped outside like the wrath of God. Faye followed me at what she judged to be a safe distance, not knowing that if there was so much as a scratch or a dent, or a whisper of timing being off, that the next county wouldn't be a safe distance. The next *country* might not be a safe distance.

Perhaps I was a little unreasonable on the subject of Petite, but I was literally the only one who'd driven her since I got her when I was sixteen. She was a junker I'd rescued from somebody's barn, and I'd put more time, energy, and love into that car than anything else in my entire life. I'd rebuilt her from the bottom up. Her engine had been in remarkably good shape, with fewer than fifty thousand miles on it. It was creeping toward a hundred now and I had a storage locker full of parts and plans to rebuild it from scratch. Her bucket seats were black and I'd hand-sewn the leather, replacing entire panels when they were damaged. The paint job was custom and entirely my own work. The driver's seat was set to my specifications and nobody had ever moved it except me. Petite was my *baby*. She'd gotten wracked up badly back in January and it'd taken most of the intervening five months and a lot of money to get her back into shape. I wouldn't have let God himself drive Petite, much less some twenty-year-old chickadee with no driver's license.

Who must have had a hell of a time driving it, because she hadn't, in fact, moved the driver's seat, and my legs were a good six inches longer than hers. I started Petite up and she rumbled to life without complaint or suspicious sounds. I glowered at Faye. "You get a stay of execution. Don't ever, *ever* drive my car again without permission." Poor Petite had already had a very bad year, and I was more paranoid than usual about her. Faye looked on the verge of tears. I was too bent out of shape to apologize.

"I'm sorry," Faye warbled. "I just thought you'd want it here. I thought it'd be safer than the park."

I ground my teeth together. She had a point. "You have a point." Grr. "Just...don't do that again, okay?"

"I won't." She sniffled. I suddenly felt like the Big Bad Wolf, so I put Petite in Drive and roared out of Faye's parking lot with unnecessary but satisfactory noise.

CHAPTER NINETEEN

I went into my garden still pissing vinegar. In the greater scheme of things, Faye'd done the right thing, moving Petite away from University Row and the out-of-control frat houses in the area. That, however, was reason, and I was in no mood to listen to it.

My garden reflected that, wind howling through it and whipping up low, heavy clouds into a boil. I stomped around, kicking at the edge of my pond and swearing when wind-induced waves splashed over my feet. In response, the skies opened up and deluged me with cold, pelting rain that stung my skin.

"It's summertime!" I bellowed at the clouds. "It's not supposed to rain in Seattle in the summer!"

The rain intensified. Thunder rumbled beneath the

clouds, ominous and low. I tilted my face up, eyes closed against the stinging drops, and watched the garden flash bright with the crack of lightning. My clothes were drenched through, stuck to my body. The wind changed into lonely frustrated sobs that struggled to rip the tiny leaves from the branches of my trees. I felt them clinging stubbornly, refusing against all good sense to give up purchase. The ground beneath me softened and began to drink down the water that pounded against it. The grass needed it. Maybe the concrete garden walls needed it, too, a hard strike of rain to work away the mortar that held them in place. I remembered Gary's untamed garden, wondering if it had walls at all.

I stood there in the rain, pretending it was that, and not tears, running down my face.

By the time Judy showed up it'd stopped raining. I sat on a bench with my head on my knees, arms wrapped around my shins. The air smelled fresh and clean, and with my eyes closed I could feel the grass growing, thankful for the rainfall.

For the first time, I felt her arrival. It was subtle, like slipping between shadows. I thought of the snake and said, "Hello," without lifting my head. "I don't think I've said thanks for putting up with me, so thanks."

A little silence answered me before Judy said, "You're welcome," in a mild voice meant to disguise startlement. "How is your friend Colin?"

I shook my head against my knees. "I haven't had time to go see him yet."

I felt, rather than saw, Judy's nod. "You took part in a great magic last night."

"Ah yes. Always an excuse." I lifted my head and rubbed my eyes. My vision was bizarre again, even inside my own garden. The edges of everything were faded just badly enough to be a distraction. I spent a few seconds trying to straighten it out, like I was clearing dust away from a windshield, but nothing happened and I gave up. If my own maintenance was this poor, how did anybody expect me to make the world a better place? "Accept," I said to myself.

"Hmm?"

I shook my head. "Nothing. Just reminding myself of something." Judy studied me for a moment, her eyes bright and black as the raven's. Then she nodded, striking her hands together sharply.

"Are you ready?"

"I doubt it, but let's go anyway. What's the deal today? Can I talk to Virissong again?"

She went still. "No. He's begun his journey between worlds. Contacting him would require more energy than you have available."

"You mean it'd kill me."

"Yes."

My eyebrows went up and I pursed my lips. "Right. Didn't want to talk to him anyway." Judy went into motion again, smiling, and I gave her a half smile in return. I didn't know what I'd say even if I could talk to him. It wasn't as if he'd say no if I asked, *Is this all really a good idea?*

Judy came to sit down on my bench, took in my expression, and chose the one opposite me instead. I relaxed a little. "Today," she said, "I want to explore the nature of sacrifice."

"Sacrifice?" That didn't sound good. Amusement curved Judy's mouth.

"I've never been able to think of a better way to describe it. Think about it, Joanne. What is change but sacrificing the old way to the new? Isn't that the nature of what you are?"

I rolled back on my sit-bones, absorbing the questions and the concept with genuine surprise. "I guess so," I said after a minute of honest consideration. "I'm incredibly *bad* at it, but yeah, I guess so." Wow. What an idea. Somehow it gave me a little more of a grasp on what I'd become.

Why sacrifice was an easier concept to come to terms with than healing, I neither knew nor much wanted to know. I was still taking baby steps as far as gut-level acceptance was concerned, even when the world was pushing me to take giant leaps for the good of mankind. Healing was hard. *Let's go shopping!* I thought irreverently, then snorted laughter. Judy's eyebrows lifted curiously and I waved my hand, dismissing my humor as I settled in to have a think about sacrifice.

Healing *was* hard. It fell outside the realm of logic and sense that I preferred to deal with. Not entirely: I did expect paper cuts and broken bones to heal up, given time, and for worse ailments to at least have a chance at being beaten back. But the wholesale version I was supposed to embrace—the entire precept of *change* upon which shamanism was built—was pretty much beyond my ken, and was entirely beyond what I was comfortable with. People and things didn't heal because they wanted to. They healed because nature dictated it, and in more drastic cases, because of the right use of medication and care. I thought of chemotherapy patients, and could acknowledge without flinching that very often, people made dramatic sacrifices in order to achieve the end result of health.

Somewhere very deep inside me, where I didn't think Judy could catch it, I thought of a tiny baby girl sacrificing herself for her brother's strength, and a scared teenager sacrificing her own confused love for the boy's future.

"Yeah," I said out loud, my voice rough in my own ears. "I get sacrifice. You're on to something. I never thought of it that way."

Judy curved a smile that darkened her eyes, taking the light out of them until they were like the snake's. I rubbed my own eyes, then my sternum, wishing my vision would stop misbehaving. "Are you all right?" Judy asked solicitously.

"Yeah." I sat on my hands to make them stop rubbing. Maybe there was something I could sacrifice to fix my vision. I'd think about it when my lesson was over. "So do I get a lesson, or what? Or is this just a 'make Joanne think' day?"

"Your energy is low," Judy said. "Are you up for more than thinking?"

My energy was lower than a snake's belly. I chuckled, more of a shoulder roll than a sound. "I don't know. I could use about a week's worth of sleep."

"Not with Virissong coming in two days time." Judy's voice deepened, becoming stern. I put my head against my knees and made an *mmph* sound.

"I have other things to do, too. Besides help a godling back into the world. He *is* one of the good guys, right?" I looked over the arch of my knees. Judy lifted her eyebrows.

"What does your heart tell you?"

My heart, upon consultation, told me *thud-thud, thud-thud*, which was reassuring if not particularly helpful. My mind, which I trusted more as a vehicle for telling me things, was still conflicted.

"Stop thinking so much," Judy said sharply. "You must learn to trust your feelings, Joanne Walker."

I exhaled noisily through my nose, pressed my eyes shut, and tried to stop thinking.

All kinds of thoughts immediately filled my mind. Whether or not my black shoes, the ones that went best with my dress uniform, were polished, and if I was going to have time to polish them before the funeral. Why exactly it was called a parkway when you drove on it and a driveway when you parked on it. Whether all of this was real or a manifestation of my overactive imagination, in which case, couldn't I at least have Keanu Reeves or Carrie Anne Moss as company?

Gradually all that noise faded away, although I kept an eye out for Keanu showing up. Less likely things had happened.

A quiet part of me acknowledged that the basic problem was I thought the members of the coven were, in general, nuts. Virissong, with his semi-godlike powers and his ambition to make the world a better place, didn't sound half-bad. If he were a little more concrete—like, oh, say, Ted Turner, with his billion-dollar gift to the United Nations—I'd be right there waving a little "Go Viri!" flag. It wasn't that hard to see the world needed some help. In my good moments, I even thought I could step up to the plate and offer a little myself.

An even quieter part of me admitted the really basic problem wasn't the coven at all. It was my own skepticism. The coven, at least, believed. They were willing to take action and risks to make the world a better place.

I was supposed to be dedicated to that sort of thing myself. Instead I was sitting on the benches, pissed at the coach for making me turn out for the team.

Maybe it was better if I stuck to car analogies. The point was, I didn't want to believe, and my recalcitrance kept me stymied. And that was exactly what my spirit animals had told me would be my hardest battle. Accepting.

"Yeah," I finally said out loud. "Okay. I get it. I donno how long it'll last, but I get it." It never lasted long, in my experience.

"Why do you fight so hard?" Judy asked. Hairs stood up on my arms and I shivered, envisioning shields rolling up around me like car windows. I didn't want to answer her question, not out loud and not to myself. All I wanted to do was sit and struggle with acceptance. I didn't need an audience for that.

"Fade to black," I said, and everything did.

* * *

The fade stayed with me even after I opened my eyes, back in my own body. I wasn't even sure I *had* opened my eyes, until I lifted a hand and poked myself in the pupil. Sparks flew through my vision and my eyes watered, darkness fading back into light. I turned to look at the VCR clock, where blinking green numbers told me it was six-thirty.

Six-thirty meant I could get a two-hour nap in before getting ready to meet Morrison for Cassandra's funeral. It also meant I could grab a shower and dash over to see how Colin was doing. I was still thinking that sounded like a good idea when the alarm woke me up again.

Morrison was early. I don't know who was more surprised I was ready, him or me. He knocked on the door at nine-twenty, and I went to open it, holding my shoes in my hand.

I saw the same curious expression cross his face that I felt cross mine. With me barefoot and him shod, he had a good two inches height on me. It felt extremely peculiar to be looking *up* at my captain, and judging from his drawn-down eyebrows, it felt just as peculiar to be looking down at me. He looked down at my feet. I dropped my shoes and stepped into them, putting myself at a half-inch advantage. "Better?"

He rolled his shoulders back, filling my doorway considerably more than he had a moment before. "Yeah." He sounded growly. I didn't blame him. Finding myself on unequal footing—literally—with him made me uncomfortable, too, especially since when it normally happened, it was because I was deliberately wearing heels so I'd be taller.

I stepped backward so I could see him better, my wretched vision notwithstanding. In dress uniform he didn't look like a superhero going to seed. He just looked heroic, broad-shouldered and strong-jawed and capable. He had his cap tucked under his arm with military precision. I wondered if he'd ever been in the military, or if he just had clear ideas about how a police captain should present himself.

"You look good, Captain." Could I get sued for saying something like that? We were both off-duty. Well, I was off-duty. I thought Morrison was, but sometimes me and thinking didn't get on so good. At any rate, whether he could sue me or not, it was true. In the hall light, my inverted vision wasn't so bad, and his shoulders had sort of a silver glow where his shadow should've been. It didn't quite make him look like an angel—that would've been too much for me to stay polite about—but it gave him an aura of confidence and strength that made me sentimental again about working for him.

"Thank you," he said gruffly. "You ready?"

"Yeah." I crooked a smile at my feet and shooed Morrison out of the way so I could step out and lock my door. There wasn't any real reason for the little sting of disappointment that the compliment hadn't been returned, other than me being a fickle, fickle beast.

The ride to the cemetery was a quiet one. I had enough sense to not suggest we take Petite. Morrison drove an unmarked police-issue Ford, the sort that isn't fooling anybody about being a cop car, and I rode shotgun, silently watching the streets slide by. We drove into Crown Hill Cemetery and parked, walking over tired green grass toward a gathering crowd. We couldn't have been more in sync if we'd tried, our paces matching exactly. Morrison pretended not to notice.

Nerves and guilt bubbled in my stomach and I tried to chase them away with a quiet question. "No service?"

Morrison said "Only the graveside service," and volunteered nothing else, leaving me to my churning stomach. I'd never gone to one of these, not for a victim, not in an official capacity. I felt like I should've done more, like I should've been there in time to save Cassandra Tucker. I wondered if he felt the same way, as if he'd failed the girl whose funeral we were about to attend. I wondered if any police officer could *not* feel that way, doing this.

I hadn't anticipated seeing anyone I knew, but the coven members were all there, pale with grief. Faye stood with her arm around the waist of an older black woman whose face was veiled under the black hat she wore. She was leaning heavily on the girl. Morrison turned his head and murmured, "Ruby Tucker, Cassandra's mother. The girl with her is Faye Kirkland, Cassandra's best friend."

"Yeah. She's the one who accosted me." That sounded better than *dreamed about me*, somehow. I glanced over the little group surrounding Ruby Tucker, then asked, as quietly, "Her father?"

Morrison shook his head. "He died a few years ago. Mrs. Tucker's had a hard time of it." He kept his voice so neutral I could hear the ache he was hiding. I reached out and touched the back of his hand with my fingertips. He looked down, then at me with his eyebrows lifted, and I let my hand fall without saying anything.

My inverted sight seemed to have settled down. The edges of things were still dim, but it was a vast improvement, allowing me to watch people as they arrived and paused to offer their condolences to Mrs. Tucker. She stopped letting Faye support her and stood straight and tall, taller than I expected. Through the shadows of her veil I could see traces of Cassandra's youthful prettiness, and her determination to conduct herself with dignity. She did not look at me or Morrison, although other people did, some with sympathy and a few with anger. It wasn't that we were white in a predominantly black crowd. What made them angry was the same thing that made me guilty: we were cops, and we hadn't been there to save Cassandra Tucker. What good were we, if we couldn't save one young woman's life? Their anger and frustration was as misplaced as my own, but I couldn't blame them for it. I held my hands still, fighting against the urge to make unhappy supplication to the men and women who had been Cassandra's friends.

A church bell rang, counting off the hour at ten o'clock, and the crowd fell back, making an open path to the grave. Planes droned overhead, and I could hear the distant sounds of traffic, engines revving and horns honking. Closer to me, people sniffled and cleared their throats and lifted their chins, but the silence, for a city morning, was nearly complete. Almost as one, heads turned to watch the six men who carried Cassandra's coffin approach her grave. The young man at the right front held his jaw so tightly set that mine ached in sympathy.

A bewildered little girl wailed and flung herself at the men who walked by, solemnly carrying a coffin on their shoulders.

Déjà vu hit me so hard I clutched at Morrison's sleeve to keep myself upright. I'd been here before, not all that long ago. Only then it'd been in the desert of my mind, with the big coyote, not real.

The girl's cry cut through the silence, sharp as knives. The young man in the lead flinched, eyes darting down to the little girl before he yanked his gaze forward again. Morrison murmured, "Siobhán."

"What?" My fingers refused to unwrap from Morrison's sleeve as I stared up at him, the funeral forgotten. It was all I could do to keep my voice down. "*What?* How do you know that name?" It wasn't anywhere on my paperwork, and the only person who'd ever used it was dead.

Morrison frowned at me. "The little girl. Cassandra's daughter. Shevaun Tucker."

Faye darted forward to scoop the girl up. Shevaun buried her face against Faye's shoulder, sobbing with misery and confusion.

I stared across the grave at the little girl who shared my name, and wondered if the universe could get any less subtle.

CHAPTER TWENTY

Shevaun Tucker was tired and bored with the ceremony long before it was over. She squirmed unhappily in Faye's arms, toddling over to hide behind her grandmother's skirt when Faye put her down. She watched all the solemn, sad faces with wide dark eyes, and put her thumb in her mouth in the fashion of a child who thought she was too old for that, but couldn't find any other source of comfort. She caught me looking at her, and for a few moments we held each other's gazes. The guilt came back, stronger than before, and I looked away. I heard her snuffle a protest, and when I looked back, I couldn't see her anymore. Ruth Tucker's skirt swung, though, as if a little girl might be hanging on to its far side.

It was over startlingly quickly, then. Someone laid a wreath of daisies on Cassandra's coffin, and her mother, grim-faced, put a handful of pansies in the middle of that. She stepped back, and the coffin-bearers lowered the coffin into the ground on taut ropes. Ruth threw a handful of dirt onto it, then turned away, shoulders knotted, unable to watch any more. I could see Shevaun again, trailing after her grandmother with a fistful of the woman's skirt in her hand. The crowd began to break up a little. Morrison touched my elbow. "Come on." His voice was low and strained. "We should offer our condolences."

"Didn't know cops knew big words like condolences," I said almost as quietly, hoping to get a smile out of him. The corner of his mouth turned up a little. It would do. We made our way to the back edge of the crowd and worked our way around it, toward where Mrs. Tucker stood with the young man who'd led the coffin-bearers. Shevaun was hanging on his pants leg now.

"Her brother?" I asked Morrison in as discreet a voice as I could manage. He shook his head.

"Shevaun's father. Cassandra was an only child."

God. Her poor mother. I dragged in a deep breath, trying to break apart the bands of aching sympathy around my heart. Then we were shaking hands with Mrs. Tucker, whose weary expression held none of the blame or anger that I'd expected. She accepted our condolences graciously, inviting us, with more quiet dignity than I imagined I'd be able to summon, to come back to her home with everyone else, for funeral meats. Morrison shook his head in apology; he had to get back to work. Mrs.

Tucker nodded her head without surprise, and we broke away, heading for the car.

"Joanne! Officer Walker!"

I screwed up the side of my face that wasn't facing Morrison. Faye's voice wasn't one I'd wanted to hear calling after me. Morrison lifted one eyebrow and we both turned back to the blond girl, who had somehow collected little Shevaun as she approached us. "I didn't know you were going to be here," Faye said as she came up to us. Shevaun stared at us both, round-eyed and suspicious as she sucked on her thumb. No, I realized after a moment: she was gnawing on it. Poor kid.

"I wanted to come. Faye, this is my boss, Captain Michael Morrison. Captain, this is Faye Kirkland. We met the day after Cassandra died."

"Did you," Morrison said, a perfect example of neutrality as he offered Faye his hand. She tried rearranging Shevaun so she could take it, and the little girl abruptly put her arms out to me. Taken aback, I lifted her out of Faye's arms, and she gazed around, apparently pleased with the new height she could view the world from.

"Thanks." Faye shook Morrison's hand, then put her arms out for Shevaun again. "C'mon, Shevaun, honey. It's almost time to go, and you've been awful good. I've got cookies for you back at the house."

Shevaun studied her with much the same suspicion she'd examined Morrison and me with a moment earlier. Then she swung her head around and checked my expression. I smiled at her. "Shevaun's a very pretty name," I told her. "Why don't you go with Faye and get some cookies now?"

Evidently it was a convincing argument. Shevaun put her arms out again and leaned toward Faye. I managed to not quite dump her into Faye's arms, but it was a near miss. I wasn't used to handling children. Morrison and I watched them walk away, and I waited for the storm.

"I didn't know you were good with kids," he said, taking me completely off guard. He turned without waiting for me, walking across the grounds to the car. I shook myself and caught up after a couple of steps.

"I'm not, really. I like Billy's kids, but I don't really know anything about them."

"She didn't scream when you held her. That's something."

I let out a breath of laughter. "We Shevauns have to sti—" My mouth was always surprising me with the things it said. I swallowed the words too late. Morrison's eyebrows shot up.

"You what?"

I wondered if it was some kind of felony to be hired as a police officer under a name that wasn't your own. "Nothing," I said, and bit my tongue until we got back to the car. Not until I was inside with the doors closed and the windows rolled up, in exactly the same kind of physical shielding that I used mentally, did I dare speak again. Even then I had to put both hands on the dashboard and lean into it, like I was drawing strength from the car, before I could manage the words. "My name is actually Siobhán. Hers is probably spelled differently, but it's the same name."

Morrison stared at me like I'd grown another head. I sucked on my upper teeth, leaned back in the seat so I could fold my arms around my ribs, and stared just as intently out the window. The car was hot, far too hot for comfort, even if I wasn't making myself uncomfortable already. The bone-deep sunburn made itself noticeable again. Eventually it became clear Morrison wasn't going to so much as start the car until I finished what I'd started. I pressed my lips together until it hurt and kept my focus out the window.

"I've been called Joanne my whole life. My mother spelled Siobhán the Gaelic way, S-I-O-B-H-A-N, which is just impossible for an American to say." Even I'd spent most of my life half-convinced it was pronounced *See-oh-bawn,* despite having looked it up dozens of times to correct myself. "My dad took one look at it and started calling me Joanne." My toe tapped against the floor, rapid tattoo displaying my discomfort even if I didn't want it to. With conscious effort, I stopped it from tapping.

My finger started tapping against my thigh. I gave it up as a bad job and let my toe go back to it.

"Siobhán," Morrison said carefully. He hadn't had a problem with the name earlier, when it belonged to the little girl, but attaching it to me appeared to take some serious thought and consideration. "Siobhán Walker?"

I tilted my head back, looking at the ceiling of the car. Black fuzzy mat, nondescript and able to hold in the summer heat. *In for a lamb,* I thought, and said, deliberately, "Siobhán Grania MacNamarra Walkingstick." That was the full name written out on my Irish birth certificate. I honestly had no recollection of ever saying it aloud before. Part of me wondered why Morrison got to be the Father Confessor. The rest of me didn't want to know.

Morrison didn't say anything else. He turned the key in the ignition, put the car in Drive, and drove me home in silence.

Monday, June 20, Noon

I felt as if I deserved the bawling out Morrison had failed to give me on the way home. That, perversely, was my excuse for going down to the station after changing out of my dress uniform. I was off-duty, so I wore shorts and a tank top, and wished my skin didn't ache like it was sunburned.

The precinct building's air-conditioning was out. It seemed like the whole city's air-conditioning was out. The heat was oppressive, as if it was deliberately trying to crush the life out of anything that breathed. I wasn't sure if it was compounded by the coven's activities the night before, or if it was just my very own personal screwed up power loop. I was afraid it was me.

Morrison's door was open and he stood by the windows in shirtsleeves, talking on the phone. I tapped on the door and he scowled, but gestured me in. I sat and took slow deep breaths of the still air, trying to shake off the feeling of suffocation.

"What do you want, Walker? It's your day off." Morrison came back to his desk and dropped the phone in its cradle.

"I know." I leaned forward, putting my forearms on my thighs, and then wished I hadn't. I wasn't sure I was going to be able to unstick from the position. "I just wanted to talk about Cassandra Tucker, Cap."

Morrison folded his arms over his chest, leaning against

his desk as he looked down at me. "What is this 'Cap' thing, Walker?"

My train of thought derailed and I frowned at him. "Sir?"

"Sir is fine," he agreed. "Captain is fine. You used to call me Morrison, or boss, when you really wanted to rub it in. Now it's Cap. What is that?"

"It's an abbreviation for Captain," I muttered, but that wasn't what he wanted to know, and all things considered, I felt like I should tell the truth. The problem was I hadn't noticed me calling him Cap until he pointed it out. I moved my gaze to his kneecaps, and talked to them. "Pretty much I feel like I'm kissing your ass if I call you Captain or sir."

"They're my job title and an honorific worthy of the position," Morrison pointed out dryly. I looked up from his kneecaps.

"Yeah, but this is me…" I couldn't help it. A little grin slid into place, and I finished the sentence with, "Cap." He didn't smile back and I looked away again. "You always look like you're waiting for the other shoe to drop when I use Captain or sir," I said with a shrug. "I guess I was just trying to find a way around that. Look, Morrison, about Cassandra Tucker…"

"The case is closed, Walker. It's closed, and she's buried. Leave her alone."

"It's just that I feel like there's more to it." My tongue and throat struggled over what to call him at the end of that statement, and couldn't agree on an answer, leaving me feeling like I'd cut it off too abruptly. Christ. I was going to have to start calling him Michael, now that he'd made me self-conscious about all the other names I used for him.

I could not for the life of me imagine calling him Michael.

"There isn't." There was a flatness to Morrison's tone, a lack of curiosity and a whole lot of barely controlled impatience. "The case is closed. Let her rest, and get out of my office. It's your day off, and God knows I need it."

I left feeling out of sorts, sticky, and a little confused. It was marginally cooler outdoors than inside, although I could feel heat radiating off the sides of buildings as I walked by. A bus rambled up in front of me and while I didn't want to get on it, it made me notice the waiting bench it stopped at. I sat down, waving the vehicle on, and rubbed my eyes. My contacts were as sticky as I felt. I couldn't remember the last time I'd taken them out. I wore the extrapermeable extended wear types just for that reason, but most days I remembered to take them out in the evenings. I was pretty sure I'd had them in for three days straight now. I wondered if I could manage to heal my own near-sightedness, then found myself rubbing the thin scar on my cheek. "Arright, yeah," I muttered to myself. "Some things don't need healing."

A white-haired old woman on the far end of the bench looked at me nervously and scooted another scant inch or two away. "Sorry," I said to her. "I'm not crazy. Of course, that's what a crazy person would say, isn't it?"

She got up and left.

Maybe I was crazy. It was possible. It was also possible Cassandra Tucker had had a heart attack brought on by too much use of magic, but the idea just made me itch. I'd been to the Dead Zone before. The bit with the snakes and the god-awful serpent monster was all new, and I didn't believe Cassie'd died of something as ordinary as a heart attack. Not with that kind of welcoming committee on the other side. Even though Coyote told me my method of investigating the Dead Zone potentially opened me up to anybody who wanted to have a go at me, I still didn't believe Cassandra's death was natural.

I actually laughed out loud, looking up at the sky. "Satisfied?" I asked my invisible spirit animals. I couldn't feel them with me, but I assumed they had to be around somewhere. "For once, I'm the believer. I'm the one who thinks something kooky's going on when the perfectly mundane explanation makes everybody else happy. I'm getting good at this acceptance thing, huh?"

I was also getting worryingly good at talking to myself. Out loud, no less. A surly faced pair wearing black leather—which had to be really uncomfortable in this weather—took the long way around me, trying not to meet my eyes. I shrugged an apology and unstuck myself from the bench, heading back to Petite. I had two days off. I might as well see if I could prove myself right.

CHAPTER TWENTY-ONE

"Hey, legs!"

I recognized Billy's voice behind me, but it didn't occur to me to turn around. He sprinted—for some value of "sprint;" the extra ten pounds made his solid footfalls sound heavy enough to shake the sidewalk—the few yards to catch up with me and dropped a hand on my shoulder. "Hey, legs. What, you're not talking to me anymore?" He let out a puff of air and fell into step beside me as I wrinkled my forehead at him.

"You were talking to me?"

"You see anybody else with Julia-Roberts-inseam legs walking around here?" he demanded. I glanced down at my pale knees and my pair of really comfortable men's sandals. Then I looked around at the passersby. Plenty of them were in shorts. Most of them weren't women a smidgen under six feet tall.

"I guess not. You never said anything about my legs before."

"Two reasons." Billy steered me into the Missing O, where I hadn't been planning to go. "One." He lifted a finger. "Melinda'd kill me. Two." Another finger. "It's sexual harassment. Three."

"You said two." I got in line for a drink, Billy still directing me. It was blessedly cooler in the O, and the place was packed, everybody taking advantage of the functional air-conditioning.

"Shush your mouth. Three. I never saw your legs before."

"Now that," I said, offended, "is not true. I wore a dress at one of the Policeman's Balls." I was almost certain I had. Practically positive. At least once.

"You wore your uniform," Billy corrected. "The midcalf dark blue skirt. Six inches of shin doesn't count."

"You have an amazing eye for detail, Billy." I'd worn the same skirt to the funeral.

"That's why they pay me the big bucks," he said with a cheerful snort. "Frappucino and a bottle of water," he said as we stepped up to the counter. "What's your poison, Joanie?"

Joanie. The name made me smile a little. It was so much friendlier than Judy's rigid Joanne or Morrison's terminally exasperated Walker. A thump of loneliness chilled my blood. I hadn't seen much of my friends the past few days, and it was making me feel isolated. Especially in face of Faye's adamant comments about me being one of the coven now. It was like she was trying to surgically remove me from the life I already had, although I was pretty sure that was giving her golden retriever self way too much credit.

"Italian soda," I said to the barrista, suddenly more cheery. "Orange, vanilla, cream, no whip." That was my summertime drink, just like hot chocolate with mint was my winter drink. It was normal, it was me, and it wasn't complicated by anybody's magical ritual or their expectations of me. "Billy, I'm not supposed to be working." I dug change from my pocket, counting out nickels and dimes to pay for my soda. Billy eyed me.

"Going broke?"

"Getting lopsided from carrying too many pennies in my pocket. Did you need something?" My vision was still playing havoc, and the edges of the coins kept fading into shadow, making them hard to pick up.

"Backup," he said. I took a step back. He eyed me again, more maliciously this time.

"Oh," I said, and stepped forward. "Sorry. I thought you were…never mind."

"I'm meeting Mel for coffee," he explained.

"Mel. Mel, Melinda, your wife?"

Billy nodded furtively.

"And you need police protection for this?"

"See, I accidentally let slip that you figured out she was, you know." Billy rolled his eyes expressively and I grinned.

"Crazy for marrying you?"

Billy laughed. "Yeah, something like that. So she's on

the warpath, figuring I shot off my mouth to the whole department."

"What, you? The picture of discretion? Your nail polish is chipped, by the way."

Billy lowered his head and stared at me. I fought off another grin and picked up my soda, swirling ice with the straw. "So I need you to go the whole feminine intuition route," he growled. "To get me off the hook."

"You know I don't believe in that stuff, Billy." Grinning again, I staked out a table while Billy stopped to shake some cocoa over the frappucino. I was looking forward to seeing Melinda on the warpath. In the almost four years I'd known her and Billy, I'd never seen her so much as annoyed, not even while herding their ever-increasing tribe of children.

She made her entrance as I sat. Melinda always managed to make an entrance, whether she was wearing an apple-yellow sundress—which is what she wore now—or sweats and a T-shirt. The door breezed open, chiming *ding-a-ling,* and she paused, surveying the coffee shop. In response, the coffee shop paused and surveyed her in turn: patrons glanced her way, smiling, and she wiggled her fingers at a couple of the cops she knew.

The door chimed shut behind her, and the shop's usual hubbub reasserted itself. Melinda skirted her way around the tables, smiling, and caught up with Billy a step or two from the table I'd scored, standing on her toes—as if the gesture made a difference in the heels she wore—to steal a kiss.

"If this is the warpath, Billy, what's she like in a good mood?" I stood up to give Melinda a hug.

"A monster," Billy moaned. "Impossible to live with. A bear." He held Melinda's chair for her, then settled the frappucino in front of her. I sat back down, smiling broadly.

"Ah-huh. It's rough to be you, isn't it? It's good to see you, Mel. You look great."

"I look like a cow," Melinda pronounced gleefully.

"You do not." It was the only appropriate response to give a pregnant woman, and besides, it was true. "But Billy's starting to look like a prize bull."

Billy sat back. "I think I'm offended."

"Well, let us know when you're sure." I beamed at him. He snorted. "See? Now you're sounding like one, too."

"Hey," he said, injured, and lifted his water bottle. "See, I'm being good. No calories."

"So how's it work?" I asked Melinda. "If he goes on a diet, does that mean you start gaining the weight?"

"I don't know," Melinda said. "He's never been able to stay on a diet for more than two days."

I grinned. "Congratulations to you both."

"For being unable to stick to a diet?" Billy asked. I kicked at him under the table and he grinned back at me.

"Thank you," Mel said serenely. "You should come over for dinner."

"Any excuse to not eat my own cooking," I agreed without hesitation. "When?"

"We're having a barbecue on the solstice," she offered. "My darling William is supposed to have invited everyone."

"Really? The whole city?"

Mel gave me a look I'd seen her give her children. It

made me giggle, which probably wasn't the desired effect. "Just our little neck of it, Joanne. Don't be difficult."

"Yes'm. I'd love to. I'll be there—" Oh yeah. Major big juju going down on the solstice. "—if I can be."

Melinda's eyebrows rose an expressive fraction of an inch. "Hot date?" she inquired, somewhere between disbelieving and hopeful, with a good dose of curiosity thrown in.

"Not exactly." I wrinkled my nose. "I'd tell you more—"

"But then you'd have to kill me, yes, of course. Well, I'm going to tell the kids you're coming, and you won't dare disappoint them, so you'll come."

"That's not fair." I liked Billy and Melinda's kids. They ran roughshod over me, but I liked them anyway.

"Were you masquerading under the impression that I should be playing fair?" Melinda smiled. "You should come, Joanne."

"I'll try," I promised. "Look, Billy—"

"What?" He shook himself dramatically. "Sorry, must've fallen asleep. I wasn't needed for the conversation, was I?"

I laughed. "Be glad we weren't talking about you. Look, you don't really need backup, so I'm going to head out. I've got some people to visit."

"How's Gary doing?" he asked, suddenly much more serious.

Mel's eyebrows wrinkled with concern and she leaned forward. "Tell him we're thinking of him, all right?"

"He's better," I said to Billy, and grinned a bit at Mel. "I will. Pretty Hispanic ladies thinking of him will make him that much better again. Thanks, Mel."

"Any time. We'll see you Tuesday." She waved me off.

The heat hit me like a pile driver. I actually staggered, trying to catch my breath, and leaned against the O's outer wall for a few seconds. It didn't help: heat sluiced off the building, too, making my tank top stick to my spine within two breaths. I took a too-large gulp of my soda and coughed, but it was better than not getting something cool down my throat. It wasn't as hot as the coyote desert, but the mugginess might've been worse. I took a deep breath and felt like I was inhaling another sip of my drink.

"Hot enough for ya?" somebody asked as he strode by. I couldn't even work up the energy to give him the glare he deserved, it was that hot. My brain functions slowed down again and I squinted at the sidewalk, trying to remember what I was doing. Petite. Hospitals. Visiting Gary and Colin. That was it. And then maybe I'd go home, spend the afternoon in a cold shower, and try to talk with my coyote. On the one hand, if he was my spirit guide and wasn't turning up to guide me, I was probably doing okay. On the other, I still wanted to apologize for being a jerk in the Dead Zone, and to ask if he had any ideas on how I might further investigate Cassie's heart attack.

A plan in place, I tried to schluck up another sip of my Italian soda, but it was already empty. I looked in dismay at the cup in my hand, honestly not remembering having drunk it. I was pretty sure, though, that I'd remember someone *else* drinking it, so I'd probably done it.

The heat pressed on me all the way back to Petite. I could hear it affecting other people: arguments barking up through the thick air and little kids whining that they wanted to go home. I figured nobody was going to get in a real fight. It would take too much energy. I certainly didn't have enough energy to stop them, anyway. Besides, I was off duty. Morrison didn't want to see me around. I should thank God for small favors, and get out of there while the getting was good.

Climbing into an oven would've been just about as comfortable as getting into Petite, although she had more leg room. I wiped sweat away and drove to Northwest Hospital.

The hospital was miles more comfortable than outdoors, but I could all but hear the air-conditioners grinding and chugging as they attempted to beat back the heat. I bought a bottle of water from a machine just inside the front door. It was gone by the time I met a nurse outside Gary's door. She smiled wearily as I asked how he was doing.

"He's lost his mind," she said. My eyebrows shot up and she laughed, the sound surprising in the humid halls. "He keeps cackling about tortoises winning the race. The doctor is pleased. He's in the shower for the third time today."

"The doctor is?" I didn't mean to be a smart-ass. I was just drawn that way. "What's he doing, cooling off? Do you think I could join him?" I laughed. "You know what I mean."

"You're too young for him," the nurse said, grinning.

"Not if we were in Hollywood," I argued. "You know. Michael Douglas gets the girl, even though she's Gwyneth Paltrow and he's old enough to be her grandfather." One of my secret vices was entertainment magazines. Those, and romance novels. I couldn't let it get out, because it would completely ruin my tough girl-mechanic image.

"Michael Douglas got Catherine Zeta-Jones," the nurse argued.

I laughed while I scouted the hall for another vending machine. I thought I'd already sweated out the entire bottle of water I'd just drunk. "Good point, and he's only old enough to be her father. Anyway, I'd rather have Gregory Peck. I like him better."

"Better than who?" Gary demanded. I spun around. Unlike either me or the nurse, Gary was fresh and clean-looking, though he swept me into a hug that assured he wouldn't stay that way for long. He looked so much more like himself that I bit my lower lip as I returned the hug, trying not to get all sniffly. The nurse patted me on the back and went down the hall.

"You look good," I mumbled into his shoulder. He put me back, hands on my shoulders, and beamed genially down at me.

"'Course I look good. Doc says I can leave Wednesday. Hundred percent better. Just gotta take it slow an' steady." He winked broadly, making me laugh. "Don't suppose you sneaked me a burger?" Gary put on his best hopeful puppy dog look, which was somewhat diminished by his wild gray eyebrows.

"Don't suppose I did," I allowed. Gary managed to appear not too crestfallen as he ushered me into his room. The window shades were drawn shut and the air conditioner chugged along, pouring semicooled air into the room more effectively than it had in the hall. I groaned and dropped into a chair. "I may move in here until this heat breaks. It's nice and cool here."

"If this's nice, maybe I'm glad I'm stuck here," Gary said. "I think I lost ten pounds of water weight already."

I pried one eye open. "I didn't even know men knew what water weight was."

Gary looked affronted. "Just 'cause I'm an old dog—"

"Tortoise," I said.

"—tortoise," Gary said without missing a beat, "don't mean I can't learn a thing or two. How 'bout that light show last night, Jo? You have something to do with that?"

I puffed out my cheeks and slid back down into my chair. "You saw that, huh?"

"The whole Pacific seaboard saw it, sweetheart. It's been all over the news. What, you haven't watched? Folks think Judgment Day's comin'."

"God, I hope not." I sank farther into the chair, my tank top sticking to its back and rucking up. "Anyway, yeah, it was me. Well, me and some other people."

"The coven," Gary said with relish. I couldn't help it. I laughed. He looked offended.

"Sorry, Gary. It's just that you like this so much more than I do. You should've been the one to get mixed up in all this."

"Next time," he promised. "Next time the old ticker won't give me any trouble and you won't be able to keep me out of it."

"That," I admitted, "seems extremely likely. Unless I can make you behave."

"Behaving never got anybody anywhere fun," Gary proclaimed. "C'mon, Jo, gimme the story. Poor old man, cooped up in a sweaty hospital…" He trailed off, eyebrows drooping with pathos. I laughed out loud, and he grinned.

"You're a bad, bad man, Gary Muldoon. I—"

Memory assailed me, abrupt and powerful. Six months earlier, just a day or two after meeting me, Gary nearly died in much the same way I'd nearly died: a sword rammed through his torso. That he'd healed without a scar was one of the few things that made me feel like I was doing the right thing.

But reluctance had me in its grasp now. I didn't want to risk him again, not if I could avoid it in any way. "I'll tell you about it when it's over, okay? I can handle this one." I smiled at him as brightly and confidently as I could. My vision narrowed down to dark pinpoints. "I want you to concentrate on getting well, not on me and the insane things I'm up to. Okay?"

Gary's bushy eyebrows drew down and he held me in a frown for a long time before he nodded. "Arright. Arright, darlin'. Just this once. You be careful, though, you hear me?"

"Always," I promised. I stayed a while longer, and let myself out feeling guilty.

CHAPTER TWENTY-TWO

Monday, June 20, 6:45 p.m.

By the time I went to the coven meeting I was in as bad a mood as I could remember, including all the sulking teenage funks I'd tried to wipe from my memory. I'd spent most of the afternoon trying to find Coyote through one inner landscape or another, and instead had barely been able to get out of my own body for more than a few seconds at a time. I hadn't even made it to my own garden, and that just seemed like bad news all around. I imagined thunderstorms going on there, and thought that would be a relief, compared to the day's heat.

I put Petite through her paces, revving the engine and taking corners much too fast. People honked and shouted and swore like they'd been doing all day, but now they were shouting at me. I knew I was being an asshole. I just didn't care very much.

I also had no clue where I was going. I finally slammed Petite into a parking place at Faye's apartment complex and stomped up the stairs to find her.

I found a note on the door instead, directing me to where the coven was meeting. Apparently I was predictable. That pissed me off, too. Maybe I could go find Morrison and get him to kick me a few times, just to round everything out a bit. I stomped back down to Petite and drove over to Lake Washington, ripping up the long stretch of road on its western side without hitting red lights or getting caught by ticket-happy cops. The shadows among the overhanging trees were peculiarly bright, letting me see the shapes of cars pulling down side roads as dark blotches that were easy to avoid. If my infuriatingly reversed vision kept up, at least it'd make nighttime and winter driving easier.

I peeled into the Matthews Beach Park parking lot at a dangerous but pleasing speed, and braked hard. Despite the heat—or maybe because of it—there were surprisingly few cars there. I was comparatively early today, because most of the coven were gathered together at one end of the parking lot instead of already getting ready to do their thing. Only comparatively early, though, because as I got out of the car and glanced them over, it was clear that they were only missing me and Garth.

Several of them were still dressed in the somber funeral colors from that morning, Marcia included. She looked at my shorts and tank top disapprovingly. "I didn't work today," I said, feeling obliged to make excuses. "It was too hot to wear real clothes." Marcia's mouth drew down and she nodded. That's me, Joanne Walker, social faux pas in the flesh. I muttered under my breath and went to sit on a too-hot concrete parking bumper where my bad mood wouldn't spread.

It looked like it was too late. Everyone was long-faced and grumpy. The good-natured lightness that had been a part of the coven's makeup, even with Cassie's death hanging over them, had been eaten away. They were standing together, clearly all part of one group, but there was a lot of distance between shoulders, and most people had their arms folded or hands stuffed in their pockets in very distinct keep-away body language. Even Faye's typical golden retriever look was dampened by the heat, although she was moving from one person to another, trying to strike up conversations. Every time someone scowled and looked away, she looked a little more miserable. I felt sorry for her, even when I tried to be annoyed about her driving Petite. "Hey, Faye."

She lit up like a puppy who thought it was going to get a treat and scampered over as I said, "Sorry I yelled at you this morning." It was possibly the surliest apology in the history of the universe, but the tone didn't seem to put Faye off.

"It's okay. It was a tough night for all of us. Thanks for coming to the funeral this morning. That was your boss, huh?"

I bit my tongue until I was sure the impulse to snark at

her had passed. I had, after all, told her Morrison was my boss. "Yeah," I said after a few long moments, as evenly as I could.

"He's kind of handsome, isn't he?"

"Is he? I don't know." I did know. A man I was inclined to describe as an aging superhero almost had to be handsome. But the phraseology let me work my way around the admission that Morrison was a handsome man without actually having to say it out loud. Or think it, for that matter.

"Well, he's awfully *old*," Faye allowed. "I mean, he's what, like forty?"

I almost laughed. It hadn't been that long ago when I thought forty was pretty old, too, and I wasn't sure exactly when the idea that it wasn't had settled in my mind. Or when eighteen-year-olds started looking like kids, for that matter. "Late thirties, anyway."

"Old," Faye agreed, nodding. "Too bad."

"Why? Is he your type?"

"Ew!" She leaned back, stretching her mouth in horror. "I was thinking you could date him, jeez."

"*Me?* He's my boss, Faye."

"So? Like people don't have work relationships?"

"I don't," I said firmly. Then, hoping to sidetrack her, I asked, "Where's Garth?"

"I don't know where he is." For the first time, I saw Faye look a little uncertain. Then it cleared, replaced by the sunny look. "But he'll be here. He's never let us down. Tonight we give the spirits body. He won't want to miss that."

"All those things we let loose last night? Body like real physical body? So there'll be monsters tromping around?"

"Magic," Faye corrected me, happily. "Magic, finally returned to the world."

"Only Seattle, for the moment," Marcia said above me. I looked up, watching her colors inverse. I was getting used to it. I almost couldn't tell what was the right color and what wasn't anymore, except I was pretty sure the frosted ends of Marcia's hair hadn't glowed purple when I first met her.

"Only Seattle?"

"We still give the spirits their strength in roaming this world," Marcia said. "We're still their link, and so for now they can't travel far from us. When Virissong himself has crossed back into our realm, then they'll be free and the world will share what Seattle has already come to know. That's tomorrow night, the final binding of the spirits to their bodies. That'll bring Virissong to us in his whole and complete form. And it may take some time," she admitted. "Even when we've brought him across, it'll take a while for him to regain his full strength. He's been away from this world a long time."

"Yeah." I suddenly felt much better. Seattle was a tangible scale. Knowing the light show and the spirits were confined to the immediate area was surprisingly reassuring. The coven held enough power to clean up any messes that went wrong, in a Seattle-sized scale. Hell, *I* held enough power, if it came down to it, although I didn't like thinking that way. It made goose bumps run up and down my arms, and made my stomach queasy. Still, I thought it was true.

And no matter how I tried, I didn't truly believe Virissong was up to no good. He was tremendously powerful, but I'd spoken with him and shared memories with him, and his desire to help his people three thousand years ago had been a genuine one. Tangled with ambition, maybe, but there wasn't anything wrong with a little ambition. Without it, he wouldn't still want to try to save *this* world, the one I lived in now. The one I'd screwed up.

I stood up, abruptly bubbling with energy. The oppressive heat seemed to fade away a little. "All right," I said. The enthusiasm in my voice wasn't forced, and it surprised not just me, but several others of the coven, who all looked toward me as if I'd sprouted wings. "Let's go ahead and shake this city around a little. Do we need a fire like we did last night? We can get that started so it'll be ready when Garth gets here."

My ears began to burn and itch in the silence that followed. Faye and Marcia glanced at each other, then at everyone else, then at the trees—everywhere, in fact, but at me.

"What? What'd I say?"

Faye cleared her throat delicately. "We need a fire, but it isn't the same kind of ritual."

"Well, then, what is it? Do we all get naked and dance around trees and yodel to the moon this time? This is all new to me, guys. I don't know wh—" It took that long for the slight smiles to register in my mind. The smiles that had started with "get naked." "Uh," I said, very loudly in the faintly grinning silence. "Uh. Guys?"

"It's a ritual of body." Faye's eyes were very, very wide. So wide, in fact, that I suspected she was holding them that way deliberately, to keep herself from laughing. "It's a, um…"

"Sexual ritual," Marcia said dryly. Faye blushed. I backed up so fast I fell over.

"What? A what? A *what*?"

"Performed specifically by the Mother and the Father," Marcia went on. I shot one horrified look at the Father—I couldn't even remember his name—and was offended to see that he looked just as dismayed, if less surprised, as I felt. Then I remembered I didn't care if he didn't want to have sex with me, because, "I am not having sex with him!" Pause. "No offense."

He waved his hand in an understanding gesture, his expression bordering on strangled. I scrambled to my feet and put my hands on my hips. "No way, no how, no *way*—"

"But you must," Marcia protested. I overrode her, my voice getting louder and louder as I repeated, "No way, no *how*, no WAY—!" It wasn't the most eloquent argument I'd ever made, but it was right up there in the running for most heartfelt.

Garth pulled into the parking lot before we went through another iteration. We all broke off to watch him park. He tumbled out of the car nearly before the ignition was off, taking a dozen long steps to me.

I had never actually been swept off my feet before. Garth, who didn't have the height advantage, managed it. He lifted me off my feet and spun me around in such a tremendous hug that my back popped. I staggered when he put me down, and he grabbed my face with both hands and kissed me. I gaped while the coven members laughed and broke into applause. "The part of the Father will be played by Garth tonight," someone said in a dry, amused tone. Garth picked me up and spun me around again.

"They say they've never seen anything like it." His grip on my shoulders hurt, when he put me down the second time. He shook me, a little vibration that felt like it wanted to explode into enthusiastic violence. "It's like all his healthy cells finally noticed the cancer and are all like, 'What's this bullshit going on?' They're tearing it apart, Joanne. He's getting better!"

More applause erupted around us. The coven moved in like a swarm of bees, hugging and back-patting and cheering, getting close and making contact despite the sticky heat. I stood there staring at Garth, feeling a slow, crooked smile start to work its way across my face. "Seriously?" I asked beneath the coven's happy babble. Garth nodded so hard I thought his head might pop off.

"You should see him, Joanne. You've got to come see him as soon as we're done here tonight. You won't recognize him."

"I will," I promised. "I will, as soon as—I am *not* having sex with him!"

Garth's jaw dropped in horrified astonishment, eyes going round. "Not *Colin,*" I said impatiently. "—the Father." Crap. I still couldn't remember his name.

"Duane," he offered.

"Duane! I am *not* having sex with Duane!"

"Joanne, can't we discuss this reasonably? It's an act of sharing and—" Marcia honestly sounded like she expected to get her own way. I set my jaw and dug my heels into the ground.

"No. No, we can't. I appreciate that there's power in sex, okay? I even appreciate that we're trying to save the world, here. And you know what? I can even appreciate that maybe Cassandra was willing to go through with this, but I'm guessing she *knew* Duane here. How long'd she been with the coven?"

The corners of Marcia's mouth pulled down. "Two years."

"And Duane?"

"We only brought this coven together a year ago," Duane said. "I used to work with an all-male coven. Still, you're right. We'd discussed this ritual pretty thoroughly and had worked out our discomfort. Marcia, you know it's not going to work with unwilling participants anyway. I'm not any more comfortable with this than Joanne is. No offense," he said back to me, and I waved it off just like he had.

"Nothing else has the required power." Marcia kept frowning. "Have we come this far to turn back now?"

"I am *not*," I said adamantly, "having sex with Duane. I'm sorry if I'm screwing up your ritual, but there are limits. We're going to have to find another way."

"There is another way." Faye's voice was deep and hollow. We all turned to stare at her, alarmed sounds erupting from everyone's throats. Her eyes were rolled back in her head, glowing bright black in my frustrating vision. "He guides me." She sounded like her tongue had fallen back into her throat, making her words thick and glottal. "We have to hurry."

"Shouldn't we call an ambulance or something?" I

asked nervously. No one paid me any heed. Marcia and Garth stepped forward to take Faye's elbow, leading her around a parking bumper and toward the woods. The rest of the coven flowed around them, hurrying forward until I was the only one left in the parking lot. At the last moment Duane turned back, expression curious. "Aren't you coming?"

I flung my hands up. "Yeah. Yeah, I guess so. Wait up." I jogged over asphalt and caught up with him, walking into the woods with everyone else.

It took absurdly little time for the fire to build up. It was as if the branches sucked the heat right out of the air and turned it into flame. Well, it was like that except the air certainly didn't get any cooler, and the fire's dry crackle didn't seem to wipe any of the mugginess from the air. I felt like somebody'd wrapped my head in a wet wool blanket and put me down to roast.

Faye was still functioning with her eyes rolled back in her head, bright blackness tracking like she could see. I was the only one who seemed disturbed by it, which struck me as wrong. How did people get used to weirdness being an ordinary part of their everyday lives?

By accepting. I puffed out my cheeks until air squeaked through my lips, and sat down on a log to wait out the preparations.

Five of the coven members, including Garth, had finished drawing a tremendously large circle around the fire. Where trees intersected the circle, they'd stopped and spoken with the tree before doing what looked like drawing a thread through a needle, where the tree was the needle and the circle, the thread. It was extremely polite. I had the peculiar feeling I could feel the trees' pleasure at being asked to take part in the ritual. I wondered if anybody'd asked the branches in the fire if they'd like to be burned. Probably.

They stood at five points. It didn't take a genius to figure out they were the points of a pentagram. I worried my bottom lip, thought of heeding my teacher and accepting and honoring, and tried to see. Rather: to See.

I wasn't very good at it. I didn't know if it was my own reluctance, or if it was that they practiced a different kind of magic, or if it was something else entirely. If I stared at the fire and unfocused my eyes, I could almost see the lines of power misting up like gray fog between the five points of the pentagram. They came up one at a time, from Garth to Roxie, behind my left shoulder, then to Sam the underwear model off in front of my right shoulder. Five lines, all of them nearly touching the fire, making it the pentagram's heart. The five creators murmured a binding spell—I assumed it was a binding spell, and tried not to wonder where that particular bit of knowledge had swum up from—and then stepped away from their points in the circle, the pentagram completed.

The circle itself shimmered very faintly, just like the air had been doing all day with heat. It had a sense of purpose to it: the intent to disguise, although not to hide entirely. To an outsider, it would look like more trees and grass, as if the circle were reflecting the natural state around it. I knew if I left the circle now, I'd be able to see them, because I knew they were there, but random passersby wouldn't see any more than I had last night. No wonder the coven preferred to meet outdoors. The illusion wouldn't work nearly as well inside.

"We're ready."

I startled out of my contemplation of the circle and got to my feet. The rest of the six stood together, Faye pointed in slightly the wrong direction, her rolled-back eyes wide. I fought off a shudder and shoved my hands in my pockets. "Okay, so what do we do?"

Marcia frowned at me. She was good at that. Very imposing. I hunched my shoulders and felt a little smaller. "Do you agree to partake in this ritual willingly, Joanne?" Beside her, the Elder asked Duane the same question. He said yes. I squinted.

"There's no sex, right?"

Everyone but Faye looked exasperated at me. Faye looked exasperated at something over my left shoulder. I stuck my jaw out, stubborn. I wanted a guarantee on this one before I went through with it. Marcia sighed rather dramatically.

"There is no sex."

"Okay. I agree, then. But no sex."

"Give me your hand."

I eyed Duane, who put his own hand out to the Elder without a fuss. I shrugged and put my hand out, too. "Okay."

Marcia sliced her fingernails against my palm and laid the flesh open to the bone.

CHAPTER TWENTY-THREE

I stared at the blood welling up with an astounded sense of déjà vu. It would hurt. Pretty soon it was going to hurt a lot. The bone was already gone, hidden by pooling blood. Yep. Any second now, it was going to hurt a whole lot. But right now, pure astonishment was keeping the pain at bay. It was very interesting. I blinked up at Marcia, wondering if she would suddenly reveal herself to actually be my teacher.

She didn't. She looked just like herself. "Blood binds us to this earth," she said sonorously. "Put your hand together with Duane's."

"That seems like a bad idea." One of the things I got to learn at police academy was how diseases like hepatitis were spread. Smearing bloody hands with somebody else wasn't the best way to avoid that sort of thing.

"For pity's sake, Joanne! Must everything be difficult with you? Get a bowl," Marcia snapped to someone else. I cupped my left hand beneath my right, catching blood that was now flowing over and between my fingers. It still didn't hurt. For the moment, I was grateful.

"I'm not trying to be difficult." I really wasn't. If I was trying, I'd have gone tearing off to an emergency room, at the very least. "Just, you know. AIDS, hepatitis, all that sort of thing. We didn't exactly exchange blood tests, you know?" I thought I was being very reasonable, for somebody who was dripping her own blood all over the place. It probably helped that it didn't hurt yet. Neither, I remembered, had the cut on my face that had left the thin scar on my cheek. I nearly lifted my hand to touch the scar, but Marcia grabbed my wrist with a painful grip. "Ow!"

Then my palm started to hurt. It was worse, shockingly, than having a sword stuffed into my lung. That had just been going to kill me. This was crippling. I could conceivably be unable to use my left hand again. The line of pain burned up my arm and all the way down into my stomach, making me heave. If Marcia hadn't had an iron grip on my wrist I'd have fallen. I wasn't particularly grateful for the prevention. I wanted to scream, but my teeth were clenched together and my throat was locked up, so I just stood there staring at my bleeding hand. The edges of the wound pulsed with my heartbeat, blood popping up in little bursts with each thud. My stomach rolled again, cold sweat sticking my tank top along my spine.

Someone pushed an earthenware bowl beneath my hand and Marcia turned it palm down. My fingers curled over my palm all on their own, which gave me hope that the tendons were all right. Blood splooshed into the bowl, then began dripping down my hand like macabre fingerpaint. After a moment Duane's hand joined mine above the bowl, his blood pooling down into it as well. I could feel it when it mingled with mine, tiny electric shocks snapping back up into my hand like drops of blood reversing their fall. It stung all the way up into the nerve in my elbow, and made my stomach twist again. I felt cooler for the first time in days, like all the sunburned heat was running out of my body through the cut in my palm.

I looked up to see Duane's face as white as mine felt, his nose pinched and strong lines standing out around his mouth. "Well, crap," I whispered. My voice sounded like it came from far away, possibly another planet entirely. "Next time, let's go for sex."

His laugh cracked over me like a whip, a sharp sound of surprise that made us both wince. Then we were leaning on each other for support, shrieking with laughter that was mixed with tears. Marcia and the Elder kept the bowl beneath our outstretched hands, but the rest of the coven stood back nervously, dismayed by our howls of laughter. I couldn't have explained it to them if I'd tried, but Duane and I got it. We kept leaning on each other, giggling, until my knees went out and I hit the ground in a silent rush.

When I woke up my hand was bandaged. Duane was sitting up a few feet away from me, cradling his own hand, swathed in bandages as well. He looked as sick as I still felt, all the desperate humor gone from his eyes. My palm throbbed so badly I could feel it in the back of my throat and in my stomach. If I made it through the rest of the night without puking, it would be just shy of a miracle.

I rolled to hands and knees, or more accurately, hand and knees, my left hand curled up against my chest, and hitched over to Duane. "Give me your hand."

He looked wary. "No offense, but last time somebody said that…"

A bubble of laughter popped through the nausea, making me feel better for about two-thirds of a second. I managed a smile. "No more bleeding. Promise." I didn't know what was going on around us. Marcia said, "She's awake," but no one came to check on us. Duane, who looked too tired to argue, gave me his hand. I cupped it in my right, afraid to even try touching anything with the left. "Do you believe in magic, Duane?" All things considered, it was a ridiculous question.

He half smiled and shrugged. "Yes, I do."

"S'good. Close your eyes." I closed mine, partly because I was too tired to keep them open. The heat had come back while I wasn't paying attention. I felt it bearing down into the cut on my hand as if it were trying to get in. I didn't have the energy to keep it out.

My heartbeat, thick and slow, matching the throb in my hand, was enough of a drumbeat to put me under. The heat probably helped, too, and maybe the blood loss.

I retained a vague sense of awareness of the world around me. Duane's hand in mine had a little weight to it;

the popping fire lit the insides of my eyelids to strange reversed colors. Distressingly, my garden didn't appear around me. I wasn't used to doing this when I couldn't fully reach at least some level of the astral realm.

I wrapped Duane in my image of a damaged vehicle: a blue minivan, with thin white racing stripes and a baby rattle hanging from the rearview mirror. I couldn't tell if it was my own concoction or if Duane had a secret inner minivan, which didn't seem inappropriate, given his role as the Father.

The left front wheel well had been keyed, a deep scored mark that cut through paint and into the metal. I ran my thumb over Duane's palm without quite touching the bandages, and, behind my eyelids, ran my hand over the mark on his car. The scoring ran deep, almost through to the other side. It would take heat to fix it, a soldering iron that would let the metal reach viscosity again so filaments could blur back together. That was how it worked in my mind's eye; I understood on some level that a more practiced shaman should be able to just see the damage as whole, and through that strength of vision, make it happen. I wasn't that good.

And I didn't want to leave Duane with burns where I'd just cleaned up a cut. I reached out my damaged hand toward the fire. Pulling heat from the image of the minivan I was fixing while continuing to solder the injury was more difficult than I expected. I wanted the heat to bleed off through my outstretched fingers, but it stayed in me, my own blood heating up. I wondered just how hot I could get before I caused some sort of irreversible damage. I tried to stop worrying about it, and concentrated instead on Duane's injury.

Gray metal melted and merged back together, overlaying the idea of the cut on his hand. I could feel, if not quite see, the flesh knitting back together, wholeness working its way up from the bottom of the slice. It should have been easy, but the core of power inside me didn't want to respond. It was as if it, too, was oppressed by the weather, unwilling to do anything.

Duane believed, though, and I thought that might be the only thing getting us through the healing process. I was able to put the idea of the soldering iron away after a few minutes, replacing it with a noisy airbrush. The heat within me didn't fade. By the time I had the image of smooth, unblemished blue paint in my mind, I felt parboiled. Sweat rolled down the bridge of my nose and through my eyelashes. I didn't want to open my eyes and feel its sting. "There." My voice was croaky from heat bubbling inside me. I wiped my arm across my forehead before blinking my eyes open. "You should be okay now."

Duane lifted his eyebrows a little and began unwrapping the bandages from his hand. A handful of the coven surrounded us, watching him curiously. "I'll be damned." He turned his palm up, unblemished, and stared at me in pleased astonishment.

For an instant my vision crashed back to normal. His skin looked healthy and whole in the mix of firelight and dappling sun. I could see the unscarred lifeline wrinkling across his palm. I smiled and it made me dizzy.

The image of a windshield, sun-baked and spiderwebbed with age, slammed into my line of sight. I recognized it with a catch of my breath, although I hadn't seen it in months. Coyote would say it was my soul, and right now I wouldn't have enough in me to argue. As I watched, a handful of the spiderweb lines along the outer edges of the windshield crackled and hissed, melding together again. Healing.

My vision smashed back into reverse. The windshield fled to black. Silver-clear splinters of spiderwebs glowed an unhealthy throbbing white against it. The fractures that had just healed split apart again, reaching all the way to the edges of the windshield. My windshield. The car, if my vision drew back far enough, would be Petite. My heart and soul. Poor damned Petite. My head hurt. I blinked, and the vision of the windshield was gone.

Someone touched my shoulder. Dull white pain curdled through me at the touch. "Joanne, are you all right? You're all red."

I looked down at my own hands. My below-the-skin sunburn had surfaced, flushing my skin to dark reddish pink in the failing light. I might tan, from this burn. Sometimes I did, when a bad sunburn peeled away. It was the only time my Cherokee heritage showed up in my coloring, and it made my green eyes look weird and bright in contrast with suddenly darker skin.

Now that I was aware of the burn, my skin ached and itched. I was still sweating, the heat inside me pushing moisture out. I climbed to my feet, trying not to touch myself. I couldn't bend my arm enough to cradle my left hand against my chest like I wanted to. I felt tears burgeoning, but they would sting my face, so I didn't let them fall.

"Come on." My voice sounded hollow in my ears, like it was echoing through an empty cavern. I wondered if my brain had boiled away. I wondered if I'd notice. "Let's finish this thing up." I couldn't take my eyes off the fire, black-tipped wings licking at the air. My hand throbbed in time to the pops and crackles of the embers. I felt like I was putting off more heat than the fire was.

Everyone else apparently felt like I was, too. No one stood near me. Several of them wouldn't look directly at me. I wondered if I hurt to look at. I thought I probably did, because it certainly hurt to be me.

I didn't know what Marcia and the others had done with the blood. I wasn't sure I cared. All I could feel was the cut on my hand and the heat in my body. Everything was starting to make sense, in the heady, rushy way that came with heat exhaustion. There needed to be a sacrifice to initiate the change we were after. That was the real reason I was there: to apply what I'd learned from Judy. I was pretty sure I knew the sacrifice that needed to be made. I just hadn't quite talked myself into doing it yet.

The coven took up their places around the fire. Marcia hesitated, then left me where I was. I was facing the wrong direction, or at least, I was facing a different direction than I had the night before, but I thought it was probably wiser to rearrange everyone around me. I wasn't sure I could walk, for one thing, and for another, I was quite sure I didn't want anyone touching me to guide me into place.

It seemed reasonably certain that I was going to spontaneously combust at any moment.

Which thought distracted me while the coven began a
chant, a different, deeper song than the night before. Did
people who spontaneously combusted do something like
I had? Draw heat off something and then be unable to release it? My vision swirled down to pinpoints while I
struggled to follow that idea through. I was missing something there. There was something about this heat that
was clear and obvious and…gone. My mind was too over-
cooked to hold on to the thought.

I closed my eyes, swaying on my feet. Maybe if I could
direct all the heat to my head I would be able to lift off
and fly away, like a hot air balloon. I concentrated on that
for a few minutes. I succeeded in giving myself tiny fits
of giggles that made the other coven members cast stern
looks at me. I could feel the frowns even with my eyes
closed, their irritation like cool points of pressure against
my skin. Possibly if I annoyed them enough they would
scowl hard enough that their cool anger would bleed off
all the extra heat in me. I started a hopeful little dance,
shuffling my feet around and waggling my hips back and
forth. I lifted my hands above my head, squeaking in pain
as my tank top shifted against my skin. More of them
scowled at me, but it wasn't enough to cool me down. I
usually thought of anger as being hot. I wondered if they
were actually coolly annoyed, or if I was just so hot that
anger felt cold against my burning skin.

I giggled again, not because it was funny, but because
it was a choice between laughter and panicked tears. The

disapproval was stronger this time, hitting my skin in cool waves. I thought I could hear the hiss as it hit me and turned to steam, but I didn't want to open my eyes to see if vapor was coming off my skin. It seemed like the precursor to the whole combustion thing, and I was pretty sure I didn't want to have my eyes open when that happened.

I could feel things starting, a low rumble from the belly of the earth. I thought my soles were shaking, though judging from the unbroken chanting around me, it was probably just my imagination. No one else seemed bothered by it. Still, I thought the ground might split open beneath my feet and spew out the bodies we were trying to call forth. I wondered if they would erupt upward in solid form, lions and tigers and bears, oh my! and then come crashing back down onto us. It would be an ignominious death, squashed by zoo animals. I wondered what the epitaphs would say. Morrison would probably write mine, and it would probably say, "Thank God."

The earth groaned and stretched. I stumbled to the side, crashing into Sam. He caught me, a hand wrapped around my forearm. I made a high-pitched sound of pain, a squeal without enough air behind it. He let go as fast as he'd caught me, staring at his hand. To my eyes, his palm turned white, blood rushing up where I'd burned him. On my arm, where he'd caught me, there was a bleached black hand-print against the sunburn. The earth grumbled and I lost my balance again. This time Sam yanked his hands away, making sure not to touch me. I couldn't blame him.

I didn't want to touch me, but I couldn't get away from myself. I broke out of the circle, moving toward the fire.

"Can't you feel it?" I didn't know if anyone else could hear me. I wasn't sure I was speaking out loud, or if my voice was making it through the tight heat that clenched in my throat. "Can't you feel it coming?" I didn't know how they could miss the pressure building, the impatience buried beneath the land.

No one answered. I spun in a reckless circle, coming too close to the fire. It ripped my breath away, leaving my lungs empty and burning, too. Faye, across the circle, met my eyes. Her eyes were back to normal, but her gaze was sharp and intense, like it could flay the burning flesh from my bones. "You feel it," I panted at her. She tensed and looked away, gaze skittering to the fire. I couldn't tell if it was denial or encouragement. I swung to face the fire myself, and shrugged. My tank top scraped my skin and I found myself savoring the rough, painful feeling. It was the last time I'd ever feel it. I knew what the demanding earth beneath my feet wanted. I knew what the burning in my skin wanted. And really, I didn't think I could hurt anymore than I did already. It might even be peaceful. I was ridiculously glad I'd met Judy and had learned enough in a few short days to understand what was going on, and what I needed to do.

I took one last look around at the coven and shrugged again. "Hell with it." My voice was breathy and light, like flame itself.

I walked into the fire and let it burn.

CHAPTER TWENTY-FOUR

Exultation boiled through me, peeling the skin from my flesh. The fire gobbled its way inside me, meeting up with the heat I'd taken into myself. Together they tangled and tore me apart from the cellular level out, exploding my bones and my brain and leaving me in a floating haze of pain and delight. Breathing didn't seem to hurt anymore. I had a vague sense of wrongness about that, like there ought to be pain in *not* breathing, but it swept over me like a runner's high. The fire had forced me over a threshold: pain was good. Agony was a decadent ending to the build of heat inside me. It ached through my fingertips and curled my feet, and I tried to breathe it in more deeply, grateful for it.

I couldn't hear the coven anymore; even the popping fire had faded into a song that rang high and sweet against my eardrums. It sounded like freedom, like bells calling everyone home. The stinging purity brought tears to my eyes, like liquid goose bumps, involuntary and a little startling. They heralded change and acknowledged me as the conduit. I tilted my head back, lifting my arms to embrace the old world and the ancient creatures that had roamed it. I invited them through me, the Mother, bound by blood and fire to the earth.

It was the utter opposite of the thunderbird. Wolves and bears, wild-eyed things I'd never dreamed of in my nightmares and gentle monsters with the light of hope in their souls fed themselves to me a hundred at a time. Some were malignant and dark, tasting of ash and tar. They came hand in wing with lighthearted, benign creatures that left the scent of clean air and roses in my throat. Some were tricky, and stuck like molasses, only to be washed down by the cool water and straight-forward dedication of their counterparts. I couldn't name most of them even if I'd wanted to, but they fed me and grew fat on me, and through me were born out into the world.

I tore apart with the birth of a thousand creatures, feeling the earth tear with me. I didn't think I cried out loud, but I didn't need to: the earth itself shrieked and rumbled with the influx of things from the otherworld. I burned, no longer inside my skin, but in my core, spinning eternally, creating life. Time stretched and snapped and twisted until it was meaningless. I had no sense of age, no sense of purpose; I simply was, and would be until I ended. Nothing could change me, not the life I brought forth nor the death that inevitably cycled with it. I drifted in that complacency, warmed by my core and no longer worried about anything. The world went on. It always would. Birthing pains faded away. I felt nothing, no conscious thought or fear to disrupt me. I spun, bound to my own heat and nothing more.

Something tickled inside my ear.

I ignored it, then swatted at it, writhing with irritation. The tickle turned into a stab of pain and I clawed at it, feeling like I was trying to scrape a needle from my eardrum. The pain grew, wriggling and pricking and poking, until it became a fierce, furious shriek, like a raptor's call. *Raptors don't hunt at night,* I thought peevishly. The idea bounced through me, shocking in that it was made of words and images. I clutched my head, an ache pounding through my temples and reminding me of myself. Reminding me of consciousness and of choice, rather than the act of simply being.

Faye's voice cut through the screeching birdcall in my head, whispering to me. I could feel the power of the coven behind her, lending her the strength necessary to work through the layers of earth that held me away from them. "Joanne, don't forget us. Remember our purpose. We can't lose you. Without you we'll fail and the world will die with us." Her voice was deeper than usual, older than I remembered it sounding, like it carried the weight of more than one speaker. It reverberated through the earth, making my skin itch and shudder as if I were a horse trying to dislodge a fly.

Remember. I struggled after Faye's words, trying to make sense of them. Remember what? Remember—

Remember *Gary*. Colin. *Coyote*. Remember the heat wave burning Seattle, spreading out to the world. Remember *who I am (Joanne Walker),* a back part of my mind said. A part further back, noisily, said, *Remember the Alamo!* and beneath that whispered another name to me, so hidden and soft that I couldn't let myself even think it, but I knew what it was. Who it was. Who I was.

I uncurled with a gasp, struggling back to my feet, grasping at an awareness of things like up and down and hot and cold. The earth shouted, ripping apart, as if protesting my actions and my free will.

The fire fell away from around my feet. I hung suspended in the air, my bones shaking and twisting and roaring disapproval. The coven disappeared, out of my inverted sight and out of my ability to sense them, leaving me alone with nothing except stars in the night sky and the treetops I was surrounded by.

A tremendous release of power hit me in the gut with the intensity of a waterfall. It knocked me ass over teakettle, endless roaring filling my ears. I slammed upside-down into one of the trees, crunching into branches with enough force to break them. I tumbled down, catching my shoulder on another branch and flipping right-side up again in time for a solid Y in the tree to catch me in the crotch and hold me. Disorientation smashed over me, leaving my mind blank of anything except an appreciation for excruciating pain. I hadn't done that since I was a kid, and I didn't miss it one bit at all. Poor men. Getting caught in the crotch made me wheeze and want to vomit. I couldn't and didn't much want to imagine what getting kicked in the nuts felt like.

Then a giant ripped the tree I was in out of the ground and flung it to the earth with a resounding, wet crash, and I stopped caring about anything for a while.

Tuesday, June 21, 5:45 a.m.

I was cold. Goose bumps were all over my skin, and my tank top was clammy and sticky against my back. I kept shivering.

After the last couple of days of heat, and the episode with the fire, I was surprised I could even be cold anymore. I lay there thinking about it, and wondering if I was broken anywhere or if I was just cold. There seemed to be a tree lying partly on top of me, which overall struck me as somewhat peculiar. I remembered being in the tree, but without opening my eyes—which I didn't much want to do—it felt like I was now lying in mud.

I moved my right hand very slightly, prodding at my resting place. Yes. Yes, it was mud. It schlucked and gooed and generally behaved like mud. Which was all wrong, because last time I was conscious it not only wasn't muddy, but hadn't rained in several weeks. Mud was very unusual. I wondered where exactly I was. There was a sound like thunder somewhere nearby, confusingly alien to the whisper of wind through trees that I last remembered. Well, that I last remembered in a world that made sense. There were dark places in my memory that I was reluctant to prod at yet. The mud and the thunder were enough for the moment.

My hand explored a little more, apparently content to

do this without me opening my eyes. I was grateful. Perhaps I could get my hand something nice later on, when I'd gotten up again. A manicure, perhaps, or a ring. No, not a ring. A ring would get all nasty with oil and grease. Didn't matter if I was a cop with a beat these days. I still thought of myself as a mechanic. I could start wearing the copper bracelet my father'd given me. It would look nice on my wrist, close to my hand. I thought my hand would like that. It seemed like a good idea, and I was satisfied.

There were branches and twigs in the mud, and then a puddle. The puddle surprised me enough that I opened my eyes.

It didn't help. Not that I couldn't see: I could. It was more that what I saw made no sense. Tree roots stuck up in the air, globs of dark earth hanging from them. Broken branches were strewn in every direction over a shattered landscape. There were huge humps of earth standing with their sides sheered away, looking precarious and wobbly without the support they used to have. One of them had a tree still standing on it, perfectly serene and unbothered by the changed world around it. Its roots stuck out of the sides of its earth pillar, reaching down for ground that had fallen away around it.

I lay in a low point. I pushed up on my elbows, the mud sucking at my face and chest before releasing me. The puddle my hand had discovered wasn't a puddle at all, but a stream that hadn't been there the last time I'd looked. It was muddy and thick and quite determined. If I listened I could hear its burble under the sound of thunder.

The thunder came from behind me. I pushed myself up

to hands and knees in slow motion, my entire body stiff with mud and sore muscles. I had to scrape my leg out from under the tree I'd fallen with, but I didn't seem to have taken much damage. As my hand sank into the mud, supporting my weight, I found that the tree was still beneath me, as well, just buried in the muck. It had very probably prevented me from drowning. I patted it with a fingertip and said, "Thanks," absently, then crawled around in a half circle to see where the thunder was coming from.

Even looking at it, it took several moments to wrap my mind around the idea that the waterfall I was staring at had formerly been the western side of Lake Washington. The ground had collapsed at least fifteen feet. I couldn't be sure if it was more, from where I rested on my hands and knees. It was a lot, anyway: fifteen feet is a lot when you're talking about where the ground used to be and isn't anymore.

The waterfall was broad and enthusiastic, tumbling down noisily and creating the stream my hand had discovered. I wondered if they'd let me call it Jo's Hand Stream. Probably not. That was okay. It was a terrible name. I sat back on my heels, cautiously, and stared. The sun was rising, painting the falls and the lake behind them a startling gold color. I had no sense of how long I'd been out, or how long the ritual the night before had gone on.

"Oh, Jesus." I staggered to my feet before consulting my body on whether it was a good idea or not. It wasn't an impossible feat, but I hung on my fallen tree for a few moments, trying to regain my sense of balance. The coven must have been caught in the earthquake just as I'd been. If any of them were still alive, I had to find them and get help.

"Jesus Christ, there's somebody over there. Hey. Hey! Lady! Are you okay?"

I wobbled around, trying to place the speaker over the sound of the waterfall. A man a few years older than I was appeared from around one of the tall earth humps, leaping gingerly over the stream and approaching me. "Hey, are you all right?"

"I'm not dead," I offered. The guy split a grin and jumped over another stream rivulet.

"Well, thank God. We didn't expect to find anybody alive down here."

My stomach fell through my feet. "You've found dead people?"

"Not so far. It's a goddamned miracle. Usually this time of year the parks are all madhouses, but it's so damned hot everybody's been at home with their air-conditioning." His expression darkened. He had sandy hair and blue eyes and the complexion of someone who spent a lot of time outdoors. "Not that that hasn't caused its own problems with this quake."

"What time did it hit?"

"'Bout ten o'clock last night. 6.2 on the Richter. You don't remember?"

"I got hit by a tree." My voice scraped and I coughed, trying to swallow the dryness away. "I don't remember much after that."

"Well, you're goddamned lucky," he opined. "We've got

to get you to a hospital, get you checked over. You know your name?"

I blinked at him. "Yeah." He waited, and I blinked some more before startling. "Oh! It's Joanne. Joanne Walker."

He stuck his hand out. "My name's Crowder. Geologist."

"Is 'Geologist' your first or last name?" I cracked a little grin as I shook his hand. He laughed.

"David Crowder, geologist. Damn, you are one lucky woman. C'mon. Let's get you out of here. Hey! Ricky! C'mon, help me get Miss Walker out of here! Somebody call an ambulance!"

"I don't need one," I protested. "As long as my car's still there. Oh God." Panic hit the pit of my stomach again. "Is it? Is the parking lot still there?"

Crowder hesitated. "Kinda. There are islands of it. What do you drive?"

I swallowed and knotted my hands into fists. My left hand suddenly cramped and split through the mud, starting to bleed again, and I fought back tears of pain and dismay. "A Mustang. A purple 1969 Mustang. License plates say PETITE."

Dismay washed over Crowder's face and he took a step back like I might kill the messenger. "I saw it tail-down in one of the crevasses. Looked like the back end got pretty badly crunched. We called it in. I'm sorry."

White rose up over my vision for a few seconds, static hissing in my ears. "How badly crunched?" My voice was hollow, and I don't think I expected Crowder to give me a real answer. The words just came out as an effort to not start screaming. "Were there any other cars up there?" My hands were cold and my stomach cramped, making some-thing go wrong with my eyesight. More wrong than usual: it was all blurry and stinging, the itch of unshed tears. I could handle pretty much anything, but not my car being destroyed. Between that and Gary I thought I might just throw up.

Crowder took my elbow and started leading me out of the mess that used to be a park. "I bet you can get it fixed." His encouraging words could've been coming from several light-years away. My head rang until I was dizzy, tipping over as I tried to put my feet on solid ground. "Might cost a bundle, but it can probably be winched out, or maybe helicoptered, and then you can really see the damage. But that solid steel frame'll keep it from being smashed up as some of the others up there, right? You're the first person we've found down here," he added, clearly hoping to change the subject. "Were you down here with anybody?"

"Some friends." My answer was low and fuzzy to my own ears, like somebody'd sucked all the life out of me. "I don't know what happened to them. I'm not sure when they left. Is there a search and rescue team out here?"

"Yeah, yeah, I'm part of it. You, ah, not sure when they left, huh?"

Oh, for God's sake. He thought we'd been doing drugs or something. I put my teeth together against a flare of rage that had more to do with my car than his assump-tion. "I wasn't paying a lot of attention to the time. No funny business going on. I'm a cop."

"Oh, no shit. You work in the North Precinct?"

"Yeah."

"No wonder."

I didn't like the sound of that at all. "No wonder what?"

"When we called in your car the dispatcher got a little freaked out. Said she had to verify it and she'd get back to us, but—"

"—but they recognized her. A lot of people know Petite." I groaned and closed my eyes, then opened them again swiftly, not trusting the ground or my feet. My left hand was still clenched in a fist. I didn't want to drip blood all over everything and have Crowder insist I go to a hospital. I wanted to look at the injury first and see if I could fix myself, preferably without a repeat of last night's heat-intense performance. I wanted to curl up in Petite's bucket seats and sob, too, but I didn't think I was going to get much of what I wanted. "I'll call them when we get up there."

"C'mon, this way." Crowder led me through a ravine of sharp drops and inclines, ushering me up a hill that I tried climbing without using my left hand. He noticed and stopped me, putting his hand out for mine. I sighed and opened my palm.

Blood seeped through cracks of mud, dripping off the back of my hand. It only hurt on a dull, ignorable level, but Crowder hissed dismay and yanked a handkerchief out of a pocket. "It's clean," he promised as he wrapped it around my hand. "That looks deep. You're gonna need to get it looked at."

"I know. I will. I just want to get to my car and go home and call my friends and make sure everybody's okay first. How…is the city okay? I mean, are people…dead?"

"Some injuries." Crowder started up the hill again. "A handful of heart attacks, a couple dozen women going into labor, that kinda thing. It happens, when there's an earthquake. Lotta property damage, but it's pretty localized. Weird behavior. That Corvalis woman on Channel Two is trying like mad to tie it together to the aurora the other night. Swear to God, those people, making news when there's so much real stuff to report. Here you go, just over the guard rail here." He boosted me up and I swung my leg over the railing, trying not to think about whether there was a connection between the aurora and the earthquake. People don't cause earthquakes. It was a ludicrous idea. Of course, people don't cause massive auroras to come sweeping down, either, and I knew perfectly well the coven and I had been responsible for that, even if the interpretation was wrong.

The parking lot was a disaster. Petite's nose poked up out of a ditch several yards away. Between me and her, there were pits of earth that had opened up or split apart. The car Garth had driven was stuck halfway in one of the pits. It'd be okay if it could be winched out. I jumped a crack in the earth and hurried toward Petite, swallowing against sickness as I looked down into the crevasse at her smashed back end. She was a heavy vehicle, but Crowder was right about the steel frame. Even from above I could tell that the damage was probably more to the tail lights and back fender than to the body. I couldn't, at least, *see* any wrinkles in her body, which didn't necessarily mean they weren't there. I was going to have to find a way to get her out of there and into a garage where I could really survey the damage. My hands were shaking and my throat was tight. I didn't want to burst into tears in front of the helpful geologist, but I wasn't sure I'd be able to stop myself. I turned my back on him deliberately and knelt by Petite's front end, putting my forehead against the wheel still hooked over the broken earth. "I am so sorry, baby. I'll get you out of here and I'll get you fixed up, okay? And then we'll go on a really nice long drive out to Utah where we can go super fast on the salt flats. That'll be fun, right, sweetheart? I'm so sorry, baby. I'm so sorry."

"Miss Walker?" Crowder's diffident voice came from behind me, a polite intrusion. I looked up, swallowing back the tightness in my throat, expecting the geologist to be offering some kind of sympathy or suggestion.

What I found instead was Morrison vaulting the parking lot gates and coming at a run toward me and my car.

CHAPTER TWENTY-FIVE

Morrison had me by the shoulders before I had time to think through the idea of hiding. His grip was hard enough to hurt, although I noticed the skin-tenderness of the sunburn was gone. He had the slight height advantage even though he was out of uniform, and for a few seconds he stared down at me as if making sure I was real. Then he shook me, let go of my shoulders, and started yelling.

I didn't listen. I just looked up at him, trying not to smile. He would have gotten up at five in the morning for a report that any of his officers was missing. I knew that. What I hadn't known was he'd get up if the officer in question was me. I wrapped my filthy arms around my ribs and watched him rant. Crowder hovered nervously on the next island over, trying to decide if he should interfere. I hoped he didn't. I'd never felt so warm and fuzzy at receiving a dressing-down. When Morrison finally paused for breath I said, "Thanks, Captain."

He didn't start up again. Instead he pulled his mouth long, scowled, and gave me a curt nod. Then he turned away, jumping to Crowder's asphalt island with more grace than I would've expected from him, and offered the geologist his hand. "Thanks for finding my officer. I'm Captain Michael Morrison, SPD, North Precinct."

"Well, she was up on her feet already when I found her. She would've been just fine even without us." Crowder shook Morrison's hand. "David Crowder. Pleasure to meet you, sir. I'm glad to say it looks like Officer Walker was the only person caught in the park last night. Looks like we may have no casualties from the event itself. We've been very lucky."

I closed my eyes and leaned on Petite's upended nose. No one in the coven had mentioned earthquakes accompanying the body-to-earth ritual. I wondered if they hadn't known, or if it had been an error. I was hoping for an error. Knowing you were going to set off a 6.2 quake and opting to stay in a populated area was criminal, not that there was the slightest chance they'd—we'd—ever be prosecuted for it.

And I wondered if it had worked. From what I understood, there ought to be all sorts of strange and mystical creatures wandering Seattle's streets now, but Morrison hadn't mentioned any while he was yelling at me. I'd have to find Faye or one of the others.

Or, I supposed, I'd have to go look for myself. I opened

my eyes again and studied the parking lot without seeing it, trying to figure out how long it would take to get Petite out of there. I didn't want to leave her, not with the lake pouring a new stream into the neighborhood. I was afraid the exposed earth would be cut away and she'd fall.

"What happened, Walker?"

I jostled myself out of studying the parking lot and looked back at Morrison, who'd rejoined me while I wasn't watching. "Sir?"

"What happened out here last night? What were you doing here? And have you been tanning?" He was getting over his relief that I was alive and was becoming more interested in the bones of the matter, which probably meant in relatively short order he'd be yelling at me again.

I looked down at myself. My vision behaved itself for once and I realized the sunburn had done more than come to the surface. It'd already peeled, or the mystical equivalent thereof. I was brown, tanner than I could ever remember seeing myself. I resisted the urge to peer down my shirt to see if I was tan all over. I hadn't been naked in the desert of my mind, but I wasn't at all sure a sunburn like the one I'd gotten there would care about clothes. I suspected there were no tan lines.

"I was meeting Faye. The girl from Cassandra's funeral." It wasn't exactly a lie. I didn't think Morrison cared all that much about whether I'd been tanning, so I skipped that part.

"Walker, I thought I told you to leave it alone." He didn't sound exasperated, much less surprised. More like resigned.

"Yeah." I looked away. "Meeting her was set up before you told me that."

"What were you seeing her for?"

"...she was working on a project with Cassandra before she died. She thought I might be able to help out with it." Again, not exactly a lie. I was pretty sure Morrison would be happier if I didn't tell him Cassie was part of a coven and I was taking her place. My vision swam to inverted again, giving me a sudden headache as the rising sun turned black. I winced and put my hand against my temple. Morrison reached out and caught my wrist, turning my palm up.

"What happened?"

I stared at Crowder's bloody handkerchief wrapped around my hand and sagged. "I was gouged. It was kind of a rough night."

"So I see. You need to get cleaned up and get this looked at. My car's up at the head of the street. You're not getting yours out of here without a helicopter."

I clenched my jaw against dismay and patted Petite's nose carefully. "It's okay, baby. I'll figure out how to get you out of here." I didn't think I'd spoken loudly enough for Morrison to hear, even though he was barely two feet away from me. The look he gave me said he had.

"What is it with you and cars, Walker?"

"They're easier than people." I tugged my hand out of Morrison's grip, trying to be gentle enough about it that it wouldn't seem rude. He let me go without a fuss. I felt him watching me as I hopped to another broken island. After a few seconds he followed me.

We walked in silence up to the head of the road, jumping over broken land where we needed to. I felt like I should say something just to fill up the quiet between us, but I had no idea how to make small talk with Morrison. He pulled ahead of me by a couple of steps and my mouth asked, "How old are you, Morrison?" without consulting my brain about it first.

Morrison threw a startled look over his shoulder. "What? Thirty-eight. Why?"

"Faye wanted to know."

"I don't need setting up with a girl half my age, Walker." Morrison pulled ahead of me again, leaving me blinking at his shoulders. There wasn't, as far as I knew, a Mrs. Morrison. He didn't wear a wedding band, and he seemed the type. I reengaged my brain before it asked him any more questions, and scowled at my feet as I followed him. My hands wanted to go into my pockets, but my left hand kept screeching protest. In order to give myself something to do, I caught up with Morrison, matching my pace to his.

"How old are you?"

"What?" I missed a step, caught my toes on broken earth, and regained my balance before Morrison had time to help me, which I wasn't sure he would.

"How old are you?" he repeated with a reasonable degree of patience.

"Isn't that kind of thing on my official records?"

"Yeah, but so's 'Joanne Walker.'"

I pursed my lips. "A very palpable hit. Twenty-seven." I hesitated. "Did you look?"

"At your records? Yes. They're all under Walker. Why?" Morrison didn't sound even slightly apologetic. I wouldn't have either, in his position.

I shrugged. "Defining myself by my own rules, I guess."

"There's no paperwork filed for an official change of name."

"You did your homework, didn't you?" I shrugged again. Morrison's car was at the head of a cross street, parked just before a dark crack in the road. "I didn't feel like I needed to, I guess. I broke into my school computer to change my last name to Walker on the transcripts and never had a problem with the university systems, so why bother with the paperwork." I was pretty sure the statute of limitations on hacking my own transcripts was long past. I hoped so. Morrison would probably arrest me if it weren't. He lifted an eyebrow at me, then nodded at the car. I jumped the crevasse—it was deeper than I expected, probably six feet—and waited for him to unlock the doors. He was already on the radio, reporting me as alive and well, when I crawled in. There were actually cheers from the dispatch room. I felt my cheeks sting with color, and stared out the window. The sunlight, still inverted in my vision, bled silver and black over the horizon as it climbed. "Crap."

Morrison glanced at me as he put the car in drive. "What?"

"I'm late for a meeting."

"It's six in the morning."

"I know. Can you just drive me home?"

Morrison's silence was profound before curiosity got the better of him. "You've got a 6:00 a.m. date at home?"

I slumped in my seat. "Yeah. You know. That boyfriend you didn't believe in."

Morrison snorted. I guessed he still didn't believe. "You need to get that hand looked at."

"I need a shower. If I can't fix it I'll go to the ER."

"If you can't fix it." The skepticism in Morrison's voice was thin. He'd watched me recover from impossible injuries enough times to know I could do it, even if he didn't want to believe it. I felt an unexpected pang of sympathy for him.

I pushed myself up in the seat, toes pressed against the back of the footwell. "Forget I said anything."

"Walker—"

"Really, Morrison, forget it. You'll be happier that way." I glared out the window, wishing I'd kept my mouth shut and just gone to the damned hospital with him. A ten point buck, its antlers glowing an unhealthy neon yellow, bounded out of the greenery at the side of the road and into the car. I yelled, flinging my arms up as if I could ward off the animal's impact. Morrison yelled, too, slamming on the brakes.

"What the *hell* was that?"

"The *deer!* It almost hit the car!"

Morrison stared at me with furious concern that almost masked a complete lack of comprehension. "*What* deer?"

"The—" It dawned on me that there'd been no impact, nor any scrape of hooves over the car's roof. I flinched forward, looking beyond Morrison at the street. There was no sign of the animal anywhere. My voice got very small. "You didn't see it?"

"See *what*, Walker? Jesus Christ! What the hell's the matter with you?"

I stared at the quiet street. "I thought I saw a deer. A buck. Come out of the woods and jump at the car."

Morrison frowned and reached for my head, running a hand through my dirty hair. Mud flaked away, showering down the back of my tank top and leaving his fingers a muddy tan. I pulled away, frowning in return. "What?"

"Seeing if there are any lumps on your head. You sure you didn't hit your head, Walker?"

"No."

He kept frowning at me. "We're going to the hospital."

I sighed and slumped down in my seat again. "Yes, sir."

I had enough sense—barely—to bite my tongue when I saw the grizzly roaming unconcerned down the middle of the street, and to close my eyes and count to ten and hope the eagle sitting on the stoplight would disappear when I opened my eyes. It didn't, but that gave me enough time to be absolutely certain Morrison wasn't seeing it. Bald eagles do not hang out in suburban Seattle frequently enough to go uncommented on. But an utterly gorgeous thing with a bear's head and a glittering body, scaled like a fish, made me gasp out loud and sit forward, which in turn made Morrison frown at me even more deeply. I couldn't help it. It was beautiful, covered in iridescent reds and blues, with enormous teeth and tall deer horns. Beautiful and totally alien. It belonged in a picture book of mythology, not on a corner with its tail lashing, looking as if it were impatient to cross the street.

Whatever else had happened last night, we'd clearly succeeded in giving the spirits body. What I didn't understand was why Morrison wasn't seeing them. I clenched my eyes shut and my teeth together as we drove through a hippogryph, which I wouldn't have betted on recognizing before I saw one. And that gave me some of my answer: there had to be a third step to the ritual that would make them solid. I could see them because…

God. Because I believed. The very thought made my head hurt. I put both hands against my temples and groaned. Morrison frowned at me again. "You okay?"

"I don't know. Ask me again tomorrow."

"I'll ask you again after you've seen a doctor." Morrison flicked a blinker on and I groaned again, watching Northwest Hospital come into view. I was spending way too much time there. A minute later he found a parking place, meaning I wasn't going to get away with watching him drive off and then running home. "Out," he said.

I got out, thinking that at least Judy and my spirit animals would be pleased. I was taking their advice to heart, and to active effect. I, on the other hand, wasn't thrilled. I was happier with the world when I couldn't see the magical things in it. Even if this was exactly the path I was supposed to be on. I made a gurgling sound of frustration in the back of my throat and Morrison shot me a concerned glare. "Walker?"

I was clearly too unused to having somebody else around. I needed to learn to stop vocalizing my internal annoyances. Either that or I needed to obtain a significant other so I could just tell people like Morrison to hand me over to him and stop worrying about me. At this point, the former seemed more likely. "Nothing. I'm fine. Honest. Can't I just go home?"

"No."

I slunk off to see a doctor. Morrison told them I was having hallucinations, and they tested my eyes after they'd stitched my hand up. The light shining into my pupils looked black to me, but my responses were all right and they told me I could go home. I very carefully didn't mention the bright-eyed rabbit spirit sitting in the corner.

Morrison dropped me off at home, still scowling. "Get some rest, Walker. That's an order."

I got out of the car, smiling. "I'm not on duty, Captain."

"You will be tomorrow, and if you don't do what I tell you now, I'll make your life a living hell," he said pleasantly. I laughed, straightened, and saluted the roof of his car.

"Yessir, Cap'nsir." I thumped the car and watched him drive off before heading into the building. About twenty-four hours of sleep sounded really appealing, truth be told. Of course, there were about eight reasons why I wasn't going to get that, so dwelling on it would probably only make me miserable. I climbed into the shower, sat down on the tub floor, and went to see if Judy was still waiting for me while hot water beat the night's grime off my skin.

CHAPTER TWENTY-SIX

She was, and she was agitated, pacing my garden with her skirt a-swirl. I sat where I was for a few seconds, watching her. Unlike Phoebe, she was far from an economy of motion. Every step she took seemed to eat up too much space, as if there was too little control behind it. She looked like she might fly apart at any moment.

Moreover, my garden looked terrible. The grass was curling brown and the sky flat with dust. Even the pool was dull, like someone'd poured charcoal over its surface and the particles hung there, distorting the water's ability to reflect. I looked up at the sky, wondering if I could convince it to rain. It didn't start to, so I shrugged and looked back at Judy. "How do you end up here, anyway, when I'm not here?"

She flinched, hands rising up from her sides a few inches, like a startled bird fluttering its wings. I hid a grin, suddenly seeing her as the black-eyed raven. She spun to face me, skirt whirling again. "*There* you are. We were worried. Where have you been?"

"We?"

Her eyebrows crinkled together. "The spirit animals and me. You're late."

"I didn't know spirit animals got worried." I glanced around, didn't see them, and shrugged it off. "Sorry I'm late. It was a rough night. Anyway, so how can you be in my garden? How can you be waiting for me here?"

"You expect me to be here," Judy said. "It gives me access."

For a moment I thought I heard Marcia's voice saying, "It's a matter of expectation," and frowned at Judy. She didn't look anything like Marcia, even after the whole knife incident. The truth of the matter was probably that expectation colored a lot of what I did, or what I was supposed to do. I said, "Okay," through a yawn, and nodded. At least I'd gotten a night's sleep, even if it'd been in a fallen tree.

Judy came and crouched in front of me. "You've changed a great deal."

I tried to speak through another yawn and gleeked instead, then coughed as I clapped my hand over my mouth. My eyes teared with the effort of the whole thing and it took two swallows before I was able to say, "I have?" I glanced down at myself again. My new suntan hadn't followed me into my garden. Too much self-perception tied up in being pale-skinned. The tan probably wouldn't last long enough for that to change. Still, it was a nice compliment. It made me feel like maybe I was doing something right with the whole mystical lifestyle thing.

Judy's pause stretched on long enough to be audible. I blinked up at her, curious, to find her mouth pursed. "I meant the world around you," she said gently. "You've changed a great deal out there."

"Oh." I felt foolish, a blush burning my ears. The tan might've been useful to hide that. And here I thought I'd been doing so well. Judy put her hand on my shoulder, smiling.

"I'm sorry. I didn't mean to hurt your feelings. I think that you're able to affect these changes means you're finally beginning to accept your own gifts, Joanne. The world around you isn't the only thing that's changed." She sat down across from me, folding her legs under herself tidily.

A little surge of happy pride tingled through me. I ducked my head, feeling ridiculous. I'd practically asked for the clarified compliment. It made me happy anyway. "So what's on the agenda for today, bo—" I bit off the word. I called Morrison boss. For some reason I didn't want to share his word with Judy.

I'd never put it in so many words, but it occurred to me that I had some interesting hang-ups about Morrison.

I put the thought firmly out of my mind. "What's on the agenda?"

Judy leaned forward, suddenly full of intensity. It lit her eyes, making them blacker and brighter, reminding me of

Virissong as he'd told his story to me. Which also reminded me that I'd wanted to ask him more questions, but
it was going to have to wait until after the solstice ritual.
At least then I'd be able to talk to him face-to-face. "I want
to talk to you about tonight's ritual."

I sat up straighter and looked around with a nervous
laugh. "Are you reading my mind? I was just thinking
about that."

Judy smiled. "No. I can't read your mind."

"Really? Everybody else can."

Judy's eyebrows rose slowly. "They can?"

I waved it off. "Never mind. What'd you want to talk
about, about tonight?"

Judy's eyebrows remained elevated for a few moments,
but she nodded. "You'll be asked a great deal tonight, Joanne. More than has been asked of you in the past."

More than having a sword stuffed in me? I didn't ask the
question out loud, just nodded attentively like a good
student. "Virissong will complete his journey tonight and
return to the Middle World. He may need to rely heavily
on your strength."

"How do you know that?"

Judy smiled. "Teaching you isn't the only thing I do.
Since you mentioned him and have spoken with him, I've
been looking in to the rituals you and the coven are pursuing. It's quite clear that they have the desire, but you
have the power, to help Virissong bridge the worlds. It's
part of why I'm so pleased at how far you've come in acceptance the past few days. Your belief strengthens us all."

I felt another warm little glow of pride tingle around the

back of my neck. Doing things right could get addictive, if people were going to keep complimenting me for them. My vision went inverted and I shook my head, rubbing my eyes. Judy's voice lifted with concern. "Are you all right?"

"Yeah. Just, my vision's been all funky for a few days. Ever since—" Reticence popped through again. I hadn't told Judy about the talk with Big Coyote in the desert, and didn't really want to. I didn't want to talk to anybody about that yet. The déjà vu brought on by Cassandra's funeral after the desert still made me uncomfortable, sufficiently uncomfortable that I didn't want to think about it. My vision narrowed down again and I pressed the heels of my hands against my eyes, making black sunbursts behind my eyelids. "Ever since the first ritual." It was close enough.

"Ah." Judy didn't sound surprised. I squinted my eyes open to find her nodding wisely. "It's the power you're using, almost certainly. Think of it like stretching muscles you're not accustomed to. You'll adjust."

"Before I go blind?" I muttered. I stopped rubbing my eyes, but the after-images of darkness still hung around the edges of my vision. It was like looking into binoculars. "Anyway, thanks. So I've noticed some people aren't seeing the spirit animals out there. What's up with that?"

"A matter of faith." Judy hesitated. "And maybe something more. You released a great deal of power last night. I'm not entirely sure it went the way it was intended to."

I made a face. "Yeah, I kind of got that with the whole massive earthquake thing. I hope that was an accident."

Judy shook her head. "I'm sure it was. And tonight's ritual should finish everything and put it all back to rights. You'll have to be brave tonight, Joanne. It's going to be hard."

"I can handle it. I just lived through being the epicenter of an earthquake, after all." My, wasn't I brash and cocky. Judy smiled at me.

"Good. I think we'll move on to your next lesson in the morning. You should save your strength for tonight, now. You'll be ready, in the morning."

"You sure I won't be all burned out?"

"Positive. It's the nature of sacrifice, after all. The more you give, the more of you there is to give."

That sounded very mystical and reassuring. "All right. I'll see you tomorrow, then."

Judy nodded. "Tomorrow. Good luck tonight."

"Thanks." I opened my eyes, still sitting under hot shower water. I felt cleaner and almost ready to face the day, even though my vision was still tunneled. I tried blinking it away and succeeded in blinking water into my eyes, nothing more. Oh well, it'd faded before.

The phone rang and I leaped out of the tub, all elbows and knees and flailing as I ran for it. I didn't know why I was in such a hurry; my answering machine worked just fine. Telephones caused a Pavlovian response in me. Someday I was going to spend a few weeks training myself out of it, so that when a telemarketer called I didn't compulsively leap up and race to see who it was. Possibly the whole training prospect would be more successful if I got more than one phone call a week.

I knocked the phone's base off the nightstand as I snatched the receiver up, gasping, "Hello?" into it. Thank God genuine video phones hadn't been invented. I hadn't even grabbed a towel. Ford Prefect would despair of me.

"Joanie? You okay? This's Billy."

"Oh. Hi. Yeah. I was in the shower, that's all. What's up?" My heart rate slowing down, I edged back into the bathroom to reach for a towel. The phone cord wouldn't reach. I stretched as far as I could, an awkward naked ballet, trying to snag the towel with my fingertips as Billy spoke.

"What the hell happened last night?"

"You sound like Morrison. What do you mean?"

"Earthquakes and monsters roaming the streets? Ring a bell?"

My foot slid out from under me. I seized the towel on my way down, but it didn't provide any kind of support. I crashed to the floor, banging most parts of my body on the floor, the doorjamb, and the falling towel rack, variously. I lay there, afraid to even groan while I judged whether anything was badly injured, then fumbled for the phone, I'd dropped sometime during my dramatic descent.

"Joanie? Joanne? Are you all right? Joanie? Jesus Christ! Jo—"

"I'm okay," I announced, hoping it wasn't an overstatement.

"What the hell happened?"

"I fell." I sat up cautiously, trying to extract my leg from around the door frame. "I think I'm okay. Um. Monsters roaming the streets?"

"Don't play dumb with me."

"I'm not. I just didn't know anybody else could see them." Although if anybody could, of course it would be Billy. My friend the True Believer.

"Well, I promise you, it's not just me. The station's hopping like a madhouse. Calls coming in from all over the city, some of them from people who're seeing things and lots from people who think their friends have lost their minds."

"You the only one there?"

Billy understood what I meant, even if the question hadn't come anywhere near asking it. "No, there's me and Jen Gonzales in Missing Persons and a bunch of people from your little séance back in January. I donno who else."

"It wasn't a séance."

"Joanne!"

I'd never heard Billy sound so annoyed. I winced, clutching my towel against my chest. "Yeah, sorry, not a good time for arguing details. Look, I'll…" What the hell was I going to do? "I'll come down to the station. I don't know what good I can do, but somebody else on duty can't hurt, at least."

"Forget coming to the station, Joanie. Figure out what's going on. Gimme a call when you know. Maybe we can figure out how to fix it."

"It'll be fixed tonight," I said without thinking. I could all but hear Billy shake his head.

"Tonight might not be soon enough. Get busy, Joanie. This is important." He hung up. I got dressed and went to find Faye.

* * *

Actually, I got dressed, went outside, and discovered my car wasn't there. How quickly we forget. I swore and went back upstairs to call a cab.

It took forty-five minutes to arrive. I desperately wished Gary was on duty, and not just because he always managed to dump his current fare and come skidding to my doorstop when I needed a ride. He'd delivered me to a crime scene back in March, and had been terribly sulky that Morrison wouldn't let him hang around and gawk. I wanted him to be there to gawk with me.

I made two loops around my block while I waited for the cab, checking out the havoc caused by the earthquake and the spirits running amok. There was often a drunk or two sleeping it off in the park across the street from my apartment building, but this morning everyone, even the drunks, was awake and a little wild-eyed. Apparently seeing spirits all over will sober a person right up.

And there were more and more of them, and they were becoming more solid. I watched a moose cross in front of me and dent the grass it stepped on, although it didn't stay bent. I kept side-stepping around things that weren't quite real, often into things that were, like a jogger who stopped and yelled at me for three minutes straight. At least he was keeping his heart rate up. Just about everyone was crabby, either from seeing animals that couldn't possibly be there, or from having to deal with people who were having hallucinations. I didn't know which group I felt sorrier for. Both, maybe. The coven and I had disturbed the natural order of things. I wondered if it'd ever really been like this, thousands of years ago, with so many spirits roaming free. I wasn't sure our modern world could adapt to it.

The cab ride to the station was frustrating. There were now creatures settling themselves in the middle of the road, deliberately springing toward moving vehicles as if they were prey. Sometimes vehicles ended up with visible impact marks from monsters smashing into them; other cars would just suddenly swerve and crash into something. Earthquake debris littering the streets made more than enough targets to bash against, even if other vehicles weren't on the roads. I clenched my fingers around the cab's armrest and threw banishment thoughts at the spirits with all my strength. It didn't help.

I wished again Gary was the one driving my cab, partly because I suspected he'd be able to see the monsters. Even if he couldn't, it didn't matter, because he wouldn't think I was crazy, which would be good enough. He also wouldn't let the meter run up—probably—while I got out to try to deal with both wrecks and spirit animals. My teeth began to hurt from pressing them together so hard. I wished Coyote was there—my coyote, Little Coyote— to tell me what to do, but I couldn't even concentrate enough to slip into the otherworld. I was going to have to help on my own.

I overpaid the cabby and went into the precinct with my shoulders hunched around my ears. There weren't that many spirits infesting the precinct building, except near the windows. Too much concrete and too many straight lines, I thought. Cernunnos and his lot hadn't been overwhelmingly delighted with rigid man-made structures either. Maybe it was something otherworldly creatures had in common. I didn't care: it was a little relief from the bizarreness outside, and I took what I could get.

"You been on vacation, Joey?"

"What?" I nearly started out of my skin, then wished I didn't feel like that was a genuine possibility. A friend of mine, Ray, leaned out of a doorway I'd passed. He wasn't wearing his hat, but I could see the ring where sweat had matted his hair against his head.

"You're tan. Been on vacation?" Ray was short and bulky and solid, like a human bunker. Explaining to him about my mystically induced tan would've been like explaining quantum physics to a hippo. I wasn't up to either task.

"Got too much sun, anyway."

"Looks good," Ray offered, then tilted his head back at the main doors. "It's balls-busting nuts out there." He disappeared back into the office, having delivered his piece. I rubbed my breastbone, blinking, then shook my head and went looking for Morrison to see if he'd let me borrow a patrol car until I could rescue Petite or get a rental.

I found Billy instead. He came around a corner like a wrecking ball, nearly bowling me over. I stepped back, flattening myself against the wall, and he lumbered past me, then drew up and turned back with a glare. Sweat rolled down his face, too pink with exertion and the lack of air-conditioning. "You're not supposed to be here."

"I don't have a car, Billy. I need to see if I can borrow one. And Christ, somebody needs to be here. It's nuts out there." I twitched my nose, annoyed at my mouth for stealing Ray's words. At least I'd avoided the balls-busting part.

"Yeah. Look." Billy curled his fingers around my upper arm and drew me aside, not that there was a great deal of traffic that required avoiding. His voice dropped low enough that I leaned in to hear him better. "I couldn't talk about this on the phone, Joanie. Whatever's going on here is upsetting Mel in a big way."

My stomach tightened up as I looked at Billy's expanded paunch. "How big?"

"Bad cramps and nerves. The doctor told her to stay on bed rest for a couple days. It's almost impossible with the rest of the kids, especially with me not being there, but—"

"But she is, isn't she, Billy?" My voice rose too high and Billy tightened his fingers around my arm. I knotted my right hand into a fist, my left too damaged to curl more than a few centimeters closed. "You want me to go take care of the kids? Is there anybody else with her?"

Relief paled Billy's face so sharply I thought he must be in pain. "Her Mom's flying in, but she's in Arizona and can't get here until tomorrow. If you could—"

"Yeah." I cut him off with a sharp movement of my hand. "Of course, Billy. I'll try to see if there's anything I can do about—the rest of it, but at least I can take care of the kids and take a load off Mel's mind. Is there anything I oughta pick up on the way over?"

"Tranquilizers," he said, only half-kidding. I pulled up the best smile I could.

"For the kids, or for Melinda?"

Billy laughed, startled. "I meant the kids, but it might

be more effective to give them to Mel. Look, I'm sorry if I was short with you on the phone—"

I grabbed his hand. "You weren't. It's okay. I'll go take care of them, Billy. Isn't that what cops are supposed to do? Don't worry. It's going to be fine."

CHAPTER TWENTY-SEVEN

Billy called ahead to let Mel and the kids know I was coming. I stopped for loot on the way over and pulled up their driveway in the borrowed patrol car. I got out and pushed the gate—an actual white picket fence—open and wended my way through the overgrown herb garden that made up the Holliday front yard. It was almost cool under the shade of a couple of enormous birch trees that filtered sunlight down to the ground.

The two oldest kids, Robert and Clara, met me at the front door with serious expressions. I put my bag of loot down on the porch and ruffled Rob's hair. At eleven, he was starting to have distinct opinions about his own dignity, so when he didn't duck out from under my hand, I knew things were dire indeed. "Hey, guys. How's your Mom?"

"Grumpy." Clara hooked her arm around my hips and leaned on me. "She doesn't like staying in bed."

"Me either. Where's Jacquie and Erik?"

"Taking a nap," Robert reported. "I told 'em they had to be extra good 'cause Mom's sick. Is she gonna be okay, Joanne?"

"Yeah." I pulled Robert over to my other hip to hug him. "And I'm here to sit on you guys and make sure everybody's good and take care of your mom if she needs it, okay?"

"We're *being* good," Clara insisted. "It's awful hot. Can we go get some ice cream?"

"Maybe later. How about a drink now? Lemonade?" The kids were so assured it made me feel better.

"Can't," Robert said. "There's a thing in the kitchen."

So much for feeling better. "A thing?"

"A Thing," Clara repeated, imbuing the word with a capital letter. "We didn't want to tell Mom."

"The doctor said she had to stay in bed," Robert explained. I smiled a bit.

"Yeah, and a Thing would probably make her get up. You guys are good kids."

"Yeah," Robert agreed. I grinned more broadly.

"Modest, too. Okay. Let me go say hi to your mom, and then I'll come look at this Thing, okay?"

Robert and Clara exchanged glances, considering the proposal, then nodded. "Okay," Robert said. "Can we set up the water slide on the lawn?"

I pursed my lips. "Let me see if your mom's up to all that noise, okay? I'll help you if she is. Otherwise it'll be

Parcheesi or something. Something quiet." I inevitably lost at Parcheesi, Monopoly, and pretty much every other board game ever played. I blamed it on never learning the rules properly as a child. On the other hand, I could identify more vehicles at a glance than most people could in a lifetime, which was enough of a party trick for me.

The kids exchanged glances again. "You've never played Parcheesi with us, have you?" Clara asked. "It's not quiet."

I grinned. "We'll have to make do. Tiptoe in and check on your little brother and sister while I check on your mom."

"Okay!" They ran off, sounding less like a herd of elephants than I'd ever heard them before. I kicked my sandals off before going to visit Melinda.

The Hollidays' house was the kind of place I'd always wanted to live in and never had the foggiest idea why I should. It was in a better part of the North Precinct, far enough north that when Billy'd bought it, it'd been unfashionable and comparatively inexpensive. It'd started with four bedrooms and had expanded to six, with hardwood floors scarred from kids and dogs running rampant over them. The backyard was enormous and usually had a croquet set and a badminton net set up. It looked exactly like the kind of place a person would want to raise a herd of children. I couldn't imagine what I'd do with it, but I coveted it anyway.

The stairs up to the bedrooms squeaked as I took them two at a time. Somehow the kids always ran them without making them squeak, although it didn't do a thing for silencing their approaches or departures. Melinda heard me coming and called, "Joanne? Is that you?"

"Yeah." I appeared in her doorway, smiling. "I squeak too much to be the kids, huh?" Clara was right: Mom was grumpy. Her color was off and for once she didn't look perfect. Her hair was up in a tangled ponytail and she was wearing an orange shirt that I recognized as Billy's, soft and comforting but a bad color for her. Her eyebrows were pulled down and her mouth was turned in a frown.

"Come on in. Thanks for coming over." The frown fled into a grateful smile. I padded in and sat on the edge of the bed.

"Not a problem. Are you about to die of boredom?"

"Yes. And I've only been here three hours."

I laughed. "I'm surprised you've stayed still that long. I brought you some stuff."

"If it's knitting, I'm going to poke your eyes out with the needles," Melinda warned, then shook her head. "I couldn't get up if I wanted to. All I have to do is remember how scared Bill looked and I don't even want to move." She pulled her lower lip into her mouth and frowned out the window. I touched her arm.

"Hey. It's okay, huh? You don't have to be tough if you don't want to. I won't tell anybody." My heart hurt for her. "It's gonna be fine, Mel. You just take it easy. Anyway, I brought trashy romance novels, not knitting, and a pint of chocolate fudge brownie delight ice cream."

"That's my favorite!"

I grinned. "Yeah, Billy told me. He thought maybe if you

were stuck in bed for a while he could get you to gain some weight instead of him."

To my relief, she laughed. "Isn't that just like a man. Always thinking of himself." Her eyes brightened and she looked away again. I busied myself hauling stuff out of plastic bags until she cleared her throat and said, "Thanks."

"No problem." I looked up again with a smile. "Rob wanted to know if they could put the water slide out on the back lawn. It's that or Parcheesi. What's your vote?"

"The water slide is okay. I didn't want them to get the lawn all soaked because of the party tonight, but—"

"Oh, crap, right."

Melinda gave me a dirty look. "You'd forgotten, hadn't you." Then she frowned. "Joanne, have you been tanning?"

I groaned, half-laughing. "Sort of. It's a long story."

"I may be stuck here a while," she said dryly. I lifted up my hands and she gawked, grabbing my left wrist so she could turn my injured palm up. "What happened?"

"…part of the same long story. I'll tell you about it," I said hastily. "I promise. Let me get the kids going with the water slide first, okay? We'll come play Parcheesi in here this afternoon so you're not trapped in the twilight zone alone all day, and I'll call to let people know the party's canceled."

She let go of my wrist reluctantly. "I guess so. Unless you've got a 'get out of bed free' pass handy?"

For an instant I hoped the power inside me would rise to the challenge, but it didn't so much as stir. I shook my head and pasted on a rueful grin. "'Fraid not. Just tell me where to find the guest list."

"How organized she thinks I am," Mel said to the ceiling. "Guest list, *dias mía.* Bill's telling the guys at the precinct, and I think I can give you the rest of the names."

"Okay." I produced a plastic spoon and the pint of ice cream from the plastic bag. "Eat, gain, and be merry. I shall return anon, once the kids are settled outside." And once I was done dealing with the Thing in the kitchen. I stood, saluted smartly, and left Melinda smiling behind me.

I helped the two older kids set up the slide, which is to say I set it up while they got their younger siblings and everyone, including the two-year-old, stood around telling me what I was doing wrong. Despite my incompetence, they seemed pleased with the results, and I left them alone, shrieking and sliding across the plastic mat in freezing cold hose water. Then I went to investigate the Thing in the kitchen.

I felt it when I got to the dining room. I could even see it, a malevolent silver glow that bled through the walls. My steps slowed until I felt like Cinderella stuck in the pitch. I had to look at my feet to realize that I was not, in fact, moving forward anymore. No wonder the kids hadn't wanted to go into the kitchen. I lifted my chin and kept going, feeling like I was trying to walk through a marshmallow. The air pressed back at me, soft and sticky and thick. I breathed through my nose, deliberate deep breaths, and pushed through it. When I reached the kitchen door, the thickness shattered like a soap bubble and I was able to draw in one normal breath.

It seemed like a long time before I took the next one.

There was more than a Thing in the kitchen; the Thing had filled the kitchen almost entirely. Enormous silver coils piled on the counters and stuffed the corners of the room. A shadow of my own reflection bounced across glittering white scales that weren't quite solid enough yet to make a true reflection. A heavy head lifted out of the coils and flat white eyes stared down at me.

It was smaller than it had been in the Dead Zone. Its head was only the length of my body. When it opened its mouth, hissing silently with the gray-white tongue flicking out to taste the air, its fangs were only half my size. As I watched, though, it…popped. Cartilage and muscle bulged with audible cracking sounds, expanding a few inches in every direction. The spires along its back snapped and pulsed to a larger size, and its skull jerked out, stretching skin that suddenly didn't fit it anymore. The scales shattered and reformed, larger now to accommodate the new size. The fangs were a hand's-length longer when it hissed again.

It was very nearly solid already. Whatever was keeping most of the spirits from realizing their bodies wasn't affecting the serpent. Maybe it had more strength of will or more conscious awareness. It sure as hell knew I was there, gaping up at it. It all but smiled, lowering its flat nose to within centimeters of my face. Then it opened its mouth and snapped its jaws shut over me.

Agony cramped my hamstrings, dropping me to my knees with a gurgle that wanted to be a howl. I fell through the not-quite-solid serpent's mouth, feelings its jaws scrape up my bones, and lay curled with my forehead on the floor, shuddering. The serpent seemed to chuckle above me, and I thought I felt its tongue lash along my backbone. I curled my hands into fists and whispered, "Houston, we have a problem."

I'd thought I could vanquish the Thing in the kitchen. I hadn't been real clear on how the vanquishing would work; I'd had vague ideas of playing maiden-and-unicorn and leading the Thing outside. The minor detail that I wasn't a maiden hadn't seemed relevant, since it'd seemed unlikely that the Thing would be a unicorn. I didn't think kids would call a unicorn a Thing. Then again, I'd never met a unicorn. They could be very Thing-like, for all I knew.

I admired how my brain was trying to derail me. It didn't want to think about the Thing being semisolid. It didn't want to think about the Thing growing larger even as I watched. It certainly didn't want to think about the Thing being the Dead Zone serpent with a particular vendetta against me. Well. Vendetta might be a little strong. It wanted to eat me. I had, in fact, agreed to let it, too. It just wanted what I'd promised.

I decided that from the point of view of the one who was going to be eaten, that was enough like a vendetta. Then I bonked my forehead on the floor and set my teeth together. *Focus, Joanne.*

I wasn't going to be able to get the serpent out of here by playing maiden-and-unicorn. I wasn't at all sure the damned thing would fit through the door. I heard it pop through another growth spurt above me, and revised that upward: it wouldn't fit through the door. Then again, in its semisolid state, that might not matter; doors might be irrelevant. I began to crawl backward, whispering, "Hee-eere, snakey snakey snake. C'mere, snake." I heard it rustle upward, the sound more in the backs of my ear bones than in my ears, and dared to peek up.

Only then did I realize my vision was completely inverted, the sunlight through the window spilling in black and making patches of shadow against the serpent. I'd adapted. Funny what a body can get used to. I wondered if Melinda's shirt was really orange, or if I'd lost my color vision before that.

The serpent, staring down at me, didn't look inclined to move. I whispered, "Here, snakey snake," again and backed up a few more inches. It followed me with its gaze, stopping when its head came up against the doorjamb. It would fit, if only just. The damned thing's head was three feet wide. The spires on its back might not fit at all. I bit my lip and backed up some more. "C'mon, master serpent. I owe you one, don't I? Why don't we go outside where you can eat me."

It flicked its tongue out, looking amused, and settled back down in its coils. I swore and hit the floor with my fist. "Look, goddamn it, you're going to be stuck in here anyway, if you don't come with me. This room's not big enough for you. Just come on already." I sat back on my heels and glared at it. It flicked its tongue complacently and shivered a few of its spires before the whole creature cracked and popped and enlarged again. I watched it fill another six square inches of the kitchen, and understood.

It didn't need to fit into the room. The room would fit

it, eventually. The bigger and more solid it got, the less the building structure would be able to accommodate it. The serpent would destroy Billy and Mel's house unless I could get it out of there. I got to my feet. "It's not going to be this easy," I warned it. It blinked lidless eyes at me and hissed, as close to a laugh as I ever wanted to hear from a snake. I shook my head and nerved myself up to turning my back on it.

I had a plan.

Mel looked more cheerful with a half pint of ice cream in her, but her expression darkened as I came into the bedroom. "What's wrong? Are the kids okay?"

"The kids are fine." I sat on the edge of the bed. "What time's Billy get off work tonight?"

"Seven, if there aren't any crises. Why?" Melinda tightened her fingers around her plastic spoon like she'd use it as a weapon against me. I twisted my mouth, studying her and trying to judge how much truth I should impart. "Dammit, Joanne," she said, "stop looking at me like that. I'm a cop's wife. I can handle it. What the hell is wrong?"

"There's a monster in your kitchen." I winced as the words came out. Mel's eyebrows went up a fraction of an inch.

"You mean besides my terminally hungry eleven-year-old son?"

I smiled a little. "Yeah, besides that. There's, um… Crap. Before you got assigned to bed, did you see, like, weird animals and things around?"

Melinda exhaled, her shoulders dropping. "Of course

I did. The last two days, everything's been nasty. The
weather's too hot and everyone's crabby, like they're waiting for the other shoe to drop. My grandma was a *bruja*,
Joanne. Me and Bill met at a paranormal events conven-
tion fifteen years ago. Oh, and don't give me that tight-
mouthed look. You think I don't know what's been going
on with you? Even if you hadn't gone tearing off from the
equinox dinner like your tail was on fire, Bill tells me everything anyway."

"Yeah?" I smiled weakly. "Did he caper around you saying, 'I told her so'?"

"Yeah, some." Melinda grinned, but it fell away almost
immediately. "So what's in the kitchen?"

"A serpent. I mean, not just a serpent, but a sea-serpent.
I don't know what it's called, but it's huge. I want to call
in some backup and see if we can get rid of it. I'd rather
have you and the kids out of the house, but I'm not sure
we've got that much time."

Melinda started to sit up farther. I put my hand on her
shoulder, shaking my head. "No way, no how, sweetheart.
You're staying in bed. When Billy comes home he can
pick you up and carry you out of here, but you're not
walking around, young lady. And I honestly don't think
there's any immediate danger."

Mel eyed me skeptically. "Honest," I repeated. "I'm gonna
cancel the solstice party and get my friends to come over.
With any luck we'll get this thing out of here before Billy
even comes home, and I think that'll make you feel better.
Meantime I'll keep an eye on it and the kids and you. If anything starts to look worse, we'll figure out a plan B, okay?"

Melinda sucked her cheeks in and glared at me. "All right," she said. "All right, but you've got to keep me in the loop, Joanne. It's the only way to make it work."

I grinned lopsidedly as I stood up. "Is that police procedure, or relationship advice?"

Melinda's eyebrows quirked again. "Some of both." She nodded at the door. "Go on. Get that Thing out of my house."

CHAPTER TWENTY-EIGHT

By six-thirty, the serpent overflowed the kitchen. Rounded stretches of scales and muscle curved through the walls and spilled onto the backyard lawn and into the dining room. Robert's bedroom was directly above the kitchen; when I looked into it, the serpent lifted its head through the floor and gave me a flat, silver-eyed stare. The house was still standing, even though if I put my hand against one of the creature's shining scales and pushed I felt resistance before falling through. I had a half-assed theory at the back of my mind that because I was sentient and able to accept the thing as real, it was more real for me than for the house, which dealt solely in things which were there or not there. There was no in between stage. I had a few moments of longing for the days when there'd been no in between for me, either, but the wish didn't last long. It was easier to accept in the thick of things than from a remove of a couple months, or even just a day or two.

"Joanne?"

I pulled out of Rob's doorway and closed the door behind me. Garth stood at the head of the stairs, smiling so hard it felt like he might lighten the mood in the whole house. No one was exactly grumpy, but everyone, even Erik, the two-year-old, was nervous and twitchy. Melinda was gnashing her teeth with the frustration of being useless. Faye'd taken up a post at Mel's bedside, keeping her occupied with stories while everybody else arrived. "Hey, Garth. You made it. Is that everybody?"

"Marcia's not here yet. But there's somebody downstairs who wants to see you."

Morrison. Cold nerves laced around my stomach and tightened so hard I burped. Garth blinked and grinned. I rubbed my hand over my stomach and managed a smile. I couldn't think how the hell Morrison had found out what was going on here, or why he'd care. Well, Billy would've told him, maybe, but why would he care? I straightened my shoulders and put on my best brave soldier face. "Okay." I thumped down the stairs behind Garth.

Colin, looking ridiculously healthy, sat in a wheelchair in the living room, beaming around at everyone. He turned the chair as he heard us coming down the stairs. I could see the shadows of his spirit snake around his shoulders, but the weight didn't seem to affect him at all. His grin got wider. "Amazon!"

"Colin! My God, they let you out? You look fantastic."
He did. My inverted vision didn't bother me at all anymore. It seemed normal for his hair to be black and
streaming bits of light when he moved his head. His color
was better and there was more meat on his bones, although how that could be affected in the two days since
I'd last seen him, I wasn't sure. "My God, you look *great!*"
I bent to hug him and kiss his cheek. His temperature was
a little high, but everyone's was, in the hot weather.

"I'm just out on temporary leave," he said. "One of
modern medicine's miracles, they keep telling me. Never
seen a reversal like this. I made the big eyes at them until
they agreed to let me out for a couple of hours. I've got to
get back before nine."

"I hope you don't mind him coming along," Garth said
behind me. The smile in his voice buoyed me up.

"Nah, of course not. A little good news'll help us all get
through the rest of the night."

Garth's voice lowered. "Is it going to be bad?"

I shrugged my eyebrows. "Looked in the kitchen yet?"
He shook his head no, and I tilted my head in the right
direction. "Go see for yourself."

He came back a few moments later pale and wide-eyed,
just as everyone else had done. "How're we going to take
care of that?"

I shook my head. "I wish I knew. I don't really understand spellcrafting, Garth." I sat down on a couch, rubbing the scar on my cheek. The couch sucked me in; four
bouncy kids did in even the best of springs. I edged forward, trying not to disappear entirely into the cushions.

"I've watched it tear a hole in the sky and another one in the earth. Can we make a spell to just move something?"

"Translocate," Marcia said from the doorway. I lifted my head, relieved. "This isn't exactly where we agreed to meet," she said as she came in.

"I know. Something came up. What's translocating? I mean, how do you do it?"

"There has to be an exchange. We can't simply move something from one place to another. We have to take something back in order to make up for the mass of the thing we've placed elsewhere. Where is it?"

"The kitchen."

Marcia was grim, not pale, when she came back from the kitchen. "I don't know if a translocation spell will work on something that's not solid. It *may*, and then all we'll have to translocate is air, which would be the best-case scenario for the house."

"But," I said, hearing it hanging on her words.

"But it may not be possible. The ritual to bring the spirits across, and Virissong with them, may have to be completed before we can make the exchange."

"Solidifying that thing will destroy Billy and Mel's house, Marcia. There's got to be another way." I put my hands on my thighs and pushed myself upward.

"What is 'it'?" Colin asked. I looked at him, then at Garth.

"It's a…" I looked at Colin again. "Oh, hell, I'll just show you. You're here anyway." Despite the knot of worry in my lungs, I couldn't help grinning at Colin. "God, it's good to see you out of there. You look so much better."

He lifted an arm and flexed the biceps. "I'll be breaking all the girls' hearts soon. C'mon, I wanna see this thing that's got you guys all spooked."

I put my hands on the wheelchair handles, waving Garth away. "I'll take him. Being an Amazon's gotta be good for something."

"Wait till I tell the guys back at the ward I've got an Amazon girlfriend," Colin said cheerfully. I laughed and wheeled him down the hall to the dining room and kitchen.

The serpent's silver glow was bright enough to hurt my eyes. Colin didn't lift a hand to protect his own eyes against the brilliance, and after a moment I remembered it was probably black to his eyes, like it had been when I first saw it in the Dead Zone. I wondered if it glowed black to him, or if the glowing was just a spiffy side effect of my stupid inverted vision.

It heard us coming and lowered its head through the door to flick its tongue at us. It was nearly full-sized now, its head longer than I was tall. It was going to destroy Billy's house, and I couldn't figure out how to stop it.

"Jesus," Colin whispered. The serpent's cold eyes focused on him and it thrust its head forward a few feet, until its flat nose was almost touching his chest. I backed up several steps, pulling Colin with me. The serpent flicked its tongue and followed, then opened its mouth and hissed a wave of hot irritation over us. I could see the sides of the door through its translucent skin, its body already too wide to fit through the opening. For the first time I thought I heard the house creak protest against the thing's tremendous weight.

"It's kind of gorgeous, isn't it?" Colin whispered. I gaped at the top of his head, then at the monster.

He was right, though: it was. Not like a snake; it was too much more than a snake to simply have a snake's deadly grace. It rolled forward another foot or two, its gleaming spires slicing through the wall and ceiling above it. That time I did see the wall shudder, plaster loosening from the ceiling. I backed up another couple of steps, watching first the ceiling, then the serpent. "It is," I admitted. "It's gorgeous in a kind of 'I'm going to crush you to death in my gigantic coils' way. Seen enough?"

"I guess," Colin said reluctantly. I backed out of the dining room, entirely unwilling to turn my back on the serpent. It reared up a few feet and spat. Colin and I both flung our arms over our faces, yelling. The venom passed through us, harmless as a breeze, and hit the floor behind me with a wet splat. The hardwood gave an acid hiss, a foul odor steaming up as the varnish was eaten away and the wood beneath it scarred. I twisted to stare at it, then jumped backward, avoiding the damp ruined floor as I yanked Colin's wheelchair back over it. The rubber tires melted and stretched, sticking him in place for a few scary seconds before my determination overcame the gooey residue and the chair schlucked loose.

"Joanne," Colin said in a small voice. I looked up to discover the serpent's head pushing through the dining room door we'd just abandoned.

"Oh," I said. "Shit." I backed up faster, hoping there weren't any toys to trip over, and led the serpent into the living room.

"Out of the way, out of the way, please get out of the way." I dared glance over my shoulder so I could navigate the living room without knocking anyone or anything over. The gathered coven members leaped to the sides. "I don't know why," I said, still very fast, "but it's following us—"

"Me," Colin said. I stepped on my own heel and nearly fell over, staring at the top of his head again.

"Jesus. You're right. It's following Colin and I'm going to see if I can lead it out of the house." By the time I was done explaining my clever plan, I was out of the living room and nearly to the front door. I fumbled it open and pulled Colin onto the porch. The serpent stopped and reared its head up again, mouth open wide with anger. "C'mon, big guy," I said to it. "Just a little farther."

Then I took a step back and realized I had no good way to get Colin off the porch. I wasn't sure I was strong enough to maneuver the wheelchair without dumping him on his ass, even if he was still slight and I was reasonably strong. "Shit," I whispered again.

The serpent struck so quickly the only thing we had time to do was fall over. Its blunt nose slammed through the wooden floor of Billy's front porch. Colin and I crashed backward down the stairs, landing in a painful tangle of wheels and legs and elbows. I kicked the wheelchair away and struggled to my knees, getting my shoulders under Colin's arm. He was both pale and grinning maniacally, which made me wheeze laughter despite the circumstances. "Having fun?"

"This is a whole lot better than the cancer ward," he said, still grinning.

"You're crazy."

"Yeah, but I'm cute."

We surged to our feet, which is to say mostly I surged while Colin leaned. The serpent lifted its head, shaking it violently, while I stared in dismay at the ruin of the porch. It wasn't quite rubble, but the laws of physics were starting to apply to the giant monster, and there was a sizeable, nose-shaped hole in the wood. The house creaked and groaned as Colin and I backed up, the serpent following us. We crashed into one of the trees and scrambled around it. The serpent screeched anger and struck again, sending tattered branches and leaves to the ground.

"If we can get it to do that one more time, I think it'll be out of the house entirely." The larger part of the serpent was coiled in the garden, though its tall spires still ripped through the front of the house. I could see boards starting to come loose as paint flecked to the ground in a blue snowstorm.

"Oh, sure," Colin said. "That's a great idea. Let's get the monster snake to attack us again."

I giggled, once more despite myself. "You actually sound like it is a good idea."

Colin gave me a surprisingly rakish grin and staggered away from my support, leaning heavily on the tree we'd hidden behind. "Oooh Mr. Snake!" he yelled. "Over here!" Then he turned and ran pell-mell, elbows and heels flying every which way, for the far side of the front yard. I yelled something panicked and incoherent and went after him. There was a tremendous tearing sound behind us and we both turned to look.

The last of the serpent's spires had torn a foot-wide slice through the front of Billy's house. It began over the front door and reached more than halfway to the roof, not quite splitting the building entirely. Staring at it, all I could think was, *insurance companies don't cover acts of gods,* and then the serpent struck at us again.

I don't know if it missed or if its brief acquaintance with solidity came to an end. There was crashing and banging and someone who sounded suspiciously like me yelling, "Begone, foul beast!", after which there was a bout of semihysterical giggles. When I dared open my eyes, the serpent loomed over us, black sunshine streaming through the silver tentacles that danced around its head.

"Are we dead?" Colin whispered. I shook my head.

"Nope."

"Are you sure?"

"Yeah," I whispered. "I've done dead before, or at least mostly. It doesn't look like this."

"Oh." Colin was quiet a few seconds. "Was that supposed to be reassuring?"

"Yeah," I said again. Colin nodded.

"It wasn't." He looked up at the thing. "What's it doing?"

"I have no idea."

It coiled itself taller above us, its head pointed up into the sky. Its gills flared, making a wide silver hood. Air screeched through them, a high, lonely howl. Colin and I both shivered and hung on to one another harder. "That wasn't a mating call, was it?" Colin asked nervously.

"Christ, I hope not. Okay." I closed my eyes, hoping not

being able to see the thing would help me think. It didn't, but at least I got to sit there for a moment in the blissful darkness without worrying about the world on the other side of my eyelids. "Okay, it's not in the house anymore, which is a huge improvement. We can do the ritual now without destroying everything." I opened my eyes and looked around the garden. "Without destroying the house, anyway. Wanna run for it?"

"To where?"

"Back inside. Where everybody else is."

Colin held his breath, then nodded. I got his arm around my shoulders and pushed us to our feet. The serpent didn't move, still fixated on the sky. "Okay," I whispered. "Let's go."

We took one step. The serpent snapped its gaze back down to us, glaring. Hypnotizing, even. I suddenly understood the compulsion some people had with watching snakes. Except I was afraid this thing could actually hypnotize us. "Um…"

Colin straightened up, shrugging out from under my shoulder. The serpent's head moved a fraction of a foot, watching him instead of me. "I think it wants me," he said, keeping his voice low. "I think you can go."

"Are you nuts?"

He flicked a smile at me without turning his gaze away from the hulking serpent. "Yeah, but I'm cute. Go on, move, see what happens."

I took a reluctant two steps away. The serpent's silver gaze followed my movement, but it didn't move. I took one more step. It was interested in Colin. "This," I hissed, "is not really convincing me I should leave. What if it eats you?"

"Hey." Colin shrugged. "It beats the cancer ward, Amazon. Go on, go get everybody. Maybe it won't eat me."

"Shit," I said, and went.

CHAPTER TWENTY-NINE

Maybe it was just me, but personally, if I'd just watched a couple of people playing Pied Piper with a seventy-foot serpent, I'd have followed the leader outside to see what happened. I'd want to know if the rats had all jumped in the river and drowned, or if they'd decided en masse to attack the Piper and have him for lunch.

The coven apparently didn't share my curiosity. Maybe that was what too much exposure to the magical world got you. There was an animated discussion going on when I snuck back into the living room, most of it about how to best translocate the serpent and whether or not such an action would entirely disrupt the remainder of the ritual. Faye'd come down from Mel's room to join the argument, her voice rising and falling over the general hubbub.

"Guys," I said into the wall of noise. No one noticed. "Guys! *Guys!*"

Everyone fell silent, looking at me in surprise. "Okay, look, guys. Not getting rid of this thing? Not an option. This is my friends' house and whatever the hell else we've done, however good our intentions, we're responsible for that thing being in their front yard right now. We're going to make it go somewhere else. Comprendé?"

My vision reverted to normal so abruptly a headache stabbed through my right eye. I winced and stretched my face, trying to get rid of it, then blinked around in confusion. Normal colors looked garish and wrong. The sunlight was too bright and made knots of discomfort in my stomach.

"Joanne is right, of course," Marcia said. Faye, in all her golden retriever-colored glory, looked exasperated.

"I wasn't saying she wasn't. I was only saying that I thought we'd have more luck if Melinda helped us—"

"What are you, crazy?" I demanded. "She has to stay in bed!"

Faye's eyes narrowed. "Hear me out. This is her home. She's got more natural power here than any of us, even you, Joanne. Her participation would make a big difference in establishing the territory as unfriendly."

I twisted my mouth, looking at Marcia. She sighed and spread her hands. "Faye's right. It could make all the difference."

"Couldn't one of the kids do it?" I was grasping at straws.

The Elder looked apologetic. "As an adult, Mrs. Holliday's presence is more forceful. Also, the land belongs to her and her husband, not to the children."

I set my teeth together. "All right. All right. But she can't walk around, you guys. If she's willing to do this—"

"She is," Faye interrupted. I looked at the ceiling and ran through a silent litany of words nice girls shouldn't say, then pressed my lips together and looked back at Faye.

"You already discussed this with her."

"Of course. It's her house."

She had a point. I might not like it, but she had a point. "…okay. Look, we're going to have to—"

"I'll get Colin's wheelchair," Garth offered. "Duane and I can just carry her right down the stairs. Um. Joanne?" He looked around. "Where's Colin?"

"Outside," I said brightly. "Staring down a serpent."

They were a little slow on the uptake, but I had to give them this: once I said that, they all went running for the front door. I shook my head and went upstairs to talk to Melinda.

She looked better in natural color than she had inverted, although she was still pale. The shirt turned out to be blue, which helped a lot. The kids were settled around her bed, all wide-eyed except Erik, the littlest, who was sacked out on a hand-woven throw rug in front of the dresser. "Joanne," Melinda said. From the tone of her voice, I knew my arguments were already lost. I held up my hands.

"Okay. You win. The only thing is, I'm not sure we can put this off until Billy gets home to watch the kids. The Thing in the kitchen—"

"In the front yard," Robert corrected. I eyed him.

"Right. In the front yard. It seems to be getting more real of its own accord. It made a mess of the front of the house."

"I heard," Melinda said grimly. "Robert, can I trust you to take care of your little brother and sisters while I'm busy?"

The kid puffed up. "'Course, Mom."

"Okay. I need you guys to stay in—" She glanced at me. "The backyard?" I nodded, and so did Mel. "The backyard until Joanne comes and gets you, or until Daddy does, okay? Joanne's going to bring you down there now."

"What if it gets dark?" Clara asked. I put on a smile.

"Either me or your dad should come to get you way before it gets dark," I promised. "Even before it starts to get chilly. This all shouldn't take very long."

"What're you gonna do?" Robert asked.

"We're going to get rid of the Thing."

"What're you gonna do to it?" That was Jacquie, the younger girl, who looked curious and hopeful. "Are you gonna turn it into a banana?"

I blinked at Mel. Mel shrugged and hid a grin. "Um," I said. "Probably not. But if we do, you can eat it, okay?"

She beamed. I struggled not to laugh and went to collect Erik off the floor. "If you guys have a tent, we could put it up in the backyard and you could pretend you're camping," I suggested. Rob lit up and went pounding off to his room. Mel gave me a thumbs-up, and I went with the kids to set up their tent. Really, I went with the kids to watch Robert and Clara set the tent up. If they'd been relying on me, they'd have been there all night and all the exciting vanquishing would have happened without me. Fortunately, Rob knew what he was doing, and they had it together in less than ten minutes. I left Jacquie dragging sleeping bags out to the backyard and Erik still asleep, tucked inside the tent.

The coven was gathered in the front yard by the time I got done, Melinda sitting regally in her wheelchair beside Faye. I stopped to give her a hug. "You have great kids."

"I know." She smiled back, almost disguising the worry lines etched around her mouth and eyes. "Thanks for taking care of them, Joanne."

"Not a problem." I gave her another quick hug and stood up, glancing at Marcia. "So do you have a spell for this?"

"First we have to finish bringing everything into this world. I think we can translocate the serpent as soon as that's done, so long as we're all prepared for it."

"Mmm-hmm. Is it going to eat Colin as soon as it's solid?" The serpent hadn't stopped watching the young man, who was now sitting against a tree, as entranced with the monster as it was with him.

"I don't think so."

I puffed out my cheeks. I liked a world of absolutes, with less of this wishy-washy thinking stuff going on. On the other hand, I didn't see a range of stunningly good choices. "Yeah, well, you get to explain it to Garth if his brother gets eaten."

Garth elbowed me, his smile crooked with concern. "We're not going to let it eat him," I promised.

"I know."

"Joanne, will you help us?" Faye had left Melinda's side and was standing on the far end of the yard. Marcia, the Elder and Duane had already taken up points opposite her, and the Youth was on his way to a fifth. Even I could figure this one out.

"Yeah, but what do I do?"

"Make the circle around us. With luck we'll fit the whole serpent into the pentagram—"

I saw the light. "And it'll be trapped in there when it becomes corporeal. It shouldn't be able to eat Colin, right? We should be able to hold it."

The serpent swayed its head, looking away from Colin for the first time to eye me with its black gaze. I decided I liked the silver better, although my eyes were readjusting to the normal color spectrum. "Shh," I said to the serpent. "Never mind us. Just go on staring at Colin."

"Gee, thanks," Colin muttered, but kept grinning. I wasn't sure I could blame him. If you had to die, being gobbled up by a gigantic serpent really did seem like a less dismal way to go than a slow cancer. The serpent hissed, noisy enough even without a solid form to make hairs on my arms stand up. Then it turned its gaze back to Colin, which didn't exactly make me feel better, even if it got me out of the spotlight. I scooted over to where Marcia stood and looked around the garden uncertainly.

"This isn't going to be the roundest circle ever," I warned.

"It's lopsided," she agreed. "It's all right. It's more for us than anything else. Protection and familiarity. If we trust in it, it will do what we need it to do."

"Okay. I've never done this. What do I do?" This was a different way to build the pentagram than I'd seen the night before, but for all I knew, there were a hundred ways to do it.

"Touch each of our shoulders as you pass, binding us to the Goddess and the God. Invoke their protection and their grace." Marcia's mouth quirked. "And try not to look too much like you think we're all idiots while you're doing it."

I actually blushed, hoping it wasn't visible through my new tan. "I don't think you're idiots," I mumbled. Crazy. I thought they were crazy. It was a small but important difference. Also, they were the kind of crazy that clearly packed a punch, so I wasn't going to sneeze at them. Or mention it out loud, for that matter. I can, on occasion, be taught.

Nevertheless, I felt completely ridiculous walking around the five points and muttering thanks and prayers and invocations to a pair of deities I wasn't at all sure were listening. My skepticism didn't seem to thwart the power lines that shot up between the other five coven members. For an instant, they were brilliant gold, the color of the sunset. Then my vision went inside-out again, and they fell into the familiar silver lines I'd seen the night before. I sighed and pressed my fingers over my eyes, hoping my vision would be all right again when I stopped. It wasn't. Tomorrow I'd go see my eye doctor.

The others had taken up their places around the circle, leaving the serpent in the center. Only Colin was outside of it, still leaning against his tree, the serpent watching him. Mel made up the thirteenth of the coven, with Faye on one side of her and me on the other, as I filled in the last obviously empty space in the circle.

Another jolt of power stung through me as I took my place. It was brighter and more distinct than the gold/silver protective barriers that had gone up around the pentagram. It felt hard and pure and white: Virissong.

Joanne, he said fondly, inside my skull. I flinched from the belly out, like somebody'd poked me. "What?"

Mel and Faye and Duane, on my other side, all looked at me. "Um." God, I was so clever I could hardly stand myself. "You guys didn't hear that, did you?"

Faye's eyes brightened. "He speaks to you again?" She had the note of zealotry in her voice again, making me hunch my shoulders against it. "What does he say?"

We'll be together soon, Virissong said, sounding pleased. *You should be able to almost see me now. You've done well, Joanne. I owe you a great debt of gratitude.*

"See you?" I asked hoarsely. By and large, all I could see was the tremendous silver serpent, and four or five coven members all peering at me with interest. Beyond them, Colin gazed up at the serpent, the spirit snake around his shoulders a physical burden I could nearly see. It seemed to be settling farther into Colin, as if its bulk were adding to his. He looked healthier and stronger. I threw a thought of thanks to the spirits again, shaking my head at the same time. "I don't see—"

My eyes snapped back to Colin and the snake. *"Virissong?"*

The spirit snake lifted its head and flicked its tongue

at me. Inside my head, Virissong chortled, pleased. *I've lent him my strength, as you asked. In exchange, he'll lend me his body.*

"But I thought—!" I cut myself off with a strangled sound as Virissong chuckled in my mind again.

That I would return to my body? Three thousand years dead, Joanne? I think "ick" would be the technical term. Colin and I are agreed on this, he said more flatly. *This is the price of sacrifice.*

I crossed my eyes, completely distracted and trying to see inside my own head. "'Ick is the technical term'? Are you sure you're three thousand years old?" My heart was pounding too hard, pushing up lumps of nausea and worry from my stomach. I was sweating and cold and too hot all at once, my hands clenched in fists. Virissong was right, I knew he was right: there had to be an exchange, a price of sacrifice. My vision was tunneling down, getting narrower, and breathing was getting harder. It wasn't the pain of a sword through my lungs. It was a little more like the desert heat pressing down on my chest. I swallowed and shook my head. "Colin?" My voice went up a register and broke. "Are you really okay with this?"

He didn't look away from the serpent swaying overhead. "It's fine, Amazon. It's cool. I'm fine. Go ahead and finish this up so we can all get out of here." He flashed me a smile without really looking my way. "I'm supposed to be back at the hospital by nine," he reminded me.

Beneath the conversation with Colin, Virissong smiled, the expression warming the voice inside my mind. *I am, yes, thousands of years old. But I've always had—how would you say it. Avatars? In the Middle World. Men and women who do my will and who have helped keep me up on the changes in language. And Colin,* he promised, soothingly, *will not go back to the hospital tonight, or ever again. My strength will be his for eternity.*

"Who?" I asked, bewildered. "Who's your avatar? Colin?" Underneath that, the sarcastic voice in my head said, *eternity's a very long time,* but Virissong didn't respond. Instead I found my head turning to the left, my tunneled vision blocking out everyone except Faye, with her bright puppy eyes and smile.

Colin is the host, Virissong caroled in my head. *I sent her the dream of you, and she brought you here so we can rebuild the world, Joanne Walker. There is so much that we can do!*

The slice across my left palm itched and tingled so badly I slapped my hands together, rubbing gingerly at the stitches to try to relieve some of the pain as I stared at Faye. There was a little hurt in her eyes: she knew, I realized. She knew Virissong had passed her over and was talking to me. "Last night," I said numbly. "The blood ritual. You knew because he actually told you how to do it."

More injury darkened her eyes. Brightened them, in my inversed vision, making them hard white agates that perversely reminded me of Judy's bright black eyes. "That's what we said happened, Joanne. Didn't you believe us?"

"I didn't quite understand."

"But you understand now." Faye's mouth was set somewhere between angry and hopeful. "We only have to finish the ritual, Joanne, and he'll help us right the heat wave you started. Not just in Seattle, but all over. Global warming. And so much more, too." She clasped her hands together over her stomach, leaning toward me in her intensity. "We're on the verge of changing the world. Can't you feel it?"

I looked from Faye to the enormous serpent that dominated the pentagram. It waited, patient, never taking its eyes from Colin. It knew him. It knew the strength he was gaining from Virissong. Colin watched it serenely. The snake settling into his shoulders coiled around him snugly, becoming more and more a part of him.

The few coven members I could see looked absurdly distant, the confines of my vision pushing them away. I felt like I'd lost all my depth perception; like my mind knew I was looking at people who stood hundreds of feet away, rather than half a dozen steps from me. They held themselves terribly still, as if they were caught in amber, waiting while the world around them prepared to change.

"There's only one more step to take to bring him back," Faye whispered to me. "One more sacrifice to make, and the world will be ours. Are you ready, Joanne?"

"What sacrifice…?" My own voice sounded like it came from as far away as the coven members appeared to be. I felt thick and uncertain. Faye pressed something into my hands, a handle. I looked down to discover a bone knife, the ivory blade glowing black and deadly in my reversed vision. "It's beautiful," I said remotely. It throbbed with power, matching the itch and tingle in my left hand. It took the strength out of my legs. I knelt, feeling awkward and jerky, though my knees touched the ground so lightly it seemed like I'd borrowed a swan's grace. I felt like I had the night before, before I walked into the fire. I knew what had to be done. It was just a matter of preparing myself mentally. I could do it.

"It was Virissong's," Faye whispered reverently. "The sacrifice must be made, Joanne. Are you ready?"

I put the knife across both my hands and lifted it, then twisted my right hand beneath the hilt so I could grab it. I thought the blade would slide between my ribs tidily, maybe without much pain. The idea made me want to laugh, but I couldn't quite reach the laughter. The sacrifice had to be made. It seemed a pity to not be able to go out laughing, but at least I could change the world. I lifted the knife, taking a deep breath.

"I'm ready."

Faye twisted the knife in my hands, reversing the blade so it pressed outward, no longer angled to be buried in my heart. Melinda, wheelchair-bound and frightened, came into my narrow line of vision. Her eyes were huge, frightened, all pupil that glowed silver and beautiful in my inverted vision. Faye's voice rang out over our heads:

"Then take her!"

My vision went black.

CHAPTER THIRTY

"Are you out of your fucking *mind?!*" I didn't know if I'd screamed the words out loud, but they ricocheted through my skull like the bells of Cork. My arms were uplifted but frozen, waiting for the fall that would end Melinda's life and bring Virissong back into the world.

"*Me!*" I screamed. "*I'll* be your sacrifice! Mel, the *baby,* they're not part of this deal!"

I fled backward, into myself, terrified and angry. Earth encompassed me, drowning me before it erupted and spat me out. I lurched into the sky and collapsed on my back in my garden. I could smell the old dying grass, the heat that stung the air and made my little pond rancid and flat, but I still couldn't see, not even inside myself. "Judy?" I was high-voiced and desperate, sounding like a frightened child. "Judy, everything's going wrong. Please, I need your help."

"Joanne." Judy spoke from somewhere behind me. I rolled to my hands and knees and whipped around blindly.

"Judy? Judy, I can't see. Please, I need help, everything's going wrong." That was me, the broken record. I was shaking too hard to even get a ghost of humor out of myself. I knelt, putting my hands out. My heartbeat slammed in my chest and in my ears, drowning me in panic. "They want me to kill Melinda, Judy, they're insane. You have to help me stop them."

"Joanne," Judy repeated, calm and reassuring. I felt her hand on my shoulder and clutched at it.

"It's all right." She knelt before me. I was astounded how much I could sense through hearing alone, how easy it was to place her. Even the sound of my heartbeat didn't stop me from knowing where she was. Maybe I'd turned into Matt Murdoch. Judy's weight shifted as she put her other hand on my shoulder, pulling me closer to her. "I told you," she murmured. "I told you much would be asked of you tonight."

"But they're *nuts!* This is *Mel,* they're *nuts!* Nobody could—I can't—not this! This is—no! No!" I shook my head violently, knocking her hands from my shoulders. "This is *wrong!*"

"This is the path you've chosen." Her voice was soft and soothing, making the horror in my stomach bubble even more, until it lodged in my throat and gagged me. "There must be sacrifice to make change." Her hands came to my shoulders again. I fumbled for her wrists, blindly knotting my fingers around them. My left palm ached, throbbing with every heartbeat, as if the cut traveled all the way up my arm and into my heart itself.

"No," I whispered again, hoarsely. "This isn't—shamanism isn't about death. It's life. It's change. It's—" I tightened my hands around her wrists, hard enough that I could feel the bones grind. My palm hurt so badly it made me want to vomit, but the pain was something to focus on besides not being able to see. "This isn't even witchcraft." I could taste the desperation and fear in my own gasped words. "Even I know that. Witchcraft isn't evil, and this—this is! Judy, there's some kind of mistake, this is evil, this is *wrong!*"

"No," she said again, shaking her head. My blood went icy as I felt the motion. As though I saw a ghost of the vigorous movement. Shivers split my belly and ran down my arms, making me want to cry. I held on to her wrists more tightly. I thought I might break them from the pressure, but she didn't complain. "It's sacrifice," she whispered. "You understood that, Joanne. What did the spirit animals tell you?"

"Heed," I croaked. "Heed my—my teacher. Accept. Study." The light that had teased me with Judy's movements had been false; blackness swept over me again, enveloping me in soft, frightening comfort.

"Yes." I felt her nod. Then she caressed my cheek, brushing her knuckles over the thin scar. "I'm your teacher, Joanne. You've come so far. You've learned so much in just a few days. Won't you honor what you've been taught?"

My heart fluttered like a dying bird, a rapid tattoo against my ribs that sent sickness through me again in waves. "I've tried." My voice was weak and tired. "I'm trying, Judy, but—"

"There are no buts!" Her voice rang out strong over mine, suddenly filled with anger. "Joanne, there are no buts. You must accept."

I closed my eyes, as if it could somehow diminish the darkness that ate away at me. "Why do you call me that?" I asked. No, I whimpered. I had neither pride nor shame left, just the blackness encroaching on my soul.

And I felt her smile, a gentle amused thing as she touched my cheek again. "Because it's your name, of course. What else would I call you?"

I opened my eyes again, slowly, to no glimmer of light. "But it's not my name," I whispered. *Jesus, Joanne.* I knelt there, staring blindly at my teacher. And I'd thought the coven was slow on the uptake when they didn't chase the serpent out into the garden after me and Colin. They had nothing on me.

I felt Judy's surprise and bewilderment, rolling off her like cool fog. I remembered fog in the North Carolina hills being like that, silent and motionless until I held still myself. Then it had life, soft edges that swept around me and made me a part of it. Judy's startlement tried to draw me in, but it failed. I had found a line, and suddenly, embarrassingly, it seemed ridiculously obvious. "Joanne," I whispered. "It's not my name. And you know what?"

"Of course it's your name." Her voice turned sharp, and beneath the sharpness rode fear. "Don't be absurd."

I straightened my shoulders, my hands still tight around her wrists. "No," I said, more strength in my words now. "No, it isn't my name, and the thing is, Judy, so far all the good guys have known that. It's just the bad guys I learned to protect it from." My very first concept of shielding came back to me, dark-tinted car windows rolled up tight and safe around the center of my being, around the name that Coyote, both Big and Little, had known from the start. The name that the shamans had pulled from me easily. The name I'd protected from the banshee Blade, and the name that I'd protected, without understanding or realizing why, from my teacher. Herne and Cernunnos had learned it, but I'd been an utter neophyte then.

"Your name is Joanne Walker!"

"No. It isn't. And I can't accept this." My voice grew stronger, more confident. "This is wrong, Judy. Sacrifices should be willing, if they have to be made, and this is— this is blood sacrifice, this is ritual sacrifice. This is sorcery, Judy! It's wrong, and I won't do it."

"Your name is Joanne Walker, and I command you by it!"

I surged to my feet, dragging Judy with me. "My name," I roared back, "is *Siobhán Walkingstick, and you have no power over me!*"

Darkness ripped away, streamers of light bursting through my vision and tattering the shadows. Pinpoints of brilliance sparked into the back of my eyes, burning along the optical nerve and bringing understanding with them. At first all I could see was Judy, caught in my grip, furious and frightened all at once. Her eyes were hard and black, eyes I'd seen a dozen times in different places without recognizing what I saw. "I know you," I whispered. A grin was pulling at my mouth, distorting it with wicked triumph. "Give me your name."

"No!" Tears of fury filled her eyes. "I don't know what you're talking about, Joa—Si—"

I tightened my grip, bearing down. Judy's cheeks went white and her knees buckled. I brought her all the way to her knees, using my weight above her. "Your charades aren't going to work anymore. I know you," I repeated. "The eyes have it, isn't that what they always say? But I didn't see until now. Bright black eyes. Just like the spirit animals. Were they real, Virissong? Or were they your creations?" *God*, what a sucker I'd been! "They were yours," I added. "The eyes, all the bright eyes. Even the snake I brought Colin. Give me your name, Virissong! I want the truth!" My anger was more for myself than my so-called teacher, but for the moment I needed it. Even an instant of doubt would undo me, especially now that I'd thrown my name at the thing that had invaded my garden. Judy held on to silence almost long enough. I set my teeth together and shook her, yelling without words.

And her face split in an ugly grin. The corners of her mouth tore open wide and bloodless, stretching around her head. Pieces of her face fell away, dropping in fleshy chunks. It continued down her body, over her shoulders and breasts, exposing a new shape beneath them. Virissong's passion-lit features appeared, mouth pulled wide in a sneer.

"You were *so* easy," he whispered. His shoulders broadened, wrists thickening. I kept my grip, even as the power of his transformation made my palm scream in agony. I was afraid blood from it might spill onto him and bind me to him again, but my hold was so tight I imagined it bloodless, and in the garden of my mind, imagination trumped reality.

"I was." I held on to anger and pushed embarrassment away. There'd be time to be humiliated later. Right now I'd screwed up so monumentally that I couldn't afford to kick myself about it. "I was," I repeated. "I fell for it hook, line, and sinker. And so did the coven. How did you do it, Virissong? How did you keep Faye's power pure enough that it couldn't be detected by the rest of the coven, while you corrupted her?"

He laughed, staccato sound that lifted the hairs on my arms. "Ask yourself, *Walkingstick*." He hissed the name, searching for chinks in my armor. I only grinned down at him, rictus of forthright fury that made an impenetrable shield.

"You shouldn't have involved Mel," I whispered to him. "I would've gone all the way. I had faith." Another bolt of light shattered through me, making me laugh breathlessly with anger. "Faith. That's why our power wasn't corrupted. We thought we were doing the right thing. *Faye* thought she was doing the right thing. God, what power faith brings you," I whispered. My laughter disappeared and left me trembling with rage all over again. *"I want your name!"*

"Oh, no, Walkingstick. Not when I'm this close. It's not going to be that easy." Virissong set his teeth together in an openmouthed grin that bordered on a snarl. Power surged through him, hot and volatile as electricity. I clamped down on his wrists, struggling to hold him as my hands burned. He got one foot under himself, then the other. I shoved forward, trying to knock him off balance, but he stayed in his crouch, then shoved to his feet, stronger than I was. I thought, inexplicably, of Morrison. Strength shot through me and I squeezed Virissong's wrists harder, trying to bring him to his knees again.

He kneed me in the crotch.

I couldn't even tell if I was hurt. I was so astonished I loosened my grip, which was all he needed. He skipped backward, breaking free of my hold, and winked out of my garden. I set my teeth, too angry to even swear, and followed.

Good news: when I fell back into my body, I could see in full, glorious Technicolor. Bad news: getting hit in the crotch still hurt a lot, and my vision swam with tears as my eyes crossed. Semigood news: that was something to concentrate on instead of Melinda's terror. The time inside my garden had passed with no noticeable correlation in the outside world: Faye still stood behind Mel with an enthusiastic grimace. Zealot's smile. The rest of the coven hadn't had time to react; the serpent still loomed hungrily over Colin. Concentrating on the pain from being kicked made it easier to stagger to my feet. As I did, Faye's expression twisted in anger and dismay.

"You can't—"

"*Shut up!*" I loosened my grip from around the bone

knife and backhanded Faye with all my strength, knocking her away from Melinda. I heard a tiny squeaked sob and wasn't sure if I'd made it or if Mel had. It wasn't Faye: she flew to the side and hit the ground, bouncing up again so fast it looked inhuman. She snarled, lips pulled back from her teeth like a wild dog's, and leaped for me.

I vaulted Mel's wheelchair, my left hand screaming with injustice as I put my full weight on it. My knees hit Faye in the chest. The wheelchair tilted under my weight. Melinda screamed. I shoved the chair as I landed, hoping to right it before it spilled Mel. Faye hit the ground and bounced up again, launching herself at me, her hands extended for the knife I still held. I reversed the blade, snapping it back so it lay along my forearm, and met her attack with my elbow driven at her throat.

It was luck, not skill, that let her deflect the blow. She lifted her head to scream and I hit her collarbone instead of her throat. It slowed her, but wasn't debilitating. She made claws of her hands and raked them across my arm, reaching for my face and eyes. I grabbed her wrist, dropped the knife, and twisted her arm down and back into a half-nelson. She screamed again, in pain this time, and I brought her to the ground with my knee in the small of her back. They'd taught me how to do that at the police academy. I could tell that later on I was going to be amazed it worked. I leaned forward, keeping her arm twisted between her shoulderblades. "Faye, goddamn it, this is crazy. You're crazy. You're being used."

In retrospect, I was pretty sure they also taught me in police academy not to get my head that close to a violent suspect's, but I'd stopped moving like a cop and was trying to bring somebody back from the edge. Faye, it turned out, was perfectly happy over the edge. She popped her head back with as much force as she could, slamming the back of her skull into my nose. Blood and tears went everywhere as I toppled over backward, clutching my face. Faye sprang forward, lunging at the bone knife. I flung myself after it and missed; she came to her feet over me, brandishing the blade.

"I'm not going to let you fuck everything up," she snarled. I leaned back a few inches, my hands spread, watching her warily as I got to my feet.

"Come on, Faye. Let's talk about this. This doesn't have to end this way. We can fix all of this." The rest of the coven was finally moving, leaving their appointed places to watch the fight. I felt like they were absurdly slow, but knew they were moving in real time. Time for me had stretched.

"Fix it?" Her laugh skirled high and sharp. "I've done all this *to* fix it, Joanne! You think it was easy, killing Cassie? But we needed *you*, and she was too dedicated, she'd never leave the coven!"

"What?" There was nothing to my voice, just a whisper of shock.

"He sent me the dreams of you! Cassie was in the way! My best friend, and I had to kill her so we could get you! You can't stop now! I won't *let* you!" She flung herself at me, the knife raised high. I fell backward, catching her wrists numbly. I had the advantage of reach and strength, dulled by shock. Faye twisted and kicked my shins, screaming with rage.

"You killed Cassandra Tucker?" I felt like my mind had been dipped in a vat of glue. Time wasn't moving slowly anymore: it was stuck. Faye sneered at me, furious.

"She had a congenital heart problem. The autopsy told you that, right?" Her arms trembled with the effort of bringing the knife down, but I held her fast, leaning into her in order to keep her hands held aloft. She smiled, wide-eyed and manic, her teeth still bared. "Crafting a spell to make the hole a little bigger wasn't so hard. Just a little bigger, and the heart can't work anymore. Know what was harder?" She sneered, then lunged like she'd tear my throat out with her teeth. "Your old friend. *His* heart was healthy. It took a lot of work to damage it. I'd show you the scars, but—" She writhed in my grip, proving that she was too well-caught to be able to show me anything. "It took a long time, but witchcraft can do a lot with little things like that."

Emotion so cold I had no name for it slid through me, utterly quelling the power centered in my belly. Faye's skin felt shockingly hot under my hands, so hot that I thought if I let go there would be blue marks around her wrists from my fingers. "Gary?" I honestly didn't know if I'd said the name out loud, but Faye heard me anyway. "You gave Gary a heart attack?"

Faye surged forward again, kicking and snarling without touching me. "I thought the old bastard would just kick off. He was supposed to. It was supposed to keep you from asking questions." She bared her teeth again, a smile without soul. "And it worked, too, didn't it?"

It had. I remembered being on the verge of questioning something Virissong had said, when the phone rang to tell me about Gary's heart attack. I couldn't pull together the memory right now to pursue the question, but I would in time. I whispered, "Sorcery. Faye, oh, God, Faye, don't you see what you've done? Faith isn't enough. We have to use judgment, too." She was so close to what I was it made my heart hurt. It made breathing hurt, tears knotting in my throat. I had so very nearly become her.

"Virissong used you to get to me, Faye. This is all going to end right here and right now. I'm so sorry, Faye, but you're under arrest for the murder of Cassandra Tucker." I had no idea how I was going to make it stick in a court of law, but that hardly mattered at the moment. "Anything you say may be used against you in a court of law. You have the right to an attorney. If you can't aff—"

A scream of rage erupted from Faye's throat, so furious it became a strangled gurgle. She stopped fighting me, strength going out from her arms so abruptly that I nearly fell into her. I caught my breath, caving my chest in, away from the knife. Pure fanatical light brightened Faye's eyes.

"You won't stop it," she whispered. "You can't stop it. I'll stop you."

"You can't, Faye. It's too late. It's over."

"No," she said, "it isn't."

She flipped the knife blade around and drove it into the hollow of her own throat.

CHAPTER THIRTY-ONE

"Faye!" My scream tasted like blood. My own blood, not the hot splash of crimson that spattered my face and hands as Faye's eyes widened in shock and she began to topple. I grabbed her forearm and the back of her head, trying to bring her to the ground gently. Power bubbled in my stomach for the first time in days. I wanted to close my eyes and hit my head against something. For the first time in days. For the first time since Judy had come into my garden. For the first time since I'd let myself be led down a bitterly wrong path. I had been a massive fool, failing to see the warning signs at every turn. No wonder Little Coyote hadn't responded to me. I deserved to have to dig my way out of this mess all by myself.

Rage and self-directed fury lent all that power focus as

I fumbled for the knife buried in Faye's throat. I was afraid to pull it out and didn't know how the hell I could heal her with it still in. It was like slapping a patch onto an inner tube I couldn't afford to lose any air from.

Lousy analogy, but it would have to do. I wrapped my fingers around the bone hilt, focusing on the idea of patching the tube. Around the blade, under my hand, Faye's skin felt sticky in a way that had nothing to with the blood. More like it was covered in inner tube glue. The analogy was apparently working, even if it made me want to let go a hysterical giggle. "You're gonna be okay, Faye," I whispered.

Her eyes rolled back in their sockets until she stared at me. I pulled up the best reassuring smile I had, still fixated on her throat. There were so many layers to patch, and they had to be done all at once. I held my idea of patches in place, building up layer after layer of silver-blue glowing power around the knife. I would have one chance to seal the wound after I took the knife out, and I was willing to take a few extra seconds now to make sure the patch would be airtight.

Or not, given that it was her throat and airtight would make her suffocate to death.

Shut up and concentrate, Joanne.

"You're gonna be okay," I whispered again.

The knife stuck when I tried to pull it out in one swift motion. Not badly, but it was harder to remove than I thought it would be. I wondered, very briefly, if removing the sword from my lung back in January had been as difficult, and then I slapped my patch into place, layer after layer of cellular rehabilitation.

And encountered resistance.

The "glue" I'd imagined, edges of cells and skin and muscle softening to be melded back together, refused to stick. The silver-powered patch slid away like I'd never held the idea, leaving the bloody gash in Faye's throat spilling red wetness over my fingers. I jerked my eyes to hers and met a gaze of hard determination and ultimate victory.

"Faye, no."

She took the last air from her lungs and spat a mouthful of blood at me. Then her head rolled to the side and I felt, with sickening clarity, the life leave her body. A clammy chill swept over me, like I'd stepped from the muggy Seattle heat into shadow sixty degrees colder. I looked up so fast it made me dizzy, honestly expecting to see Faye's spirit slipping away into the sky.

Instead I saw the serpent, bellowing like a bull elephant gone mad. The sound hit me like a wall, as if my hearing had been shut down while I concentrated on Faye and now was playing catch-up for everything I'd missed in those few seconds.

The coven had gone absolutely insane. Marcia and the Elder had their hands locked together and were screaming at the tops of their lungs. I could see it in the mottled color of Thomas's face and in the strain in Marcia's throat, but I couldn't hear them over the sound of the serpent's trumpeting to save my life. Roxie and Sam were both on their knees beside me, Roxie shrieking so loudly that I could hear her, tears streaming down her face as she reached for Faye's body, then stopped, then did it again.

Sam didn't move, just sat there staring at Faye without comprehension. I knew exactly how the poor kid felt.

I could only see two others. Garth was trying to reach Colin, who still stood with his head flung back and his arms spread wide, gaze of ecstasy on the serpent as it reared up, towering above the trees in the Hollidays' front yard. And Duane was only a few yards away, helping Mel. Everything else was blocked by the serpent's huge body rising higher and higher until it seemed to blacken the whole solstice sky.

Holy sweet Christ, I had fucked up.

I shoved the thought away as violently as I pushed to my feet. There was still no time for it. It seemed that there was no time for anything, anymore. I needed to see clearly, and I needed to do it right now.

I'm not any good at this, a little voice inside my head protested. I crushed it, not with anger, but simply because I had no time for a crisis of faith. The last time I'd deliberately looked at the world with two sets of eyes had been back in March, when Morrison asked me to. I'd barely been able to hold on to the power then, but the world as I knew it hadn't been about to end. Desperation brought out the strength in me.

I was going to have to work on that.

But not right now. Right now I set my teeth together and reached for the coil of energy inside me, all too aware of its lack of response lately, and the reasons why it had failed me. But the sky behind the rearing serpent was hot summer blue and the monster itself gleamed black the way it had in the Dead Zone, which boded well for seeing clearly. I closed my eyes, feeling the sting of wind-shield wiper fluid washing over them as I fell back on my car analogies.

When I opened them, I could see in two worlds. The physical world was almost a distraction, but I didn't want to let it go. The other world was translucent and made of astounding colors that meshed and melded and slammed against one another.

Mel was okay. I could see her life force entwined with the baby's, both of them much stronger than I'd feared. Mel's good-natured personality shone through, butter yellow that deepened to an intransmutable golden core. The little girl she carried inside her glimmered with the color of dark pink roses, soft and sweet and probably hiding thorns. For a moment it was all I could do to keep my feet as relief staggered my heartbeat.

Only for a moment. There still wasn't time to relax. I turned my Sight on Thomas and Marcia. Power roared off them, pulled up from the earth and drawn down from the sky to mix together into a spell. Marcia's power was graying out, the color blanching, as if she was drawing too much too fast. I grabbed Roxie's arm and pulled her to her feet. "Take your place! Everyone! All of you! Get in place around the circle! The elders need you!" My own voice thundered through the racket the serpent made, sending shockwaves of sound bouncing around the overheated air. Roxie stumbled away, but Sam gave me a look of despair.

"We can't. We can't do anything, we don't have a full coven. Faye's dead."

"Go!" I yelled. "It'll be all right!" I had absolutely no

freaking clue how it was going to be all right, what with missing the Maiden, but I couldn't tell Sam that. His eyes widened with trust and he ran for his place.

I could see through the serpent's bulk again, though it was no longer because the creature itself was only partly manifested. It was my own power lending semitransparency to solid objects and giving my vision depth. On the monster's other side, coven members were tottering into place, strength seeming to come to them as they reached their points around the pentagram. Only Garth was still trying to get to his brother. His movements had a viscosity to them, as if he tried to slog through tar in order to reach Colin.

And Colin, a few feet beyond Garth's reach, was wrapped in black. There was no hint of life to his aura, no neon glow that made him beautiful and unique and one of many, but matte and flat and deadly, pressing in to him without the slightest protest from the slim blond boy. The snake I'd brought back from the spirit realm tightened around his shoulders and began unfurling like a cloak, becoming Virissong's strong, slender spirit. I wondered if anything I'd done in the spirit worlds in the last few days hadn't been wholly orchestrated by one Virissong aspect or another.

Images flashed behind my eyes, the icy Upper World and the astounding thunderbird. Big Coyote in the desert. The cheerfully warring spirit animals and the tortoise that had returned with me to lend Gary his strength. I hung on to those memories, taking them for the lifeline they were. I'd screwed up monumentally, but not everything I'd done had been tainted by the dark sorcerer who now settled into Colin's body. There seemed to be things out there that still had faith in me.

Clinging to the scraps of hope that I hadn't fucked up beyond redemption, I wove my own power together into a silver-blue net and swung it toward Garth, not so much to capture him as gain his attention. He wrenched around toward me, rage and fear in his eyes. "Get in place, Garth," I said as gently as I could. "We're going to fix this. But we've got to work together."

"But Colin!" His voice broke, youthful terror, and my heart clenched at the sound.

"I know." My stomach hurt around the power centered there, sorrow and pain that touched the net I'd woven and rode out to tell Garth that I understood and shared some of his agony. "But the coven needs you if there's any chance of making this right." There was a peculiar ring to my words, like they'd been processed through bells made of pure silver. They sounded as if they carried inexorable truth, and for a dismayed moment I hoped I wasn't going to get stuck having to tell the truth all the time. I'd never be able to speak to Morrison again.

But Garth seemed to hear the truth in my words as well. He reluctantly broke away from trying to reach Colin, his steps coming easier as soon as he moved backward instead of toward the blond boy. I could feel power growing as the coven members each offered up what they had, and slowly their voices began to lift over the sound of the serpent's bellowing.

"Joanie." A hand touched my elbow, startling me. I

turned to look down at Mel, who glowed so brightly I had to squint to see her clearly. "You've only got twelve."

"I'm trying not to think about that." I was pretty sure that we needed a full coven in order to vanquish the serpent and Virissong, but taking my place in the circle and harboring doubts would only sabotage the whole attempt.

"Joanie," Mel said, more urgently. "Your maiden's dead and I don't think any of those girls is old enough to be the Mama. You're playing with a shit hand and you need a full house."

"One of them must still be a maiden," I said doubtfully, and turned to glance over the girls, wondering if my Sight could verify that. Mel put her hand on my arm again before I'd figured out how to figure it out.

"Is it a boy or a girl?"

"What?" I stared down at her again, watching her colors flex with agitation.

"The baby." Mel's voice showed none of the twists and flaps of frustration that her aura danced with. "Is it a boy or a girl? Can you tell?"

"Oh. It's a girl," I said as if announcing such a thing was an everyday activity for me. Mel took a deep breath.

"Then I can be both."

My double vision was doing nothing to help me understand her. I shook my head, feeling especially slow and dull. "Both what?"

"Mother and Maiden," Mel said a bit impatiently. "I told you, Joanne. My grandmother was a witch. This isn't entirely new to me."

"Mel, you don't have to—we've—I'm—" I had never

once in my life said out loud that I'd had children. Plenty of people back in North Carolina knew, but no one in my life since the day I left Qualla Boundary had any idea.

Except maybe Morrison, depending on just how much digging he'd done. The idea made a knot in my stomach.

"You need thirteen," she said, long before I could find a way to break through more than a decade of self-imposed silence and admit I'd been playing the role of the Mother. "The baby and I make twelve. You're the thirteenth. The focal point. You're the one with the power, Joanie."

"You're the one who's pregnant! Mel, this could be really dangerous—"

"You won't let anything happen to us." She smiled, full of serene confidence, and that was it. I'd lost the argument. I could tell, because she walked over to take a place in the circle and folded her hand into Marcia's. As soon as she did, Thomas left Marcia's side and darted around the serpent to clasp hands with two other coven members.

I was the only one left outside the circle. The coven had gathered into four groups of three, one at each cardinal point of the compass. Power swept off them like a river in flood, their concentrated, trained efforts blowing away the magic that the cops had helped me call up back in January. There was more than just good will and hope behind their power. I could feel their spellcrafting, words chanted above the muggy wind and the serpent's howls, and knew if I could harness all that power I could set straight the things I'd messed up, and send Virissong back to the Lower World he'd been so long accustomed to.

But I couldn't do it from outside the circle. I stared up at the serpent, screwed my courage to the sticking point and walked into the center of the pentagram.

Unexpected silence assailed my ears, so loud I stumbled and put a hand on the gigantic serpent to steady myself. I was much, much too small for it to notice, yet it hissed and twisted at me, spitting venom. I didn't have time or enough presence of mind to duck, but the acid spattered against a silver-blue sheen instead of burning my skin to the bone. I blinked at my arm in astonishment, then blinked again, looking more carefully with the Sight I'd called up. Filament-thin power sparkled over my skin, like a shield made of sparkling lamé. I wondered where it'd come from, and thought Coyote would be proud of me if I'd had the foggiest idea how I'd done it.

The coven's spell was reaching a crescendo. I could feel it in the bones of my ears, even if I couldn't exactly hear it, and despite the hissing serpent above me I spread my arms wide, listening with all my being.

And then I knew what to do, like instructions were being poured into me. I couldn't borrow the coven's power the way I'd done with the cops in January. Theirs was much too focused, the spell they were casting meant to do a specific thing: translocate the serpent somewhere less dangerous than the Hollidays' front yard. They could create the spell, but I needed to provide the power boost that would force a creature this massive into motion.

I dug down into the core of me, reaching for the bubble of power that spent so much time lying dormant thanks to my refusal to use it, and which had not unreasonably stopped answering when I called. It wasn't exactly sentient, but I found myself *asking* it to respond, instead of bludgeoning my way into using it like the proverbial bull in the china shop.

It responded with joy, as if I'd finally, finally taken the right approach. I lifted my hands up, feeling the need to actually *push* the serpent away, and discovered I could see through my skin. Networked vessels carried blood that glowed with life, bone caressed by the warmth of muscle and sinew against it. I could see the serpent through my own hands, and felt a surge of confidence. Last time I'd gone transparent on myself things had turned out all right. I wondered if my eyes were the wrong color. Morrison'd watched me last time I'd done this and said they'd turned gold.

It didn't matter. All that mattered was focusing the coven's spell and protecting the Hollidays and their home.

I laid my hands on the serpent and everything went horribly, critically wrong.

CHAPTER THIRTY-TWO

The serpent snatched the power I was bringing to bear, draining it from me so fast that black thunder pounded through my skull. Spikes of light shattered behind my eyelids like unhealthy warnings that my life was in the balance. I dug my hands into the edges of the serpent's scales, struggling to keep my feet as I began to feel stretched thin as taffy. I had one frivolous moment of sympathizing deeply with Bilbo Baggins, and then knowledge began slamming into my mind with each of those bright bursts of lightning, and I had no more time for superficial thoughts.

It wasn't some great epiphany on my part. It was that in opening itself to take my power, the serpent also revealed itself to me. Memory assailed me, flat and eager and hungry.

* * *

I waited restlessly in a place where fragile human conceits like time had no meaning. There were constants in my world: there was power, and with power, temptation. *Time* meant nothing when I had these things, because the creatures who had birthed me with their fears and petty dreams were endlessly weak. There would always be those willing to sacrifice anything for power, and I waited for those ones, secure in the knowledge that they would come.

Sometimes others came, traversing the dark places that belonged to me and my kind. Those ones could be tempted but rarely caught, their purpose at opposite ends to mine. They led the weak out of darkness, slipped them from my grasp and turned them back to light. I always knew them when they came into my place, because they were touched by the Enemy.

I shifted, scales sliding over one another in comforting hisses. Darkness cradled me, and I waited, for time meant nothing when I had power and temptation and most blessedly of all, the Enemy to rise against and fight again someday. So it was and so it would be until the small things that had given life to me and the Enemy no longer had life of their own. I did not think I would fade away then. I had been brought forth from nothing and believed I would continue in darkness so long as there was light. It was the way of things. If meaningless *time* ended, then perhaps so might I, but I belonged to something larger than mere life and death.

A shard of blackness, bright against the dark. A path, leading out. A man, youthful and arrogant and strong, untouched by the Enemy. Better still, I could see the mark on him, blazing black in endless night: *rejected* by the Enemy, his power tainted with the need to make himself a hero, to be beloved of his people and to stand above them all as their god-king.

I wondered, at times, why the Enemy did not fold ones such as this under its wing, choosing to reject rather than to guide and protect them. Should one of the Enemy's fall so far as to walk my path, I would welcome him with sweet words and gentle teachings, until his power was so corrupt and so great that I could break free of my waiting place and into the Middle World forever. Surely the Enemy could use one of mine so well as that, to burnish and embrace such aspirations until *its* dream was the one dreamed by all the creatures of the world.

But perhaps the Enemy can only squint at heat illusions and bright horizons, blinded by too much sunlight. Those who dwell in dark must learn to look farther than we can see, depending on the imagination of ambition to free us from our cages.

He is so easy, this newcomer. His people freeze and starve and he believes without hesitation that it is the spirits who are to blame. That there is a great and terrible battle waging in this other world he walks in now, and that the creatures who fight here are so powerful that their war spills into his world. And his people are hunters, so it is very easy to convince him that the dark things must be brought into his world in body, so that men might slay their physical forms and thus weaken them in this, the spirit world. Then his people will be safe and warm once again, with food in their fat bellies and no more thoughts of darkness in their small minds.

He agrees, with all the naiveté and arrogance of his kind, and never understands what he will be giving up to me. For this one has power, an unusual power, and my bargain this time will cost him everything, at a price he will think a gift: time. Meaningless, endless time.

The serpent shifted, its scales cutting into the palms of my hands and yanking me out of memory and into my own mind again with a flare of pain. Panic sickened my stomach, a foreboding feeling of awareness that I should have understood more from the brief moment of sharing the monster's memory than I did.

I had seen those memories once before, from someone else's point of view. From Virissong's point of view. I clenched my eyes shut, trying to remember. He and Nakaytah had built a power circle, he'd said. *Said*, not shared; the memories were too painful and I'd been willing to listen instead of see. And the monsters tried to become them. Virissong's spirit animals had been strong enough to protect him. Nakaytah's had not.

I had the horrible feeling I was Nakaytah in this scenario, and I already knew the spirit animals I'd met were manifestations of Virissong's power. Black eyes, bright eyes, all like the serpent towering above me. All like Virissong himself. All meant to draw me in—successfully—to the web he built for me.

I desperately wanted to burst into tears or throw up or

run crying for help, but I was pretty sure the person I needed to get help from was me, which left me shit out of luck.

I leaned back without releasing the serpent, literally digging my heels into the ground, as if doing so would help me cut off the rush of power that it siphoned from me. The bubble in my belly stretched a little, not far enough to snap, but enough to encourage me. I was almost certain it was psychological, but what the hell: if vehicle analogies and physical action did the trick, I could work with that. All I needed was a moment to think, time to unjumble the memories and thoughts I'd shared with the monster I held on to.

Exhaustion swept over me, leaving me trembling and unable to haul backward on the serpent anymore. Screw understanding. I needed to cut off the flow of power, or better yet, do with it what we'd intended: translocate the damned monster somewhere safe. I gritted my teeth together, leaned forward, and shoved as hard as I could.

The monster smashed forward, dragging me with it.

Not in to some other place, outside the Hollidays' front yard. No. That would have been good. That would have been what I wanted. No, it splintered through the pentagram walls like they'd never been there, and dove into Colin's chest.

I went with it, all the way through the pentagram lines, and let go the instant before I, too, was absorbed into Colin's body. I had too much momentum and stumbled forward, planting my hands on the tree behind his shoulders, so I was right there, half an inch from his nose, when his eyes went black and hard as obsidian, bright and dark like Virissong's. Like Judy's.

Like the snake I'd brought back to give him strength.

For one brilliant, aching moment I understood.

I understood something even Virissong hadn't. There *was* no separation of one creature and another. The serpent was Virissong, and Virissong the serpent. They hadn't always been one and the same. That much I could tell from the serpent's memories that still lingered in my mind, their meaning becoming ever-more clear. Virissong's spirits hadn't protected him at all. He'd become a vessel for the serpent, allowing it into the Middle World. My world. He still thought he was in control, that the serpent did his whim. That the hunt he'd begun for the monster that had destroyed Nakaytah, so many thousands of years ago, was his own hunt.

But the serpent's memory whispered to me that like the serpent itself, Virissong had only been trapped in the Lower World, unable to free himself and regain the Middle World that was the serpent's own goal. With Virissong's human face, they could together influence receptive mortals from time to time. Faye had been one, but her mistakes paled next to mine.

Because the black snake whose weight Colin's slender shoulders had borne carried a thread of Virissong's essence within it. A thread that *I* had carried back from the Middle World to make this all possible.

There'd never been any chance the pentagram would hold the serpent, not with a real and true shard of its self outside the star's safe walls. Not with a willing host waiting to carry it into the world, and not with a helpful conduit shuttling pieces of its core back and forth from the Lower to the Middle World. Faye had done badly by beginning the process that would release Virissong, but I was the one who'd actually brought a piece of him into my world.

Virissong's grin split Colin's face in a nasty gash, his laughter a rich deep delight edged with diamond razors. He said, "Thank you," the whisper rattling the small bones of my ears and sending chilly waves of nausea down my spine and into my fingertips. He swayed his head, watching me with cold flat eyes, snakelike, and split another vicious smile. "Perhapsss the Enemy cannot bind those who walk my path, asss I could not fully bind you. Perhapsss the Enemy is wissser in not trying," he whispered, "but perhapss that iss not sso. In sso little time of following me, look what you have wrought, Walkingstick." The hiss in his voice faded with each sentence, as if he was relearning the way a human tongue made speech. "You have brought me forth fully, as no one has been able to do in thousands of years. And there is no Enemy to bind me again, shaman. You are my greatest achievement."

"Buddy," I whispered, "I don't know who your Enemy is, but whoever it is, I'm pretty goddamned sure he's my friend." I lifted my voice, hearing it crack as I called out, "Marcia? Take care of Mel."

Then I wrapped my arms around Colin's no longer frail body and let go with all the power I'd been collecting, focusing the coven's spell on myself instead of on Virissong.

* * *

Air imploded around me with a soft *bamf*. I hadn't previously known that imploding air was a sound in my repertoire of easily recognized noises, but it was. For a couple of seconds, I felt like a special effect in a movie, which was just so cool there wasn't much else in the world to worry about. Besides, it didn't hurt, and that made it even better. I'd sort of expected that moving myself from one point to another without going through the intervening distance would rupture my eardrums, or something equally unpleasant. I had some pretty recent experience with ruptured eardrums, and I was extremely pleased to not be revisiting that particular moment in my life. All in all it was a highly enjoyable two seconds.

At the end of that time I noticed I was falling very very fast toward a flat glimmering surface a long, long way below me. I was reasonably sure the part where it didn't hurt was going to come to an abrupt end in the near future.

Colin twisted in my arms, screaming outrage as he writhed. An elbow caught me in the nose and I nearly let go, then held on tighter. For some reason dropping him seemed careless, even as he flailed and shrieked. "It's gonna be okay," I yelled. The air tasted thick and sour, too muggy and too hot, even though we were making our own wind by falling through it.

He gave me a black-eyed look of unmitigated hatred, pulling his lips back from his teeth to hiss, more like a cat than a snake. "It'll be fine," I yelled again. I wasn't sure who I was trying to convince, but I suspected of the two of us, I was the one concerned about our future well-being.

Which led me to wonder what the hell I thought I was going to do next. The glittering surface below was slowly getting larger—I was pretty sure it was Lake Washington, although I hadn't ever seen it from quite this vantage before—and I wondered how high up we were and how long it would take us to hit the water, and whether terminal velocity gave any kind of softening on the odds of survival if you hit liquid instead of solid earth. It was amazing the kinds of things that just flowed right through my mind when the other option to think about was impending death.

Colin screamed again, a long thin sound that had no business coming from a human throat. His whole body bucked in my arms, wrenching itself rigid before it softened, as if the bones were melting out from under his skin. I shuddered and took my eyes away from the looming lake to try to calm him, and instead let out a hoarse yell and let him go despite my best intentions.

He *was* melting, skin molting and blending into black scales, the rage in his eyes flattened by the deadly dullness of the serpent's gaze. His body threaded longer, arms melding to his sides, legs growing together, and his hair became wild with tiny Medusa-tentacles. Spires ripped from his spine, glistening and deadly with poison, until the boy was gone entirely and I fell beside the serpent.

It flared wings, short and stubby, not nearly enough to lift its bulk through the air. Still, somehow, its fall slowed as its body thickened and lengthened, until it was the colossal monster I'd first met in the Dead Zone. I was still falling at a gravity-dictated rate of speed, but the serpent was above me now, black scales picking up sunlight and glancing the brightness through my eyes.

If I hadn't promised once upon a time that it could eat me, I might've thought it was beautiful. As if the thought reminded the thing, it lunged forward, snapping massive jaws shut mere inches from my head.

Given the choice between being eaten alive and smashing at a billion miles an hour into Lake Washington, I decided smashing sounded good. I tucked myself into a pike, then straightened out so my head was pointed down and my body was streamlined. Maybe I could out-fall the thing. Anything was worth trying.

An unexpectedly powerful buffet of wind crashed into me, ignoring wholesale my attempts to streamline myself. It knocked me back up into the air, far enough and fast enough that the serpent's second lunge missed by yards instead of inches. For one startling instant, the whole thing felt very familiar, like every falling dream I'd ever dreamed had just come real.

Only it wasn't a dream I was reminded of.

I arched back, closing my eyes against the warm wind, and let the thunderbird's golden liquid fire burst free from my chest.

CHAPTER THIRTY-THREE

I turned inside-out, my consciousness folding upward into the creature that I gave birth to. Disorientation and pain swept over me, bewildering in a muffled way. I felt like I'd turned a somersault that placed me firmly in a new body and put someone else in the driver's seat. That was good: if I'd been in control of the thunderbird's body, I'd be plummeting toward the lake at record speeds. Instead, massively powerful wings clapped against the muggy air so heavily I could hear thunder as I climbed higher into the sky.

I turned on a wingtip once I'd gained enough altitude, watching the world spiral below me in vivid colors that went beyond my second sight and into something purely inhuman. It was like discovering I'd been wearing sunglasses that'd been draining the life out of everything I looked at. Even through waves of heat rising off the earth, the leaves were more than just the emerald that gave Seattle its nickname. They had depth, wavering into gem-clear colors that made my hands—never mind that I didn't seem to have any—ache with the desire to touch them. The sky around me was the same, so pure a blue I felt like I should draw my wings in for fear of being sliced apart on the clarity of air.

Amusement that wasn't my own welled up from deep within the broad chest. Even that was so sharp it throbbed, making my own experiences and feelings shallow by comparison. Great. The thunderbird thought I was funny, with my tiny human emotions and my tiny human brain.

Disapproval, like another thunderclap. Apparently I wasn't supposed to belittle myself while sharing flesh with mythical Native American archetypes. Morrison would approve.

I don't suppose you'd like to tell me what the hell we're doing here? I asked internally, afraid to try speaking. God knows what might come out of the thunderbird's beak if I did.

Fond exasperation, like you might feel toward a recalcitrant but cute child. This was not making me feel any better about myself. I added a hopeful, *Please?*, on the principle that people liked it when I was polite. At least, people who weren't Morrison.

I wished I would stop thinking about him.

Memory hammered into me.

* * *

It was becoming familiar, this scene. I wondered how many more times I could see it played out from a new point of view, and then realized I'd never seen this actual moment before. The colors were still painfully vivid, white sun boiling cold in a pale blue sky, the frozen earth blinding with glare that made me squint until my eyes ached with the effort. No human saw in those colors, even if I seemed to be seeing through human eyes. I recognized the body I was in, but not the clarity of vision.

I stood in a power circle, holding Virissong's hand. Nervousness bubbled in my stomach where I was used to feeling the ball of waiting power, and I clutched his fingers a little harder. He gave me a brief smile, squeezed my hand, and stepped away, moving into the absolute center of the circle.

Confidence fought the sickness in my belly. Virissong had spoken with the spirits and would save our people. I drew in a deep breath of cold air, straightening my shoulders, suddenly determined to do him proud. He had done things only the shamans could: spoken to the spirits, built a power circle that would protect us when the worlds opened up to give the spirits bodies that might be killed. My faith was born of love, and it warmed me even against the biting wind.

A spark of hope flew through me. Virissong hadn't been born to the shamanic line. Perhaps I could learn to sense the magics that he'd learned, and stand with him as an equal. I saw nothing when I looked at the power circle, nothing more than lines etched in the ground. I took a few quick steps to the edge, brushing my fingers through the air.

Disappointment burst the nervousness in my stomach. I felt nothing, though Virissong swore that magic poured from the circle, protecting us. Only the true shamans among the People were meant to feel it. My shoulders slumped as I stepped away, knowing that pride would never buy the ability to sense magic.

Virissong's hand touched my hair. I looked up with a sad smile that faded into uncertainty as I met his eyes. Their warmth was gone, the laughing brown that I knew so well drained all to hard, flat black. He saw my smile go and touched my cheek, lowering his head until his mouth almost brushed mine. "Sacrifice," he murmured, "is the nature of power. I loved you, Nakaytah."

Astonishing agony slid into my belly, wiping away disappointment and nervousness. I looked down, gaping, at Virissong's bloody fingers wrapped around the hilt of his bone knife. The blade I had carved for him over one cold winter. Buried deep in my stomach, piercing what would have been my own center of power, had the body been mine. I wrapped my fingers around the hilt, over his hand, and looked up again, pain turning my vision white.

Virissong smiled at me, cold and inhuman, not at all the man I loved, and turned away to let me fall to the earth and spill my life's blood there.

Dying took longer than I thought it would, and hurt less. The cold seeped into my body, taking the edges of pain away until I could roll onto my back with my fingers clutched around the knife. Visions danced in the pale blue sky, spirits crashing against walls that I couldn't see, as if trying to break in and finish what Virissong had begun. He was right, I realized distantly. There was power in the circle. Pride filled me, then drowned under confusion. Nothing good could come of a power that had to be fed by death.

Taking the knife out of my belly almost didn't hurt at all. The part of me that was Joanne Walker struggled to separate herself from Nakaytah so I could reach for my own power, the healing magic that would save my/our life. But the body I inhabited was Nakaytah's, and she had no such power. Heedless of my attempts, she rolled to her stomach and slowly pushed herself to hands and knees, then staggered to her feet. Virissong stood a few feet away, head thrown back and arms spread wide in exultation. I wanted to surge forward and slam the knife through his ribs, but Nakaytah had no intention of becoming a killer.

Beyond the shielding I could see the serpent, rising higher and higher against the icy winter morning. Pale sunlight bled around it, making a glowing, gorgeous aura, like a benevolent god looking down at its people. Even against the back lighting, I could see its individual scales glittering and shifting against one another, my vision still too acute for a human's. Especially for a human with no magic of her own. I stared up at the monster, trying to absorb the import of that, as Nakaytah whispered, "Amhuluk," and then, in despair, "But where is Wakinyan?"

Trapped. The answer came to me—or to Nakaytah; I wasn't sure which—with absolute certainty. Virissong's sacrifice was to Amhuluk, the ancient serpent, not for his

Enemy. That, at least, was something the coven had done right. Or wrong, since it was unlikely that Virissong had intended for us to invite the good into the world along with the bad. Maybe some of those intentions the road to hell was paved with had come through despite our blindness and our guide.

While I was thinking that, Nakaytah gathered herself and tottered toward the edge of the power circle, her hands outstretched for balance.

One thing Virissong told me was true: it was Nakaytah's blood that brought down the circle. She fell toward it, strength draining from her body, and with a hiss and a spatter the shielding came down. Even she felt it, and through her, so did I, a buzz of power shorting out, like a circuit breaker flipping. It knocked her askew, and she sprawled across the circle's line, landing on her back so that she and I together watched Amhuluk come smashing down to close its massive jaws over Virissong. I saw a fang slash through his right arm, and another bite through his torso, just where he'd shown me the scars that he'd claimed Nakaytah had caused. Which, technically, I guessed she had.

"Wakinyan," Nakaytah croaked. "We need you."

For the second time in as many moments, liquid gold burst forth from my chest and I turned inside-out.

Minutes of memory-surfing meant nothing to the world outside: no more than a blink of time had passed when I resurfaced from the thunderbird's memories. And they *were* the thunderbird's memories, I realized. Powerless or not, Nakaytah's plea and her blood had made the creature's passage into the Middle World possible, a dying wish granted by the very gods themselves. Her memories had played in such vivid, inhuman color because the thunderbird had partaken of the gift she offered, just as it'd gobbled through me in the skies of the Upper World. We were all in this together, shaman, spirit, and mortal alike.

I folded my wings back and tucked my claws up, plunging through the thick atmosphere. My eyes had no tears in them as wind ripped by, a thin membrane shuttering over red pupil as protection from the speed. Color dimmed only slightly with the membrane, but my focus changed, telescoping in on the serpent beneath me, its writhing form the only matter of importance in my world.

Its stubby wings drove it upward in short, twisting bursts as it strove to reach me, its Enemy, in turn. I could sense fury and hatred pouring off it, helping to fuel its passage through the sky, and knew as long as I kept it angry I had the advantage. It was in the lake below that it would come into its own, where its long serpentine form would play in and out of the water with ease while I struggled with the weight of liquid on my wings.

Backwinging, claws extended, shocked me with the force of gravity denied. It tore my breath away, making me want to laugh, wide-eyed, like a child, but the thunderbird was in control, and it had no time for my youthful glee. Wind slammed against the undersides of my wings, supporting me as my claws pinched into—no, around—the serpent's body. Irritation surged through me, that I hadn't drawn blood, but even so, I had the thing in my talons and flung myself skyward, wings crashing heavily against the air.

The monster in my claws twisted and struck, spires on its back rigid with rage. One bite landed and I screamed as venom shot through the wound. The sound shattered the thickness of the air, cracking the sky with its strength. I released the serpent, watching it fall away beneath me, struggling to keep aloft with its vestigial wings. I struggled as well, burning heat of poison cauterizing my blood. As a bird I had no jaw to set, but the same feeling of resolution washed through me. The bite had to be ignored, and the Enemy defeated. I turned on wingtip again, and thought, rather incongruously, *hey*.

Hey. I was a healer.

Hey. I had something the spirit creature didn't.

Water in the gas line. The idea came easily, silver-sheened power rising through me even though my body wasn't my own. I wondered briefly where the hell my body *was*, and if it was alive, because I didn't see how I could've actually shape-shifted into a gigantic bird. The mass equation just wouldn't work, even taking hollow bones into account. Then my heartbeat faltered as the first of the tainted blood came to it, and I stopped fucking around with little details like physics and started worrying about staying alive.

It would have been easier with a siphon, but I couldn't wrap my mind around the idea well enough to make it work. Hell, it would've been easier if I could see what I was doing, but I didn't think asking the thunderbird to nip in for a quick landing so I could step out of its body and take a look inside it would go over well.

Instead I clung to the idea of water in the gas line, one liquid floating on top of the other. Blood below, poison on top: I could tell when it began to work because the pain intensified, pure venom corroding the vessels and veins it touched. I figured the next few seconds might make me a little dizzy, but as the thunderbird folded its wings and went into another dive, it seemed as good a time as any to risk it.

It took pressure to squeeze the poison out, like a thin tube with a semisolid matter in the bottom, the liquid on top squishing its way forward. I was right: dizziness crashed through me, and instead of diving I suddenly realized I was just plain falling. The thunderbird's heartbeat hung motionless for a terribly long time as I squeezed water from the gas line with all my concentration.

And then the poison was gone and the thunderbird somehow managed to pull out of its plummet, smashing into the serpent with such force that we all tumbled down toward the lake, tangled together. I flared my wings, slowing the fall as best I could, while the serpent wrapped itself around me, trying to crush my wings back to my body. It reared its head back, jaws agape, and lunged forward again.

To hit thin silver shielding that sparked and lit with its contact. Snakes weren't normally much for expression, but as it flinched back I was sure I saw astonishment in its eyes. I let out a cackle of sheer delight. It erupted from my throat as a skree, making the air around me seem to collapse again.

I tore at the serpent's face with my beak, and as it twisted away, rolled onto my back. Panic shrieked through me, warning me of my vulnerability, but it loosened the serpent's coil from around most of my body. I rolled again, dug my claws into the Enemy's belly, snatching it out of the air, and climbed for the sky again.

There was no sunlight left. Thick heavy clouds filled the air, like all the muggy heat of the last several days had finally coalesced together. It was my weather, thunderbird weather, and I felt the bird's thrill of pleasure as we dragged the serpent into the clouds. Its fragile wings would be easy to rip off, its unprotected belly simple to tear open. The steaming entrails would be a feast.

I gagged. I didn't even know birds *could* gag. No, I guessed they could, because mommy birds gagged up dinner for baby birds. I felt badly for the baby birds. Swallowing bird bile was not high on my list of things to do again. At any rate, I was sure eating snake was a fine thing for a bird to do, even a thunderbird, but I needed to do more than that. The coven, with my help, had opened up the passage for not just Amhuluk, but for all manner of creatures that were probably wreaking further havoc on an unsuspecting Seattle. I needed to undo that, or nothing was ever going to get straightened out. I swallowed against bile again, and tried my hand—or throat—at speaking a word with a bird's voice box.

It came out like thunder. Amhuluk, the serpent's name, the one I hoped was true and would force it to answer all the way from the depths of its being. Nakaytah, three millennia dead, had offered up the tool I needed to capture the thing and drag it, kicking and screaming, back into the Lower World.

Wriggling and screaming, said the snide little voice at the back of my mind. *Snakes don't have legs.*

It's a good thing I didn't know where my real body was. I might've convinced the thunderbird to go bite my head off.

The serpent in my claws convulsed, then surged forward, reckless action that let it strike at my throat. Silver sparkling shields flared up again, protecting me, but it had learned. Its goal wasn't to bite through me, but to grasp my neck in a crushing grip with its mouth. I shrieked, more from fear than pain, my claws opening to scrabble at the serpent's body. Its weight pulled my head down and suddenly we were falling, an uncontrolled dive back toward the distant lake. I flared my wings, but it only slowed the fall. The serpent lashed around, using its own stubby wings to generate enough lift that it could slam its body weight down onto my right wing.

The expected pain didn't come: the thunderbird's bones were less fragile than a smaller creature's might've been. But it unbalanced me badly, and the dive became a tumble, serpent and thunderbird wound about one another as we crashed through the air. I screamed outrage over and over, shattering the storm clouds above us. Rain hit in torrents, sheets of water weighing us further, driving us toward the lake's surface.

The serpent wrapped itself around my neck, crushing my throat. We hit the water with a splash that felt like it broke every bone in my body.

CHAPTER THIRTY-FOUR

I felt terribly, terribly small, beneath the surface of the lake. My wings were waterlogged, the serpent's strength much greater here than in the sky. It slithered around my neck until it held me with the end of its tail, and then began swimming deeper, dragging me farther into the stormy lake. I spread my wings, pathetic painful gesture of protest, and the serpent's speed slowed a little.

A little. Not enough. I closed my eyes and struggled to backwing, trying to pull myself back toward the surface. The serpent tightened its tail around my throat and swam harder. I wondered how long I could survive underwater, or if a thunderbird didn't need to do mundane things like breathe.

From the growing tightness in my chest, I suspected I wasn't going to be that lucky.

Why hadn't it worked? I'd sure as hell gotten the thing's attention by bellowing its name. Why hadn't it bent to my will?

Maybe because I had no ritual. It'd taken ritual to open the world walls with the coven. The water grew colder and darker and I fought to remember any of what they'd done, beyond dancing around a fire and singing in a language I didn't know. Even in the midst of drowning, I snorted at myself. Water went up my beak and I coughed out most of the air I had left.

Ritual not only wasn't my style, but I was a little short on time anyway. The serpent had only hesitated when I called its name, not been stopped entirely. I was missing something.

Virissong's face flashed through the darkness that was becoming all I could see, and I almost laughed. Didn't, quite: I'd already used up too much air. But almost. And cast down deep into myself, reaching for power at the same time that I made a promise: if I got out of this alive, I was going to spend a whole lot more time studying and a whole lot less time pretending that my gifts didn't exist.

Approval bubbled through me, not my own. The thunderbird stretched its wings farther and swept them down powerfully, dragging the serpent and its downward journey to a stop. The serpent snapped around, a silver streak in the dark lake, its fangs bared as it lunged for the thunderbird.

My power responded with a flare of brightness that turned the rain-pelted lake to white. I whispered, "My name is Siobhán Walkingstick," into the whiteness, and the thunderbird's voice roared, water shaking away from me in visible shock waves. "I live within Wakinyan, your ancient Enemy." Maybe I had a little ritual in me after all. "I know you, Amhuluk. And I know the demon whose soul you share."

I had no way to draw breath, and the impulse to do so nearly killed me. I drew water all the way to the back of my throat before coughing it out again. Dizziness brought my eyesight down to pinpoints, even the thunderbird's superb color vision unable to offer me more than tiny spots of focus. I took the last air in my lungs and someone else whispered, *"Idlirvirissong,"* from my mouth as I lunged forward to slam my talons through the serpent's skull, shattering bone and closing claw through the monster's mouth.

I had a moment to be astonished while thunder ruptured all the water away from me, sending it spouting up into the sky in a whirlpool that I was the eye of. The serpent was flung into its swirls, squealing hideously as the water swept it farther and farther into the sky. A split appeared in the sky, shredding the clouds and opening a path all the way up to the clear stars. I dragged in a deep breath, feeling warmth and life returning.

I was good with the idea of nets. Cars and nets and cages. Things that held people in, rather than releasing them. What I needed now was an opening, the same kind the coven had created, one that would let not just the serpent, but all the spirits we'd released into Seattle return to their homes.

The idea of sacrifice flirted around the edges of my mind, so obvious and simple that even now I almost fell for it. It'd been made clear to me that it was my power that'd given the coven the strength to do what they had. I was certain that a little thing like the cost of my life would be enough to pay for sending the spirits home again.

But that would be the easy way out, and frankly, I didn't think I deserved it. I tilted my head back, feeling wet feathers ruffle and stretch against my throat. I had no spell to sing, but I had the voice of the Wakinyan, and I had my own will to *change* the things that had been done badly.

I had never heard a sweet sound from a raptor's throat before. The pure noise of shattering glass played off the whirlpool's walls, bouncing higher and higher into the atmosphere, until the sound itself crashed into the gash in the sky, and tore it open all the wider.

I threw my own will behind that sound, flinging power up toward the clouds. Just to the clouds: rain thundered down all over Seattle, and I wanted to use that. I envisioned silver drops of power mingling with the rainfall, splashing down over man and beast and calling those who belonged somewhere else home again. Roofs and tree cover meant nothing, I whispered to the power-infused rain. It was the rain that carried the message, and all the creatures that heard it were bound by my will.

Amhuluk, closest to the rip in the sky and weakened by the calling of its name, went first. It threw its own black power behind it, trying to stitch the tear closed, so that the others couldn't follow. I reached up and slashed the hole open again with a silver lance of magic, the distance between it and myself meaningless.

Crystal filled the air, so sharp-edged and full of color I winced away from it. It took long moments to realize it was an aurora, more brilliant in the thunderbird's acute vision than my own mind was capable of processing. Jade faded to diamond-white at the edges, then ran and blurred into violet and crimson, so hard I thought I would cut myself if I reached up to touch them.

And littered in the colors came the spirits, their own forms faded and gentle inside the aching incandescence of the aurora. Resentment tingled from some, relief from others as they pounded into the sky.

The beat of footsteps into the sky shook the earth, and a surge of panic lent strength to my power. I didn't want another earthquake, and remembered too vividly that was how the spirits had been given body. I shouted again, thunderbird voice running deep this time, and the whirlpool I hovered in the midst of buckled and mirrored itself, opening a spigot into the depths of the lake beneath me. I was the focal point of that one, too, the center at the small end, its width growing as it spiraled down toward the bottom of the lake.

Poor fish, I thought unexpectedly, and for the first time started to worry about things like airplanes and weather patterns when there was a whirlpool in the sky. I reached out with my power, trying to feel the rest of the city, to see if I'd endangered anyone or anything.

The whirlpool nearly crushed me, water slamming in toward my body so fast it stole my breath again. Fresh panic flared, forcing the waterspout to its original dimensions, my focus entirely on it again. I gnawed my lower lip, at least mentally—bird beaks weren't really meant for gnawing—and gave the power inside me a sort of sideways glance, trying to peek at it. I'd had it drained from an external source before, but I'd kind of hoped it might be like the Energizer Bunny, left to its own.

That was clearly not the case. I was tapping the absolute limit of my own abilities, so much so that I couldn't even afford to open myself up and let the city hit me with its strength. It was pretty clear that a lapse in concentration would kill me.

The good news was that all manner of creatures were thundering into the lake below me, physical bodies and spirits seeming to separate as they hit the double whirlpool. They raced up and down the swirls, becoming part of the aurora or part of the lake, returning to the things they'd come from. I just needed to hold on long enough for the rain to drive everything home again.

Long enough becomes a strange amount of time, when it's just you against yourself. *Long enough* becomes *one more second,* each one infinite but graspable in conception. I can hold on *one more second.* Each one became the sum total of my universe, until there was nothing left of me but a shell pressing outward, holding the water back like Moses at the Red Sea. *One more second.* Meaningless, endless time lost in an aurora so intense that my eyes slowly learned to deny it. All around me there was nothing but static white light, and then that, too, faded away into a sky full of broken clouds and the scent of rain.

I beat the thin air with weary wings, turning a slow wheel on a tip so I could cock one eye at the rip in the sky. It was all but gone now, last vestiges of what I hoped was victory. The lake, far below me once again, was almost settled, a few choppy waves rippling its surface. I heaved a sigh and folded my wings, plunging toward the white-capped lake. It was over.

Slamming into my own body at two hundred miles an hour drove me beneath the surface, so deep I wondered if I'd be able to make it back up again. There was no somersault sensation this time, just a good old-fashioned kick to the gut as I sank into the water. My lungs hurt. My ribs hurt. Golden fire burned into my breastbone, doing something to replenish the worn-out power I carried within me, but not doing a damned thing for the lack of air in my system. I was too tired to panic. Hell, I was too tired to kick toward the surface. Maybe I could survive long enough to bobble that way with whatever little air was still left in my lungs.

Soft gold power drew me upward, exiting my chest as it had done before, but without taking my sense of body with it. *One last spirit to go home*, I thought hazily. The tear in the sky had to still be there, so the thunderbird could return to the Upper World.

Two spirits, someone inside my own head corrected me. Nakaytah's voice, oddly familiar in my own mind. I exhaled, somewhat foolishly, all the stress leaving my system as I finally recognized who had spoken through my mouth when I'd named Virissong properly.

I hoarded his name for all this time, Nakaytah said. *Only a shaman speaking it could drive Amhuluk and Idlirvirissong back into the Lower World.*

I wished I had some air to breathe, but I smiled a little anyway. Drowning turned out to be a surprisingly pleasant way to go after all. I was going to have to apologize to—well, somebody—for my sarcastic doubting earlier. *You're the Wakinyan's host, too, you know?* I asked her. *Your name is a part of it, too, now. It can't be banished unless the Enemy knows to call your name, too.*

Nor released, she agreed, and because I could take a hint, I drew in a lungful of water and whispered, "Goodbye, Nakaytah Wakinyan."

I like to think I was the only one who saw the golden ghost of a thunderbird rise upward from my chest and speed into the sky like a star falling in reverse.

Eventually it struck me that being dead was a great deal like floating in a giant swimming pool, my chest rising and falling just like I was still alive and breathing. My eyelids were so heavy I had to lift my eyebrows to get them far enough open to see. A handful of fuzzy bright stars came into sight, and I began to think I probably wasn't dead after all. I'd lost my contacts in the lake water, but on a scale of one to ten, with ten being dead, losing my contacts was probably somewhere around a negative fourteen in matters of consequence.

The lake water was still incredibly warm from the heat wave, though the air itself seemed to have cooled. I drifted for probably half the night before it occurred to me that I could swim to shore. Getting there took a long time, and once I crawled onto the beach I didn't want to do anything else. I sat there until the sun rose, like I was waiting for something.

And I was. A gray shape in the water became recognizable as morning sunlight began to pick its way across the lake's surface. I got up and walked into the water again, striking out in a swim when the bottom fell away, and brought Colin's body back to shore.

CHAPTER THIRTY-FIVE

Wednesday, June 22, 8:25 a.m.

I must have slept, because the next thing I remembered was Billy's hand on my shoulder as he said, "It's all right, Joanie. We've got him."

The sun was higher in the sky, and the entire coven, including Melinda, was there. Billy wasn't the only police officer, and someone had already called an ambulance. I didn't want to look at any of them, but I couldn't look away from Garth. He looked older and much more haggard, bags under his eyes that spoke both of sorrow and exhaustion.

But the worst of it was what he said. He met my eyes, then looked away, watching them take his brother's body to the ambulance, and echoed Colin's opinion: "It beats the cancer ward."

Knots twisted in my stomach, until I couldn't tell if I wanted or dreaded forgiveness. But I still had to say I was sorry. I'd fucked up so badly. "Garth," I whispered.

"Don't." His answer snapped out, hard enough to be a blow. I flinched and closed my eyes, glad for the pain. "Don't," he said again. Controlled emotion bled through his voice, anger and despair. "Just…don't."

I lowered my chin to my chest and pressed my lips together, nodding. I felt Billy's hand on my shoulder again, then heard him say, "C'mon, let's get her to the hospital, too."

"I'm fine," I said very quietly. I was not fine. Two people had died because I'd screwed up, and a third almost had. I wasn't sure I could face Gary again. I couldn't bear the idea of facing Morrison. And Coyote might have abandoned me for good, which I couldn't blame him for.

All of which was why I got to my feet and went with Billy to the hospital. I didn't care if anybody else might be able to forgive me. I was not going to let myself off the hook.

The radio on the drive over said the heat wave had broken, that a cooler front was moving in. It coincided with the end of the global warming symposium, a fact which the commentator clearly thought had meaning, because he repeated it twice with a sort of nudge-nudge-wink-wink delivery. In more local news, there was already a petition to the city to leave the new Lake Washington waterfall in place. They were calling it Thunderbird Falls. The battle over the lake hadn't gone unnoticed.

I wasn't sure I was happy with that. It seemed harsh enough that the people I knew well were being made to accept magic into their daily lives, whether they wanted it or not. Now the things I'd done were becoming a real part of the world as total strangers knew it. I already knew there was no going back, but I honestly hadn't thought I might push a whole city toward believing the monsters under the bed were real. I unfocused my eyes, feeling so disconnected that it was easy to let second sight slide over my normal, fuzzy vision.

The wrongness in the air was gone, the dark twist of power that had lain over Seattle for months dissipated. It felt and looked healthier, the murky colors washed clean again. I knew I hadn't fixed that on my own. The thunderbird had cleared the air, and if I'd had any part in it, it was in being the Wakinyan's conduit. I wasn't about to take credit for it. I kept the double vision on all the way to the hospital, feeling like it might be at least a step toward using my gifts more reliably.

I was sitting on the edge of a hospital bed, my feet dangling toward the floor, when Morrison said, "Walker," from the doorway. My fingers clenched on the mattress as I looked up.

"Captain. Didn't think I'd see you." The desert-inspired suntan was still with me, but it didn't hide the whiteness of my knuckles as I squeezed the mattress.

"Thought you wouldn't, or hoped you wouldn't?" He came into the room and pulled a stool up to lean against, arms folded across his chest. I shook my head.

"Thought. I was going to come see you after they let me out of here."

"They going to do that?"

I shrugged one shoulder, watching his shoes. They were black polished leather, and considerably safer to look at than his eyes. "Nothing wrong with me that some sleep won't cure." Nothing physically, anyway. I swallowed and made myself look up. Morrison was frowning at me. At least some things never changed. "Captain, I—"

"Every single one of your buddies," Morrison interrupted, loudly, "says that in the middle of a solstice party last night, Faye Kirkland flipped out, confessed to murdering Cassandra Tucker, and in a fit of regret killed herself. Everyone," he repeated, "told me the same story. Including Melinda Holliday. They also said that Colin Johannsen, who was dying of cancer, left the hospital for a few hours and opted to drown himself in Lake Washington rather than return for further treatments."

I stared at him. Morrison stared back, gimlet gaze. "Is that what happened, Officer Walker?"

The incredible thing was that it was the only possible real-world spin that could be put on what had really happened. I wet my lips and kept staring at him for what felt like a very long time, before straightening my spine and saying, "No, sir."

There was not a single hint of surprise in Morrison's blue eyes. "Would anyone with two rational brain cells to rub together believe what really did happen?"

I closed my eyes and lifted my eyebrows a little. "No, sir."

Morrison inhaled such a long deep breath that I opened

my eyes again, half-expecting to see that he'd expanded like a puffer fish. He hadn't. He let the breath out with equal deliberation, glowering at me. "Is their explanation a reasonable facsimile of what did happen?"

"Yes, sir." My voice was so soft even I could barely hear it. "Faye did kill herself. I couldn't stop her. I tried, but…" I looked down at my hands, thinking of the passion that had driven Faye to refuse the healing I'd offered. "And Colin did choose to not go back to the hospital." It was absolutely true. It was absolutely deceptive.

"I hate this, Walker."

"I know. I'm sorry." I looked up again. "Am I…" I didn't know how you busted a foot patrol cop back to anything. Maybe it meant desk duty. I didn't want to put the idea in Morrison's head. "…busted back to being a mechanic?"

"That what you want?"

Christ. Moment of truth. I wet my lips again and shook my head. "No, sir." I couldn't believe I'd just said that out loud to Morrison.

A very faint glint of satisfaction came into Morrison's eyes and he exhaled again, noisily. "Then you're still stuck with foot patrol." He pushed off the stool, looming over me. "There's somebody here who wanted to see you when I was done with you. I expect you at work tomorrow, Walker." He stalked out, the door slowly closing behind him.

I tightened all the muscles in my stomach, internal support to help me face the person I expected to walk through the door next. But it wasn't Gary at all. It was a tall, pretty woman I didn't recognize, holding the hand of a six-year-old girl whose eyes were big with interest. "Ashley heard on the radio this morning that Officer Joanne Walker had been brought to the hospital," the woman said. "She wanted to come by and make sure you were all right."

I blinked at them both without comprehension, until recognition smacked me so hard that I bounced off the bed. "Oh! Oh! It's Allison, right? Allison and Ashley Hampton. I didn't recognize you awake, Ashley." I grinned and knelt down, putting myself on a level with the little girl. "Thanks for coming to check on me. How're you feeling?"

The girl's grin exploded with pure happiness and she stepped forward to give me a hug. "I'm glad you're okay! I was worried." She was strong and warm and smelled like clean kid, the heat-induced clamminess long since banished. "Mommy said you made me better!"

Ms. Hampton chuckled. "I've told her how you called the ambulance about fifty times in the last few days. She thinks you're a superhero." There was almost an apology in the woman's wry voice. "She insisted we come visit."

"I'm glad you did," I said, muffled against Ashley's shoulder. "It means a lot." It was one little reminder of something I hadn't screwed up, and right now I needed it more than I liked to admit. I set Ashley back a few inches so I could grin at her again, hoping the smile wasn't too watery. "I feel a lot better now that you've come to visit me," I told her, with complete sincerity. "Thank you."

She wriggled. "You're welcome. I'm gonna be a policeman when I grow up, too."

"Yeah?" I was going to get all sniffly any second here.

I grinned wider, trying not to leak tears. "Maybe, if it's okay with your Mom, I can show you some of the police station sometime. You can be just like a real grown-up officer. How'd that be?"

Ashley's eyes widened and she spun around on her heel to look up at Allison Hampton. "Please, Mommy?"

Allison laughed. "We'll talk about it, baby. But now we have to leave Officer Walker alone. Mommy has to get to work."

"Aww." The kid said it, but I felt it too. But then Ashley turned around and hugged me again, and said, sternly, "You better take care of yourself, Ossifer—Officer Walker."

I grinned as brightly as I could. "I will, Ashley. Thanks."

Going to see Gary was a little easier after Ashley's visit. I climbed the stairs so it'd take longer, stopping to look out windows at the damage done to Seattle's streets by rampaging mythical wildlife over the last twenty-four hours. Everything was in soft focus because my contacts had washed out. It wasn't enough to hide the mess, but it took some of the edge off.

Gary was charming a nurse half his age into letting him walk out the hospital doors under his own power when I showed up in his room. The woman look flustered and blushed when I knocked on the door, and made him sit in the wheelchair whether he liked it or not. "Hospital policy," she said firmly, and I grinned as she beat a hasty retreat.

"You don't look so good, Jo," Gary said as soon as the

door whispered shut behind her. I let out a half laugh, mostly breath, and came into the room to give him a brief hug.

"You're the one leaving the hospital a few days after a heart attack and I don't look so good?"

"I," Gary proclaimed, "am fit as a fiddle. What in hell happened to you?" He got out of the wheelchair so he could frown down at me in concern.

I put my fingertips on his chest, cautiously calling for the power that lay inside me. It jumped as readily as it had when I'd healed Ashley, silver warmth spilling through my fingers to explore his arteries and heart muscle. There was no blockage anywhere, though I could feel that the muscle itself was wearier than it should have been. I still didn't know how to fix that, but I was going to learn. I left another little glimmering ball of energy behind and dropped my hand. Gary watched with fascination and I smiled a little. "Is that the doctor's diagnosis? Fit as a fiddle?"

"Pretty much, yeah. They got no idea why I had a heart attack. You're avoidin' the question, Jo."

"I know." I sat down on the edge of his bed and Gary leaned next to me, bumping his shoulder against mine. I leaned my head toward his and worked up the courage to say, "You're here because of me, Gary. You weren't supposed to have a heart attack. Somebody got to me through you, because I haven't been taking this seriously enough."

"You're nuts," Gary said. I shook my head.

"I'm not. One of the coven had a knack for messing up

people's hearts. She attacked you with a spell." Once upon a time I wouldn't have been able to say that without either snorting derisively or wincing. Right now I was too low to do either. "Right at the same time that the bad guy was lying to me," I whispered. "You had a heart attack so I'd be distracted and wouldn't question what I'd been told. And it worked, Gary. I screwed up so bad I almost got you killed."

"Almost only counts in horseshoes and hand grenades, darlin'." Gary put his arm around my shoulders and tucked me against his side, feeling absurdly strong for a man who was a few days out from death's door. "You gonna make the same mistake again?"

"No." I sounded like a little kid, my voice nothing more than a tiny, tearful squeak. Gary put his cheek against the top of my head.

"I know this ain't easy for you, Jo. You got all this new stuff inside you pushin' you one way, and all the old stuff pushin' back. But I told you this before and I'll tell you again: you got the ability to help people, and you can either keep screwin' around and pretending it ain't there, or you can stop bitching and do somethin' about it. Maybe it just needed to hit real close to home before you started understanding that. In that case, I figure a few days in a hospital flirtin' with pretty nurses is getting off cheap. You gotta remember I'm an old man, Jo. My kind don't last forever. I kinda like the idea of having some purpose to my death, if I gotta go."

"You're not going anywhere," I said in a tight voice. "Except into that wheelchair and then home. I can't afford to lose you."

"Yeah?" He sounded pleased. "Why's that?"

I managed a smile up at him. "Because I've still got way too much to learn from you."

Gary flashed me a grin full of bright white teeth. "What, now you think I'm a teacher or somethin'?"

My smile got more solid. "I think I don't believe much in coincidence anymore. I think I got into your cab that morning for a reason. Maybe it was just that you drive like a bat out of hell and I needed to be somewhere fast, but I think there's more to it than that."

"Pshaw," Gary said cheerfully. He actually said "pshaw." I didn't think people said words like that. "Now you're just buttering me up."

"Yeah." I grinned and patted the handle of the wheelchair. "C'mon, let's go home. I'll make you some nice tofu and wheat toast for breakfast."

Gary clutched his chest, sheer horror descending on his face as he sat. "What are you, crazy, lady? You tryin' to kill me or something? Tofu? You just did somethin'," he accused. "Put some kinda tingle on my heart. If that don't earn me bacon and eggs, then life ain't worth livin'."

"Okay," I said. "Bacon and eggs. But only if I get to ride the wheelchair like it's a shopping cart."

"You got yourself a deal, lady."

We charged out of the room, me balanced precariously on the chair's frame, and broke for the hospital doors with the horrified staff chasing after us.

* * * * *

What happened to Coyote?
Find out next year in
COYOTE DREAMS,
coming from LUNA Books.

C.E. (Catie) Murphy holds an utterly impractical degree in English and history, making her unfit for any sort of duty beyond Web design and novel writing. Fortunately, those are precisely the sorts of things she likes to do.

At age six, Catie submitted several poems to an elementary school publication. The teacher producing it chose (inevitably) the one she thought was the worst of the three, but he also stopped her in the hall one day and said two words that made an indelible impression: "Keep writing."

Heady stuff for a six-year-old. It was sound advice, and she's pretty much never looked back.

She lives in Alaska with her husband, Ted, roommate Shaun and a number of pets. More information about Catie and her writing can be found at www.cemurphy.net.

LUNA™

If you enjoyed what you just read,
then we've got an offer you can't resist!

Take 1 bestselling love story FREE!

Plus get a FREE surprise gift!

Clip this page and mail it to the Reader Service®

IN U.S.A.	IN CANADA
3010 Walden Ave.	P.O. Box 609
P.O. Box 1867	Fort Erie, Ontario
Buffalo, N.Y. 14240-1867	L2A 5X3

YES! Please send me one free LUNA™ novel and my free surprise gift. After receiving it, if I don't wish to receive any more, I can return the shipping statement marked cancel. If I don't cancel, I will receive one brand-new novel every month, before they're available in stores! In the U.S.A., bill me at the bargain price of $10.99 plus 50¢ shipping & handling per book and applicable sales tax, if any*. In Canada, bill me at the bargain price of $12.99 plus 50¢ shipping & handling per book and applicable taxes**. That's the complete price and a savings of 10% off the cover prices—what a great deal! I understand that accepting the free book and gift places me under no obligation ever to buy any books. I can always return a shipment and cancel at any time. Even if I never buy another book from LUNA, the free book and gift are mine to keep forever.

175 HDN D34K
375 HDN D34L

Name	(PLEASE PRINT)	
Address	Apt.#	
City	State/Prov.	Zip/Postal Code

Not valid to current LUNA™ subscribers.

Want to try another series?
Call 1-800-873-8635 or visit www.morefreebooks.com.

* Terms and prices subject to change without notice. Sales tax applicable in N.Y.
** Canadian residents will be charged applicable provincial taxes and GST.
   All orders subject to approval. Offer limited to one per household.
   ® and ™ are registered trademarks owned and used by the trademark owner and
   or its licensee.

LUNA04TR   ©2004 Harlequin Enterprises Limited